PRAISE FOR
SIX OF ONE

"*Superior is inadequate to describe this new book* by the author of RUBYFRUIT JUNGLE . . . No polemic for feminism, it is yet gloriously about women; not sensationalized, it is still passionate. True quality disdains description; there is simple satisfaction in its existence."

—*West Coast Review of Books*

"*SIX OF ONE by Rita Mae Brown is joyous, passionate and funny*. What a pleasure! . . . So delightful . . . She opens the seams to give us her vision of what was really there. We are shown not the seamy side of life, but a body ready for anything, especially celebration."

—*Washington Post Book World*

"*A madcap mixture of North and South*, folk spunk and high elegance, and defiantly its own place. The author explores the town's cultural psychology like an American Evelyn Waugh, finding dignity and beauty without bypassing the zany and the corrupt."

—*Saturday Review*

"It's like listening to Virginia Woolf and her pals gossiping and philosophizing. What fun. What sass . . . There is love everywhere in this book."

—*Glamour*

"What is especially impressive about this delightful novel is Brown's understanding and affection for older women. Her characters experience two world wars, prohibition, labor struggles and, most important, the slow aging process and death itself, yet their highly individual natures remain constant through it all . . . It must also be noted that she does not slight her male characters in this predominantly female book, as many current women novelists are wont to do. This is a lively and very lovely book."

—*Publishers Weekly*

"At her winning, fondest best, Brown has some of the same effervescent yet secure trust in her local characters that Eudora Welty feels for hers . . . Rita Mae Brown has got her mostly female characters beautifully and high-spiritedly trained; when history nicks them, they slap right back."

—*Kirkus Reviews*

"Rita Mae Brown has written a disarming, funny book. Everything about it is not quite conventional . . . With her first book, RUBYFRUIT JUNGLE, Brown proved that 'feminist' books need not be gut-wrenching proclamations. SIX OF ONE is just as free of cant . . . An exuberant performance."

—*City Paper*, Baltimore, Md.

"No matter how quirky or devilish, Brown's people cavort in an atmosphere of tenderness . . . It is refreshing to encounter this celebration of human energy."

—*Chicago Sun-Times*

"SIX OF ONE is a brilliant novel, eloquent in its tough prose, compassionate in its committed realism. It is Brown's most ambitious and best novel so far and establishes her as an artist of the first rank."

—*New Women's Times*

"The book is guaranteed to delight."

—*Rocky Mountain News*

SIX
OF
ONE

RITA MAE BROWN

BANTAM BOOKS
TORONTO • NEW YORK • LONDON • SYDNEY • AUCKLAND

SIX OF ONE

*A Bantam Book / published in association with
Harper & Row, Publishers, Inc.*

PRINTING HISTORY
*Harper & Row published August 1978
2nd printing . . . October 1978*
*Literary Guild of America Alternate
Selection January 1979*
*Macmillan Book Club Alternate
Selection June 1979*
*Woman Today Book Club Alternate
Selection June 1979*
An excerpt appeared in
Omega One *magazine, October 23, 1978 issue*
Bantam edition / September 1979
2nd printing . . . October 1979   5th printing . . . . . . July 1982
3rd printing . . . . March 1980   6th printing . . . . March 1983
4th printing . . . February 1981   7th printing . September 1983
8th printing . . . July 1984

Spine photograph of Rita Mae Brown by Skrebneski.

---

*Bantam Books are published by Bantam Books, Inc. Its trade-
mark, consisting of the words "Bantam Books" and the por-
trayal of a rooster, is Registered in U.S. Patent and Trademark
Office and in other countries. Marca Registrada. Bantam
Books, Inc., 666 Fifth Avenue, New York, New York 10103.*

PRINTED IN THE UNITED STATES OF AMERICA

H   17 16 15 14 13 12 11 10 9 8

For

Julia Ellen Brown *née Buckingham*

Born **Apparently Immortal**
March 6, 1905

Acknowledgments

I solemnly swear never to write in any acknowledgment such sentiments as: "And to my dear wife for bringing cups of coffee, mowing the lawn, and enduring my absence from routine duties, my gratitude is boundless." Even if I acquire a wife I promise never to write that.

However, certain individuals helped enormously in shaping this book. Diana Williamson spent months in the library looking up strange tidbits such as when zippers were first marketed. She also caught my spelling errors and sent me packing in the direction of my dictionary.

Sylvia Kaneko, Susan Smitman and Elaine Spaulding provided me with useful comments after reading the first draft.

Marty Gibbons and Sharon Deevey haunted the Library of Congress on my behalf. They also told me I could do anything and I believed them.

Colleen Moreland and Linda Damico lent me money so I could eat and keep a roof over my head while I wrote.

Baby Jesus, my aging cat, daily brought me a mouse to prod my labors. Knowing what a valuable gift that was by her standards, I was truly inspired. Frip, my other hairy friend, chewed many of my research materials, thereby making invention a necessity.

I do not acknowledge the person who typed the manuscript. She got paid well enough.

Since this is my book and I can put in anything I want, allow me to exhort the following people

to write their own books. That way you don't
have to depend on me for all your reading matter:

Dr. Annella Brown	Tanya Slover
Charlotte Bunch	Tina Smith
Amy Gross	Elaine Spaulding
Sally Ann Harrison	Gloria Steinem
Arnold Reisman	Joan Tewkesbury

Special Mention

This work was supported by a Creative Writing Fellowship grant made by the National Endowment for the Arts.

The Massachusetts Council on Arts and Humanities awarded me a fiction grant, which was crucial to my being able to continue work.

I hope the federal and state governments expand their programs of assistance to the arts. It's time we stopped puritanically treating artists as though they were both a luxury and a necessary evil. American artists are a national resource and critical to our spiritual/cultural life. There is no rebirth without art.

May 21, 1980

I bought Mother a new car. It damn near killed Aunt Louise. Those two have been fighting like banty roosters since 1905, the year Mom was born. The first big blowup that both recall involved a multi-colored hair ribbon, 1909. Juts (Mom) says Celeste Chalfonte gave it to her because she was such a pretty, sweet little darling. This made Louise jealous. Things have been sliding downhill between them ever since.

Louise trumpets a different version of this earth-shattering event. She says Celeste Chalfonte made a present of the ribbon to her because she was such a pretty, sweet little darling. Juts, that jealous devil, snatched it clean off her head, getting some hair by the roots in the bargain. Being seven, Louise re-frained from beating her younger sister to a pulp. Instead she reported the theft to their mother, Cora Hunsenmeir, in the hopes she'd do it. Cora, justice personified, returned the ribbon to Louise. Ever since that day Juts has been eaten up with green envy. Louise swears this for a fact.

In May of 1980 I still can't untangle victor from victim. It changes regularly like night and day as each sister revolves around the other. The front door just slammed. It's Aunt Wheeze (Louise).

"Juts, you steeping pickled eggs, I see."

"You see fine. Want one?"

"No, you put in too much sugar. I like my eggs a bit more tart."

"Figures."

"Hells bells, I can't say anything around you—or that damn kid you picked off the streets in 1944."

"Louise, she's my daughter sure as if I bore her."

"Ha! You never will know what it is to be a mother.

I

You have to give birth. Blood of your blood, bone of your bone. It's all so mystical and spiritual—but then I don't expect you to understand. You wouldn't listen to me in 1944 and you won't listen to me now."

"Piss on your teeth! Walking around like a bloated toad don't make no woman a mother. Mothering's in the raising up of the child."

"Well, a fine job you did of it. Nickel left the church, left the town, left you, and now she writes books that disgrace the whole family."

"If you don't want no one to know your business, keep your mouth shut."

"How was I to know that brat would remember everything?"

"Wheeze, the last thing to die on you will be your mouth. You don't just tell Nickel stories—you now got a goddamned CB radio and tell anyone who tunes in."

"Liar, liar, your pants are on fire!"

I can't stand it. I'm going out to referee. "Are you two at it again?"

Aunt Louise whirled around to greet me. "You got gall, Nicole Smith, showing your face in this house."

"Why? It's Mom's house."

"Writing stories that make fun of me, Grand Regent of the Catholic Daughters of America for the Great State of Maryland. I'm so embarrassed I could die."

"I doubt we'll be that lucky."

"Nickel, don't you talk that way to my sister."

"Jesus H. Christ on a raft."

"See, Juts, see—that's what comes of her leaving the church. Just throwing Jesus's name around like it was salt."

"Your Aunt Louise is right. Show a little respect."

"I am going back to the sunroom. You two are impenetrable. Mom, can I have a pickled egg?"

"Get it and get out. Me and Louise are talking business."

As I shut the door behind me I heard Louise ask in a deafening whisper, "Impenetrable? What's that mean—that we're dumb?"

"I never know if I'm being insulted or not. It's hell having a daughter that went to college."

Two pairs of feet hurried over to the big dictionary Mom keeps stashed under the coffee table. I can hear the pages rustling.

"Louise, look under *i*, not *e*."

I can picture those gray heads bending over Webster's. Once they find "impenetrable" they'll soon start in on each other with renewed vigor. Seventy-five years is a long time to love and hate.

March 6, 1909

Celeste swirled in the kitchen like a fragrant tornado. Louise and Julia Ellen looked up from their picture book.

"The birthday girl! Julia Ellen, here is something for your pretty head," Celeste handed the child a bright ribbon.

"Thank you, Miss Chalfonte."

"Miss Chalfonte, don't forget my birthday's in three weeks." Louise wanted to make sure.

"I know. How was school today?"

"Yashew Gregorivitch got a whipping."

"How exciting." Her right eyebrow arched upward. "You two play. Mother will be here as soon as she's done with the silver." Celeste disappeared through the kitchen door, leaving her scent behind.

Julia attempted to tie a bow smack on top of her head, toothache style, but her little fingers weren't nimble enough. "Wheezie, help me."

Once the ribbon was secure in her hand, Louise began trading. "I'll tie you the best bow ever if you let me wear this to school tomorrow."

"No."

"I'll let you play with my glass beads."

"No. Gimme my ribbon."

"Don't grab, Julia. It's so unladylike."

"You tie a bow or gimme my present back."

"Selfish."

"I am not selfish. It's my birthday."

"Think how happy you'd make me if I can wear this tomorrow."

"You can be happy on your own birthday. Gimme my ribbon." Julia grabbed Louise's arm and rubbed her hands over it to make a burn.

"Stop it!"

"Gimme my ribbon."

"Don't you know nothing? We're Christians. That means we gotta share."

"Gimme my ribbon."

"Do you want to go to hell and have a red tail stuck on your heinie?"

This threat caused Julie to let go. "On my heinie?"

"A bright-red tail like the devil."

"Louise, you are making that up."

"I am not. Ask Mother."

Julia tore out the kitchen door and found Cora polishing the last of the forks.

"Mother, Louise says if I go to hell I'll have a red tail stuck on my heinie!"

"Are you planning on leaving anytime soon?"

"Is it true? Do people have red tails?"

"Child, don't worry me with this stuff. How do I know what fashions are in such a warm climate?"

Perplexed, Julia walked back into the kitchen. "She don't know."

Louise seized the moment. "Because she don't know don't mean it ain't true. You don't want to go there, do you?"

"No—now gimme my ribbon back."

"You'll go straight to hell. Let me wear it tomorrow."

"No." Juts went for her again. Louise dodged.

"You gotta share. It's Christian."

Reinforced by theology, Louise spied a knife by the sink. Before Julia could stop her, she cut the lovely ribbon neatly in half. "There, I've saved you from eternal torment."

Juts took the pathetic remnant held out to her. She sat right down on the floor and cried. Her anguish reverberated throughout the cavernous house.

Cora, with purpose, strode into the kitchen. "What goes here?"

"Wheezie stole my hair ribbon."

"Liar, liar, your pants are on fire."

"Stop that, Louise. Did you steal her hair ribbon?"

"No, Mother, look—she has it in her hand."

"Such as it is."

"Waagh. She cut it in half."

"What's that behind your back? Gimme that hand."

Louise reluctantly volunteered her hand.

"Open your fist."

There in the middle of her palm rested the other half of the ribbon, wrinkled.

"Mother, Jesus said: 'Ask and it shall be given unto ye.'"

"What does Jesus have to do with your sister's birthday present?"

"I asked and she wouldn't give it to me, so I took half. This way Julia won't get in trouble with God."

"The Lord moves in mysterious ways, Louise Hunsenmeir, but I don't." Cora walloped her bottom. "There, smartypants. That'll teach you to spoil your sister's birthday. Since your birthday's coming up in three weeks, I'll divide everything in half between you and Julia Ellen."

"No! No!" Louise screamed.

"It is better to give than to receive," Cora calmly pointed out to her.

Juts, refreshed from the sight of Louise's discomfort, threw her ribbon at Louise. "Momma, she got all my ribbon. Now can I have all her birthday presents?"

Louise emitted a piercing squeal. "Never!"

"My God, you're as bad as the other one. I'm done with both of you. Now get your coats on. We're going home."

May 21, 1980

"What the hell's she doing out there?"

Juts sauntered over to the window to see what her
sister was bitching about. "Turning cartwheels in the
dandelions."

"That girl's thirty-five, ain't she?"

"Be thirty-six come November."

"Juts, call her in here before the neighbors see."

"Oh, hell, Louise, our dear mother turned cartwheels
past fifty."

"Our dear mother wasn't educated. Nickel is."

"Go turn on the TV, then she won't bother you."

"By God, you always stick up for that brat."

"She's my daughter."

"You know how I feel about that."

"Yes, and let's not go into it again. All of town
knows how you feel about Nickel, Jesus, FDR and
Amelia Earhart, to say nothing of Sonny and Cher."

"Mebbe they know what I think, but they don't see
my all. You went down to the square yesterday in
hot pants. Orrie Tadia told me."

"So what?"

"Seventy-five is too old for hot pants. And them
glasses you got on your nose are a disgrace—granny
glasses."

"I'm old enough to be a granny—you said so yourself just this minute. I heard you with these ears."

"Don't get smart with me, Julia Hunsenmeir. You
know what I mean. All the young people wear those
glasses. Why you don't get something conservative like
me and act your age, I'll never know."

"Your glasses got so many rhinestones on them,
when the sun hits you, people are blinded by the
light."

6

"You're so immature. I don't know why I bother to discuss anything with you."

"Louise sucks green monkey dicks!" Juts relished this childhood insult. Never failed to fry her big sister's ass.

"I didn't come over here to be insulted," Louise peered out the window again. "She's still at it. Juts, make her stop."

"I will not. I think I'll give it a try." Julia opened the screen door and hollered to Nickel. "Wanna watch on old lady make a fool of herself?"

"Sure, Mom."

"Julia, don't you dare. You'll break something."

"Fiddlesticks."

"Julia, when our dear mother died she told me to watch over you. Don't you dare go out there and show your bottom."

"Want me to change into my hot pants? Then my skirt won't flare up." Juts charged out the door. Louise followed two steps behind, mouth rattling nonstop.

"Julia Ellen, I take my responsibilities seriously. Those were Mother's last wishes. Don't you dare turn cartwheels out here. You'll break a hip."

"Mother, are you really going to turn a cartwheel?"

"Damn right I am." And with that, Julia Ellen took a hop, skip and a jump and over she went—not a perfect cartwheel, but a cartwheel all the same.

Louise screeched at the top of her lungs, "She broke something, I know she broke something," and ran over to a flushed but triumphant Juts.

"Mom, that was terrific."

"I ain't dead yet, kid. Wanna see another one?" Over she went.

Louise smacked her hand to her head, the other hand outstretched to heaven for divine intervention. "Mother, she won't listen."

"Criminetys, Wheeze, Mother can't hear you. She's been dead since 1962. Shut up."

"That's right. Insult our poor dear mother. Insult

me. You'll miss me just like you missed her, when I'm gone!"

"Aunt Wheeze, Mom's having fun."

"Don't you tell me what my sister's doing, you big-mouthed brat. She's out here acting a fool and it was you put her up to it."

"Me? What did I do?"

"Out here turning cartwheels. A grown woman. Old enough to have children."

"Christ, don't start that again."

"Well, I can see I'm not wanted. I'm going home. Julia, when you feel like apologizing, you know my telephone number. As for you, Nickel Smith, I'll light a candle for you." Puffed up and twitchy as an old broody hen, Louise stalked to her 1976 Buick, put the key in the ignition and then peeled out.

Juts smiled and waved good-bye. "Sucks green monkey dicks."

"Mother, you'll give her a hemorrhage."

"It's her own fault. She's got nose blisters from sticking it where it don't belong."

"Those were sure fine cartwheels you turned."

Julia beamed. "Life in the old girl yet. Come on, let's sit on the front porch. I'll fix you a Coke. We can put out the pickled eggs, too. I feel like celebrating."

"You're on."

I raced to the kitchen, put the eggs on a tray, got out some saltines, cheese and pretzels. Juts loved her pretzels. She soaked them in beer. Julia fixed me a Coke and herself a Rolling Rock beer. The little green cans got cold fast. Since they were little she could knock off a few and tell herself it wasn't the same as drinking a Budweiser.

"Ready, kid."

"Ready, Mom."

The front porch sported a big swing. All around it shrubs bloomed. Spring came late. The lilacs opened full a few days ago. Sweet air curled into Julia's nostrils, reminding her of all the spring of her life, a sum of springs, the essence of spring. Oh, she felt glad to be alive and the hell with people who make fun of old folks.

"How's your Cokey?"

"Delicious. What would I do without Southern champagne?"

"Be a fallen woman like me and drink beer in public."

"But you're a real lady, Mom—you are drinking it out of a glass."

"Ha. Do you know when I was a girl, women weren't supposed to drink, period? I remember Celeste Chalfonte, and you know what a great lady she was."

"I know you told me about her," Nickel replied.

"Momma worked for her, you know. I never once saw Celeste that everything, even down to the buttons on her gloves, wasn't perfect. She was the greatest beauty I ever saw. Where was I? Oh, juice. Well, now, as I started to say, a woman couldn't drink. I remember as a girl watching Celeste and her bridge gang sneak gin in the afternoons. By the end of the afternoon the great ladies was three sheets to the wind and dishing dirt like the rest of us."

"Bet you had fun."

"Yes, I did. When times were rough or smooth, I always managed to find a laugh somehow. You know, I truly believe that's why Louise gets so wrought up over me. She resents me."

"Yeah. I can see that. She doesn't seem to enjoy herself."

"Enjoy herself! She peddles uplift and relishes downfall. Ever since she got sent to Immaculata Academy, that's when all this started. You know, her being a religious nut."

Mother and I turned. The lilacs shuddered. Louise flew out of that bush like a steel ball released in a pinball machine. "Religious nut! Religious nut!"

She scared Juts so bad she spit out her pickled egg.

I dropped my crackers and cheese. "Shit!"

Julia recovered and was now royally pissed. "What the Sam Hill are you doing jumping out of my lilac bushes?"

"I knew as soon as I turned my back you'd talk about me. And to her. You know she'll put down everything you say in another book."

"No I won't, Aunt Louise. No one would believe you."

"That's right, that's right. America goes the way of Mammon. No one would believe me. They are all worshipping the golden calf. For once we agree."

"Now that you're here again, would you like a beer, Sis?"

"You know I never reek of strong waters."

"Pulease, Louise." Juts rolled her eyes while drawing out the "please." "I remember when you made bathtub gin."

"I never did no such thing. Nickel, don't you listen to this. Not a word. You know how Juts likes to embroider stories. Yes, Juts, I will have a little refreshment if you put it in a glass kindly." A long sigh.

"I'll get it." I went into the kitchen and could hear Louise boring into Mom. "So what if it's true? That don't mean you tell."

I came out with a tall frosted glass so passersby couldn't guess the contents. "Here, Aunt Louise."

"Thank you, dear. You always had beautiful manners."

We three sat there for a quiet moment. Louise needed to recover her breath. She had parked the car a block away and snuck into the lilacs. The excitement of it had worn her out.

"Honey, it's nice to have you home."

"Thank you, Mother."

"If you had any sense of responsibility you'da never left your mother in the first place." Louise licked her lips to get the foam off.

"Aunt Wheeze, there are no colleges in Runnymede. I needed to educate myself."

"So you got a Ph.D. and can't get a steady job. A waste of time and money, it was."

"If I put my money in my head no one can ever take it from me."

"I'd rather have a new car myself," Louise smarted off.

Juts pounced. "Nickel bought me a new car, or did you forget already?"

"How can I forget? You roll down your window at

stoplights and yell at total strangers, 'My daughter bought me this car!' " Louise was disgruntled that she had walked into that one. Why did she have to mention the word "car"?

"As I was saying, honey, it's nice to have you home."

"How long are you planning on staying?"

"I'm not sure. I want to talk that over with Mom."

"Before you go, I want to set the record straight about me being a 'religious nut,' as Juts puts it. You know I was sent to Immaculata Academy because I was very musical. Celeste Chalfonte, a good woman in her fashion, sent me there. Paid for it herself."

"I don't remember it being quite that way," Julia countered.

"What do you remember? You were six years old at the time. I was ten and very talented." Louise crossed her legs in order to look talented. She stuck her little finger out from the glass, too.

"Celeste sent you there because her sister, Carlotta, ran the school."

"That don't mean I wasn't talented."

"Well, no."

"I still play my organ that Pearlie bought me before he died. God bless him."

Uncle Pearlie died on Louise's seventy-fifth birthday, four years ago. Mom swore he did it out of revenge. Wheeze bossed her husband same as anybody else.

"That's wonderful that you kept up your playing, Aunt Louise."

"Thank you. It's about time I get a little appreciation around here."

"Play! All you do is switch on the banjo effect and strike a few chords." Juts devoured another pickled egg.

"Shut up, Julia. Me and Nickel was having a meaningful conversation. Like I was saying, Nickel, Celeste sent me to Immaculata Academy to study music. And it's true it was run by her sister, a very holy woman. When she died she sat bolt upright in her casket and made the sign of the cross. That's how all of Runnymede knew her for a saint"—she cast an eye at her nibbling sister—"in case they missed her glory whilst she lived."

"That ain't how I remember it." Julia took another slug of beer.

September 25, 1911

Runnymede sets smack on the Mason-Dixon line. Both Maryland and Pennsylvania state legislatures tried to get the town to become two separate towns since they already had to obey two different sets of state rules. But the inhabitants would have none of it. Runnymede was Runnymede and the hell with both governments. The wisdom of 1865 prevented them from seceding from the Union, but given the opportunity, the whole town would have jumped at it. True, they fought the War over and over again among themselves, but South or North, they were still Runnys. It's one thing to fight among your own kind. It's quite another to have some outsider come in and do it for you.

Runnys settled things their own way. For instance, Patience Horney was cracky. Everybody knew it. Once a doctor from Philadelphia tried to get the South Runnymede mayor to commit her, since Patience lived on the south side of town. John Gassner wouldn't do it. Then this big-city doctor goes to the north side mayor, Otto Tangerman, tells him how backward Southerners are and he should commit Patience. Otto eighty-sixed him. Patience talked out loud, very loud, about the planet Saturn and her visitors from there. She also talked about the Rife family, who owned the cannery and the munitions plant. Once she walked right up to the old boy himself, Cassius, and said, "You're a walleyed son-of-a-bitch." The town loved it. That was back in 1882. Now Patience wore a red fright wig to cover up her bald spot. Both mayors put their heads together and got her a job sitting at the railway depot selling hot pretzels and chestnuts in winter and lemonade in summer. Patience jabbered a mile a minute there but she did no harm. She could see everyone's comings and goings and felt herself to be the middle of the world. That's how Runnymede did things. On that September day in 1911 Louise had no idea that she, too, was to put Runnymede to the test.

Louise and Julia sailed in through the back door of Celeste's, as they always did after school. Cora was in the kitchen making sandwiches. "Hey, darlin's!"

The children hugged their mother around the neck.

"Don't choke me, girls. Celeste needs fortification. She's in the middle of a hot card game."

"Juts and Ev Most had to sit in the corner today."

"Is that a fact?"

"You ain't in my class. How do you know?"

"Orrie Tadia told me," Louise announced.

"Orrie Tadia sucks green monkey dicks."

"Julia, don't let Celeste hear you say that. She'll use it at the next town meeting if she hears it." Cora laughed.

In the front room, Celeste peeped over her hand of cards with a conspiratorial look. Her partner, Fannie Jump Creighton, had had entirely too much to drink and was missing all Celeste's cues. Celeste had on a pearl-gray, trimmed in maroon, dress with a touch of silver at her ears and a single shining diamond on her hand. Celeste never overdid it. Fairy Thatcher flashed a rock on her left hand so big her left bicep developed as muscular as a weight lifter's. Not tipsy, she caught all of Celeste's bids and made the appropriate counter to Ramelle, her card partner for the afternoon. Celeste enjoyed winning more than losing. She did her best not to drum her fingers on the table. She even ignored Ramelle's knee pressing rhythmically into her own, which any other time would have offered her a spasm of delight.

"Cora, where are those sandwiches?"

"Coming, Queen Bee." Cora was not one to be ordered.

"Girls, do your sums."

When Cora left the kitchen, Juts turned to her sister. "You got a big mouth. You and Orrie Tadia."

"You and Ev Most is best friends. Leave me and Orrie alone."

"Orrie sniffs school seats when people get up."

"Ugh! She does not."

"She does. I saw her myself."

"She probably saw you do it first."

Julia hauled off to belt her one, but Louise ran down the back hall. Juts was in hot pursuit. "Tattletale, tattletale."

"Pee sniffer," Louise called out from ahead.

Celeste heard this last lovely phrase. So did Fannie Jump. "Girls, did I ever tell you about the time Brutus Rife suffered the humiliation of being urinated upon by Theodore Baumeister?"

Ramelle snapped her cards together. "Fannie Jump, honey, you pay attention to this game or Miss Celeste will do worse than that to you."

"Cora, I think we ought to rename your offspring France and Germany," Celeste said in her dry voice. Cora meanwhile had been arranging the sandwiches according to a code she and Celeste had worked out years before.

"Care for refreshment, Mrs. Thatcher?" Cora offered her the tray.

Celeste now knew Fairy held two aces. Cora's a brick, she thought to herself, and her mood improved despite Fannie Jump's wobbly state.

Juts and Louise penetrated deep into the servants' quarters. An abandoned upright greeted Louise as she rounded a corner.

"Juts, look." Louise leapt onto the seat.

Julia forgot her mission and sat down next to her sister.

"You hit these two black ones regular, one, two," Louise told her little sister.

Juts obeyed and Louise went on to play a melody she had heard in school. She had an ear for music. There she sat, legs straight out, her head bent down over the keys, and every once in a while she'd jerk up in happiness. Julia Ellen hit her two keys, one, two, one two, and rocked back and forth, delighted with the sounds.

"Darling, do I hear 'After the Ball Is Over'?" Ramelle asked Celeste.

Fannie Jump didn't wait for her hostess to answer. She launched into song, swinging her card hand. Ramelle and Fairy saw everything. Celeste just closed her hand in resignation and sang along with Fannie. Ramelle giggled and joined in. Fairy hit all the high notes for her part and motioned for Cora to sing along. The five women were soon as enraptured with themselves as Louise and Julia Ellen were with their sounds.

Louise tired of "After the Ball Is Over" and knocked out something patriotic.

"Celeste, dear, what we need here is a fife and drum," Fannie crooned.

Cora left the coded sandwiches and went off to fetch her girls.

Ramelle called out, "Bring them in, Cora. Let's hear them at the grand."

A gleaming grand shimmered in the corner, the black seat covered with a silken embroidered shawl Celeste had tossed on it for effect. Cora reentered the room, with Louise on one side and Julia Ellen on the other.

"To whom do we owe the honor of our applause?" Celeste asked.

Cora whispered, "Which of you played the piano?"

"Me!" they both replied.

"I'd like an encore," Fannie Jump requested.

"Come on, darlin's." Cora led them over to the grand.

Louise looked about. Juts clambered onto the seat and waited for her sister to direct. "Come on, Wheezie." Louise put her sister's fingers on the black keys and Juts started right in. Louise began her part of "After the Ball" and soon both girls forgot about the adults and were full of the sounds.

Ramelle slipped her arm through Celeste's. "Sweetheart, little Wheezie is adorable."

Fannie waltzed over to the piano, glass in hand, and picked up the tune again.

When Louise finished, Juts continued. An elbow in the ribs stopped her one, two, one, two.

"Very good, girls," Ramelle praised them.

Fairy Thatcher and Fannie applauded. Cora folded her arms over her chest and laughed. Juts clapped, too.

"How long have you been playing, Louise?" Celeste asked.

"Never."

"Cora, how long has this child been taking lessons?" Celeste readdressed the question to Cora.

"This is the first time I heard her play, same as you."

"Brava!" Fannie cheered. "Runnymede's own Mozart."

"Do you know how to read music?" Fairy asked Louise.

"She don't read too good anything," Julia Ellen volunteered.

"I do so," responded Louise.

Ramelle put her hand on Louise's shoulder, which made her feel very special but immobilized. "Is there a piano at school?"

"There's one in the big room, but the keys don't all work."

"Is that where you play?" Ramelle continued.

"When the big kids let me."

"And they wear green." Juts added this detail, which to her meant something.

"Hush, Julia, honey. People are talking to Louise."

"Does the teacher help you?" Ramelle still had her hand on Louise's shoulder.

"No."

"That's wonderful—she plays by ear," Fannie enthused.

"Miss Chalfonte, how come you got two pianos?" Louise wanted to know.

"One for myself and one for the servants."

"The last servant you had that was musical was

Sylvanus Peaks. That was years ago. Besides, he played the banjo," Fannie said.

"Don't you think the piano gets lonesome?" Juts inquired.

"To the best of my knowledge, pianos don't display emotions," Celeste remarked. "I wish more humans would follow their example."

"Heartless," Fairy teased.

"What do you want with an old upright? Why don't you give it to Louise?" Fannie blundered on.

"Beggars mounted ride their horses to death," Celeste said, turning to Fannie.

"What?" Fannie was incredulous.

"I don't want no horse, Miss Chalfonte, but I'll take the piano." Louise got excited.

"I simply mean one can't bestow large and expensive objects on people who can't afford them."

"Celeste . . ." Even Ramelle was surprised.

"What Her Highness means is give them an inch and they take a mile." Cora was getting mad. Since when had she asked for anything?

"Money shared makes love grow stronger, money given kills it dead." Celeste was sinking lower.

"Good Lord, a piano isn't money—not really," Fairy exploded.

"It's the principle behind it," Celeste held firm.

"Celeste, you're a generous woman. What's got into you?"

Fannie was amazed.

Ramelle was amazed, too, but she'd seen Celeste get her back up on a few other occasions and there was no talking to her then. At those times the incidents seemed equally as trifling. The less she said, the better. Since she lived with Celeste, she'd bear the brunt of her discontent if, in Celeste's mind, she publicly appeared to undermine her.

"If you're so concerned over Runnymede's Mozart, Fannie Jump Creighton, bestow upon her your piano."

"Don't be ridiculous, I only have one. You have two."

"What about you, Fairy? You can't even play scales."

"Celeste, you know perfectly well one can't have a drawing room without a piano."

"Hypocrites."

Louise and Juts were frozen at the piano. They didn't want to move, but they didn't want to stay, either.

"Celeste, it was my girl that asked for your upright, not me. This beggar don't ask nobody for nothing. I work for what I get. But you are carrying on so about something you don't even use . . . I don't want to hear it." Cora looked level at Celeste. "Come on, children."

The two little ones shot off the bench, they were so glad to get out of that room. Cora walked out of the house and slammed the door behind her.

"My servants never talk to me like that," Fairy sniffed.

"Cora is more than a servant," Celeste said. "Now if you don't mind, I think I've had quite enough of the human race for one day."

Celeste propped herself up in bed and picked out Tacitus. Reading Latin calmed her. The order and clarity of the language soothed her plus there was not a soul to speak it and disturb the serenity she imparted to it. No babble of tongues, jarring accents or cursed slang; Celeste could sink into the past and master it. Ramelle, long blond hair curling around her shoulders, opened the door to the bedroom. At twenty-seven, Ramelle was seven years Celeste's junior and felt it. The first time she entered Celeste's Georgian mansion she was awed by the priceless Orientals glowing on the floor, jewels tossed underfoot. The central hallway curled upward like a chambered nautilus. Room after room bespoke Celeste's wealth and imagination. Ramelle hadn't just opened the door to a house; she had opened the door to another world, Celeste's world. Celeste read in Greek, Latin, French and German. Her library overflowed with hand-bound volumes. A stack of books kept vigil by her bed, waiting their turn. Celeste Chalfonte was no ordinary woman. For that matter, neither was Cora. Ramelle loved Celeste and made love with her, but she always suspected that in some unspoken way Cora was more central to Celeste than she was. Cora's wisdom and endurance, her ability to find joy in the simplest of events, grounded Celeste. In her rarefied world such people didn't exist. If Celeste was blessed by great wealth, she was also cursed by it. It was her saving grace to recognize that. To Cora and even little Louise and Julia Ellen, though Celeste had more money she was no different than they were. Celeste needed them. For all her wit and cool distance, she needed to be included in humanity. Cora included her as an equal.

"The best part of Tacitus is reading between the lines." Celeste loked up at Ramelle.

"I never did go for that dead stuff. I'll stick to modern novels."

"Ha. The suburbs of literature."

"Yes, dear." Ramelle crawled under the covers.

"I bet you think I've been sitting here fuming over the afternoon? Well, I haven't. I haven't even wondered if Cora will show up tomorrow."

"I can see that you haven't been thinking about it at all. Is that why the book is turned upside down?"

Celeste wondered how long she'd been sitting there like that. She closed the book and turned out the light.

"Good night, dearest."

"Good night." Ramelle kissed her on the cheek.

September 26, 1911

The next morning Cora did not cook breakfast. The gardener's wife was pressed into service. Celeste pretended not to notice. Diana, the all-round maid, brought in the *Runnymede Morning Trumpet*. Celeste exploded. "Take that contaminated rag away. I don't understand why people enjoy reading about disasters at the breakfast table. Surely I'm not one of them."

Later Fannie Jump Creighton and Fairy Thatcher called to see if the storm had passed. This made Celeste all the more furious. The grapevine hummed all day. By nightfall, both South and North Runnymede were informed of the piano incident. Brutus Rife, who had taken over the munitions factory and cannery from his father, Cassius, particularly enjoyed the news. He'd proposed to Celeste year in and year out until 1898, when he married Felicia Scott, a classmate of Celeste's. Brutus had dearly wanted the Rife and Chalfonte fortunes to blend, but Celeste would have none of him. Her troubles just proved to him that a woman alone can't handle running things.

Cora's day passed quickly. She toiled in the big vegetable garden while the sun was up. When the girls came home from school she put them to work in it as well. Louise hoped to find a piano in the living room, but all she found was Lillian Russell, the cat, with a mole she'd caught. Juts tried to cheer her sister. She offered to cut the mole open so they could see its insides. This did not cheer Louise.

At nightfall the girls could hear Idabelle McGrail playing her accordion out on her porch. Every dusk in the good weather Idabelle would sit there, one sock up and one sock down, in different colors. Stretching her accordion across her ample bosom, Ida sang songs of Ireland and Scotland. Sometimes her huge, hairy son, Rob, would accompany her on his bagpipes. Tonight the music lifted up to the top of Bumblebee Hill, where the Hunsenmeirs lived, and made Louise feel all the more miserable.

"Mother, why don't Celeste gimme that old piano?"

"Celeste has her ways."

"But she has two." Juts sat next to her sister and put her arm around Louise's waist. "It ain't fair."

Louise started crying again. Lillian Russell rubbed against her legs. Everyone tried to comfort Louise. As there was little furniture in the clean frame farmhouse, an upright would be a pleasant addition.

"If Celeste hadn't been set on from all directions, she probably woulda give up that old piano. She's not a mean woman. But now, with her pride, it would take three years and four animals to get it from her."

This provoked a fresh outburst of sobbing on Louise's part.

That night there was no living with Celeste. She was so foul Diana quietly left and so did the gardener and his wife. The only one who could tolerate Miss Chalfonte on her high horse was Ramelle, and even she was having doubts.

Next morning the piano was no longer gossip but an issue. Poor Runnys were outraged that Celeste was being so damn tight. Rich Runnys didn't like the sound of Celeste's servants leaving. Middle-class Runnys didn't want anything to interfere with business, and if servants don't get paid they don't spend their money.

Celeste, unaware of the proportions of the incident, saddled up her beautiful bay mare for her morning ride, as usual. On the way back home she rode through the north side of town. Theodore Baumeister spied her and ran out of his barbershop. "Miss Chalfonte, good morning."

"Good morning, Ted."

"Town's in an uproar over your old upright."

"That just goes to show you people have nothing better to talk about."

"Yes, m'am, but I do believe you should give that little girl your piano so folks will settle down."

"Mr. Baumeister, I'll thank you to mind your own damned business." Celeste touched the horse's flanks and headed home at a fast trot.

There was no peace at home. Fairy Thatcher and Fannie Jump Creighton grabbed her as soon as she walked into the front hall.

"Celeste, you've got to do something!" Fairy exclaimed.

"What on earth are you so agitated about?" Celeste asked her.

Ramelle, having heard their tale, stood off to the side awaiting the earthquake.

"Agitated? Marooned is more like it. Celeste Chalfonte, do you know that on this very day our servants, Fairy's and mine, walked off?"

This unwelcome knowledge took a few seconds to sink in. "What?"

"Walked off, I tell you, and over the damned piano."

"You can't be serious!" Celeste's voice rose.

"Serious! I am fit to be tied, Celeste Pritchard Chalfonte. I'm hosting the monthly Daughters of the Confederacy meeting tonight, or have you forgotten?" Fannie Jump flushed in anticipation of her plight. "You know tonight's the night we plan for the Harvest Moon Ball, and nothing must be out of place. That viper Minta Mae Dexter and her Sisters of Gettysburg already pledged the decorations. All proceeds to the poor, blah, blah, blah. You should have heard her. Why her father didn't get picked off at Big Round Top I'll never know."

"Calm down, Fannie." Celeste grew icier the hotter Fannie waxed.

"Calm down! Calm down, after the Sisters nearly ran us over last Fourth of July? We've got to have a strategic session so we can outdo Minta and her soiled doves to raise more money."

"And you know the Martha Circle has been meeting in secret over the ball. We'll not be spared their onslaught of vulgarity, as usual directed by La Squandras."

La Squandras were Ruby, Rose and Rachel, triplets who shared a brain among them. They spent enough on jewelry to keep the Brazilian navy afloat. As their father, Cassius Rife, had sold guns to both sides during the War Between the States, neither the Daughters of the Confederacy nor the Sisters of Gettysburg could abide them. In retaliation, La Squandras formed the Martha Circle, named for Martha Washington, and forced all the merchants' wives to join.

"Why can't you move the meeting to Caesura Frothingham's house? Ought to get our blood up since it's decorated in Reign of Terror style."

Fairy giggled. "Celeste, you are wicked."

Fannie was not to be amused. "Celeste, Caesura's servants are threatening to walk off, too."

"This is impossible," Celeste said matter-of-factly.

"Impossible or not, the Daughters of the Confederacy are marching on my house tonight at seven."

"Can't you have a meeting anyway?" Ramelle asked.

"I can't do anything without my servants. I don't even know where the finger bowls are kept. They magically appear on the table each time I inform Mona." Fannie was feeling her tragedy deeply.

"Fannie resents any accusation of usefulness." Celeste couldn't help saying it.

"You're a fine one to talk. You can't even boil water." Fannie retaliated.

"No, but I can saddle a horse."

"Road apples, Celeste. This is a dinner party tonight, not the Kentucky Derby." Fannie strained to think of something more awful to say, but terrible things hovered on the rim of her consciousness and then fled before she could pluck one.

"You've got to do something," Fairy pleaded.

"Why are you two matrons and pillars of society coming to me? Why don't you go to your husbands?"

"What, and lose my allowance because Horace will declare I can't manage servants properly?" Fairy wailed.

"Creighton has to be dragged out kicking and screaming from Pearl Streicher's. He's either there or up in York, Pennsylvania—Gomorrah on the Codorus." Her husband's dalliances or outright whoring didn't bother Fannie a bit. It left her more time to lead handsome young men astray. Fannie had a sharp eye for men, flesh on the hoof.

"This is your doing, Celeste. Do something," Fairy pleaded.

"I refuse to bear this cross alone. You, Fannie Jump Creighton, were the first to suggest I part with that dilapidated piano."

"Was I? Was I really, Celeste? I truly don't recall."

"Next time we play bridge, restrain yourself in the spirit department," Celeste barked.

"Now, Celeste, honey, Fannie loves her gin."

"You all are like a dog chasing its tail. If you'd stop accusing each other, maybe you could find a way out of this situation," Ramelle correctly noted.

As Ramelle was younger, quite beautiful and Celeste's lover, Fannie and Fairy stiffened. They did not like being told what to do by a relative newcomer. After all, they grew up with Celeste. In childhood the three were called Hic, Haec and Hoc by their classmates at the Fox Run School for Young Ladies. At Vassar each covered for the other, a considerable feat. Fannie shamelessly screwed young bloods from Yale, Fairy cheated like a bandit on her tests and Celeste threw herself at Grace Pettibone, a gorgeous upperclass girl. By that time the three were referred to as the Furies for all the trouble they caused. Nonetheless, Ramelle was right. After a ritual fluffing of feathers, they settled themselves.

"What do you suggest?" Fannie stared at Ramelle, wishing she could find a man that good-looking.

"Why can't Celeste go and talk with Cora?"

"Ride up to Bumblebee Hill and suffer the entire town seeing me placate Cora? Never!"

"It's your pride versus our social well-being," Fairy said.

"Now you sound like my sister, Carlotta. Bag it, Gladys." "Bag it, Gladys" was a childhood expression of the threesome that roughly meant shove it up your ass.

"Perhaps we could ask Her Holiness to come and say a prayer over all involved," Fannie sneered.

"You know, the union organizers started this." Fairy went off on a tangent.

"The Unpleasantries Between the States have been over for some time," Celeste remarked.

"No, union organizers—men who read Karl Marx and go into factories," Fairy went on.

"My house is not a factory." Celeste folded her hands.

"No, but Cora is a member of the proletariat." Fairy was rolling now. "The workers will rise against their masters."

"Fairy, have you been reading seditious books?" Celeste's right eyebrow arched upward.

"I . . . yes."

Fannie nearly fell over. "Fairy, I never saw you crack a book the entire time we were in college."

"Karl Marx, that German?" Celeste, too, was stunned. "Really, Fairy, pay no attention to the Germans. They still haven't recovered from Attila."

"However did you start reading?" Fannie wanted to know.

"Horace set me off. You know how conservative he is. After his last trip to Chicago he returned fuming about unions, unhealthy ideas, Paris in 1871. I never saw him so excited. I decided anything that upset Horace must be good. So I made up my mind to find out," Fairy said.

"Interesting though that may be, I don't think Cora's been reading behind our backs. Cora can't read," Celeste gently stated.

"Oh, really?" Fannie was mildly surprised. "I never think about that. I wonder how many of our servants can read?"

"They count just fine," Fairy complained.

Fannie returned to her original trial. "What am I to do about the Daughters of the Confederacy?"

"Can't you three stop bickering long enough to create one plan, even one?" Ramelle prodded them.

"To what do I owe this fierce outbreak of rationality?" Celeste was stung.

"Darling, the town is in an uproar. I seriously doubt it's due to organizers or anything systematic. Your keeping the piano seems a spiteful gesture. God knows, Celeste, you could purchase a piano factory if you wanted one. It's the little things that spur people, not the big ones. You know that—one small incident can trigger larger ones until everyone forgets how and why something started." Ramelle spoke quietly.

"You're quite right, Ramelle. But I'll be damned if I'll knuckle under to a batch of servants and shopkeepers!"

"Just by giving Louise a piano?" Fannie understood

perfectly well Celeste's position, but needled her anyway.

"Fannie, I'll lose face—with you tarts as well as with the town. It's a matter of discipline. One can't go about giving things because others ask."

"Strange. I thought that's what Jesus meant." Ramelle had steel in her back this time.

"The last Christian died on the cross!" Celeste was hurt.

"Christ never mentioned pianos," Fairy innocently remarked.

"Right, there were no pianos in the New Testament. All they had was David with his harp in the Old." Fannie displayed her vast biblical knowledge.

A radiant smile covered Celeste's face. "Ladies, Jesus didn't have a piano, but La Sermonette does."

"Carlotta?" Fairy was confused.

"I'd like to see that. You get your sister to give Louise a piano. All she'd give her is a blessing. She may be a religious nut, but she'll pinch a nickel until the Indian rides the buffalo," Fannie sneered.

"Oh, ye women of little faith." Celeste stretched out her hands in benediction and reproach. "My sister runs Immaculata Academy, or have you forgotten?"

"Celeste?" Fannie Jump saw it coming.

"Yes, I shall send Runnymede's musical wonder to Immaculata Academy, there for education and moral uplift."

"You're a genius," Fairy admired.

"You said it; I didn't." Celeste nodded.

"Darling, you are a wonder." Ramelle touched Celeste's hand.

"Careful, dearest. We don't want to offend Fannie and Fairy's ordinary sensibilities."

Fannie loved such rare moments. One never talked of these things directly, although as she grew older she really didn't care what she said about Creighton or her lovers. Celeste, however, was far more reserved. "Bullpucky, Miss Chalfonte. 'Twas I who stumbled upon you and Grace one cold winter's night."

"Serves you right, you rude thing. Didn't your mother teach you to knock? Anyway, we were just keeping warm. Ramelle, don't listen to Fannie. She exaggerates when she tells the time."

"Celeste, isn't this going to cost you money?" Fairy delved into more practical matters.

"You mean Louise Hunsenmeir?"

"Private academies aren't in the custom of accepting poor girls," Fairy said.

"Better to pay for it than give up that piano. If I part with that damned instrument I'd lose more than money. This truly is the best solution, and who knows, maybe Louise will learn."

"Isn't it cruel to educate the poor?" Fannie was genuinely perturbed.

"Cruel? Education is the finest gift anyone can give!" Celeste had her hand on her hip.

"No, really, Celeste, what good is an educated woman? She can't do anything. The best Louise could hope for would be marriage to a man broad-minded enough to forgive her her origins," Fannie said a bit sadly.

"Better to be unborn than ill bred?" That eyebrow arched upward again.

"I . . ." Fannie was stumped.

"Oh, God, and what if your sister gets her clutches on the child? Next thing you know, she'll want to be a nun." Fairy's lower lip quivered a bit.

"Carlotta's Catholicism mystified our family for years," Celeste said. "Why couldn't she be secure in the white bosom of Episcopalian abundance?"

"Are you sure this is the only way?" Fannie wondered.

"Yes, but that doesn't mean Cora will agree to it."

Fairy slumped. "Oh, no. I never thought of that."

Celeste saddled up again and rode off toward Bumblebee Hill, south of town. She wasn't two lengths down the Emmitsburg road before the entire town was buzzing. The land west of Runnymede rolled in gentle deep-green hills. Just above the town on the north side, Hanover horse farms bred the nation's best Standardbreds. A faint hint of fall tainted the air. Celeste loved this land. She'd seen Paris, Vienna, London, Rome,

Athens and Saint Petersburg as well as New York, but she loved Maryland best. The undulating hills gave her a strength she could never find in other places. In a sense she was blessed because she knew where she belonged. She rode past Idabelle McGrail's and strained for sight of the old girl. All Runnymede had bets going on Idabelle's socks matching. Ida was nowhere to be seen.

The hill steepened considerably. Cora's house, a frame farmhouse built around 1832, commanded the top of the hill. A small apple orchard lay behind the kitchen. A few peach trees drooped with fruit beside the barn. Morning glories smothered the porch. Celeste wondered how Cora could keep it all up. Order, cleanliness and splashes of color clearly showed Cora's hand. A big wooden washtub by the front porch burst with black-eyed Susans. Flowers bloomed everywhere. Even the hens looked happy. Cora worked this by herself. Her husband, Hansford, ran off in 1907. Wasn't women that drew him, but booze. Celeste never heard Cora complain about Hansford or anything else. Cora worked. Complaining took time. Celeste could see her, hatless, stooped over the vegetable garden in the back.

"Cora."

"Hey, Celeste." Cora put down her hoe and walked over to her.

"I've come to apologize."

Cora looked at her.

"You know how I get when my pride gets into it."

"Yes, I do. You go so far out on a limb you can hear the wood cracking."

"I think I have a solution to the piano affair."

"Don't tell me you'll give it to Louise, or I'll die." Cora laughed in spite of herself.

"You do know me, don't you?" Celeste replied softly.

"I know the fat's in the fire."

"I propose to send Louise to Immaculata Academy, run by my sister, Carlotta. She'll receive a good education there and special attention will be paid to her musical talents."

"Does she stay overnight?"

"She could if you want her to."

"No, I want her with me and with her sister."

"I'll see she's brought to and from school."

Cora didn't say anything. Celeste waited a moment and then asked, "Is that acceptable to you?"

"It's handsome of you, but I'm not the one going to school. Louise needs to make up her own mind."

This had never occurred to Celeste. "Oh—well, yes, of course."

"When she and Julia Ellen get home from school I'll put it to her, and give you her answer tomorrow morning."

"Could you possibly do something before then?"

"What?"

"Fannie Jump Creighton is hosting the monthly meeting of the Daughters of the Confederacy, and all her servants walked out. Do you think you could convince them to serve tonight?"

Cora laughed. She knew people had left work even though she hadn't stirred them up. "I'll see what I can do, Celeste."

"Cora."

"Now what? You're as bad as the children."

"I'm sorry if I hurt your feelings." Celeste never had an easy time speaking about her emotions.

"I was riled some, but it was Louise had a fit and fell into it," Cora said warmly.

"I—I'm very fond of you, Cora. I would hate to cause you pain."

"I know that and I thank you for it."

"You forgive me then?"

"Forgive you? Hell, Celeste, even when I'm mad at you I love you no end."

Startled, Celeste blurted out before she could defend herself, "I love you, too."

Cora wrapped her strong arms around Celeste and gave her a bear hug. "There now, go on home and I'll see you in the morning with Louise's answer."

Celeste jumped lightly into the saddle, touched her crop to her hat and spurred her horse into a gallop. All the way home she fought back the tears in her eyes. Why was there no one like Cora in her family? She loved her two younger brothers, Spottiswood and Curtis. She tolerated her older brother, Stirling, and her sister, Carlotta, she actively disliked. Even with love her people were starched, somehow narrow. Why weren't there more Coras in the world? Why wasn't she more like Cora?

Louise and Juts skipped up the hill until catching sight of the house, when they raced each other to the door.

"Mother, we're home."

"Hello, my little kittens." Cora gathered them up and kissed them.

"Guess what, Momma, guess what?" Juts' eyes got as big as a cat's.

"What?"

"I recited all the Presidents in order!"

"Me and Orrie Tadia coached her," Louise said.

"Louise, Miss Chalfonte rode up here today."

"The piano, the piano!" Louise clapped her hands.

"Not exactly. She will send you to Immaculata Academy, where you can study music proper—and manners, too."

Louise's jaw fell open.

Juts started to sniffle. "I don't want Wheeze to leave."

"Now, honey, she'll be home at night just like now."

"Who'll walk to school with me?" Juts cried.

"Ev Most lives down at the bottom of the hill. Surely you're big enough to get down the hill alone."

"I want my sister."

"Julia, don't worry," Louise counseled. "I'll be home every night."

"Made up your mind, did you?"

"Mother, can I really go?"

"Celeste is as good as her word."

"Then I would like to go if I can play the piano every day."

"That's the idea behind it, honey."

Juts cried some more. "I want to go with Wheezie. She needs me to play the black keys."

"Julia Ellen, good things will happen for you, too. This time it's Louise's turn." Cora stroked Juts' hair. This seemed fair to Julia. She stopped crying.

"Mother, why is Celeste doing this? What does it mean?"

"Mean?" Cora thought a moment, then kissed Louise on the cheek. "It means you can reach the Lord through the back door as well as the front."

The next morning Cora reported Louise's decision. That very afternoon Celeste took Louise out and bought her uniforms and shoes. The morning after that Celeste rode with Louise to school, properly introduced her and made certain the child would not be too frightened. Above all, Celeste didn't want Louise to look out of place or poor. She remembered how cruel children could be. Louise was deliriously happy. Teachers lavished attention on her and Carlotta, sensing a cloth that would easily absorb a religious dye, took Louise under her wing. Louise would look back on these days as the happiest of her life. Julia would remember them as when Louise got religion and piss elegance at the same time.

April 11, 1912

Orrie Tadia, an animated pudge, waited for Louise to come home from the academy. She and Juts walked around Runnymede's square, looking in the shops, pausing to admire the Yankee general on his horse on the north side of the square and then crossing the line to look at the Confederate statue: three soldiers fighting, one on his way to the ground from a wound.

"Orrie, think you'd like to be in a war?"

"Only if we won."

"Celeste Chalfonte's brother is in the army, but there's no war." Juts wondered about this.

"I think it's something men gotta do. Like women having babies."

"Orrie, you gonna have babies?"

Being four years older than Juts, Orrie breathed deeply and said in a far-off voice, "You're too young to speak of such things."

"Now you sound like Louise. High-tone. One minute she talks regular and the next she talks funny."

Celeste's work carriage pulled into the square, driven by the gardener, Dennis. On bright days he let Louise out on the square so she could play with her Runnymede friends. Otherwise he took her straight up to Bumblebee Hill. Juts and Orrie ran over to Louise, resplendent with long curls.

"Louise, you'll never guess what Yashew Gregorivitch did today!"

Louise couldn't wait. "What? What?"

"He kissed Harriet Wildasin on the cheek."

Louise slowed their pace toward home. "I hope Harriet atones for this blotch on her character."

Juts intruded into the big girls' gossip. "Harriet don't have no pimples."

"Really, Julia Ellen, you're too young." Louise frowned at her.

"You'd let Yashew kiss you," Juts asserted.

"I would not."

"He can't get to you 'cause you go away to school."

Orrie defended her newly sophisticated friend. "Louise doesn't kiss. It's vulgar."

Louise took this moment to make a revelation. "I'll never kiss anyone. I'm becoming a Catholic." She whipped rosary beads out of her book bag.

Juts stopped walking. "What's wrong with being a Lutheran, Louise?"

"I've seen the light."

Orrie swooned. "Oh, Louise, you're so deep."

Yelling "Louise sucks green monkey dicks" was on the tip of her tongue, but Juts held back. She sensed a new dimension. As the two friends blathered about their mutual sensitivities, Julia searched for ammunition.

"If you're a Catholic you gotta take orders from the Pope."

Louise was unmoved. "So you take orders from the President."

"Oh, no I don't. I don't take orders from nobody," Juts barked.

Orrie questioned, "Do you take orders from the Pope?"

"No, I take them from Mrs. Van Dusen," Louise answered. Van Dusen was Carlotta Chalfonte's married name.

"Is she a Catholic?" Juts pressed.

"Yes. She's a saint."

"Then she takes orders from the Pope." Juts was adamant.

Louise rolled her eyes toward heaven. "Mrs. Van Dusen's got a telegraph line to the Pope."

"Whatcha gonna do if Mrs. Van Dusen says one thing and the President another?"

Orrie stared at Juts. Why did she and Louise always get stuck with her?

"Mrs. Van Dusen's got a telegraph line to the Pope and the Pope's got a telegraph line to Jesus, so I must listen to him and Mrs. Van Dusen."

"Louise, you're a bad American." Julia Ellen pronounced judgment.

"His Holiness is Christ's Liquor on Earth."

"What's that mean?" Orrie, a Methodist, puzzled.

"That's like being Vice-President if the President ascended into the highest clouds. He's on earth," Louise calmly explained.

"Well, I don't give two shits, Louise. I think you are making this all up."

"Liar, liar, your pants are on fire!" Louise sang out.

"Talking through your hat," Juts sang back in the same tune.

"I am not. Mrs. Van Dusen and Sister Mary Margaret told me I must obey God."

Orrie envied Louise. "I wish I could go to school with you."

Juts was totally disgusted. "Anyone who takes orders is soft."

Louise clapped her hands prayerfully. "May the Lord forgive you your smart mouth, Julia Ellen Hunsenmeir."

"You know what else?" Juts continued, undaunted.

"What?"

"The Pope is Eye-talian."

"He is not. He's Christ's Liquor on Earth."

"He's Eye-talian, nummy. You are taking orders from a wop!"

"He is not."

"Does that mean he's like the Constantinos?" Orrie asked.

"No!" Louise shouted.

"If he's not Eye-talian, then he's like Idabelle McGrail. She's Catholic." Juts grasped for connections.

"You don't know anything," Orrie disdained.

"Idabelle McGrail is Catholic and she kisses Mr. McGrail. And Mrs. Constantino kisses Mr. Constantino."

"So?" Louise walked faster in order to lose Juts.

"If you become a Catholic it doesn't stop you from kissing," Juts triumphed.

"Some Catholics kiss and some don't. I'll be the kind that don't."

"Some things are too fine for you to understand, Julia," Orrie pointed out to her.

"Pay no attention to her, Orrie. She's out of sorts."

"Maybe she has worms." The bigger girls laughed at this and ran away from Julia Ellen, who would be damned if she'd cry even though she felt awful.

May 21, 1980

"Are you going to sit here all night? You're hanging on like a tick," Juts said.

Twilight embraced the porch. Crickets carried on conversations and Louise did seem stuck to her chair.

"God knows what you'll say when I'm gone."

"Oh, Louise, you think everyone talks about you. They're watching television."

"I don't think everyone talks about me, but I know you do."

"Out of sight, out of mind." Juts rocked herself in the big porch swing.

"So that's the thanks I get."

Juts ignored her.

"All I've done for you, sister mine."

"This ain't no pity party, Louise. I asked for nothing."

"You do talk about me. Orrie told me you said I meddled."

"I don't talk to Orrie."

"No, you talk to Ev Most and she talks to Orrie."

"I didn't say you were meddlesome."

"You did too."

"I said you got a nose blister from sticking it in everyone's business."

"You're trying to insult me. Trying to get me to leave so you can tell Nickel more stories about me. I know you, you sneak."

"You gonna sit on the porch for two weeks?"

"I'm not sitting on the porch for another two minutes. It's getting cool." I got up, pushed open the screen door and headed for the sofa. Outside, the two sisters continued negotiations. I missed part of their bargaining.

"Promise?" Aunt Louise asked.

"I promise."

"Don't tell her about our dear mother and Aimes, neither."

"I won't."

Satisfied, Louise cut through the back yards to her car. Mother came in, sat down on her upholstered rocking chair and checked out the *TV Guide* before switching on her set. We heard Louise's car motor start up. Louise loved to rev her motor.

"She's got so many medals hanging from her rear-view mirror I don't know how she can see the road. And that Jesus on the dashboard with the open-heart-surgery pose—that's downright gruesome. If I had to look at that I'd have an accident. The only time I wish my cataracts would get worse is when I'm in my sister's car: Saint Christopher, the Blessed Virgin. If I'm gonna go blind then I wanna go fast. I'm sick of looking at all that religious crap." Mother let out a war whoop.

"Mother?"

"What?"

"Who was Aimes?"

"None of your business."

July 3, 1912

The night before, Celeste, in her wildness, had torn off Ramelle's blouse. Though she was a strict believer in good manners, there were no rules for the bedroom as far as she was concerned. Still, suspecting she might have behaved a bit beastly, she had ten new blouses arranged like the rainbow on the breakfast table.

"Celeste, how beautiful."

"They're not beautiful until you put them on."

Ramelle paused between sips of coffee, then said, "Do you think other women feel the way we do?"

"About each other?"

"No—I mean about physical things. My mother never breathed a word about it. I'm not at all sure how she conceived children. Aside from the fact that we're together, do you think we're odd because we enjoy . . ."

"Sex?"

"Celeste!"

"Ha! You can do it but not say it!"

"No one we know seems to enjoy such things except for Fannie Jump Creighton."

"Darling, I never think there's anything wrong with me or you for that matter. As for the rest of the world, they are their own problem."

Cora dropped a spoon in the small pantry off the breakfast room. Ramelle jumped in her seat. Celeste, eyebrow arched to her hairline, turned toward the noise. "Show yourself!"

Cora opened the pantry door, hand on hip. "What do you want, Miss High and Mighty?"

"You heard everything, I presume?"

"I ain't deaf."

"And what, might I ask, were you doing in there?"

"Polishing the silver, like you told me."

Celeste, remembering that she did assign her that chore, put her napkin next to her plate. "I rely on your discretion, Cora."

Ramelle sat motionless while color slowly returned to her cheeks.

"Hell, I've got no one to talk to."

"Lest you think harshly of Ramelle, I want you to know I am the one who initiates such acts."

Ramelle spoke up. "Spare us your Southern sense of honor, madam. I'm in this as much as you are."

"What are you two squawking about?" Cora still had her hand on her hip. "All I see is love. There's precious little of that in the world. Finish your breakfast." She stepped back in the pantry to finish the silver.

Before Celeste or Ramelle could say anything to one another, Diana burst into the room. "Miss Celeste, Spotty's here."

Bounding right behind Diana came Celeste's adored younger brother. "Twinklie, darling." He kissed Celeste on the cheek, then kissed Ramelle's hand.

"You look marvelous," Spotty enthused.

"And you, my dear brother, are a fashion plate." Celeste motioned for him to sit down. "Cora, Cora, come out of that cursèd pantry. Spotty's here."

Cora hurried out the door, wiping her hands on her apron. "Mr. Spotts, welcome home." She yanked him out of his seat and hugged him until his bones rattled.

"Cora, how good to see you. I never worry about the infamous Celeste when you're with her."

"You sit right there. I am going to fix you spoon bread." Cora started for the kitchen.

"Spoon bread?" Celeste asked.

"Yes, and don't worry—I'm nearly done with that damned silver. Why the hell can't you own a simpler pattern?"

"I don't care about that. I want to know why you don't fix spoon bread for me?"

"See you all the time." Cora laughed and opened the kitchen door.

"I can't imagine life without her, can you?" Spottiswood held his sister's hand.

"No, although some days it would be easier."

Ramelle leaned forward. "How was Paris?"

"Paris!" he said with a definitive lilt to his voice. "Paris is bereft of your presence. What the most beautiful city in the world needs is the most beautiful woman in the world."

"Don't stop now." Ramelle laughed.

"I can't tell you how good it is to see you all," he said softly.

"We're delighted to see you. I thought you'd be in tomorrow."

"I would have, but I cut my duty call to Carlotta short when she breathed down my neck that the thunder chariots would roll if I didn't resign my commission from the United States Army."

Celeste clapped her hands together. "How you and I could have shared Charlotte Spottiswood Chalfonte's womb with Carlotta is beyond comprehension."

"Have you never wondered if Major T. Pritchard Chalfonte fathered all five of us?"

Cora came into the room and poured more coffee, blithely adding to the chatter. "Major Tom was everybody's father, all right. You all look alike."

"Me look like La Sermonetta!" Celeste was indignant.

"You got the same forehead, chin and cheekbones. Her hair's brown and yours is black," Cora stated.

"Cora, what an awful thought," Spotty kidded her. "Course, that crown of thorns wore Carlotta out. She's looking older than God." Cora chuckled.

Ramelle's eyes opened wide in surprise, while Celeste glowed. Carlotta was a royal pain in the ass. Her lectures on penitential lusts delivered over the telephone had been mounting in the last month. Stirling, the oldest of all the Chalfontes, received a daily dose as well as Celeste, and always at the office, where she could irritate him the most. Curtis, the youngest Chalfonte, out in California, waded through letters discussing Saint Thomas Aquinas.

"Cora, perhaps you should present Carlotta with spoon bread in the shape of the cross," Spotts suggested.

"Louise could present it to her at morning mass," Ramelle added.

"If she didn't eat it first," Cora said, heading back toward the kitchen.

"Wheezie has been in our sister's clutches for almost a year now. She returns this September—happily, I might add." Celeste sighed.

"Might you persuade her to play for me before I return to Washington?"

"Of course—but you will stay a few days?"

"Yes, but I must get back within four days. The army needs me for a polo match," Spotts fiddled with his coffee cup.

"Polo?" Ramelle questioned.

"Being a Chalfonte carries with it certain obligations, my dear Miss Bowman. I declare, the army exploits my social position shamelessly. I doubt I will ever fire a shot in anger at anyone—except perhaps Brutus Rife."

"Everyone wants to do that," Cora, back in the room with more goodies, chimed in.

"All of Runnymede." Celeste buttered a muffin. "What made you think of Brutus?"

"He's in Washington quite frequently, you know."

"Actually, no, I didn't know that. I pay as little attention to that viper as possible."

"Celeste, you insult vipers by comparing them to Brutus." Spotts continued: "At least vipers refrain from buying congressmen like they were peanuts at the ball park."

"With the administration we have today, I don't find the commercialization of Congress terribly shocking."

"Brutus shocks even the debased," Spotts told his sister. "I can barely avoid the man, because he courts the army like a feverish lover. Now he's peddling artillery improvements. I fully expect the shells to arrive as empty casings."

"He's a crook, yes, but he does seem genuine about munitions advancements." Ramelle startled the others.

"What makes you say that?" Celeste placed her knife across her plate.

"I get around," she remarked lightly.

"Oh, you mean his hysteria about another war in Europe?" Spotts asked. "He's promoting catastrophe all over Washington while simultaneously appealing to military nationalism, which promotes it."

"Do you think there will be another war? Is there talk of such things in France?"

"Darling, my leave there was short and I scarcely approached the topic with our old friends, who were far more interested in raising glasses—but everyone is arming, heavily."

Celeste and Ramelle paused for a moment, then let the dark thought flee from their minds.

"I saw Grace Pettibone, Elder Gorgeous. She and Sigourny command all the bohemians."

"Sigourny Romaine, that damned gossip posing as a novelist. Betrayal is more important to a writer than grammer," Celeste sniffed.

Spottiswood stared for a long moment, then asked, as though speaking from another room, "Did they ever prove that Cassius Rife killed Cora's father?"

Celeste blinked. "Whatever made you think of that?"

"I don't know. I honestly don't know."

"When was that?" Ramelle snapped to attention.

"Eighteen ninety-two," Spotts answered.

So many things in Runnymede were quietly taken for granted. Births, deaths, loves, hates grew up through the town like a vine around a tree. Distinguishing the vine from the trunk or the leaves from one another took concentration.

Spotts continued: "Hans Zepp, Cora's father, opposed many of Cassius Rife's business deals. He was killed in a carriage accident on a rainy night up by Dead Man's Curve, you know, about a mile from the munitions factory. To this day no one knows why Hans was up there. He had nothing to do with the factory."

Celeste picked up the story. "No one could prove that Cassius Rife had him killed, but most people in the town believed, and still do, that Hans was murdered. Brutus was twenty at the time. Many think Cassius hired his own son for the kill."

"God, what a chilling story! I've never heard Cora talk about it." Ramelle shuddered.

"You know Cora's philosophy: 'Talk of old troubles may bring on new.'" Celeste smiled weakly.

July 4, 1912

"They all turn out for the Fourth—young and old, rich and poor, black and white, drunk and sober," Spottiswood sang out, watching the ladies preen themselves before the hall mirror.

"A Fourth without a disaster—do you think it's possible?" Celeste adjusted her "Votes for Women" pin.

Spotts looked out the window. "The weather's beautiful, so it won't be hailstones."

"Who leads the parade this year—South or North?" Ramelle tried to center her hat.

"It's an even year. Increase Martin will charge out with Old Dixie, pumps gleaming." Exhilarated by the sunshine, Spotts couldn't sit another minute. "Darlings, I'll meet you at the gate."

"Fine." Celeste eyed her button suspiciously as it tipped in the direction of her right breast even though she'd pinned it on three times already.

"Maybe the vets will start in again. I never will forget the year Captain Tibbet took off his wooden leg and swatted Keeper Baines."

"Darling, you missed 1901, when Runnymede enjoyed a saber clash. The Southern fire department broke it up, but not before Diller Beard spewed a fountain of blood from his left ass cheek." Celeste's laughter rang out clear.

"Something has to go wrong. Shall we bet on it?"

"I wager that Caesura Frothingham takes her Daughters of the Confederacy regiment too fast around the square and collides with Minta Mae Dexter, rear guard of the Sisters of Gettysburg." Celeste savored the vision of two busty matrons boiling over in front of God and everybody, while Fannie Jump Creighton, Caesura's second in command, would try to break up the fight.

"If only I could bet on Yashew Gregorivitch, but he's off the floats this year." Ramelle thought out loud.

"Well, I guess after that scandal last year."

"We never will see the equal of it."

"The Dorcas Aid Society still won't speak to his mother. La Sermonetta prayed for his soul publicly lest the Lord strike him dead for portraying gentle Jesus on the cross."

"I didn't mind him hanging on that cross with paint on his hands and feet, but the screaming was hard to bear."

"I thought the float number on his back rather a nice touch."

"Celeste, you are wicked."

"For once you and La Sermonetta are in accord."

"Will she be in the parade this year?"

"My sister miss an opportunity to waddle in public with a Bible clasped to her bosom? She'll no doubt have a float constructed that allows her to walk on water."

"Then I will bet that she creates the spectacle."

"Ramelle, her drawing breath is a spectacle. Here—your hat isn't rakish enough. Let me tilt it for you. Yes, that's better. I doubt anyone will watch the parade. They'll be gazing at you."

"Base flatterer, are you ready?"

"Quite."

The two beauties sailed out the door into a shining July day. Spotts, flawless in his captain's uniform, raced between them and they linked their arms through his. As they promenaded down to the square they could see the bands, politicians, various societies and clubs backed up all the way to the Hanover road. The children on the floats nearly got the rash from excitement.

Cora posted herself at the edge of the square so she could get a good view of Louise and Julia approaching the square and then circling it. Louise had won the singular honor of being the Statue of Liberty for the annual float "Liberty Enlightening the World." Several years before, Delphine Bickerstaff was Liberty and now she was an actress on Broadway. Louise, all of eleven, knew this was her magic moment. Julia Ellen had to be content with being a tugboat in New York harbor.

Orrie Tadia skipped over to Cora. "Mrs. Hunsenmeir, do you see anything moving down there?"

"No, Orrie, not yet."

Cora caught sight of one enormous white hat with golden hair cascading underneath. Celeste, waspwaisted in her apricot dress, disdained a hat and let her black hair shine in the hot sun. Spotts simply sparkled in the middle.

Ramelle dipped her parasol. Celeste waved to Cora and Spotts called out, "Happy Fourth."

A quick drum roll and bugle blast riveted the crowd. From a few blocks away huge horses' hoofs were heard and everyone got goose bumps immediately. Increase Martin turned the corner, driving a sparkling fire engine, Old Dixie; enormous black horses pulled in unison, their manes and tails braided with gray and gold. The giant engine glided smoothly behind all that power. A few paces behind Old Dixie rode Lawrence Villcher with four dappled grays, their manes and tails interwoven with blue and gold. The North Runnymede fire department boasted a white engine. Increase and the boys said it had no more power than a grasshopper urinating. Today the rivalries melted under the sun. The first band came into view. The new band uniforms were as loud as the music—rooster red, with gobs of gold braid hung all over their bodies. Behind the first band marched the Yankee war vets. Those that couldn't walk were in caned wheelchairs. Theodore Baumeister, highest-ranking officer alive, led the way. While many a paunch could no longer be contained by a blue coat, the fellows marched in good order. Following them, the Olive Branch Petition band, all women, banged on their tambourines. Tubas and trumpets flashed in the light. The girls introduced a two-step this year, swinging their instruments in time. People cheered and clapped. This Fourth started out smoothly. Behind the Olive Branch rode the men in gray. Officers, ever mindful of the feminine eye even though they were too old to enjoy the results, wore their capes and had placed ostrich feathers in their cream-colored hats. The men on foot stepped briskly. As always, the women sighed. Never failed to burn Theodore Baumeister and his men to see these damn rebels play the cavalier. He called out to his straggling line, "Let the ladies swoon. Remember, we won the goddamned war."

"Think it's going to be the war again?" Ramelle whispered to Celeste.

"How unimaginative. I hope not."

Theodore settled himself. One of Old Dixie's horses reared up as a firecracker exploded near her.

Orrie touched Cora's hand. "I don't see Louise and Juts anywhere. Maybe they didn't get off."

"Hold your horses. Floats come between the third and fourth bands."

"You know, Wheezie and Juts flew at each other today like wet hens. Maybe Louise threw Juts off the float," Orrie tattled.

"Hush. Those two can't do anything but fight."

The Irish band pulled into view. You could barely hear them for Caesura Frothingham belting out to her Daughters of the Confederacy, "Hup one, hup two, hup three, hup four." Each Daughter wore a large ribbon from right shoulder to left waist. Minta Mae, preceding Caesura as the tail end of the Sisters of Gettysburg, kept changing her pace in an effort to throw Leather Lungs off her beat. As the Irish band moved closer, the first float came into view, Rife's Munitions and Cannery. A huge cannon stuffed with canned peas was as far as Rife's imagination ventured this year. Now Cora and Orrie could just make out the back of Louise's head with all her silver prongs glistening. Julia Ellen and three other little girls bobbed up and down between thin wooden waves. Each child wore a big smokestack over her head, with two tiny peepholes. The smokestack ended at her waist and a chicken-wire deck, covered with cloth, made up the rest of the costume. Julia's tugboat had "Cora" painted on the prow. She was already bored with bobbing up and down the length of the float between two wooden waves that marked her channel. Louise stood in her glory, flaming torch aloft and tablet cradled with accuracy, just like the statue itself. The old mule pulling the patriotic sight plodded at a steady pace. Louise looked neither right nor left but straight ahead. Cora and Orrie applauded when they beheld this noble apparition. Even Celeste took notice from her vantage point. Idabelle McGrail walked directly in front of the float, playing "America the Beautiful" on her accordion. For the grand occasion her socks matched.

The heat and the applause went to Julia's head. Rolling back and forth, yelling, "Toot! Toot!" she decided right then and there to exact her revenge on Louise. As she made her pass in congested waters, she gave Louise the slightest nudge. Wheezie pretended not to notice. Making her turnabout, Juts picked up steam and this time bumped the base of Liberty hard.

Louise warned through the side of her mouth, "Cut it out."

"Toot! Toot!" Julia Ellen churned to the end of the

float. On her return trip she gave the symbol of freedom quite a jolt.

"Piss on your teeth, Juts," Louise spat.

"Mommy, the Statue of Liberty said a dirty word," a child remarked to her mother.

By now more than the child noticed all was not well in New York harbor. Liberty began to rock with rhythmic regularity. Cora couldn't ignore it as much as she'd have liked to. She pushed her way along the crowd and out onto the road. Walking up to the float, she cupped her hands to her mouth. "What are you two doing?"

"Mother, it's Juts."

"Toot! Toot!" Julia whirled by for another slam.

The mule got skitterish with all the commotion and picked up speed. Idabelle tried to clip along a little faster, but she was not built for speed. She did manage to play "America the Beautiful" faster than anyone had ever heard it before. Cora and Orrie ran to keep up with the float.

"Ramelle." Celeste touched her elbow. "Liberty Enlightening the World."

Julia Ellen lurched forward, both out of vengeance and from loss of equilibrium. *Bam!* This time she knocked a snarling Statue of Liberty flat on her ass.

"Goddamn son-of-a-bitch, I'll kill you, Julia Ellen Hunsenmeir!" Louise swung her tablet and—*crack!*— she smashed Juts' smokestack down around her ears. Now Juts couldn't see a thing. In all the commotion, the torch, beacon to huddled masses, flew into the crepe paper and the float caught fire.

A man yelled out, "America's on fire!"

Coolly Celeste remarked, "Perhaps."

"I don't know about America, but Louise Hunsenmeir is sure going up in smoke," Ramelle noted.

Juts, blind as a bat, crawled over the last set of waves, feeling her way, and then slid off the edge of the float, followed quickly by the other crying tugboats. Juts ran through the crowd, bumping people and leaving pandemonium in her wake.

Cora bellowed, "Orrie, catch that devil!"

Orrie tore off in the opposite direction, wanting no

part of the debacle. A slowed Juts parted the crowd, ramming people with her prow.

Smelling fire, the mule shot off without warning. Louise, already on her bottom, bounced off like an old pear. Prongs bent all over her head, she was bawling to beat the band. Cora hurried to fetch her as fast as her dress shoes would allow.

Lawrence Villcher atop the white engine spied the blaze. "Turn her around, boys. Float's afire." Not to be left behind, Increase wheeled his beasts and Old Dixie raced Villcher to the blaze. The Irish band, caught in the middle, jumped for the sidewalks. The instruments they had left strewn all over the road were flattened in the rush. The water stopped both the fire and the mule. That blast of water cleaned every tick right off the terrified animal.

Cora had Louise firmly in hand. Celeste hurried over to offer assistance between peals of laughter.

"Cora, which girl started this mess?" Increase hollered at her.

"Six of one, half dozen of the other," came the reply.

The other was being towed over toward the fire chief by a stocky, powerfully built man with a bristling mustache. He handed Juts to Cora, saying, "I believe this sinking ship belongs to you."

"Julia Ellen, what got into you, girl?" Increase was amazed.

"Toot! Toot!"

Cora rapped the sorry smokestack. "Juts, take that damn thing off your head and answer the man."

Juts wriggled out of her smokestack.

"Well?" Cora demanded.

"It was Louise's fault."

"Liar, liar!" Louise took a roundhouse swing and missed. Cora grabbed an ear apiece. "Simmer down, young ladies. I've had just about enough of this. As far as I can see, you're both party to it. Now apologize to Chief Martin and Chief Villcher."

"I'm sorry," Juts whispered.

"I apologize for both myself and my ratty sister," Wheezie offered.

"Louise." Cora squeezed her ear, then let both of

them go. "You two stay right here until you get this pile cleaned up, you hear? When you're done, I'll be at the pavilion." She turned her back on them. Louise leapt for Julia's throat. A hand caught her by the back of her costume and held her suspended.

"Louise, revenge is a dish best eaten cold." Celeste deposited her on the ground again.

Louise had time to ponder her meaning as she picked up broken waves, a splintered tablet and squashed trumpets.

Juts' catcher stood off to the side. As Cora headed for the pavilion, he took his cap off and walked beside her.

Cora turned to him. "Thank you, sir, for fetching my girl. I was so wrought up before, I forgot my manners."

"I enjoyed it. It isn't every day I get to chase a tugboat." He laughed, then he put out his hand. "I'm Aimes Rankin."

"Cora Hunsenmeir."

"May I accompany you to the pavilion?" The man tried not to hold his breath.

"I'd be pleased if you would."

September 13, 1914

Ev Most's head was smothered in tiny brown curls. Her merry eyes darted around the street. Julia Ellen, too, carried a spark of devilment in her eyes. To look at the two of them, you knew they were up to no good. Juts carried the *Runnymede Clarion* to Celeste Chalfonte's. "German Line Retires, Hotly Pursued," blared the headline. "Report Kaiser's Son, Prince Eitel Friedrich, Killed" was squeezed in underneath a story about a French aviator performing heroic feats over Troyes. Juts paid no attention to the front page. She and Ev tried to look at the movie announcement without smudging Celeste's paper.

Although it was Sunday, Celeste pressed Louise into service. Louise played "By the Light of the Silvery Moon" while Celeste, Ramelle, Fairy Thatcher and Fannie Jump Creighton languished in boredom. Celeste's two Persians, Madame de Staël and Madame Récamier, sprawled underneath the piano, enjoying the vibrations. Cora and Aimes were back up on Bumblebee Hill, tending the garden. Aimes had been living there nearly two years.

"Louise, that's lovely," Ramelle praised her.

"Here's your paper, Miss Chalfonte." Juts and Ev burst through the door.

"Thank you, Julia Ellen." Celeste opened the folded paper and read the headline. "According to this, the Germans will collapse anytime now."

"That's not what the *Runnymede Trumpet* said," Fannie avowed.

"I know. That's why I had Julia Ellen and Ev run over to the north side of the square and get the *Clarion.*"

"I wish Grace Pettibone and half our friends weren't in France," Fairy moaned.

"What does Spotty say?" Ramelle brushed back a lock of hair.

"Yes, what does your brother think of all this? He's a military man." Fannie's gin voice scratched.

"Spotty hopes we escape the pull of the maelstrom. He writes that we have barely two hundred thousand men in the armed forces."

"What makes a war?" asked Juts, all of nine years old.

Ramelle noticed the other women hesitate a moment, so she tried. "Have you ever seen two boys at school fight over marbles?"

Louise piped up, "Juts smashed Rupert Speicher smack in the jaw Friday over a clearie. Orrie told me."

"Shut up, Wheeze." Juts glowered.

"Julia Ellen, can't you conduct yourself like a lady?"

Louise spoke with the wisdom of thirteen years, fortified by long, feminine curls.

"Then you know what war is about," Ramelle concluded.

"Only it's on a larger scale." Fairy thoughtfully amended the conversation.

"I feel vaguely frightened," Fannie said.

"Why?" Celeste's voice sharpened. "Since the French Revolution we have all become habitués of terror."

Louise struck up "In the Good Old Summertime."

"Wonderful, Louise," Fannie called to her. "Yes, let's forget this whole thing. After all, there is an ocean between us. Celeste, how about some magnolia droppings?"

"Spirits on the Sabbath?" Celeste mocked her.

"Communion's wine, is it not?" Fannie persisted.

Louise stopped playing and became solemn. "Communion is a sacrament, Mrs. Creighton. That's what Mrs. Van Dusen says. Take, eat, this is my body—"

Celeste interrupted. "Thank you, Louise, but we needn't hear of cannibalism on such a radiant day."

Ramelle returned from the pantry, balancing a tray. Fannie leapt for it and poured herself a drink before Ramelle could place the tray on a table.

"Ah, I'm ready to face the Hun."

"He can't be any worse than Creighton." Celeste couldn't resist.

"Miss Chalfonte, may I be excused? Orrie and I have a social engagement," Louise asked.

"Social engagement, ha! You are going to use Orrie's curling iron." Juts couldn't believe her sister wanted to fry her hair.

"At least I don't show myself in public all strubbly."

"I comb my hair."

"With a pitchfork," Louise sniffed.

"You two." Ramelle sighed. "You may go, dear, and thank you very much for the concert."

Louise scooted out the door. Juts and Ev eyed the glasses.

"Mrs. Creighton, may I have a sip?" Ev put her hands behind her back.

"Well . . ."

"She has to learn sometime."

"You've got a point there, Celeste." Fannie's eyebrows furrowed. "Here, Ev, one little sip. Let it go down very slowly."

Ev's mouth puckered. "Ohh, it's bitter."

Juts grabbed the glass. "Gimme some." Before anyone could stop her she gulped down the contents.

"Ack!"

"Here, child, quick drink this water." Ramelle handed her a glass. "There, doesn't that feel better?"

Ev, not to be outdone by Juts' boldness, picked up the lovely crystal decanter and swallowed a healthy mouthful of gin. Tears came to her eyes, but she wouldn't cough. Juts snatched the bottle from Ev, but before she could challenge her friend's bravery Celeste plucked it from her hand.

"Young ladies."

"The girls have the right idea, Celeste, honey. Let's get stewed," Fannie urged them all.

"On Sunday?" Fairy was incredulous.

"Fannie, my ally against normality, a deliberate eccentric." Celeste poured herself a glass and toasted a beaming Fannie.

Juts and Ev sat down to better calm the fire in their throats. The four women downed two toasts in quick succession.

Fannie twinkled. "Girls, I have it."

"Go to your doctor, not us." Celeste smirked.

"Celeste, really." Fannie feigned an indignant expression, took a breath, then stepped out before her comrades like a speaker. "A perfect Sunday afternoon. Just listen to me. We'll ride into the country. I know there's a fortune in antiques stashed in those farmers' houses. They don't even know their doodads are worth anything. So we ride out and tell them we're the Mission Sisters. Then we espy the houses for goods and ask them to donate this spinning wheel to the mission and that musket to the relief of the unfortunate. You see?"

"Fannie, that's pirating." Fairy helped herself to another swig.

"Caveat emptor." Fannie flourished her glass grandly.

"We're not buying anything." Ramelle laughed.

"You know what I mean," Fannie insisted. "If they don't know the value of what they own, why shouldn't they be relieved of it?"

"Are you sure you aren't from the Rife family?" Celeste asked her.

"Oh, come on. Just for fun. We can give all our treasures back the next day." Fannie's voice rose. "Come on. All this war news be damned. Let's have some fun."

"Why not?" Celeste sailed gracefully out of the room.

"Now where's she going?" Fannie wondered.

Her question was answered a few minutes later when a horn honked. Celeste sat in the front of her beautiful Hispano-Suiza. The grownups raced for the door. Juts and Ev followed.

"Can we go? Can we go? Please, Miss Chalfonte?"

Fannie peered at them shrewdly, then put her foot on the running board, much in the manner of a man at a bar. "Children will provide our cloak of innocence."

Ramelle laughed behind her hand, while Fairy sputtered. Celeste motioned to the children to come near her. "Do you promise never to reveal this afternoon to anyone?"

"Yes, yes," they agreed.

"All right then, climb in. You are now Mission Sisters."

Fannie, ever mindful of her priorities, concealed the gin decanter in the folds of her expensive dress. As the car headed for the countryside, safe from townspeople's eyes, she passed her booty around the car. Two miles down the Frederick road, a lovely farmhouse came into view.

"Shall we try it?" Fannie eagerly asked.

"No. Bumba Duckworth's. He'd never believe us." Ramelle leaned backward and shouted, so Fannie could hear above the motor's roar and the gin.

Celeste passed the farmhouse and pulled over to the side of the road amid honeysuckles.

"Celeste, what are you doing?" Fairy asked.

"It occurred to me that we'd better practice our routine."

"Good idea." Fannie nearly fell off the running board.

Ev and Juts skipped around the car, grabbing honeysuckles to suck the syrup out of them.

"Julia Ellen, Ev, you stand here." Celeste positioned them in front of the grownups. "Good. Now, Fannie, Ramelle and Fairy, you stand behind them. Try putting your hands on their shoulders. Hmm. Girls, fold your hands. Very good. Does everyone know 'Love Lifted Me'?"

"Let's try it." Ramelle was enjoying this whole ridiculous scene.

The impromptu choir did quite well. Celeste ran them through it three times. "Good. Forward."

They scrambled back in the car. A few miles down the road, their first victims appeared. Two old people dozed on their porch. Celeste stopped her cream-colored car, adjusted her riding bonnet, cleared her throat and whispered in a low voice, "Ready?"

Julia Ellen and Ev got out first. They folded their hands and waited to feel the adults' hands on their shoulders. Celeste stood in front of them, hummed the right note. They started in unison, "I was sinking deep in sin," while they approached the porch. Julia started to giggle but Fannie pinched her. That stopped that.

As their hymn faded, Celeste said in the kindest voice imaginable, "Good Sabbath, sister and brother. We are the Mission Sisters, come to bring you the Word. Won't you let us in your hearts on this the Lord's day?"

The old man looked at the old woman. She spotted Celeste right away. "Celeste Chalfonte, what in the hell are you up to now?"

"I don't believe I have the pleasure of your acquaintance," Celeste intoned, unruffled.

"Hell, no." The old lady was tough. "You're too rich for my blood."

Juts, hands still folded, tried to rescue the cause. "You don't know me. Can I go in your house and look for antiques?"

Fairy raced back for the car, chicken-hearted.

Fannie, looped, called out, "Goddammit, Fairy, hold your ground."

Ramelle laughed out loud and Celeste started to laugh, too. The old lady didn't think it was so funny.

"You just be on your way, all of you. Coming out here to make a fool of me."

Unceremoniously, the Mission Sisters bounded into the car. Celeste turned around and headed for home.

Fannie squeezed Fairy's elbow until it hurt. "Fairy, degenerate coward—how could you?"

Ramelle, in the front seat, couldn't stop laughing. The entire affair was absurd, but you have to be absurd sometimes. Nothing is more deadly than routine rationality, she thought.

Juts and Ev started up on "Love Lifted Me" between giggles.

"How did they know me?" Celeste pondered the failure of their mission.

"Dearest, how many people in Maryland own a Hispano-Suiza?" Ramelle said.

"Hadn't thought of that."

"Celeste, can you pull over? I must relieve myself." Fairy wiggled uncomfortably.

One more time the car came to a halt. Fairy got out to survey the territory. A large locust tree stood by the side of the road. The rest was deep-green pasture.

"Go behind the tree," Fannie told her.

Fairy walked behind the tree, waited a moment, then came out the other side. "I can't."

"You can't what?" Celeste stared at her.

"Are you going to get sick? You simply have no capacity," complained Fannie.

"No, I'm not sick. I must answer nature's call."

"Do it then," Fannie bellowed.

Fairy Thatcher once more disappeared behind the

tree. Juts and Ev strained to catch sight of her bottom. Visibly upset, she came out again. "I can't."

"Can't what, Fairy? We haven't got all day," Fannie rumbled.

"I can't unburden myself behind that tree."

"Would you like us to ride down the road to see if you can find a more suitable place?" Ramelle asked her.

"I can't wait that long."

Fannie jumped out of the car. "Do you want me to stand guard?"

The thought of anyone observing her in this state horrified her. "No!"

"Good Lord, Fairy, pull your underpinnings down and just . . . go." Fannie put her hands on her hips.

"Julia Ellen, will you empty the contents of my purse into your lap?" Fairy requested. Julia Ellen did as she was told.

"Fannie, bring me my bag—please."

"Fairy, I don't understand you. I don't understand you at all. Here's your purse." Fannie handed it to her.

Fairy disappeared behind the tree and shit in her pocketbook. She closed it and came back to the car. Celeste started up. They rode through the beautiful September sunshine.

"Fairy, what stinks?" Fannie asked her.

"My purse."

"What?" Fannie shouted.

"I evacuated myself in my bag." Fairy was truly embarrassed. The children squealed. Celeste almost drove off the road.

Fairy explained herself in a high-pitched whine. "I just couldn't do it on the ground, Fannie. I just couldn't. It's so rude."

"Rude! Rude! My God, if you're going to have a bowel movement in your purse, you could at least leave it there instead of making us suffer."

Fairy receded into the seat. "It didn't seem proper to leave a bag full of—well, you know—by the side of the road."

"Fairy Thatcher, you're not right in the head. Give

me that goddamned purse." Fannie lunged for the bag. Grabbing it out of Fairy's hands, she felt the contents squish beneath her touch. Disgusted, she threw it out of the car. "That's the end of that."

Humiliated, Fairy kept silent for the rest of the short journey. Fannie sat in the back muttering. Celeste, Ramelle, Julia Ellen and Ev roared all the way home.

"Takka takka yogi tonda," Juts called out as she passed Idabelle McGrail's house. Louise, on Bumblebee Hill, heard her little sister's yell and hollered back, "Takka takka." Cora and Aimes played a mean card game on the front porch called Oh Hell. Cora whistled behind her cards.

"Wheezie, Celeste took me for a ride in her car."

"La de da." Louise pretended not to care.

"What'd you do to your hair? Looks like the ends got singed."

"Shows what you know. Curls are all the rage."

Cora smiled behind her cards. "What's the rage—looking like something that the cat drug in?"

"Mother." Louise plopped down on the worn steps. Juts sat next to her and twirled Louise's frizzed ends.

"Don't."

"Let me touch it."

"Julia, stop."

Aimes hummed, then stopped himself to look over his cards at Cora. "Gonna get you this time."

"You say."

Since the girls stayed out most of the day, Cora and Aimes enjoyed a little time to themselves. At night they were both so tired they could barely make love. Today was a treat. Cora adored going to bed with Aimes because he was slow, gentle and grateful. He didn't hop right on her and then roll off like Hansford. When Aimes made love it was as though he was trying to tell her something with his body. Cora felt the same way toward him. There were places words couldn't go but bodies could.

Cora threw a card down. "Gotcha."

"Well, I'll be damned." Aimes sighed.

"I'm gonna set your hair on fire and see if your fingers fall off," Juts tormented Louise.

"Mother, I'm hungry." Louise ignored her sister.

"You don't need to know much to eat, but you do to cook." Cora gathered up the cards.

"It's too hot to cook." Louise sidestepped the issue.

"Go inside and put out the greens and cornbread. We'll eat a cold supper tonight. Juts, go on and help."

The sisters dragged inside.

"You think you're so smart, Julia Ellen. Orrie and I spent hours on our hair today and now I look just like Myrtilla Kidd at school."

"So?"

"Myrtilla Kidd, the Kidd of kid gloves." Louise breathed this news with a superior air.

"You lie."

"I do not." Louise's voice rose.

Cora didn't get up from her chair but reprimanded them. "Enough."

"Oil and water." Aimes smiled.

"Since the day Julia Ellen was born." Cora shuffled the cards.

"Keeps them busy. For all their feuding, one couldn't get by without the other." He leaned back in his chair. "Makes me wonder sometimes."

"What?"

"What makes people mad. Those two bicker over hair and overseas men die over not much more, I'm thinking."

"You ever been mad enough to kill someone?" Cora held the cards in her hand. She didn't deal them.

"Sure. Haven't you?"

"Once or twice."

"But you didn't do it?" Aimes crossed his legs.

"No."

"Me neither. Something stopped me."

"You and I wouldn't make very good soldiers." Cora patted his hand.

"I wonder. If someone sticks a gun in your hand and into the hands of thousands of other fellas and tells you it's your duty to kill other men just like you who now have guns in their hands . . . I wonder. Like cattle, you know? Or a body without a head."

"Takes the weight off." Cora slid a card on the table.

"It seems to me if I ever kill anyone I'd like it to be someone I know. Someone I hate enough to kill."

"I can't conjure you hurting anyone. I can't see you hating."

"I come close."

"At work?"

"Yes. What goes on around the munitions factory just ain't right." Aimes paused. "The men trust me some. Might get them to fight for a union yet."

"People get hurt."

"People get hurt more if they don't fight back."

"Maybe that's what Kaiser Bill tells them in Germany." Cora started shuffling again.

Aimes sat up straight, his eyes brightened. "Cora Hunsenmeir, you don't miss much. But it ain't the same, I promise you."

"Dead is dead. Does the reason matter?"

Aimes stroked his mustache. Cora made him think. She struck deeper than those college men back in Baltimore. In that city he had given speeches to factory workers. Sometimes professors and students from Johns Hopkins snuck in to listen to him. Took them longer to ask their questions than it did for Aimes to make his speech.

"Maybe the reason doesn't matter to the dead, but it matters to the living."

October 10, 1914

Brutus Rife stepped out of his dark-blue Gräf und Stift to go into Runnymede Bank and Trust on the square. He was forty-two years old, a slender man with large blue eyes and an angelic face topped with blond curly hair. The light color hid the gray. A certain hardness around his small cupid's-bow lips was the only hint at his character. His three sisters, ravaged by prosperity, pulled up after him, one in a Pierce-Arrow, one in a Packard and one in a Rolls-Royce; each car driven by a chauffeur. After a half hour in the bank the three sisters emerged, followed by their brother, who saw each sister to her automobile. He was heading for his own car when he glimpsed Celeste Chalfonte walking through the square. He long ago had married her old school chum Felicia Scott. Dashed were the dreams of merging Rife with Chalfonte. What an empire that would have been, he thought to himself. Still, he longed to make love to her. The fact that she lived with Ramelle Bowman only increased his ardor.

"Miss Chalfonte, what a pleasure to see you." He gallantly removed his hat.

"Hello, Mr. Rife."

"You've heard that Antwerp fell to the Germans?"

"Yes."

"I've visited Washington frequently. If we do find ourselves at war we must be armed."

"By Rife Munitions, of course." She looked at him without blinking.

"I've seen Spottiswood quite often. He, like myself, fervently hopes we can steer clear of this European madness."

"Spotty did mention to me that you buzz around senators and congressmen."

"Are you expecting your brother to come home anytime in the near future?"

"We hope to see him for Thanksgiving, but his duties are very pressing."

"Yes, of course. Stirling expanded your business admirably. I wonder Spottiswood doesn't wish to join the company."

"Manufacturing shoes holds no appeal for my younger brother, Mr. Rife."

Brutus pinned her by conversation as long as he could just so he could look at her. "And what of Curtis?"

"Curtis buys up land in a little town called Los

Angeles. His preference for California is a mystery to all of us."

"Miss Chalfonte, won't you do me the honor of dining with me soon?"

"With you?"

"Dinner . . . with Felicia and myself." He exhaled.

"Brutus, I am fond of Felicia, but you know what I think of you."

"I'm not my father, Celeste."

"Brutus, you're a no-good son-of-a-bitch. It makes little difference whether you or your father carried out dishonorable policies during the Unpleasantries Between the States. You continue them."

"You're prejudiced by the past. I'm a businessman like your brother Stirling."

"Stirling doesn't traffic with the Order of the White Camellia."

"You blame me for that? I can't control my employees. Do you realize how many men work for me? Besides, I find it rather odd that you feign dismay because a few smoked Yankees were lynched."

"The dark people have harmed no one in this town. You have your diabolical reasons for promoting this sort of disease. I can't fathom it." She moved away from him.

"Celeste." He grabbed her elbow to keep her with him.

"Don't touch me, you scorpion."

"You'll regret insulting me." Brutus crumpled his glove in anger. Still, insulted or not, he wanted her. The sight of those broad shoulders, narrow waist and erect carriage burned him. He'd thought of forcing himself on her many times. Back in the 1890s he'd grasped both her arms and tried to kiss her. But he couldn't rape a Chalfonte; another woman, perhaps, but not a Chalfonte. Her brothers would kill him. For that matter, he thought to himself, she'd probably do it herself. Celeste was a crack shot. Damn her.

May 22, 1980

The back door opened. Louise sauntered in and tossed her white purse on the kitchen table. Juts didn't look up because she was icing a spice cake.

"Thought I'd stop in on my way home from the beauty parlor."

Juts put her knife carefully by the icing bowl and turned around. "Had it done again in Rinso Blue, I see."

"At least it's all my own."

"Once, just once, I wore a wig to see how I looked."

"Ha! You wore it to cover up your bald spot."

"Louise, I do not have a bald spot. I burned my scalp on that damn home Toni."

Juts' poodle, freshly clipped so he looked like a little black marine, scampered into the room. First he kissed Juts' hand, then he danced over to Louise and jumped in her lap.

"Henry Kissinger, oh, you pretty thing. Your Auntie Wheeze is so glad to see you. Gimme kiss. Thata boy. Henry Kissinger comes and goes and what he does nobody knows." The dog wriggled affectionately in her lap. "Where's Shakespeare?"

"Still asleep, I think."

"Laxybones."

"You mean Lazybones, don't you?"

"Hmm? Oh, yes. My dentures hurt me today. That girl sleeps so late."

Juts put the finishing touches on her cake. "She works at night. Says it's the only time she gets peace and quiet."

"Tell her to set up in the cemetery. It's quiet there." Louise laughed at her own joke.

"Did you eat breakfast?"

"Had my two cups of coffee and a BM. Why? You fixing to serve me cake?"

"Sure, if you want it."

"No. What else you got?"

"Nickel's about ready to wake up. Soon time for her. I thought I'd make some poached eggs."

"Toad in a hole?"

"All righty. How many can you eat?"

"Two. Nice and soft, won't hurt my teeth." Louise scratched the dog's ears. "You know what I thought of, riding over here?"

"Surprise me."

"Remember the time you and I had the big fight over the Baltimore singer coming to town?"

"God, yes. That goes back."

"You wanted to go with Orrie and me and we didn't want you."

"Didn't I sneak into Saint Lou's Church and steal communion wafers?"

"You most certainly did, and fed them to the birds. I was horrified." Louise laughed. "I thought God would throw a thunderbolt at you right then and there. When he didn't I was disappointed."

"Birds need saving, too." Juts warmed up the coffee, an impish grin on her face.

"We had good times, looking back."

"Remember what Momma would say? 'Take the rough with the smooth.' Somehow it's easier to remember the smooth." Juts opened the cupboard and pulled out two cups and saucers with a cherry pattern on them.

"Don't seem to have fun like that anymore." Henry Kissinger jumped off Louise's lap.

"Speak for yourself," Juts said.

"You have Nickel; makes all the difference in the world. Even when she's bad she's funny. She always had that knack from little on up." Louise's voice adopted the familiar oh-pity-me ring. "With Pearlie gone and Mary taken to heaven back in 1955"—she inhaled deeply—"then Maizie in '78, taking . . . I never expected to outlive my children."

"Don't start up again, Louise. You just upset yourself to no end. Here—put some cream in your coffee. Real cream, too. Taste it."

Louise made quite a show of being valiant, put the cream in her coffee, then held the cup in both hands for a pregnant moment to savor the full effect of her suffering. She drank a touch. "Cream—are you celebrating?"

"You bet." Juts whirled around the kitchen, getting the bread, the butter, the frying pan, a saucepan and big brown eggs.

"What?"

"Life!"

Another sigh. "Oh, I thought it might be something special."

"Horse's dubbers, Wheezie. I've got no time for grexing."

"You've only lost your husband. That's not the same as losing a child. What can I expect? You'll never understand. Nickel isn't yours anyway."

"Piss on your teeth," Julia enunciated without any emotion.

A pair of feet plodded into the bathroom. The door closed. The sisters could hear the water running. Juts became more animated and put water on for Nickel's tea. The kid couldn't abide coffee. She turned on her radio now that her daughter was awake and kept time with the music.

Louise checked to see the bathroom door was shut tight. The sound of a shower satisfied her that Nickel couldn't hear a thing. "Juts, have you seen anything she's done since she's home?"

"What do you mean?"

"You know, anything she's written."

"I don't go through her stuff. For all I know she could be back there doodling at night."

"Go look."

"No."

"I'll go with you."

"It ain't right," but Juts was tempted.

"She's in the shower. Quick. One fast little look."

"Well . . ." Juts dried her hands on a dish towel, then walked to the bathroom door. "You gonna wash your hair, honey?"

"Yes."

"O.K. I just want to know so I don't pour your tea water too early."

"Thanks, Mom."

Julia motioned to her sister and they tiptoed back to Nickel's old bedroom, unchanged since she left home at seventeen. They zipped over to the small wooden desk. Julia started looking through the papers.

"See anything about me?" Louise became excited.

"No. All I see here is stuff about Runnymede."

"Gimme that." Louise snatched the papers out of her hand.

Julia Ellen snatched them back. "She's my daughter. I get to see first."

The bathroom door opened and the two old women froze.

"Mother, I forgot my comb. Mom, where are you?"

"Uh—right here, dear. I'm coming." Juts raced to the bureau, grabbed the comb and buzzed down the hall. "Here."

"Thanks." The door closed.

Juts returned to find Louise straining her eyes over Nickel's scrawling handwriting. "How can a writer not make good letters, I ask you?" Then she found her name: "Louise Trumbull née Hunsenmeir born 27 March 1901." "Here's my name! Here's my name!"

"Is mine there?" Julia leaned over her sister's shoulder.

"Yes, here next to mine. See: 'Julia Ellen Smith née Hunsenmeir born 6 March 1905.' There must be more."

"Looks like history stuff to me."

"Maybe she's doing research. Writers do that, you know. She's gonna write about us. Sneak." Louise uttered the word "sneak" without much venom. Hide it as she might she was dying to be written about.

"Louise, let's get back to the kitchen. She'll be out of there any minute."

Reluctantly, Louise put the papers back on the desk exactly as she had found them. She even remembered to place Nickel's prize Mont Blanc fountain pen on top of the papers. The two scurried down the hall and took up their former positions in the kitchen.

"I know she's going to write about me."

"You're not the only one." Juts dropped butter in the pan.

"Julia?"

"What?"

"Do you think you could get her to make me fifteen pounds lighter in the book? I need to fall off a little."

Juts started laughing. This set Louise off and then Henry Kissinger got to barking.

"What's all the racket about?" I opened the door. "Hi, Aunt Louise. Morning, Mother."

"Sleeping Beauty," Louise said.

"I don't know about the beauty part."

"Nickel, you're a pretty girl." Mom bobbed a Lipton's bag up and down in the hot water to hurry it along.

"Mother, I'm thirty-five."

"Girl, woman—hells bells." She shook the pan with bread in it and reached for an egg.

"Aunt Louise, you mentioned someone last night— Aimes. Who was that or is that?"

"None of your business." Louise took a determined sip of her coffee. "Juts, turn the flame on under the coffee, will ya?"

Julia flipped on the burner and cracked, "I'm not getting paid for this, you know."

"Come on, Aunt Louise, please. I'll buy you a piece of the true cross next time I'm in Italy."

"Blasphemer," Louise said without much conviction.

"If you don't tell me I'll go down to Orrie Tadia. She tells all."

"Ain't that the truth." Mother wielded her spatula.

"You've got a point there, kid," Louise agreed.

"Does she still dye her hair change-of-life red?" I asked.

"Ha!" Mom liked that.

"She favors auburn tresses." Wheezie pretended to defend her old crony.

"How old is she?"

"Same as me, seventy-nine," Louise answered.

"Seventy-nine, going on twelve," Julia offered.

"Me or Orrie?"

"Take your pick."

"You should talk." The promise of combat enlivened Louise, already flushed by considering herself a literary model.

"Come on, Aunt Wheezie, tell me about Aimes. It's not fair to bring something up and then not tell."

"Ask your mother."

"Mother?"

"You opened your big mouth, Sis. You tell her."

Louise glanced over to Julia. "How's the toads in the hole?"

"Are you making that, Mother?"

"Uh-huh." She flipped one over.

"Great. Come on, Aunt Louise, no changing the subject."

A flash of electricity leapt underneath those blued finger waves. Louise gathered herself, made sure she was the center of attention, then began in a low voice. "Aimes Rankin was our mother's boyfriend. They never married. They couldn't get married, although they would have. Let me be clear about that: red tape fouled things up."

"What do you mean?"

"Our father, Hansford Hunsenmeir, walked out when Julia was tiny and we never saw or heard from him again. So Mother couldn't extricate herself from that unfortunate marriage." She folded her hands, pleased with her choice of language. Immaculata wasn't all for nothing, she thought.

"Is that what you all were fussing about?"

"Living together out of wedlock is nothing to take lightly, missy." Here comes old-time religion. "You young people of today behave like rabbits. It's disgraceful, and mind you, the good Lord is writing this down in his Tablet of Tablets." Louise rapped her knuckles on the table.

"Almost ready, Nickel. Set the table."

I got up and counted out plates, utensils and napkins. "Don't look at me about this rabbit business."

"You're worse," Louise denounced. "You like men

and women. You don't have the sense to pick one over the other."

"What happened to Aimes?"

"He died, like everybody else." Mother enjoys final-moment stories immensely.

"Back up a minute. When did this man live with Grandma?"

"Let's see now—I musta been around seven."

"I thought I was telling this story," Louise interrupted.

All the food on the table, Mother and I sat down. Mother makes the best breakfasts.

Louise broke her yolk, then continued. "Aimes came to live with us around 1912. He was a labor organizer, you know. This was just before the U.S. got in the Great War. All kinds of union activity then."

"What do you know about union activity? You were too busy watching *The Perils of Pauline*," Mother said with her mouth full.

"Julia, I did go to Immaculata Academy, remember? We were much better educated than you public-school people. Mrs. Van Dusen was keen on keeping us informed of current events—the war, temperance, unions, Knights of Columbus."

"Did you like Aimes?"

"Oh, yes. He was a kind man. I guess I liked him because I knew mother liked him," Louise said.

"I loved him," Julia added. "He was soft-spoken; not a rowdy man at all. I do think he loved our mother a great deal."

"What'd he look like?"

Louise reclaimed the floor. "He was stocky but not fat. You couldn't call him handsome, but once he started talking to you you thought he was handsome. He had a way about him."

"I remember a big broad mustache. Used to tickle when he kissed me." Julia got up to get jelly out of the refrigerator.

"Where did he organize? He sounds like someone I would have something in common with."

"With all your women's movement work, I guess

you two woulda hit it off. He read those kind of books, too." Mother sat back down.

"He roused the men over at Rife's Munitions." Louise tried to sound historical.

"Rife Munitions, right on the Pennsylvania side of town?"

"Oh, yes. We had quite a bit of trouble in those days, don't you know. Even Celeste's factory had union organizers. Course, Stirling, her brother, accommodated them. Especially when the shoe business started exporting a lot during the war."

"How do you know all this? I don't know about Celeste's shoes." Julia poured more coffee.

"I was just that much older, so I paid more mind to the goings on."

"All I can remember is going to the movies with you once a week. I don't recall you getting political."

"Aunt Louise, who ran Rife Munitions then?"

"Brutus. Before him it was Cassius, who set the whole works up—that and the cannery, where Pearlie used to work before he started house painting."

"Brutus was kin only to Lucifer," Mother said.

"That's the truth, Nickel. And to look at him—well, he looked like a painting from Europe, all blond and pretty. Pericles—you know, Pericles Rife, who runs the business now—looks something like him."

"That's his grandson. Once Brutus departed this earth, his sons, Napoleon Bonaparte and Julius Caesar Rife, ran the business up through World War II." Mother filled in while Louise ate one bit of egg.

"Sounds like they never recovered from Latin class," I said.

Mother relished this tidbit. " 'Cept Brutus had two more sons besides Julius—Judas we called him, the son-of-a-bitch. Robert E. Lee Rife and Ulysses S. Grant Rife—that's the other two. Well, Runnymede had blocked bowels over that, I can tell you!"

"They didn't want to run the business."

"Robert E. Lee became a missionary. His mother got real religious, I guess to atone for the old boy's sins. Robert never came back. They say cannibals ate him. And the other one, Ulysses, shot himself at Harvard."

"Living in the midst of Yankee heaven drove him to it," I smarted.

"Shame. It was shame." Louise rose to her material. "The sins of the fathers."

"So Aimes took Rife on?"

"Yes, that he did." Louise sounded final.

"He won. The unions are here."

"He set it in motion, I guess," Mother thought.

"What happened to him?"

"That's the hard part," Louise said. "Here I've been talking so much my eggs got cold."

March 17, 1917

The Perils of Our Girl Reporters flickered on the screen. Louise and Juts crouched in their seats, breathless. Ten days before her sixteenth birthday, Louise Hunsenmeir began to notice boys. They noticed right back. Juts, just turned twelve, jammed her hand in a candy bag, miffed at Louise's primping. A cold, rainy March evening and her sister carries a frilly parasol. It was too much—Louise, who swore she'd never kiss boys. Juts fervently hoped the flicker would bring Lou to her senses so they could get back to the serious business of raiding Celeste's pantry when neither Celeste nor their mother was looking. Louise was breathless, all right, but not over the screen. Behind her sat Paul Trumbull, Pearlie to his friends. Seventeen, Pearlie'd already worked in Rife's Cannery for three years. Age rules bent like rubber around that place. Pearlie received a lower wage than a full-grown man but he made enough to buy himself snappy trousers, a crisp shirt, well-fitted jacket and dashing hat. A short, dark young man with a pleasant face, he strutted in the square with the rest of the young bloods in good weather. Tonight he had ducked into the theater as much to get out of the rain as to tremble for the fates of the girl reporters. Recognizing Louise, he positioned himself one seat off right behind her so he could study her features.

"Madam, would you please remove your hat?" Pearlie leaned forward so he could see Louise's face.

Chills shooting through her body, Louise quietly answered in her best big-lady manner, "Yes, of course, young man."

"Thank you."

"Yeck." Juts tossed a bad piece of candy on the floor.

Kaboom! The theater rocked. Louise screamed, along with plenty of others. A man yelled out, "Great God Almighty!" People began tearing down the aisles.

"Fire! Fire!" called an unseen man.

Louise yanked Juts up to her feet. Pearlie leapt over the seats to their row. "Wait, miss. I don't smell any smoke. You'll get hurt in the mob."

"Goddamit, Louise, you made me drop my candy, Piss ant!"

"Julia Ellen, mind your mouth!" Louise dropped her younger sister's hand. So many people crammed for the door that a few fell and were walked over. Juts observed this and forgot about her candy. Louise swooned because of the panic and because in his haste to help her Pearlie grasped her hand.

"Here, miss. Sit down."

"Pay her no mind, mister. She can piss up a rope." Pearlie ignored an unsympathetic Julia Ellen and fanned Louise with his program. In the dim light he made out her deep widow's peak and very feminine features. The mob crashed its way outside. He wrapped his arm around Louise's waist and helped her up the aisle. Although recovered, Louise wasn't going to pass this up.

"Brother!" Juts trudged behind, dragging her sister's prized parasol.

Outside, the three witnessed a raging blaze coming from a hill on the north side of town.

"Oh, thank you. I feel much better now."

"Please, let me buy you a beverage. Hattie's is only a block away."

Hattie's was the south side drugstore, right on the square.

"Me, too?" Julia asked.

"Sure," he said.

Julia decided to like this good-looking small fellow. Placing his hand under Louise's left elbow, Pearlie correctly walked on the outside. Careful not to be one hundred percent recovered, Louise tried to walk as slowly and gracefully as possible. People raced around them.

"What happened?" Pearlie called out to Theodore Baumeister, who'd just run the few blocks from his apartment over to the barbershop.

"Rife Munitions blown up!"

"My daddy works there," Julia piped up. "He's not really my daddy. We don't know what happened to the real one, but he lives with us. So he's more my daddy than my daddy."

"Quiet." Louise pinched her.

The light drizzle magnified the red sky.

Celeste and Ramelle rolled around in bed, carrying on like trash. The explosion vibrated through the whole house. Celeste, never at a loss for words, cracked, "I know the earth is supposed to move, darling, but this is ridiculous."

Another report got them out of bed. Curiosity won over pleasure. Standing to the side of the window, shivering without clothes on, Ramelle said, "My God, looks like the whole north ridge is on fire."

"The war! A Black Tom explosion like the one in New Jersey last year."

"Not yet, darling. A saboteur wouldn't last long in Runnymede and the Germans don't have a gun that shoots that far."

"Ramelle, it must be Rife Munitions. Dollars to doughnuts." Her voice rising, Celeste threw on her riding clothes.

"What are you doing?"

"Driving up to Cora's."

"Why?"

"Didn't you read tonight's papers?"

"You mean the revolution in Russia? 'Czar abdicates'? What's that got to do with Rife?"

"That's only part of it. Didn't you read through the whole paper?"

"No, dear. If you will recall, we didn't even finish our dinner tonight." Ramelle smiled.

"In the left-hand column of the *Trumpet* there was an article about Wilson, Gompers and the Council of National Defense stepping into the breach between the railroads and the four brotherhoods—the unions."

"A strike?"

"Possibly. The important point is the government is intervening."

"We really are mobilizing for war, undeclared or not." Ramelle's voice lowered.

"Yes, but the workers at the plant see the handwriting on the wall. Darling, hurry. Aimes may be in this somehow. I've got to get to Cora."

She tore down the steps two at a time, picked the phone off the hook and rang her gardener. "Dennis, please bring the motor to the front door."

Then she went into her study and took out the beautiful high-caliber pistol, German made, Spotts had brought back from his European holiday. She checked it. Loaded and in good order. She strapped the holster around her waist.

Ramelle opened the door. Dennis sat in the driver's seat, a shotgun across his knees.

"Thank you, Dennis." Celeste made for the driver's seat.

"I'm going along, Miss Chalfonte," Dennis muttered through a plug of tobacco.

"You'll do nothing of the kind."

"Might be trouble."

"I haven't got time to argue with you. In the back seat." The headlights barely dented the veil of rain. Celeste roared along, heedless of weather and road conditions. At the top of the hill, Cora's soft gaslight filtered through the windows. The two women got out of the car. Dennis stayed in the back seat, shotgun still resting on his knees.

"Cora." Celeste knocked at the unpainted front door.

The door opened. Inside, Ida McGrail wrung her hands.

"Where's Aimes?" Celeste asked.

"Out," Cora answered. She was worried, too, but Idabelle was on the edge, so she kept as calm as she could.

"My Rob went up to the munitions tonight with Aimes. I begged him not to go. I begged him," Ida wailed.

"Mrs. McGrail, did he tell you anything?" Celeste didn't want to push her too hard.

"Said they was gettin' even. Said Rife buying off all of Washington to stop the unions. His factory being part of war things. Unions gonna be unconstitutional." The poor woman's eyes gleamed, bloodshot.

"Did he say what they were going to do?" Celeste kept on.

Cora interceded for Idabelle. "Look outside."

"I was afraid of that." Celeste stuck her hand in her pocket.

"Who goes there?" Dennis's gruff voice could be heard.

Ramelle jumped. Celeste shifted behind the door and pulled her gun. Cora took Idabelle by the shoulders and sat her down.

"Rob—Rob McGrail."

"Robby, Robby!" Idabelle flew to the door. Her huge son stooped to get inside. Soaking wet and scratched from brambles, he was winded but unharmed.

"It's all right, Ma. I'm all right."

"Where's Aimes?" Cora tensed up.

"I don't know. I lost track of him when the factory guards chased me."

"Well, where did you see him last?" Celeste asked.

"We was running from the factory. We planned to split up if there was trouble. Two's an easy target. The guards heard us. I bumped into a loading cart.

I headed south. He headed north. They was shooting, but in the rain they couldn't see any better than we could. Maybe the explosion drew them back to the plant," Rob hoped.

"Didn't Brutus import some York boys for dirty work?" Ramelle asked.

"He did that. He knew Runnys wouldn't fire on their own. Not since 1861, leastways."

"Rob, you'd better leave town for a while." Celeste reached into her pocket and drew out a wad of carefully arranged money. Every jacket and coat she owned carried a small stash in it. It was one of her eccentricities.

Hesitating, the large man took it. "I never figured you for this."

"Neither did I," she quietly replied.

Cora walked over to the hooks by the door and put on her coat.

"What are you doing?" Idabelle's eyes were as big as saucers.

"I'm going for my man."

"But what if he comes home?" Ida asked.

"He ain't coming home."

"How do you know?" The old woman's head was fogged from her terror and subsequent relief.

"They'd send men here to kill him." Cora looked at Celeste. "Will you take me up there?"

"Yes."

Ramelle, considering all possibilities, inquired, "Where are the girls?"

"Down at the theater."

"Perhaps you ought to leave them a note in case they come home early. The whole town's in an uproar. They might return soon."

"I can't write," Cora stated.

"I'll write a note for you." Ramelle found a scrap of paper in one of Juts' schoolbooks on the kitchen table.

"Let's go." Celeste herded everyone out the door. "Ramelle, I'm dropping you off home."

"No you're not. I'd rather be in danger with you than worried sick about you."

"There won't be room in the car if we find Aimes."

"That's a damn flimsy excuse, Celeste. No!"

Cora, her voice low, begged, "Miss Ramelle, do me the great favor of finding my children and taking them back to your place."

"I—of course, Cora. Don't worry."

Celeste dropped Ramelle off at the theater. The rain splashed against the windshield.

"Cora, we can't go right up to the plant. There will be a huge crowd by now."

Dennis spoke up. "Miss Chalfonte, you can get close if you use the old Littlestown road. We can circle around on the north side and get within a half mile of the plant. That road is hardly ever used. It'll ruin your car, though, in this weather."

"The hell with the car." Celeste hunched over the wheel.

"Go up to Dead Man's Curve," Cora said softly.

"What?" A cold hand seemed to smash Celeste's chest.

"Dead Man's Curve. Brutus is like a dog with another bone."

The curve hooked treacherously over a bluff. Celeste switched off the engine. Cora, unmindful of the downpour, ran to the sharpest point over the drop.

"Can you see anything?" Celeste was right behind her.

"No," Cora shouted above the rain.

"Cora, he got away. This place is like a grim magnet for you. Let me take you home."

"He's down there, Celeste. I can feel it."

Shivering and soaked, Celeste was more chilled by Cora's intuition than by the weather.

"You stay up here. I'll go down."

"Miss Chalfonte, I'll go with you." Dennis had already started his slow descent.

"I'm coming along."

"No, Cora. You'll hurt yourself. I don't want to be impolite, but you're too big. Please."

Cora stayed transfixed at the edge. A great sadness washed over her—and a terrible question. How can these things happen? How can murderers walk among us, untouched? She knew he was down there.

Slipping, sliding, Celeste lowered herself down the steep incline. The rain nearly blinded her. Dennis's form lurched before her. His foot gave out from under him. He grabbed a naked bush. She stretched for his hand.

"O.K." She grasped him. "Keep hold of my hand. You feel your way down. I'll try to balance you as best I can." The rain swilled in her mouth.

Not thinking she would be on a grim search, Celeste hadn't brought a lantern. Finally at the bottom, amid a tangle of bushes, neither she nor Dennis could see much.

"I'll go left. You go right."

"No, Miss Chalfonte. Can't hardly see your hand in front of your face. We'd better stick together even if it takes twice as long."

Sinking up to their ankles in mud, they hugged the bank. Neither one wanted to say it, but they were sweeping the area as far as a body could go, if a body did go over the curve.

"See something." Dennis's voice was clipped.

A dark mass lay about two yards off. Groping toward it, Celeste felt her heart rip at her rib cage. She fought back an almost uncontrollable urge to run. She wondered if Dennis felt the same way.

His voice cracked. "It's a man."

Celeste got down on her hands and knees to peer at the face. Revolted, she reeled back.

"It's him. What's left of him."

Even with the rain and darkness she saw they had bashed half his face in.

"Dennis, we have to bring him up."

"Oh, God, Miss Chalfonte, let's wait until the morning. Don't let her see this."

"I know Cora. If we don't bring him up she'll crawl down here herself and break her neck. If we forcibly take her home she'll walk back in the night."

They could hear her calling through the noise, but couldn't make out what she said.

"If you lift under his chest, I can get my shoulder

under his legs. We might be able to climb up like that."

"Worth a try. We can't hurt him anymore." Dennis bent over and hoisted Aimes on his shoulders. Celeste stood behind him and wrapped her arm up around the dead man's hips. Slowly they made their way to the path down. It took them forty-five minutes to get to the top.

On seeing Aimes, Cora let out one piercing cry of impossible anguish, then lapsed into silence. Celeste and Dennis rested the body in the back seat, where Cora sat with his bloodied head in her lap. The whole torturous way back to Celeste's, Cora wiped his caved-in face with her apron. She ran her palm over his brow like a mother checking a sick child for a temperature. Rocking back and forth, touching her crushed lover's body, she never uttered a sound.

Celeste felt like a bathtub with the plug pulled. Shaking, empty, she sternly concentrated on bringing both the living and the dead safely home.

April 6, 1917

Celeste rested in a blue wing chair. Spotty's bold, clear handwriting made reading easy.

Dear Twinklie:

I hope everyone is mending. Forgive me for not writing you since the funeral, but as you may have already guessed, pandemonium reigns here. We expect a war declaration this week. I estimate, given the usual snarls, I will go to France sometime in June. At least that's what Colonel Raider tells us. You know Bunny Cadwalder was shot down behind German lines. How hard it was for me to sit here in Washington amid papers, people and patter while half the fellows I chummed with joined Lafayette Escadrille!

Colonel Raider also told me Brutus got his contract as well as covert funding to repair the damages. Given the situation, any hint of a strike will be met with federal troops. I am afraid Aimes Rankin died in vain. Brutus gathers more power daily. Steel, railroads and munitions are interlocked here like the Three Musketeers. As a soldier I am to be above politics—above politics and beside the point. I find myself wishing Father were alive. What was it like then? What internal petty army politics did he endure for the sake of the Confederacy? What alliances between Richmond and cannon-makers insulted his sense of honor? Worse, my dear sister, I am beginning to question honor. You and I were raised with a code, a duty, a sense of place, position, responsibility to others. We may bear as much relation to this society as a dinosaur does to our own.

Forgive me, darling. I am morbid today. I feel overpowered by events and out of step with my associates. I keep it to myself of course. You are the only soul to whom I can unburden myself, and forgive me for such indulgence. You are carrying your own heavy sadness. Remember last Harvest Moon Ball when I consumed too much champagne and conceived of myself as the planet Jupiter? I laugh to think of it and to think of Fannie Jump Creighton resorting to lewd palm readings. This hour my mind wanders to thoughts of the firmament, though less jolly. Perhaps, dear Celeste, pain is the experience of a marred universe.

Since I can't stop myself, I shall stop this letter and relieve you. I believe I'll be able to come home mid-May. I do so look forward to that.

Your loving brother,
Spotty

Placing the letter on a cherrywood table, Celeste considered the past three weeks, Spotty's letter, the new doubts breaking into her well-ordered brain. She recalled her old cliché: "Revenge is a dish best eaten cold." Cold . . . How cruel the cold was that night up by Dead Man's Curve. Then she thought of something Cora said days afterward: "A snake that swallows too large a prey loses its swiftness." Celeste began to wonder about wealth, war, women. She was so taken with those swirling impressions, ideas, tremors, she didn't hear the uproar outside. Firecrackers and guns crackled. Cora stopped dressing the leg of lamb and hit the back screen door just as Ramelle pushed it on her way in from the garden. Julia Ellen slammed the front door. She was not to enter the house by the front door. This startled Celeste.

"Julia, why are you home from school?"

"War. We declared war on Germany!"

May 19, 1917

A gentle west wind played with Spottiswood's black hair. The extensive, well-clipped lawn provided a green counterpoint to the gold and maroon decorations Celeste had put up in his honor. Spotts had to laugh, because he knew full well those were also the colors of the suffragists. A large tent housing cold chicken, champagne, truffles, caviar and other delights stood next to the perfect garden. Hundreds of guests gloried in the gentle weather and Spotts was touched by the pains his sister had taken in his behalf and by the large turnout. He used to love going to France. He certainly never dreamed there would be a time he'd rather remain in Runnymede or Washington. Starched, shining, he looked the warrior in his captain's uniform. To his surprise and Celeste's, Curtis arrived from California, also in uniform. Spotty threatened to reveal Curtis's age, thirty-three, to the enlistment officer since he knew his younger brother had lied. Curtis simply replied, "I am a Chalfonte. It is my duty to go." Nothing more was said of the matter, except that Spotty turned to Celeste and remarked, "Good God, Twinklie, don't you try to go as well." The three of them had a good laugh over that.

Juts wore white for the occasion. Her high-button

shoes drove her bats, but she did her best. Louise went whole hog. A large summer hat, replete with feathers from countless unfortunate birds, dwarfed her small head. After much begging, Celeste had allowed her to wear one of her pin-on watches. To complete her wardrobe Louise carried an embroidered handkerchief in her left hand. As she walked she cast it to and fro. She could barely wait for the dancing to begin, as she knew Captain Spotts would ask her at least once and then she could transfer the pink flag to her right hand and have it trail while she twirled. The height of romance, she thought.

Bullpucky, Juts thought. She'd seen her sister snitch a pinch of rouge from Celeste's vanity. Loose as ashes! I hope I never get that daffy, Julia grumbled to herself.

Carlotta, La Sermonetta, towered above everyone else. She was the tallest of the Chalfontes. Striding among the well-dressed guests, she paused here and there for a counseling word, a prayer, a magic moment.

"There goes Carlotta, despotically improving our lot," Celeste said gaily to Spotty.

"Apparently she hasn't heard of the Great War and the Twelfth Commandment," Spotts replied.

"And what might that be?" Curtis asked. Overhearing a dig at Carlotta, he had moved closer.

"Each against all," Spotts solemnly intoned.

"Oh, that's good, Spotty, that's very good." Curtis roared. "Perhaps the family could inscribe it on a tablet or even a giant domino and have it installed in the chapel at Immaculata Academy."

"You are wicked." Ramelle tiptoed up behind him. Curtis was hopelessly smitten with Ramelle.

Cora, though invited to the party as a guest, stuck close to the food tent. Celeste had hired people from Baltimore to come and create their gastronomic concoctions.

Seeing her headmistress, Louise assumed a saintly air. "Good afternoon, Mrs. Van Dusen."

"Why, Louise, don't you look very grown up. And who is this?"

"Permit me to introduce my little sister, Julia Ellen."

"I'm pleased to meet you, Julia Ellen."

"I'm not little." Juts forgot her manners, never her strong point anyway.

"Shut up, Julia."

"Louise, suffer the little children to come unto me."

"Suffer is right, Mrs. Van Dusen. Julia's a brat."

"Now, now, dear, she's younger than you and therefore must look to you for spiritual and social guidance."

This puffed up Louise like a blowfish.

Seeing her sister and two soldiering brothers, Carlotta moved over to them. Louise pulled along with her, caught in a religious undertow. Juts stomped at her heels.

"Darling Celeste, I want to thank you again for bringing Louise to my academy. She is our best musical pupil."

"Oh, hell," Julia muttered under her breath.

Spotty began to smirk, although he tried to hide it.

"Thank you, Mrs. Van Dusen."

"Apple polisher," Julia whispered in Wheezie's ear, which she had a hard time finding beneath the mounds of hair.

"I'm thinking of requesting Louise to give a performance for this year's graduating class."

Louise, beside herself with joy, blurted out, "I can do Bach's Tobacco and Fugue in D Minor."

Celeste exploded with laughter.

Carlotta corrected her charge. "Toccata, dear, Toccata. Tobacco is one of those sins of the body, staining the temple the good Lord bequeathed us to inhabit. A sin you will notice both my brothers indulge in freely and my sister, too, when no one is looking."

"Spare us Salvation in Tremolo just this once, won't you, Carlotta? The war will be ever so much easier to face if I don't have to bear your blessing."

"Spottiswood, you and Celeste imagine yourselves terribly clever. God will forgive you your transgressions, although I confess I am not yet the Christian

I would like to be. I find it hard to greet your snide comments with charity."

"Dear sister, you ooze charity as long as it isn't connected to your pocketbook," Celeste flared.

"Your sins are unmentionable, especially in the company of children, unstained yet by vice."

"Ha, Louise is full of vice," Julia butted in. "Once she had lice, too."

"I did not!" Louise's face burned red.

"Now, now, Julia Ellen, you and your sister are tied by bonds of blood. The Lord placed you two here in his wonderful, mysterious way so that you could offer sustenance and comfort to one another as you travel through life's perils."

"How come you know so much about God, La Sermonetta?" Julia unwittingly repeated the nickname she had heard Celeste use countless times in connection with her sister. Carlotta, however, had missed hearing her epithet until now.

"Such a sharp-tongued little girl," she gasped.

Celeste, Spotty, Curtis and Ramelle spilled their drinks from laughter. Louise was mortified.

"My sister resists the Lord," Louise dug.

"Little girl—" Carlotta began.

"I ain't little!"

"Julia, then, not a sparrow can fall to the earth but that the Lord in his infinite wisdom and kindness knows. Think then how he must attend to your life and the lives of other lit—I mean, young ladies."

"God can't be all that great—everything he makes dies." Juts spun on her heel and walked off.

Carlotta stood there, the milk of human kindness curdled on her face. The others had their mouths hanging open. Recovering, Carlotta said in a terribly understanding tone of voice, "Her recent loss, poor dear."

Juts wandered over to the cascading peonies, where she observed Fannie Jump Creighton, looped again, reading palms.

Caressing a gentleman's upturned hand, Fannie crooned, "Oh, you big naughty man."

Once Carlotta floated off to uplift more souls, Celeste

and her gang noticed Fannie Jump, in her cups and hot to trot.

"Darlings, I have the most sensational idea."

"No, I am not offering myself up on the altar of Fannie's lust," Curtis warned her.

"Heartless man—but I will."

"Celeste, are you mad?" Ramelle wanted to know.

Spotty and Curtis shifted uneasily. After all, no one talked about these things.

"Curtis, would you say Spotts and I are close to the same height?" Celeste's eyebrow arched upward.

"Give or take an inch."

"There's meaning to my madness. Spotts, let me wear your uniform. I'm going to let Fannie read my palm."

"Wonderful! In fact, I have an extra."

The two scurried off into the house, where Spotts initiated his sister into the mysteries of proper military attire. With a dab of gum spirits and trimmed hair, they created a very believable mustache. It was uncanny, but Celeste really looked like Spottiswood's twin. On their reappearing, Ramelle and Curtis were amazed at the resemblance.

"Introduce me as a distant Chalfonte cousin." Celeste lowered her voice.

"It would help if you didn't have your ears pierced," Ramelle said, giggling.

"Fannie'll never notice."

Fannie, in fact, didn't notice. With the practice of many years, she shooed off Spotts after the introduction, sensuously picked up Celeste's hand and put it in her lap. Curtis, Ramelle and Spotts huddled behind the peonies.

"Oh, you big naughty man."

"Tell me, Mrs. Creighton, what do you see in my future?"

"Travel and many adventures." Fannie paused and then looked invitingly into the captain's eyes. "Romantic adventures with the opposite sex." She hissed the word "sex."

"I hope not," Celeste sarcastically remarked.

This startled Fannie Jump.

Celeste quickly amended her reply to: "I hope not without good reason."

Fairy Thatcher, champagne in hand, came over and lingered by Fannie's shoulder.

"Fairy, I need all my powers of concentration to call up the forces of the beyond," Fannie told her irritably.

"I say, you do look like a Chalfonte. I'm Fairy Thatcher, a bosom friend of Celeste."

"Fairy, this adorable young captain isn't interested in Celeste's bosoms."

Celeste couldn't resist it, "Quite right, Fannie. May I call you Fannie? But your bosoms—such mountains of pleasure."

Fannie forgot to be shocked, even in front of Fairy, as she was moving in for the kill. Celeste charged on. "I can't stand it, Fannie. Your lips tempt me. You are Venus and I a poor mortal."

"Oh, my." Fairy was riveted to the spot.

"Fairy, do you mind?" Fannie snapped, then turned back to bestow a grateful smile on this ardent fellow.

"Your skin glows like a Renaissance portrait. Your hands indicate such compassion, and oh, your smile; you beguile me like the Mona Lisa." With that Celeste impetuously kissed Fannie, who loved it. Fairy smacked her hand over her mouth in shock and forbidden delight. The peonies shook suspiciously.

Triumphant, Celeste tore off her mustache and whipped off her officer's cap, letting her black hair fall around her epaulets. Fannie wobbled to her feet.

"Damn you, Celeste. This is the limit!"

"Ha, you shameless seducer. Let that be the last time you crow about walking in on me and Grace Pettibone at Vassar. You're just as bad!" Celeste's eyes filled with merriment.

Celeste's prank stirred the sedate lawn party. By dusk all manner of devilment broke loose. Carlotta, after making the sign of the cross over the revelers, left.

Later that night, as the family and Ramelle chatted in the wicker-furnished sun porch, knocking off the last of the champagne, Celeste lifted her glass and toasted her brothers. "From Waterloo to 1914 was a brief interlude of civility. Shall we rejoin the mainstream of violence?"

September 26, 1918

Cora dusted the massive relief map Celeste had set up in her drawing room. Allied Command Headquarters couldn't have been more elaborate. The Western Front, all six hundred miles of it, covered half the room, on a raised platform built for the occasion. On the walls she had pinned maps of the Eastern and Southern fronts. Small blocks of wood represented troops: British = red, French = blue, Germans = yellow, Russians = black, U.S. = white, and Anzacs = green. For the wall maps she used colored pins. Since so many nationalities collided in this conflict, she put the armies of smaller nations under the colors of their heavier comrades. She scanned both her brothers' letters for clues as to their true whereabouts. She read between the lines in the newspapers. Often she was not far off in her calculations. Fannie Jump Creighton and Fairy Thatcher eagerly came every day for briefing. Ramelle sidestepped the martial show and Cora alternated between amusement and irritation. Juts was fascinated by the whole setup and since she displayed aptitude for math she was pressed into service after school to help figure out sectors, vectors, rates of advance, shell trajectories and other exotic numerical puzzles, which ultimately meant carnage. Louise, in her last year at Immaculata, prayed over the map, to everyone's horror. Her saintly streak deepened because Pearlie Trumbull had enlisted in the navy and was somewhere on the high seas in a dreadnought.

"Orrie Tadia accosted me yet one more time today to 'Do My Bit, Save the Pit,'" Celeste informed her war room generals.

Fannie hummed "Our Boys Need Sox, Knit Your Bit."

"Ha! You can't sew a button on, much less knit," Fairy tormented her.

"Indeed, that's why I'm rich," Fannie retorted, swinging her British officer's crop.

"Fannie Jump Creighton, does this mean you are cheating on wheatless Mondays, meatless Tuesdays, porkless Thursdays and gasless Sundays?"

"Well . . ." Fannie swung her crop less vigorously.

"Any more news from Spotty?" Fairy asked.

"He no longer complains that this war is boring as bat shit. He's working with the 78th Division, 312th Regiment. Finally got himself transferred off staff. Sinking amid a horde of boys from New Jersey doesn't sound too thrilling, but he says it's better than the tedium of being the bright young thing at HQ."

"He's hardly a babe," Fannie muttered.

"Compared to those elderly gents he is," Celeste remarked.

"What's that saying? Old men start wars and young men fight them?" Fairy wondered. "You'd think after all these thousands of years fellows would catch the hint."

"Rationality is a failed belief, darling. Whatever gave you the idea humans learn from experience, theirs or others?" A slight smile twitched on Celeste's mouth.

"Marx is very rational," Fairy threw in.

"Lenina among us," Fannie growled. "I don't see it, Fairy, I just don't see it. Russia is Russia and the U.S. is the U.S. You can't go grafting systems onto one another. Besides, what is a wealthy woman like you doing waving the red flag? You're getting obsessed with this, you know!"

"You haven't read a word yet," Fairy accused.

"Bother," Fannie growled again.

"Puritans are the plague of revolution. Just wait. They'll strangle this one, too. Besides, Fairy, your Bolsheviki wrecked hell out of the Eastern Front. What have you to say for that?" Celeste kept on the war, as always these days.

"Each nation must find its own solution." Fairy liked the ring of that.

"They're all a bunch of scorpions ringed by fire, if you ask me," Ramelle said. Her quiet statement produced the usual disquieting effect.

Celeste chose to ignore it. "All right, girls, let's review today's positions."

The three old friends placed themselves around the huge table and began moving the colored wood blocks. Fannie's bearing intensified during these sessions until she swaggered. Ramelle left the room and went into the kitchen.

"Hey, Ramelle, honey," Cora greeted her warmly. "What can I get you?"

"Nothing, Cora. I think I'll put on a pot of tea. The generals are at it again."

Shaking her head, Cora began to throw together a batch of muffins. "With brothers over there, I guess Celeste wants to keep up with them."

"You know as well as I do this project has gotten out of hand."

"Well, it's not my business to judge the ladies."

Ramelle watched over the stove. "I wish I could be as gentle as you, Cora."

"Why, thank you, but I'm sporting no halo."

"You are to me."

Cora walked over and kissed her on the cheek. "Thank you, punkin, but I'm no angel. As for sweetness, you are the one."

"On the surface, but I entertain dark thoughts."

"We all do."

"You, too?"

"Yes, many's the time I wonder why the Rifes of this world go on while the kind souls drop away. There are times when I question God's will. I see no justice."

"They are sons-of-bitches."

"They may be sons-of-bitches but they're our sons-of-bitches." Cora sifted flour.

"I see what you mean. Water's boiling. Dare I take this back to the High Command or do you think whiskey more appropriate?"

Cora laughed. "Here, let me put that on a tray for you, and some sweets, too."

The three heads didn't turn as Cora and Ramelle brought in the refreshments.

". . . shifting troops from Verdun," Fannie Jump was saying.

"Can't risk the loss of prestige. I don't think they will," Celeste countered.

"Well, what do you think is happening, then?" Fairy insisted.

"I don't really know," Celeste confessed, "but I feel we must be preparing for something. If we wait too much longer we'll be immobilized by cold. Spotts writes it's already raining and quite foggy where he is."

"Where is he?"

"He's got to be on the Meuse somewhere. Did I tell you his last letter mentioned that communications from behind the lines always begin or end with 'All Quiet on the Western Front'?"

"Would you ladies like something to eat or drink?" Cora took advantage of the pause.

"You bet." Fannie raced over. "Love your cakes, Cora just love 'em. Now, Celeste, be a good hostess and break out the ale."

Cora walked over to study the map.

Celeste noticed her. "Incredible, isn't it?"

"Yes, but I still think they're all loose as ashes."

"The impersonal selection of victims and survivors grates on the nerves. It does all seem so insane—and yet oddly exciting."

"Exciting," Fairy garbled through her tea, "because you're here and not knee deep in mud."

"Of course, Fairy, but the reality of hundreds of thousands of men, millions really, swarming against one another . . . the sheer weight of it numbs one to the horror. I wonder could Napoleon have imagined it." Celeste leaned on the map table.

"I still don't know why we're in this thing. Democracy be damned." Fannie munched another sweet.

"We're in it so Rife can get richer," Cora calmly asserted.

"He sure as hell is doing that," Fannie concurred.

"I do wonder, though, what madness impels normally decent men to hurl themselves at one another." Ramelle looked at the three generals.

"Fear." Celeste spoke as though laying down the law.

Fairy perked up. "Of what—the enemy?"

"No, of being thought a coward by one's associates."

"Celeste, you can't mean it. I certainly wouldn't fling myself into machine gun fire because some creature next to me is dumb enough to do it." Fannie filled her glass again.

"You're a woman," Celeste reminded her.

"How good of you to notice." Fannie swallowed her favorite gin mix.

"Women fought in the War Between the States." Fairy paraded her historical sense.

"True, but only when the war intruded on their personal sphere. Our mothers and grandmothers neglected to form up in battalions." Celeste pursued her line of thought. "Don't you know killing is a sacred privilege?"

"Drivel." Fannie rolled the contents of her glass, imagining life on a battleship. "That still doesn't explain why a man is more afraid of his mates than the enemy."

"Men must prove they are men. We don't need to prove anything." Celeste finally hit home.

Cora listened to the debate with curiosity, but it answered few of her questions. "For all that, Celeste, don't you wonder? Half of Runnymede carries German names, but our boys go over there and kill their cousins, if you think about it."

"Hell, little more than fifty years ago we killed our brothers," Fannie added.

"Don't seem right, for all the reasons." Cora stuck with it.

"No one could argue it's right, but it's there." Celeste's voice rose slightly. "It's them and us . . . always them and us."

"Maybe the first division really was men and women." Fairy's eyebrows drew closer together, her concentration apparent and somehow endearing.

"Oh, I don't know." Cora smiled. "Maybe it was the right-handers against the left-handers."

Celeste stood straight. "No, the first division was plants versus animals. Inside you, microbes dine unmolested. One insect eats another and is consumed by a bird, who becomes tabby's feast. And so it goes. The nature of this world is combat. We're not plants. We're in the kingdom that kills."

October 23, 1918

The 78th had been in it for days now. No one had time to count how many Americans rotted in the Meuse-Argonne. Spotts didn't have time to think about it. Attack, attack, attack. These death orders issued relentlessly from Black Jack Pershing. Spottiswood Chalfonte, far from headquarters, carried no overall picture of the battle plan. All he knew was his small plot of ripped earth. Orders from above seemed intent on massacring as many Americans as possible. He thought of General Grant, who massed men and squandered them in ways unthinkable at the time. Pershing must have learned a lot from the bastard, Spotts thought. So many officers were already killed he was jumped up to major, the same rank his father held in the War Between the States. There'd been no time to write Celeste of the useless honor.

He wondered where Curtis was in this fresh hell. He'd lost track of the California fellows. He hoped Curtis was spared what happened to the group his own men had followed up; four hundred of the six hundred men of the 1st Battalion, 308th Infantry, were dead.

"Canned heat," yelled out a voice. Spotts rolled into a ball. An explosion shot up dirt some hundred yards off. He and his men were pinned down on Talma Hill, a steep incline festering with Germans at the top. The 312th had tried to take this place before. Why they were ordered in again after that past meat-grinding he didn't know.

The Germans on the heights of the Bois de Bourgogne as well as on Talma Hill dumped an avalanche of fire on the Americans. They couldn't believe the Yanks were edging upward. How could they know the 312th was a patchwork of poor men from Jersey—Irish, Poles, Slovaks, Germans, Italians, Jews—and one blueblood Chalfonte. Even if the Germans could have known who faced them, they would never have understood the courage of these men sneered at back in the States. Immigrants and sons of immigrants were earning the right to look a Chalfonte, a Creighton, a Thatcher, in the eye. Three generations later their sons and daughters would wonder if it was worth it.

"Major Spotts, any bright ideas, have ye?" a perversely cheerful McDougal called to him as they flattened themselves along the reverse slope.

"We need artillery support, Sergeant."

"Sure, and I'm for kissing a Paris mademoiselle myself." McDougal laughed.

"Only hope is a runner, Major." Steinhauser spoke on Spotty's right.

"In daylight? Not a chance," Spotts called back.

A scream and explosion slightly to the rear shut them up.

"Goddamn whiz-bangs," McDougal cursed.

The men hated whiz-bangs worst of all. The shell raced along at the speed of sound and smashed you before you heard it. A man down below shrieked.

"We'll all be in hell tonight if we get no support." Spotts crawled forward, his handsome features still discernible under the stubble and filth.

"Ah, then I'll be seeing all my friends." McDougal grinned.

"Runner?" a small fellow called over to them. "I'll go."

"Parker, it's suicide," Spotts warned him.

"I've the luck of the Irish, Major Spotts." The tough little fellow took off without waiting for a reply. No sooner up than a piece of lead flattened him. Parker Dunn jumped up once more and tore off. Ground quivered around him, jets of earth flung upward from raking machine gun fire and shells. Spotts and the men watched, muscles locked, not moving. Dunn crashed to the ground a second time.

"Done for. Shit." Steinhauser stared at the small figure. His eyes widened as Parker, gripping the pulverized earth for support, staggered once more to his feet and willed himself forward. Blood spurted out of him, but the man would not stop. A geyser of brown dirt shot upward immediately in front of Parker. Steel conquered will. He never got up again.

"Artillery or not, we're going up," Spotts shouted, crawling forward.

The men, enveloped in dirt, blood, the screeching of shells, drove upward. No one at headquarters had ever expected the 78th to reach the top. Unbeknownst to them, their objective was to keep the German flank stationary. They were being sacrificed so the 32nd and 42nd divisions could slam into the center of the German line and pulverize it. The 78th, freed from higher military knowledge, fulfilled its assignment.

"Potato masher," Steinhauser yelled as a grenade landed among them. Spotts sprinted a few yards and flung himself on the ground, rolling. It detonated, covering him with dirt, but he had all his parts intact. Hands on his helmet, he peered up from the dirt.

"Major Spotty, how would Washington like you now, and so filthy, too." McDougal slithered up to him.

"McDougal, you son-of-a-bitch, let's get 'em."

Not far from the top, the remnants of C Company surged upward and drove the Germans off. Spotts kept firing. He didn't know if he hit anyone or not. Out of the corner of his eye he did see Steinhauser jam his bayonet into a slow Hun and rip his guts out. Pausing for a moment, Spotts turned to look back down the hill. A strange hum from far off rang in his ears. He felt himself flying into the air, oddly exhilarated. He crashed to the earth. Assuming a close shell had rocked the ground, he scrambled to his feet again, but keeled over like a broken tripod. Looking down, he saw his left leg was ripped in half through the thigh. His bone stuck out like a white winter branch. Disbelieving, he tried to get up again. McDougal was at his side, though he hadn't heard him come.

"Lie still, man."

"Sergeant, how would Washington like me now?"

Tears filled McDougal's eyes. "They'd say you was beautiful, Major Spotts, or we'd take care of them."

"Thank you." Spotts felt no excruciating pain, rather a deep throbbing. Blood was pulsing out of his leg. McDougal tried to hide it from him. "Sergeant, I know."

"You rich boys think you know everything."

"Leave me. Take care of the men."

"No. The men are fine. We are taking a little vacation from Fritzie."

Spotts heard other men crying, howling. He began to feel strangely light. "I'm not afraid."

McDougal grasped his hand, leaning over him.

Flashes of light erupted like lightning. The rumbles drifted away. The sobbing of the wounded and dying pierced him. "I want to believe this is for something," he whispered.

"Major Spotts, rest yourself."

"I've got a long time to do that." Spotts lifted his head up again and saw the blanket of blood already soaking into the earth. "At least I obeyed the Bible." He laughed.

"What, Major?"

"I didn't spill my seed upon the ground."

McDougal grinned and held his hand more tightly. Spotty shuddered. A detachment reached into his destroyed body. He felt as though he could leave his flesh. Felt as though he would do this in a few moments. McDougal took Spotts' helmet off. He put his arm under Spotts' head and lay alongside him, full length.

"Thank you."

"Shh."

Spottiswood knew he had but a few minutes to live as we know life. He wished he could see Celeste one more time, just once to tell her all the things they never spoke of. He felt himself slipping. Spotts did something he had never done in his entire life. "Sergeant, I love you."

Tears flooded the gritty man's face. "I love you, too." McDougal kissed him on the cheek. Spotts smiled and died.

Celeste strolled through her garden, which was on its last gasp. She stopped and stared for what seemed a long time. Peaceful; peaceful but terrifying. She walked briskly back into the house.

"Ramelle—Ramelle, where are you!"

"Here, dear." Ramelle hurried down the stairs. Celeste looked pale. "What's the matter?"

"Darling, I could have sworn I saw my brother standing in the garden smiling at me."

Within two weeks Celeste was informed of Spotts' death. The three generals were in the war room when the news came. Celeste turned to Fannie and Fairy and said in a low voice, "All this nonsense about the lights going out across Europe. When the corpses are cleared no new order will emerge. Power, society, relationships, will descend in all their confusion on a new generation. The old, who started this conflagration, will retreat, worn out; the survivors and the young will continue the dance." She grabbed her father's sword off the wall and smashed it into the Meuse-Argonne district. The sword broke. Her two cronies stood there, paralyzed. Cora, who'd been in the next room, walked in, put her arms around Celeste and led her upstairs to her room. Neither she nor Ramelle left her that night.

May 22, 1980

"What are you going to do today, now that your hair's in order?" Juts asked Louise.

"Thought I'd go show it to Orrie." She plumped up a curl. "What are you going to do?"

"See if I can chisel Nickel into doing the yard."

"I'll do it. Your mower still work?"

"Yes, but you gotta oil it. It ain't a power kind."

"I wish I could help, but you know my back. I can't hardly work anymore. I used to like getting up in the morning and going down to the five-and-ten-cent store. I held a very responsible position, you know.

Juts smirked. "Yeah, it broke up your day between reading your horoscope in the newspaper and watching *Let There Be Light*."

"Don't get smart, Julia. You don't have regular work, either."

"My ironing's coming along just fine. When I can't work no more I'm going to lie out on the square and let the birds eat me."

"Before I go do the lawn I want to ask you two something."

"What?" Mother took off her apron.

"You wrote me that the renters left Grandma's house up on Bumblebee Hill."

"Yes." Mother's voice was even.

"You ain't living there for free. I can see it coming." Louise started in before I could finish.

"I'm not asking to live there for free."

"Hear her out, Louise. Rest your mind and hush your mouth."

"I mean what I say." Louise fired up.

"Calm down, Aunt Wheeze. I'm not asking for anything. I'll pay."

"You want to rent that old house?"

"No. I want to buy it."

Mother got interested. "With money?"

"Sure—what have I got to trade?"

"How much?" Louise suddenly was all business.

"The house needs lots of work. . . ."

"You don't find old lovely houses like that without working on them." Louise turned positively big executive.

"You've got about twenty acres up there."

"With an orchard, a crick, the springhouse stands and the barn isn't so bad, either."

Mother joined in. "Half that house belongs to me. Our dear mother willed it to both of us."

"I know, Mother. I figure it's worth forty thousand dollars."

"The land alone is worth that." Louise was jubilant. "Gimme sixty."

"Aunt Louise!"

"Sixty!" She picked up her purse and headed for the door, trying not to run, because she couldn't wait to drop this on Orrie Tadia.

"I'm going to be around for a while, so we can keep talking about this," I said.

"Sixty. Take it or leave it," and out the door she went.

"Some sister. I tell you she'd steal the pennies off a dead man's eyes," Juts grumbled.

"What do you think, Mom?"

"It's your life. Do as you please. I'd rather have you near me than in California or New York City."

"I'm ready to settle down. Besides, I love that old house and I can fix it up."

"Well, good luck bargaining with J.P. Morgan. Religion isn't all she picked up at Immaculata. Louise gets mean and hateful when it comes to money."

"Fills a need for her, like Drano."

"Ha! You really got money?"

"Not enough for sixty thousand, but I can stretch it to fifty. If she'll give me terms, or the bank. Otherwise, Mom, I won't have any money left to fix it up."

"You can pay me my half month by month. For spite, she'll make you give her her half all in a lump, then she'll go out and buy a truckload of costume jewelry, wearing it all at the same time."

"You don't seem very surprised about my wanting to come back to Runnymede."

"I could see it coming. You're at that age, besides."

"Smart, aren't you?"

"I know a thing or two." Juts threw the dog's ball and he scrambled after it. "That sister of mine can be a piano fart when she's a mind to."

"God, Mother, where do you get these expressions?"

Juts, surprised, said, "I don't know. You mean 'piano fart'?"

"For a start."

"Mebbe I started calling her that when she got musical. I don't remember."

"Will you help me work on her?"

"Yes, I'll help you, but we can't get her too stirred up or she'll rip her drapes off the window and yank the phone out of the wall. You know the phone company won't service her anymore."

"Thanks, Mother. You start thinking about how we can get around her. I'm going to go mow the lawn." I pushed open the back door.

Mother made a beeline for the phone and dialed so fast she forgot her arthritis. "Hello, Ev. How are you today? Ev, I need you for a secret mission. It's you and me against Louise and Orrie, one more time."

June 14, 1919

Louise, fluttering in her graduation white, perched on the piano bench awaiting her cue. Graduation had been rehearsed endlessly, as Carlotta Van Dusen wanted a spectacle sufficient to impress the parents to send their other daughters to Immaculata Academy. Cora and Julia Ellen wore their Sunday best and sat quietly in the outdoor chairs along with Celeste and Ramelle, as well as Orrie Tadia. Louise had used all her powers of persuasion to get Orrie invited, as she particularly wanted her friend to be overwhelmed by her position. Celeste and the others were overwhelmed by Orrie, whose hair flamed suspiciously red. Orrie was no longer a pudge; she was now a load—a load drenched in store-bought perfume. Orrie subscribed to the idea that a dab of L'Heure Bleue on her pulse points and she was ready for life.

The war was over but the peace hadn't been signed.

Many of the men were still "over there." Neither Curtis nor Pearlie Trumbull was mustered out. Celeste had recovered her wit after Spotty's death but she was quieter, and while she herself was funny, she rarely laughed.

Carlotta approached the podium. "Welcome to the class of 1919's commencement. Today as our graduation speaker we are pleased to have a home-front hero. A man whose work here made their work over there possible. Won't you join me, please, in welcoming Brutus Rife."

Celeste was shocked to find Brutus on the program. "The woman is beyond endurance. I wonder how much this 'honor' is costing him?"

"Celeste, don't trouble yourself over this." Cora patted her hand. "He ain't dead yet."

"One hopes it will come soon," Ramelle said.

"Brutus donated a building to the school," Juts piped up.

"Where'd you hear that?" Celeste demanded in a whisper.

"Louise. La Sermonetta tells her everything. Wheezie's her pet."

Orrie pretended to listen to Brutus drone on about peace on earth bought with our boys' blood. He then linked this to economic opportunity.

Celeste leaned over to Juts. "Did Louise know Brutus would give the commencement address?"

"Yeah. But she made me swear not to tell because she was afraid you and Momma wouldn't show."

"Damn my sister!"

Ramelle pulled Celeste upright. Brutus was looking right at her. Celeste glared back. She couldn't bear the sight of the man. Her sister's crass opportunism, violating Runnymede's upper-class rules, infuriated her. She leaned over to Julia again. "Doesn't it bother Louise that that man killed Aimes? How can she sit there?"

"She told me she'd get even."

An anxious look passed over Cora's face. Much as she hated Brutus and much as she was surprised at

Carlotta's greed, she didn't want Louise to get in dutch. "What's she gonna do?"

"Won't tell." Juts clammed up.

"Julia, I know you know." Celeste breathed conspiracy.

"I don't know nothing."

"Amen." Cora smiled.

"Cora, do you know?"

"Celeste Chalfonte, settle yourself. I don't know nothing. I'm just trying to keep Julia in her seat. You know if Louise starts something up there this one will be right up after her. If they're not fighting one another, they'll take on all comers." She sternly gripped Julia's arm. "Now I don't know what your sister has in mind up there, but you aren't leaving this seat, you hear?"

"Yes, m'am."

"And in closing let me congratulate you beautiful girls, the class of 1919. I know you will take your place in society as faithful wives and loving mothers. You are the backbone of America, this great country where any boy can grow up to be President. My best to you." Brutus finished with a flourish.

Celeste forgot herself. "What about our daughters growing up to be President, Mr. Rife?"

Startled. Brutus turned back to the podium. Recognizing the heckler, he smiled broadly. "My dear Miss Chalfonte, you don't have any daughters."

The crowd laughed.

"No, she don't, but I do." Cora was on her feet.

"Ladies, I don't think I'm qualified to speak on this subject," Brutus demurred. The sight of Cora disturbed him. He didn't have anything against her personally, but still she upset him.

"I am. What kind of great country is this when half the population can't vote!" Celeste warmed to her subject.

Carlotta, enraged, seized the podium and shouted her sister down. "If women vote it will ruin the moral fiber of this nation. Politics is a dirty business. We should not soil our dainty hands with it. Leave it to the men. To us falls the task of spiritual enlightenment. What are politics compared to this great challenge?"

"Money, power, the *future!*" Celeste yelled right back.

Ramelle, Cora and Julia Ellen stood alongside Celeste so she wouldn't be alone, even though they had no idea what would pop out of her mouth next.

"My dear sister, you are an overwrought woman with no children of your own, so all your passion is misdirected." Carlotta smirked. She made a sign to Louise to play, but Louise pretended not to see her frantic gesturing behind the table. Brutus sat down, jarred.

"Concern over the future of generations of women is not misdirected passion, Carlotta. Isn't that what your school is for—to train young women, to improve their minds and form their characters?" Before Carlotta could butt in, Celeste kept on. "Well, I, too, am concerned for these young citizens who are not yet full citizens. I, too, believe women are the hope of the future, but not just to sit inside a house and discuss flower arranging. Has this war meant nothing to you? Men forfeited moral responsibility for the future. You leave politics in those hands and the so-called Great War to End All Wars will be a dress rehearsal. Women must enter politics. We must fight to control the future or there won't be any future!" Celeste stopped for breath. For once in her life she let her emotion out and she didn't give a damn who saw her.

Carlotta grabbed the breathing spell. "God made man in his image, first. We are to follow man, as the Bible says. You violate God's law. Besides, everyone knows women aren't suited to work in the outside world or to run the government."

A parent called out to cheer Celeste: "Women can't do any worse than what men have done."

Carlotta, surprised to find other traitors in her midst, repeated herself: "God made man first. Adam and Eve."

Celeste, full of air: "Man was the experiment. Woman is the final product."

Many of the parents chuckled at this. Carlotta was close to foaming at the mouth. "Celeste Pritchard Chalfonte, you've spoiled this ceremony enough. Sit down."

"My apologies to the class of 1919. Young women, I hope you'll make your mark on this tired world and I wish you well." Celeste sat down. Ramelle, Cora and Julia Ellen sat down with her. Orrie's mouth was on her ample bosom, she was amazed.

Carlotta folded her hands, gathered herself, and then proceeded with the ceremony. "Will the class of 1919 please rise."

The young women, all in white, stood. Each was to walk up on the stage and receive her diploma and then shake Brutus's hand before going off the platform. Carlotta signaled Louise.

Louise began by playing "Pomp and Circumstance," as prearranged. She was to play this all through the ceremony. When the last graduate received her diploma, Carlotta would then recognize her as the piano player and Louise would walk up and get her diploma before returning to the piano. Louise did look forward to the applause.

With as much dignity as the girls could manage, they kept time to the music and walked up the steps to Carlotta. However, the graduates were not past Allston in last names before Louise slipped "By the Sea" into "Pomp and Circumstance." Millicent Allston lost her rhythm. Next Louise tossed in "Hello, My Baby" and then zip, back to "Pomp and Circumstance." Celeste started laughing out loud. Julia, fourteen, guffawed. Cora simply smiled and nodded her head. Touched by Louise's effort to keep faith with Aimes, Ramelle had tears in her eyes and reached for Celeste's hand. "In the Good Old Summertime" belted out over the graduates. Carlotta, already suffering from a bad day, tried to compose herself. She squeezed Kathy Balen's diploma into a pulp. Back to "Pomp and Circumstance," laced with "The Band

Played On." The seniors, instead of being upset, started singing the chorus of "The Band Played On." Louise hit the keys with all her might. She switched back to "In the Good Old Summertime" because more people knew the words. Soon all the seniors were swaying as they waited in line, singing as loudly as they could. Celeste was roaring with laughter. Ramelle started singing with the graduates. This rebellion quivered through the ranks of the parents. A few joined in. Some of the girls called out, "Come on, Mother"; "Father, we need a baritone." By now many of the parents joined in. A curious euphoria filled the crowd, spectators and graduates. Maybe it was the fact that the war was over or maybe it was the fact that graduation was here at last or maybe it was simple release. Whatever, the group sang with gusto "In the Good Old Summertime." Carlotta Van Dusen fainted. Brutus went to her. Juanita Weaver, class president, calmly stepped over the distraught director and took on the job of handing out diplomas. As the last girl received her rolled-up scroll, bound in black and orange ribbon, class colors, Juanita pointed to Louise. The class of 1919 went wild. Louise stopped playing and walked over to Juanita, who handed her her diploma. Amid cheers, the girls sang "For She's a Jolly Good Fellow." Louise bowed and raced back to the piano to accompany them.

Driving home, the late-afternoon sun turning the fields a deep gold, everyone in the car kept singing "In the Good Old Summertime." Celeste, at the wheel, considered Louise's musical disobedience. How hard it must have been for Louise to cross Carlotta, she thought. She must have loved Aimes Rankin very much and she must love her mother. Otherwise she would have gone through the ceremony trying to ignore Brutus's presence. Courage is an odd quality. It can crop up when you least expect it, at the most absurd moment, in someone you barely thought capable of it. Celeste thought of justice, or more precisely, the lack of it. The law allows what honor forbids.

Yes, Spotty used to say that. Singing, driving home, Celeste decided to do something about honor. She'd have to bide her time, but the time would come.

September 14, 1919

A hairy little paw reached up when Julia Ellen wasn't looking and hooked her sandwich right off the plate. Madame de Staël ate the ham out and left the bread all over the floor. Juts, immersed in her bridge game, didn't notice. Celeste and her cronies had taught Juts and Ev Most to play this, as well as poker, to fill in when any of the four got sick or bored. Juts, a whiz with mechanical and mathematical matters, could remember every card played.

Fannie Jump, remarkably sober, shrewdly watched Celeste and Julia bid. Fairy picked at her sandwich.

"Is Louise seeing Paul Trumbull?" Celeste asked Juts. She knew the answer but she hoped to throw Fannie off the track.

"Her and Orrie swoon over anything in spats."

"Is that a fact?" Fannie remarked.

"Mrs. Creighton, it's enough to gag a maggot, the way that girl carries on. She and Orrie swap clothes for their big dates. Between them they have one outfit. If they're ever asked out on the same night it'll be the end of the friendship."

"Thick as thieves, those two," Ev said, sitting behind Julia to study her hand. Ev wasn't as quick as Juts.

"Is Louise still swinging a mean pair of rosary beads?" Celeste's eyebrow arched.

"Every now and then she suffers an attack of goodness," Julia drawled.

"I say, Celeste, did you throw down that spade?" Fannie asked.

"Yes. Any objections?"

"No. Fairy, will you wake up over there? Miss Chalfonte threw down a goddamned spade."

Fairy took no notice. Fannie said, a little louder, "Fairy Thatcher, yoo-hoo."

"What?"

"Celeste threw down a spade."

"Oh."

"Will you pay attention. It's your turn."

"Pipe down, Fannie. I think I hear someone in the driveway." Fairy got up and went over to the window. "Celeste, Carlotta and two nuns are driving onto the grounds."

Light as a cat, Celeste was at the window. "Papists in the driveway!"

"That's rich," Fannie called out.

"Might as well go outside and see what La Sermonetta wants." Celeste opened the door and greeted Carlotta as she was stepping out of her Daimler.

"What are they doing out there, Fairy?"

Fannie remained the only one seated. Juts and Ev peeped around the curtains, too.

"Carlotta is gesturing," Fairy answered.

"Miss Chalfonte's got her arms folded across her chest. Whatever Mrs. Van Dusen is spouting, she don't want to hear it much," Juts observed.

"Salvation on the installment plan," Fannie muttered, and picked up the other players' hands when all were glued to the window.

"Celeste is telling her to go to hell!" Juts exclaimed.

"No doubt so she can invest in property and sell it at a higher value. Everyone's heading in that direction, you know." Fannie amused herself.

"Fannie, you are missing a good one. Sister Mary Margaret is making the sign of the cross. Celeste's language must be waxing exotic." Fairy had her ear to the window, straining for a few heated syllables.

"Carlotta still hasn't forgiven her for wrecking graduation." By now Fannie hovered at the window with the rest of them.

"If there's a way to get even she will, that pious hypocrite." Fairy's eyes narrowed.

"Asking Brutus to be the commencement speaker was insult enough, I think." Fannie looked at her.

"Carlotta traded him her family name for some money. She wasn't looking to burn Celeste," Juts wisely noted.

"Julia, you amaze me." Fannie smiled.

"He gets fatter and fatter, like a tick!" Juts spat.

"Fannie, when you consider it, how does he manage? The whole town hates him. Our people have nothing to do with him."

"When the tide's in, all the boats rise." Fannie pulled the curtain back farther. "We aren't dependent on him, but more and more of the town is. If they don't work in his factories, then they need his workers to buy goods in their stores. Look at the damned Martha Circle, now I ask you. Those storekeepers' wives mix with Ruby, Rachel and Rose whether they like it or not."

"Yes . . . God, Celeste pushed her back in the car on her ass." Fairy whispered from excitement.

"Quick, back to the table. Here she comes." Fannie raced for the cards.

Celeste slammed the door and took her place back at the table.

"Well?" Fannie demanded.

"Well what, goddammit!"

"What did Our Lady of the Cash Register want?"

"She said Brutus Rife approached her, as a Chalfonte, mind you, and asked would she allow him to place a war memorial on the munitions factory lawn—a memorial to Spotts."

"You can't be serious!" Fannie exploded.

"Quite." Celeste's mouth pressed together.

"What are you going to do?" Fairy's voice hit the high register.

"Wait until Curtis and Ramelle return and discuss it with them."

"Clever, how he bargains with the old families."

Fannie got up and fixed herself a drink. She'd waited long enough.

"When do you expect Curtis and Ramelle back?" Fairy asked.

"In an hour." Celeste picked up her card hand.

While Fannie played better than anyone remembered, Celeste thought over Carlotta's other bombshell —that Ramelle and Curtis were having an affair. She had it on good authority, Carlotta oozed, that they rented a room in Hanover for shameless purposes. Ever since Curtis's return six weeks ago, he lingered. Celeste was in no hurry to see him on his way to California. The loss of Spotts was too close to the surface for all of them. Curtis came home sporting a mustache, looking like his brother. The Chalfontes strongly resembled one another. The war had aged him. It had also increased his appetite for life. Before, he hung back. So perhaps he did finally go after Ramelle. More power to him, Celeste thought. Who could resist her? I can't. But can she resist him? I— Damn, Fannie took another trick. Yes, of course they're lovers. I know it in my bones. She loves me, though. I know she loves me. The gall of my sister. Brutus, Brutus Rife.

She uttered out loud, *"Klotzen, nicht Klechern."*

"What's that, Celeste?" Fannie leaned forward.

"Oh, I was just thinking that Brutus must come here or call to discuss this memorial sacrilege."

"You said something in German." Fairy picked up the thread.

"Don't feel with the fingers but strike with the fist." Celeste tossed out another card. "That's what I said."

Curtis and Ramelle made love all afternoon. At thirty-five, his black hair carried a few streaks of gray. A flesh wound in his left arm still shone an ugly red. Well muscled, he was a fine-looking man. Ramelle liked to run her hands over his chest, for he was covered with fine black hair, soft like the fuzz on a baby chicken. As for Ramelle, she dazzled him. He'd loved her from the moment she came into his sister's house. Spotts warned him to keep his distance. Celeste was a formidable opponent. How long ago all that seemed.

"I must return to California, you know that."

She propped herself up on one arm. "I know, darling."

"Ramelle, please come with me." Curtis's voice was low and his mouth felt dry as cotton.

She kissed him. "No."

"Forgive me. What I mean to say is will you marry me? I'd be happy, honored, if you'd be my wife." The man lay motionless.

Ramelle stroked his hair. "Curtis, I can't. You know I can't and you know why."

If he did know why, he nonetheless wanted to hear it. "Celeste?"

"Celeste. I love her. I will always love her."

"Odd having a sister for a rival. I—I can see how you would love her, but God, I wish you'd marry me. I love you." He surprised himself.

"I love you, too. I love you both." She took a deep breath. "When I used to look at you when you'd visit us, I wondered how it would be to make love with you. At Spotts' big party, when you surprised us all, I knew if you came back I'd love you, if you'd have me."

"*Have* you? I'd fight the war all over again if I knew you were at the end of it." Curtis kissed her again. He held her tight. He was afraid to let her go.

"I'm glad we're lovers. If you lived here I'd never stop." He started to say something, but Ramelle continued. "No, don't even think it. You've made a life out there in that new place. No matter how much you love me, I'm no exchange for that."

"Don't say that."

"That's one thing your sister taught me. Place. Place and the life of the mind."

"You must love her very much."

"Yes."

"Do you—" He halted, embarrassed.

"Yes. Yes, we do, and I love her for that, too.

Strange, it's all so strange. I don't feel guilty. I don't feel I've betrayed her. I feel it's the most natural thing in the world to love you. Loving you makes me love her more and loving her makes me love you. Do you think it's possible that love multiplies? We're taught to think it divides. There's only so much to go around, like diamonds. It multiplies."

"I hope so." Curtis touched her cheek, ran his finger along her perfect mouth and thought he would burst from all the emotion within him.

That afternoon when Ramelle and Curtis returned, Celeste told them of Brutus's visit to Carlotta. They all agreed there was no way in hell they'd let Brutus get away with the sly implication that he trafficked with Chalfontes. They'd erect their own memorial to Spotts as well as all the other Runnymede boys. Putting the Daughters of the Confederacy in competition with the Sisters of Gettysburg would raise money fast. Besides, both Curtis and Celeste would kick in a bundle.

That night Celeste sat up in bed reading, as usual. She was slugging through *Das Kapital* in German, but damned if she'd let Fairy Thatcher know. Celeste was forty-one; she'd be forty-two in late November. She remained beautiful, radiant even. Every morning she rode as she had done since childhood. Her body stayed tight and smooth. Ramelle, snuggling up next to her, wondered if comparing Curtis's beauty to his sister's wasn't an impossible task and a silly one at that. Let each simply be.

"Darling, do you know that Juts is becoming a razor-sharp cardplayer?" Celeste put her arm around Ramelle.

"Good. Next time I'll get her for my partner. Where was Cora today?"

"I sent her down to the theater. Gloria Swanson is in *Male and Female*. Cora's never seen a picture, you know."

"What did she say?"

"Said it gave her a headache. She'd rather listen to

Idabelle on the accordion. That way she can hear and see colors." Celeste laughed.

"Is that any good, darling?" Ramelle had noticed the title.

"It may have roused Russia but it isn't rousing me. It's hard to imagine Fairy reading this."

"She's such a birdlike creature."

"Ramelle, there's something else Carlotta said that I didn't tell you tonight."

"What?" She sat up.

"She, after careful hints and judicious indiscretions, announced that you and Curtis were on intimate terms." Celeste closed her book and put it on the night table. She looked directly at Ramelle.

Ramelle didn't falter. "We are."

"I thought so. Did he ask you to marry him?"

"Yes. Your brother is an honorable man."

"He's a good man. I don't know him as well as I knew Spotty—he was just that much younger as we were growing up—but I do know he is a good man."

"Celeste, I'm not going to marry your brother."

"My brother's not good enough for you?" Celeste's defense, her humor, covered her enormous relief. Ramelle knew her too well to be fooled.

"Curtis is good enough for me, good enough for any woman, but he is not you."

"Do you love him?"

"Yes—and I love you."

She hugged her. "I do love you, Ramelle, I do. I know I'm distant—often, too much. So much of my life is in my head, solitary. If you want him go to him. It will be an easier life in some respects."

"Oh, Celeste, I don't want an easier life. I want you. We've lived together for fourteen years. I was twenty-one when I came to you. Our lives are woven together like a braid. If I left I'd unravel everything that was dear to me, including myself."

"I wouldn't be worth much without you."

"Dearest, without me you'd be Celeste Chalfonte. You're like some element, incorruptible. You are complete in and of yourself. It's one of the reasons I love you so much."

Celeste kissed her. "I knew about you and Curtis. Ramelle, you're so beautiful and so kind I wonder that men haven't shot me to have at you."

"You know?"

"Of course. A lover always knows those things."

"Why didn't you say something?"

"It was none of my business. You belong to yourself." She looked at those marvelous eyes. "I hope you haven't hurt him. He is my brother and I love him." Her eyes filled with tears.

"What, darling?"

Celeste put her head on Ramelle's shoulder and cried. "I never told Spotts that I loved him."

Rocking her, Ramelle whispered, "Honey, he knew."

"I wish I had said it. God, it's hell to think of these things when it's too late."

"It's not too late for Curtis."

Celeste lifted her head. "No, it isn't. It isn't. You'd think telling your brother you love him would be the easiest thing in the world. I have trouble telling you."

"I know. But tell him, Celeste. Love multiplies."

Celeste turned out the light and rolled over on top of Ramelle. She kissed her and held her, then curled up behind her to sleep.

"Ramelle?"

"Mmm."

"I'm not jealous. Somehow it makes perfect sense that you love my brother. Love does multiply. I'm glad you told me."

"Me, too."

"Anyway, the advantage of telling the truth is you don't have to remember what you said."

"You!" Ramelle turned around and bit her on the neck. They laughed and fell asleep.

piete in and of yourself. It's one of the reasons I love
you so much."

October 20, 1919

Louise and Orrie covered Cora's kitchen table with
the paraphernalia of beautification. Powders, a curling
iron, magazines on the improvement of one's looks,
small strips of rags for tying the hair—the table staggered underneath their assembled potions.

"Louise, you are pretty by yourself," was all Cora
had to say about it.

"Ha, she's about as attractive as a bag of soft turds,"
Juts helpfully noted.

Cora shook her head and walked out to the garden.
"Banty roosters."

"Shut up, Julia. You are too unsophisticated to understand such proceedings," Louise sniffed.

"Unsophisticated! I'm smart enough to know you are
going out spooning with Pearlie Trumbull tonight."

"I don't spoon, as you so vulgarly put it."

"Julia, your sister is too refined for you to figure."
Orrie's hair blazed.

"For your information, little sister, Pearlie is taking
me to Hotzapple's restaurant and he's ordering a mag-
num of champagne before it's too late."

"Make it a quart," Orrie suggested.

"What do you mean—too late?" Ev Most asked.

Tracing the directions for a new hair style with her
finger in the magazine, Louise didn't look up. "The
government stops all booze come January."

"That'll kill Fannie Jump Creighton." Juts snickered.

Louise smiled a bit at her sister's joke.

Lillian Russell, the ancient cat, scratched herself in
the corner. Louise, for Orrie's benefit, intoned, "The
cat has fleas," as though to indicate she was appalled
at such an event.

"Bet you gave them to her," Juts said.

"Why don't you and Ev go outside and help Mother. You're both too young to be with Orrie and me."

"Yes, and so unsophisticated," Orrie added.

"I'm not going anywhere and neither is Ev. This is *my* house."

Louise turned her back on her. "Then do something useful and go pump some water so I can wash my hair."

"Pump your own water, Fatass."

"Chintzy!" Lousie snapped.

"What's that mean?" Ev needed to pin down the insult.

"Cheap, vulgar." Wheezie dragged out the "vulgar" through her nostrils.

"All right, I'll pump the water to shut you up. Come on, Ev. Let's prepare the princess's hair."

As the two younger girls banged the door behind them, Louise rolled her eyes and Orrie put her hand on her hip. Louise felt particularly mature, since she now worked at the millinery counter for the Bon-Ton department store on the square. Orrie worked at the fabrics counter. Millinery was very respectable work, so Louise was pleased with herself.

"How come you're giving in to Miss Priss?" Ev thumped behind Juts.

"She wants her ass kicked bad," Julia started in on the pump. Ev held the bucket, not that it needed holding, but it made her feel useful.

"So why you drawing water for her?"

"I ain't so dumb. Look." From her apron pocket Julia drew a little packet of blue dye.

Ev's hand went to her mouth. "Where'd you get that?"

"Supposed to give it to Celeste on the way down to the flicker."

"Julia Ellen."

"Scaredy cat."

"Well . . ."

"You don't have to do anything. I'll put it in the water. Water's supposed to be blue anyway."

"O.K."

Julia poured the packet and stirred the contents

in the bucket. A wicked smile crept over her face. When the brew mixed to her satisfaction, she carried it inside. Ev stayed behind at a discreet distance. She'd seen Julia and Louise go at each other before and she didn't want to get caught in the middle.

"Here." Juts slammed the bucket on the table so her sister wouldn't think her too compliant.

Orrie unpinned Louise's hair. "Thank you, Juts."

Louise bent over the basin while Orrie poured water on her hair and then a lotion. She massaged her scalp. At first she didn't notice anything. Julia edged for the door. Orrie glanced at her hands, a parrot shade of blue.

"Ack!" She held her hands up to the light.

Louise, doubled over, couldn't see. "Orrio, what's wrong?"

"Blue—my hands are blue."

"Gimme a towel. No, wait—first rinse this stuff out of my hair."

Orrie poured the water over Louise's hair. Not only was her hair a mysterious shade, but those parts of her skin touched by the dye reflected the blue quite nicely. She looked like an Indian who'd lost his touch with war paint.

"Louise!" Orrie gasped.

Louise raced for the mirror, while Julia and Ev hit the door. "I'm blue! That bitch turned me blue. I'll never be able to face Pearlie. What'll I do?"

A born soother, Orrie patted her on the back. "There, there, Louise, sit still. I'll get some more water and maybe we can wash this out."

Her scalp rubbed nearly raw one hour later, Louise bore faint blue traces but the worst was over.

"That's some improvement. If the restaurant's dark maybe he won't notice."

"Men are sort of dumb that way, Wheezie. Don't worry. He'll think you're beautiful if you wear a gunnysack."

"Thanks, Orrie. If it takes me the rest of my life I'll get even with that brat." She grabbed the curling iron and headed for the stove.

Cora came back in and placed the last of the squash

on a chair, since Louise commanded the whole table. "Your sister flew out of here."

"She put dye in my hair water."

Cora threw her head back and roared.

"I don't think it's so funny, Mother. How'd you like it if your hair was blue."

"Better blue than bald." Cora couldn't help but enjoy Julia's pranks. You couldn't stay mad at the girl no matter what she pulled.

A savage gleam shone in Louise's eye. Orrie, noticing her sudden resolve, said, "No."

"Yes," Louise answered.

Cora, unaware of the heinous plan just hatched, said, "Oh, come on, Louise, forgive and forget. After all, she's younger than you are and full of the devil."

"I already forgot."

October 21, 1919

"Darling, I'm pregnant," Ramelle stated firmly over her after-dinner cup of tea.

Celeste, without batting an eye, replied, "I'm too young to be a father."

"You are impossible and wonderful."

"I'm happy if you're happy. Do you want the baby?"

"Yes, I do. I'm a bit old."

"Thirty-five is hardly doddering. Have you seen the doctor?"

"Yes. I suspected it, but today my suspicions were confirmed."

"If it's a boy we name him Spottiswood, and if it's a girl we name her Spottiswood."

"Celeste, I'm doing all the work here. I get to name the baby."

"What do you mean? I have to go through morning

sickness and the intricacies of your plumbing. Surely that entitles me to at least a middle name."

"Perhaps."

"If you do successfully reproduce yourself, what are you going to name the baby?"

"Spottiswood." Ramelle smiled.

"I adore you."

"I haven't written Curtis, but I will. I'm afraid this will fire up his marriage dream."

"Do you think you should get married now?"

"No."

"I want you to know, Ramelle Bowman, I will not have disgrace, scandal or wasps brought into this house."

"Does that mean you want me to get married?" Ramelle was incredulous.

"No, we'll simply tell everyone a star is rising in the east."

Cora quietly came in to clear the plates. The cook had taken the day off, so she did double duty.

"Cora, wonderful news. Ramelle is going to have a baby." Celeste beamed.

Cora kissed the blond mother-to-be on the cheek and pressed her head against her large bosom. "Honey, I am so glad. Having children keeps you young."

Blushing but arrogant, Celeste bragged, "Didn't think I could do it, did you?"

"Celeste, sugar, I don't put anything past you."

"If you go around taking credit for this, I'll name the child Aloysius. If it's a girl I'll dub her Carlotta."

In mock horror, Celeste glanced upward at Cora. "No, no, a thousand times no." She confessed. "Curtis was the lucky man."

Pouring more tea, Cora nodded. "Uh-hum!"

"I hate you! I hate you!" A scream echoed from the back of the house.

The door swung open and a tearful, half-shorn Julia Ellen presented herself. Lurking way in the back, Louise and Orrie could be spied.

"Mother, she cut my hair off!"

"Julia, you look perfectly awful," Celeste blurted out.

"Louise Hunsenmeir, get in here!" Cora's voice rang with authority.

Louise minced in, not the least bit guilty. "She had it coming, Mother."

"God, you girls don't give me a minute's peace."

"Children keep you young, Cora." Celeste struggled to keep from laughing in Juts' miserable face.

"I take it back. Look at these gray hairs."

"She dyed my hair blue yesterday. Now we're even."

"You think! Just wait," Julia threatened. "That's not all. You should see Ev Most. All her little curls are laying over Runnymede Square."

"Your partner in crime." Louise folded her arms triumphantly across her breasts.

"Orrie Tadia, is that you back there by the icebox?" Cora called to her.

"Yes, Mrs. Hunsenmeir."

"You a party to this?"

"Yes'm."

"Some Christian you are," Cora accused Louise. "It ain't bad enough you near shave your sister, you drag Orrie in on it, too."

"I'm not apologizing, Mother. She deserved it."

"Yes, well, you can just go on and get out of here before I bat you one."

Louise and Orrie hurried for the back door. Ramelle took pity on Julia. "Let me see if I can fix this mess. Bobbed hair is coming in style."

"Good idea." Celeste hopped up to get a fashion magazine.

All three women fussed over Julia until satisfied. She emerged with a close-cut bob that suited her very well. Celeste gave her a cloche hat, and Juts became an instant fashion plate. She was the first young woman in Runnymede to have her hair bobbed. Thanks to her sister's vindictiveness, Julia gained a reputation for being slightly ahead of her time, a reputation she was to keep into old age.

February 2, 1920

As Ramelle grew bigger, Celeste thought more and more about being a mother or mother number two. She wondered if she could behave responsibly; she feared she'd prove a dismal parent. Grace Pettibone had sent her new books by a Viennese doctor. Such dark theories about childhood sexuality made her feel worse. Cora set her right by telling her, "You do the best you can and leave the rest in the hands of the Lord." Celeste wasn't too sure about leaving anything in the hands of the Lord, but the obsession with creating the perfect environment for the newborn gradually faded. She resigned herself to making mistakes like any other human.

Carlotta, upon nosing out Ramelle's condition, stepped up her weekly efforts to save souls, most especially the unborn's soul. When Celeste would no longer speak to her on the telephone, she resorted to writing epistles, imagining herself a female Saint Paul, and equally as dour. Despite La Sermonetta's efforts to align herself with Brutus, both Celeste and Curtis would not allow the war monument to be dedicated to Spottiswood. Rife and Carlotta got around them by having the bronze soldier look like Spottiswood although the statue did not bear his name. This proved to be the straw that broke the camel's back. Celeste no longer imagined there was justice in the world, but she seriously wondered where the line between society and individual conscience was drawn. Brutus Rife had personally killed one man, had paid to put others away, silently backed the Order of the White Camellia and held a large portion of Runnymede's population by the balls. And no one did anything. Celeste asked herself why she did nothing. The man was evil. Perhaps society could tolerate evil if it was rich enough and put on a conventional face, but could she?

The back door opened and closed. Books slammed on the kitchen table. A spirited conversation intruded into Celeste's library retreat. She got out of her wing-back chair and headed for the noise.

"I'm not taking any more dumb Latin. What do I care if Caesar came and saw and conquered? He wound up good and dead." Julia pouted.

"You take what you're supposed to," Cora told her.

"You didn't even go to second grade, so—"

"That's why I'm telling you to finish up. 'Cause I know how important reading and writing is."

"Latin ain't reading and writing. It's boring."

Celeste entered the room. "Latin might not seem important now, but as you grow older you'll understand how valuable it is."

"Everyone says that about everything. I'm tired of sitting in a seat. I want to go out and be making money. Latin's no good there."

"Julia, you'll be fifteen come March. Then let's talk about it." Cora looked out the kitchen window. The snow swirled and the sky looked a peculiar yellow. "Funny," she said.

"Yes, it almost looks like a thunderstorm," Celeste agreed.

A flash of lightning followed by a clap of thunder confirmed their forecast.

"A thundersnow!" Julia raced to the window. "Cora, did you ever see anything like it?"

"Once, years ago."

"Is Ramelle upstairs?" Celeste wondered.

"Taking a cat nap, but this thunder will wake her for sure."

"I'm going out for a short while. If she does wake up, tell her I'll be back for dinner."

"You can't go out in this."

"It's such a rare event I don't want to miss it."

"Miss Chalfonte, can I go with you?"

"No, Juts. I want the lightning all for myself." Celeste hurried into the front hall, put on a heavy coat, her boots, went into her study and threw something in her pocket and was out the door before Cora or Jutts could think of other reasons why she should stay inside.

Celeste could barely see her hand in front of her face. The snow swallowed up her footsteps and the thunder cast an eerie spell over the once familiar town. Playing a long shot, Celeste headed for a row of office buildings a block off the north side of the square. The weather slowed her. It took a half hour to make the ten-minute walk. No one was on the streets, or if they were there, the snow obscured them from view. Celeste ducked into the building. A light shone in the hallway. Sweating under the heavy coat, she opened the door to the office. "Rife and Sons," in a semicircle, graced the glass part of the door. No one was in the office. She wondered if they had all left early, fearing a blizzard. Oddly disappointed, she stood in the foyer. A sound from behind a private office door alerted her. She walked over to it and knocked.

"Who is it?" It was Brutus.

"Celeste Chalfonte."

Quick steps, the door opened, and a very surprised Brutus greeted her. "Miss Chalfonte, what are you doing here?"

"The blizzard caught me. I ducked in the front door and noticed it was your office. I'm sorry to disturb you."

"Please come in. Won't you take your coat off?"

"No, thank you. I'll take it off in a moment. I'm still quite cold."

His eyes glittered. He moved a heavy seat over for her to sit down and pulled a wooden office chair close to it so he could breathe in her face. Her beauty held him as it did twenty years before.

"Now that I'm here I want to ask you something." Celeste stared at him.

"What?"

"Brutus, do you realize what you're doing is wrong?"

"I don't know what you're talking about, Celeste."

"Then allow me to speak of the few things I know about. God knows what I don't know."

Brutus shifted in his seat. Honesty held little appeal for him. Why should Celeste bother?

"You probably killed Hans Zepp many years ago. You certainly ordered Aimes Rankin out of this world. You purchase congressmen like cigars. You hold I don't know how many second mortgages and foreclose with a missed payment. You buy what you can and who you can. Anyone who resists is run into the ground."

"Do you expect me to sit here for this?" He shifted as though to stand up.

"I want to know if you realize how low you've sunk."

"Celeste Chalfonte, you live in another world, a world of cavaliers, courtliness and romance. You don't understand how the world really works nor do you want to understand. You're too good for poor mortals."

"Yes, I do live in another world, but in any world you'd be considered corrupt."

"Corrupt? Do you think rubber is made because people like the jungle? Do you think steel is forged because men enjoy the heat? You must drive people to work. People are ignorant, stupid and lazy. The strong man must herd the weak; otherwise there's no progress, no growth."

"Ah, yes, the industrial vampire, progress." Celeste was as cold as the blizzard outside.

"You'd prefer a vague agricultural illusion? Celeste, you and your kind are a dying breed. It's men like me that make America. You people had your turn and lost it at Gettysburg. It's my turn now. What you deem corrupt is the price we pay for progress. Romans thought Caesar was corrupt, too, but he turned a republic into an empire. America is becoming an empire."

"*Alea jacta est.*"

"Yes, the die is cast. There's no turning back. Why don't you enjoy your wealth and your woman"—his voice sharpened on that reference—"and leave the business to men? You can't understand it anyway."

"You might be right, Brutus, but I do understand

simple morality and simple responsibility. Perhaps this is the ancient debate between Antigone and Creon. Perhaps nothing is new under the sun."

A thunderclap outside startled him. When he turned back from looking out the window, Celeste was holding her beautiful German pistol on him.

Half amused, half frightened, he tried to sound superior. "What do you think you're doing? Put that thing away."

"This is a matter of honor. I don't expect you to understand that."

"You're mad." He was now genuinely worried.

"Precisely."

A jagged tear of lightning cast a sickly yellow-blue light through the room. A deafening clap of thunder followed. As the thunder rolled away Brutus slumped in his chair, a perfect bullet hole between his eyes. If you didn't look at the back of his head he resembled an Indian Brahman. Celeste stuck the gun inside her coat, walked over to the window, put her gloves on and strained to open the window leading out to the alley. It was frozen shut. Without a moment's hesitation she smashed her fist through it and kicked the frame into the alley. The snow rushed through the opening, already piling up on the floor. Celeste squeezed through the window, dropped to the ground and ran for the square. Blasts of whiteness shrouded her as she made for home. She felt no fear or remorse. What she did feel was pride tainted with disgust, disgust for the human race for producing such machines as Brutus and disgust for the rest of us for allowing them to flourish unmolested.

"Is that you, Celeste?" Cora called out from upstairs.

"Yes. It's a tempest out there."

Ramelle came out of her room and peered over the stairway. "Darling you're a lunatic to go out in weather like this."

"I know." She looked up at a bursting Ramelle and said, "The fury of it drew me out."

The next day Runnymede screeched with the news. No one mourned Brutus's death, not even his wife, Felicia. Neither the South nor the North Runnymede sheriff conducted a very thorough investigation. Julius Caesar Rife, in his early twenties and already displaying the cool habits of his father, was to assume command of the family fortune. His father's murder served as a warning to Julius: You can only push so hard.

Fannie Jump Creighton flew in the front door of Celeste's house with the news. Ramelle had the uneasy sense that Celeste had done it. She kept her thoughts to herself. Cora, hearing the commotion, rambled into the living room to hear Fannie retell her story.

"They say it must have been a powerful man because when he escaped he ripped the window right out of the frame," Fannie gloated. She had hated him like all the rest.

"Is that a fact?" Celeste's eyebrow arched upward.

"No clues?" Ramelle asked.

"In that blizzard? Besides, it's only respect for Felicia that keeps the whole town from celebrating," Fannie continued.

"No one can see us, so perhaps we ought to drink a toast." Celeste headed for her supply.

"Celeste, honey, what are you going to do when your stash runs out?" Fannie was far more worried about prohibition than the murder of Brutus Rife.

"Buy it illegally, of course."

"You don't drink, not really. If my supply runs out before yours, let me have your liquor," Fannie pleaded.

"Fannie Jump, would I leave you in the lurch?" Celeste held up her glass for a toast. "Civilization means you've learned to insult people instead of killing them."

"I don't get it." Fannie gulped her toast before waiting for an answer.

"It means we have a long way to go." Celeste laughed.

Cora always possessed a sixth sense and that sense

was telling her that Celeste had ushered Brutus into kingdom come.

Ramelle observed Cora's silence. "What are you thinking?"

"Me? Oh, I was thinking of a rhyme my mother used to say: 'Right is wrong and wrong is right. And who can tell it all by sight?'"

March 6, 1920

"Julia Ellen, you start up a fire," Cora fiddled with the oil lamp.

Outside, sleet and wind banged against the windows. Cora and Juts had left Celeste's early to celebrate Julia's fifteenth birthday. Louise had promised to come home straight after work instead of hanging around mooning over Pearlie Trumbull.

"Do you like Celeste and Ramelle's birthday present?"

"You bet. That sweater came all the way from New York. Wheezie will get an inflamed bladder from jealousy." Julia enjoyed the thought of Louise's fit of envy. "Mother?"

"What? Hand me that flat blade. I wanna jiggle this wick a little. Thanks."

"It's my birthday and I want to quit school."

"What?"

"You told me on my birthday we could talk about me leaving school."

"I did no such thing."

"You did so, Mother. You forget."

"There. Got it. A light in this kitchen helps. Now what is this noise about cutting off school?"

"I'm not like Louise. I got no special talent. So why waste time?"

"Course you got talent."

"What?" Juts hoped to be convinced of hidden treasures.

"You sure can raise hell with what you have." Cora's eyes shone.

Julia smiled. She knew she was a devil. "Oh, Mom, I don't think I can get paid for that."

"Don't be so sure. Yesterday I heard Celeste say she's thinking about giving you an allowance to let up a little."

"She found out about the cigarettes, huh?"

"What cigarettes?"

Realizing her mistake, Juts waffled. "Her cigarettes. I spent the money on a nut sundae."

"Don't crawfish, Julia."

"I snitched a few and smoked them up with Ev."

"A few puffs and you're ready to leave high school, a woman of the world."

"I'm not learning anything. Look here at my history book. Did you ever see anything so dull in your life?"

Cora opened the book to the place marked for tonight's lesson. "This here looks like some kind of certificate."

"That's the Bill of Rights." Julia pouted.

"What's that mean?"

"It means I got to memorize them by tomorrow and I don't give Jack Shit about them or the Constitution. S'all a bunch of words. Money is all that counts, papers or no papers."

Straining to make out a word or two, Cora pointed to the First Amendment. "What's this big word here, the first one?"

Disdaining the subject, Juts glanced at the page. " 'Congress.' "

"You read me them rights."

"Mother."

"I wanna hear them. Only got to hear it oncet and it's mine." Cora pointed to her head.

Exasperated, Julia slid her book around and began in a singsong voice: " 'Congress shall make no law respecting an establishment of religion, or prohibiting the free exercise thereof; or abridging the freedom of speech, or of the press; or the right of the people peaceably to assemble, and to petition the government for a redress of grievances.' "

"Ain't that grand?" Cora opened her arms.

"What's so grand about it?"

"I can say what I want, believe what I want, sit at table with whom I please and nobody dare stop me."

"You do that anyway."

"True, but maybe I do it because I grew up in a place where people said what they believed."

"It's still dumb to memorize this junk."

"Read me the rest, Julia."

"Yes, m'am." She resigned herself to her fate. "Can I shorten them and tell you what they mean instead of going through this old-time way of saying things?"

"O.K."

"The Second Amendment says we got the right to keep and bear arms."

"Um-hum." Cora rose and tossed some wood in the stove and put a kettle of water on.

"The third one says we don't have to put up soldiers in our house; the fourth one says people can't fly in here and look through the house or take things out of it."

"Crooks?"

"No, I think they mean the law."

"Same difference, sometimes. Go on, I'm listening."

"The fifth one says if we're in court they got to try us by rules and we can't go up for the same crime twice. The end part declares if our land is taken for everyone's use we get good money for it."

"You mean, they can take our land without our say-so?" Cora put both hands on hips, ready for a fight should the state dare come through her door.

"I don't know." Julia shrugged.

"No one's taking my land away from me. Land's all there is. You can't grow corn on a sidewalk."

"But they gotta give you money."

"I don't want no money. I know this earth. I know when my morning glories will come up and I can feel the sap rising in the apple trees. Why, land that's yours is like your kin, your mate, sort of. Money can't buy that." Her apron fluttered; Cora breathed hard.

"Mom, I don't think you have to worry about this. Who wants Bumblebee Hill?"

"Maybe so, but I'll shoot 'em if they do, so help me, God. You read me these other rights."

"The next one says we get a fast trial by jury."

"Which one is that again?"

"Sixth. The seventh says if a legal battle is over twenty dollars you get a trial by jury."

"Do you understand that one?"

"No, but twenty dollars is a lot of money. Maybe you need a jury because you can't trust a judge."

"That could be. What's the next one?"

"The eighth says no unusual punishment and no excessive front money if you're in the can."

"An unusual punishment—people get killed if they're murderers." Her hand on her face, Cora thought this over.

"Yeah, but that's an eye for an eye and a tooth for a tooth. That's Bible, right?"

"Not so fast, Julia. That's Old Testament. Jesus came to teach love, not revenge."

"He did a piss poor job."

Her hands over her head, Cora let out a whoop. "Child, do you eat with that mouth?"

Pretending to be calm and very learned, Julia countered, "As I was saying, taking a life that took a life is an old rule. So what the Bill of Rights talks about is not that but stuff like slitting someone's tongue if they're a gossip, or burning an eye out."

Cora sighed. "Go on, read me the next one."

"O.K., this one says if a right is written down in this Constitution it doesn't mean people don't own other rights not written down. That's how I figure this one out. And the last one says any power not spelled out as belonging to the Constitution belongs to the states—you know, like Maryland. Everything else belongs to the people. That's it."

"Certainly gives a body something to think about." A large hand reached over the stove and poured the hot water over tea leaves.

"I still say it's boring and I want to quit school."

"Julia, I can't tell you how to live your life. I think school is good for you, but I'm not you. If you want out, then do it, but at least wait until this year is over in June."

"Do you mean it?"

"Yes."

A door opened. Louise could be heard taking her boots off.

"Wheezie, that you?" Julia yelled.

"No, it's Lillian Gish."

"Smartass."

Louise sauntered into the kitchen. "Don't turn wise, Juts, or I'm not giving you your birthday present. Hi, Momma."

"Hello, sweetie." Cora stood still so Louise could give her a kiss.

"What awful weather. Too bad you weren't born in May."

"You follow in three weeks, Louise. Don't bitch to me about when we got here. Looks like Ramelle's baby will arrive in May."

Louise sniffed. "She could at least get married."

"La Sermonetta the Second." Julia curled her lip.

"You mean to say you sit there and favor wanton immorality?"

"The way you are carrying on with Pearlie, you'll soon be in the same boat."

Louise slammed her hand on the table. "That's not true. Our feelings are much higher than that."

"I'd better duck before one hits me." Juts dodged under the table.

"Judge not lest ye be judged," Cora reminded Louise.

The older girl noticed the history book opened. "Quick, get me smelling salts. I believe Julia was studying." Louise faked a swoon.

"I was not!" Julia flared.

"Ha!" Louise gloated.

"She was reading me the Bill of Rights. Here—how about some hot tea to warm your innards, Louise?"

"The Bill of Rights?"

Cora stopped for a second. "All ten of them. It's something, this being an American."

Unimpressed, Louise mumbled, "I guess so."

"You sure were hot to be Liberty when you were twelve, Wheezie." A sardonic smile enlivened Julia's attractive face.

"You near burned me to a crisp."

"I could have sold you as chitlins."

"Julia Ellen, I am definitely not giving you your birthday present, insulting toad."

"Toad! Well, it's true. I'd rather eat a bug than look at you."

"Settle down, ladies." Cora threw the bread loaf at Julia, who caught it.

"Come on, Louise, gimme my present. I've got a goody for you on your birthday."

"No."

"Aw, Wheezie, don't put a mule on. You know I was funning."

"You can be so sweet when you want something. Butter wouldn't melt in your mouth."

"I can't help teasing you. It just means I like you. I tease everyone I like. You always get religious or insulted."

"That's because I'm sensitive."

"Gimme my present."

"All right." Louise went out into the front room and returned with a small, prettily wrapped box. "Here, chiseler."

"Thanks." Juts unwrapped it in an instant. Inside the box lay a pair of stylish earrings. "Ooo—help me put them on."

"Now it's my turn." Cora disappeared into the dirt-floor pantry and bustled out with a big hatbox.

Julia had the lid off before Cora could put it on the table. "Oh, Mother, just like in Celeste's fancy magazines. And the color goes with my earrings." Juts hugged her mother and kissed Louise, too.

Louise started "Happy Birthday" and Cora joined in. This made tears in Julia's eyes. Toughie that she was, she fought them back. "I love everybody!"

June 15, 1920

Runnymede looked like a brilliant palette as people ran around in thirteenth-century costume. Each year on this day the town celebrated the Magna Carta and reenacted it on the town square. Celeste remarked that King John gave the first expensive autograph. Nowhere was the activity as hectic as up on Bumblebee Hill. Cora, Juts and Louise decorated the porch with garlands; potpourri hung in the corners to spark the air. Cora put out her best tablecloth, many times mended, and its bright pattern added to the mood.

Ramelle had delivered a healthy girl on May 2. Black hair and electric-blue eyes, and she was named, as promised, Spottiswood. Cora was throwing this party in the baby's honor. Curtis had traveled from Los Angeles to be with Ramelle when she was due. He was to return in a week, so Cora did her best to see that the goings on would be special for him, too.

Fairy Thatcher arrived first with her violin. Cora had declared everyone had to make her own music. Idabelle trundled up the hill with her trusty accordion. Juts produced a tambourine and Cora had the uneasy sensation that she had clipped it. Cora'd been practicing her hambone for weeks. Slapping yourself didn't look elegant, but it made up for a drum and Cora did it with such flourish. Fannie Jump parked her Bugatti by the barn, bringing with her a harmonica. Louise zoomed around the house like Buffalo Bill with the lid off. Her mother had said she could invite Pearlie Trumbull and she was close to conniptions over the prospect of Pearlie amid all these people. She wasn't embarrassed about him, but my God, what a crew! Celeste and Ramelle were lovers. Ramelle had just had Curtis's baby. Fairy Thatcher read strange books and quoted them incessantly. Fannie Jump Creighton had a hollow leg, as the saying goes, and Idabelle was so fat, if she tripped coming up the hill she'd roll all the way to the bottom. Louise wrung her hands. How had she, graduate of Immaculata Academy, pet of Carlotta Van Dusen, got in the middle of all this? To put the cherry on the sundae, Julia Ellen, the brat, tormented her relentlessly about Pearlie Trumbull. Worse, Louise thought Julia was better-looking than she was. Here Louise prayed daily, went to mass regularly, thought elevated thoughts, and God went and made that hellraiser pretty. My cross to bear, she thought.

Knowing well Fannie's weakness, Cora made sure to have a vat of gin.

"Cora, honey, where'd you get this divine juice?"

"I'm not telling you all my secrets." As she was speaking, a flock of blackbirds dove on the field across from the front porch. "My party!" Cora clapped her hands.

"What?"

"Whenever you see blackbirds you say 'My party,' and that's how many people will come to your party," Cora explained.

"Quaint! Where are the guests of honor—the mother, the father and Celeste herself?"

"Now, you know Celeste must make her entrance."

"On an ass. Say, Cora, you got any palm fronds?"

Walking up the road, wearing a boater and seersucker trousers, came a dapper Pearlie Trumbull, carrying his fiddle.

"Who's that?" Fannie asked.

"That's Louise's beau." Cora waved to him. "Louise, your fella's here."

Louise tore out of the house like a cat pursued by a German shepherd. Suddenly realizing her behavior, she stopped and began to walk very demurely toward a smiling Pearlie.

"Carry a torch and you'll get cinders in your eye." Julia giggled.

Fairy, hearing this, gently said, "Now, Julia Ellen, love is wonderful. It will happen to you someday."

"Ha!" Julia stirred the punch.

Louise properly introduced Pearlie to the folks. Idabelle made a big fuss over him. She missed Rob, who had stayed down in North Carolina at the towel mills. Louise led him over to the punch and pushed Juts away when neither Pearlie nor anyone else was looking. Julia, lovely in her latest outfit, prepared to smear jam on Louise's behind, but a rumble down the road distracted her. A huge truck chugged up the hill.

"What the Sam Hill?" Cora leaned over the banister. " 'Zat Curtis driving?"

"Hell, yes." Fannie peered.

Curtis and Ramelle, holding the baby, sat in the cab of the pickup truck. On the back was that goddamned upright piano, with Celeste, dressed to the teeth, playing "Dixie." Pretending to ignore the gathering, she pounded away in a Confederate fervor while Curtis backed the truck around so the piano was right at the porch steps.

Celeste stopped. "Darlings, a little culture."

Hands on hips, Cora grinned. "I'll be damned."

"Pearlie Trumbull, you look strong. Lend a hand here," Celeste ordered him.

"Yes, m'am."

Curtis hopped out of the truck, dressed in white and looking better than a movie star. Julia experienced a faint flutter and decided it must be the punch; she'd put enough gin in it to punch, for certain. It couldn't be that Curtis was a handsome man. No, not Julia. She smiled at her inward strength.

Idabelle helped Ramelle out of the truck and cooed over the baby. Ramelle shone more beautiful than ever, if that was humanly possible.

"Many hands make light work." Cora got on the truck and began to help the men with the piano. Julia took up another end. Celeste sat on the bench, legs crossed.

"Fancy pants, help your brother," Fannie called.

"I will if you will."

Fannie and Celeste put their backs into it. Within five minutes the upright stood on the end of the porch. A round of punch refreshed the sweating laborers.

"Louise, I believe you requested this." Celeste put her arm around Louise's shoulder.

"Miss Chalfonte, thank you."

Beaming, Cora was speechless. Such a condition never infected Fannie. "Come on, Louise, a song."

Gliding to the piano for its effect on Pearlie, Louise could have saved herself the trouble; he was smitten anyway. Louise turned to her audience and announced in her stage voice, "I'm going to play the ballet *Les Syphilis*."

Celeste dissolved in laughter, put her hands over her eyes. "*Sylphides,* Louise, *Sylphides*."

"Wheezie Hunsenmeir has a dirty mind," Juts snidely said.

"Shut—I mean desist, Julia Ellen. This is a christening party, not a rowdy gathering. Allow me to play 'Holy, Holy, Holy.'"

Julia, stung, retorted, "Oh, stop cackling and lay the egg."

Louise smoothed out her skirt, ever so ladylike, plopped on the bench and began her religious program.

Fannie was in no mood to be saved. "Louise, faster."

The hymn speeded up, but Louise still rolled her eyes heavenward and knitted her brow together in order to appear spiritual. Pearlie thought her a noble soul. Orrie whispered something to that effect in his ear. Ev, also invited to the party, threw another belt down her throat and began to feel marvelous.

Cora put her hand on Louise's shoulder. "Hold up, sugar." She turned to the assembled guests. "We are here to celebrate Miss Spottiswood Chalfonte Bowman. Here's the rules. Everybody gets a turn to dance with the baby. The mother has the first dance and the father gets the last. The rest of us fit in between. So everyone get a noisemaker?"

Pearlie put his fiddle under his chin and stood next to Fairy, who was rubbing her bow. They tuned up together. Fannie whipped out her harmonica. Julia rattled her tambourine. Ev had a flute and she was pretty good at it. Idabelle was all excited with her accordion. How she got it over that stomach was one of life's miracles. Orrie and Celeste lacked an instrument.

"Celeste, Curtis got a zither. How about you?"

"I'll hum."

"No you won't. You and Orrie sit here by me and I'll teach you how to hambone."

Celeste sat on Cora's right and Orrie on her left. She ran them through a few quick routines. The sight of Celeste hamboning was rare.

"How about if I play 'By the Sea' just to see how we all do together?" Louise checked with her mother.

"Sure."

They ran through that pretty well.

"New Momma, are you ready?" Cora called to Ramelle.

"I'm ready."

"Is Miss Spottiswood Bowman ready?" Cora smiled.

Those little blue eyes popped wide open underneath the black curly hair. She had Chalfonte hair but her mother's chin and eyes. Some combination. Even at six weeks Miss Spotts was a knockout.

"Miss Spottiswood is very ready." Ramelle stood up with the baby in her arms.

"Ida, Wheezie, Pearlie and Fairy, do you know 'Shepherds Hey'?"

They nodded yes. Cora tapped her foot and off they went, playing a song older than all of them put together.

Ramelle danced slowly to the lively music. The baby laughed, its little arms reaching up in the air. Julia took off on her tambourine and Celeste roared all the way through her hamboning. A few turns around the porch and Ramelle handed the baby to Celeste. She adored the baby and held her up in the air for all to see. Celeste put the child in Cora's arms. Cora was thirty-seven, and the lines in her face had deepened, a few rust spots had appeared on her big hands, but rather than diminish her special beauty, these signs of age enhanced her like badges from wars lost and won. Her bursting nature knew no fashion or year. She always said, "Speak of the sun and you see its rays," but that expression really applied to Cora herself. As she bounced around the porch, the baby nestled on her bosom, Ramelle wondered if she'd ever seen anything so joyful. Her turn over, Cora handed the baby to Pearlie, which was her way of saying, You're welcome in this home. A little shaky, Pearlie kept the baby away from his body. From the strain on his face you knew he was scared stiff he'd drop the precious bundle. A quick little step and he bent over to Louise. He placed the baby in her arms. Louise thought she might faint from emotion.

Julia hit her tambourine and hopped on one foot. Two circles around the porch and Louise passed the baby on to her sister, then raced back for the piano with a sweet glance for Pearlie, fiddling away. Julia shook the tambourine by the baby as she rocked her. Fearless, little Spotts grabbed for a shiny metal rattle. Everyone cheered as the baby touched the tambourine. Julia trotted around, in heaven, and gave the baby to Fannie. Mrs. Creighton lurched, the music faltered for a moment with her. "Keep playing, I'm not down yet." A twirl and she was close to it, so she wisely gave the child to Fairy. As Fairy tiptoed to the music, she wondered how come Marx never wrote about emotion or ways of feeling. Cora and her kind did things differently from her kind. As she danced with Spotts she couldn't help but feel a slight pang that she wasn't one of these people. They had such zest, such immediacy. Lost in her reverie, she was brought out of it by Idabelle. "Come on, girl, it's my turn with our honored guest." Unhinging herself from the accordion, Idabelle oohed and ahed over the infant something terrible. She relinquished her to Ev Most, who somehow didn't look at all maternal. Orrie was next and the baby silently stared at Orrie. Must have been her flaming red hair. Orrie handed the baby over to Curtis.

At first Curtis was awkward. He turned, took a little dip and then began to feel the music. He could feel these people caring for him and his baby. He could feel his own heart opening to this new person. Curtis forgot himself and danced like an angel. Spottiswood grabbed his index finger and wrapped her tiny hand around it. Curtis laughed. Maybe there was joy in this confusing world. Maybe people's basic instinct was to love rather than to hate. He knew he'd never find the answer, but here, for this moment on Cora's simple porch filled with laughing people and with this dear baby in his arms, he wanted to live forever. He wanted to love unto eternity's echo. He didn't know he had tears in his eyes. Ramelle got up and wrapped her arms around him. Together they danced with Miss Spottiswood Chalfonte Bowman.

February 14, 1921

Ramelle agreed to spend the months of January through March of each year with Curtis in California. Celeste felt Spottiswood should spend time with her father and she rested secure in the knowledge that Ramelle would return. She made jokes to herself about Persephone climbing out of the underworld to bring spring. During the day she didn't miss Ramelle all that much. At night, however, she found herself growing lonesome. Her reading picked up, but so did her insomnia.

Tonight a light, steady snowfall blanketed all sound. The world seemed muffled. Celeste propped herself up in bed and started reading the first volume of A la Recherche du Temps Perdu. Grace Pettibone had recommended it highly in a letter. Sigourny, Grace's lover, had completed another book, which Celeste had knocked off the night before and discounted as a fragile essay in autobiography. Spare me literary lesbians, she thought to herself, but then underneath that thought she had to admit she would always resent Sigourny for spiriting off her college romance. Ah, my youth, she mused.

Within two hours she completed Swann's Way. All that French fogged her. She grabbed Aristophanes'

The Frogs, in Greek, and howled all the way through it. That finished, she sat in her bed looking out the window. It was now 3 A.M. and she couldn't sleep.

To sleep, perchance to dream. . . . Her mind wandered off. Maybe I'll call Fannie Jump Creighton. No. Fannie's in the sack with some wayward young man per usual. God, I can't possibly read another book. In the sack. I do miss Ramelle. Of course, I could always carry on some alfresco affair. Oh, but what eligible young ladies catch my fancy in Runnymede? Or elegible young men, for that matter. I'll leave the swooning to Louise and Pearlie.

She fluffed up her pillow, then rested back on it, arms folded across her chest.

Tonight's a wonderful night for making love. Snow possesses an astringent eroticism. I like that. I'll write that down.

She scribbled on the note pad always by her bedside.

Hmm. Not a woman in this town who has both beauty and wit. Ramelle returns in six weeks. That's not so terribly long. Ah, I've kissed tigers when the moon was high. I never minded men in bed, the few times I indulged my curiosity. I can understand why Ramelle loves my brother. In fact, men are fine in bed. It's out of bed that I get bored stiff. But not Curtis. He—nothing boring about him. We Chalfontes may drive one to utter distraction but we never bore. Not even goddamned Carlotta. She returned from her European tour with tears from the Virgin for her academy. Cat's piss, no doubt. I'm not jealous of Curtis. I simply miss Ramelle. Why is it that I keep hoping lightning will weld his zipper shut? That will pass. I'm above jealousy. After all, I'm forty-three years old. I should be entering my sexual decline. Seems to be going the other way. There's something about the heat rising off a woman's skin. Intoxicating. Loving a woman is touching the rim of heaven. Carlotta tells me in her low church whisper if I'd give up my peculiar vice—peculiar vice, that corrupt windbag!—if I'd give this pleasure up I'd go to her heaven. And be cursed by a God who has remarkably similar tastes to my sister. Thank you, no. I'll make my heaven here on earth. Carlotta has a tapeworm in her imagination.

I wonder if Fannie is still awake. I can't call her. It's too rude.

Celeste was terrified. Of what she didn't know. It was three o'clock in the morning and she sat safe and warm in her large bed. A vulture swept in and out of her chest, tearing her with his rotted claw. How could this be? She was a perfectly reasonable, highly intelligent, splendid woman. Flashes of irrational terror are not taught in the best schools. Not only had she not been warned such moments exist for all humans; her character strongly opposed any notion of vulnerability, which Celeste equated with weakness. Scared in the middle of a snowy night with a fire roaring in the fireplace? Lonesome. Nonsense. Of course, this refusal to embrace fear made it all the worse. She dialed Fannie, then hung up before it rang. Looking at the snow, she thought of all the poems, early writings of Western culture, associating winter with old age. Metaphors are a way to see the world, she thought. Whether or not they're related to reality is another matter. Besides, I'm not old. I'm hardly a pale lost lily at the end. I'm nowhere near death. God, I hate these nocturnal rhapsodies! Why can't I go to sleep? I'm turning out this blasted light and I'm going to sleep. Immediately.

She switched off the light. The top of her scalp burned. Breathing came hard. A pain stabbed in her heart.

A heart attack. She turned the light on and sat bolt upright. I'm too young. Her palms were wet. No, I'm not having a heart attack. Christ, I'm shaking. What's the matter with me?

She picked up the phone again and once more placed it back on the receiver. Celeste walked over to her closet and put her clothes on. She bounded down the stairs and took her plush sable, her warmest coat, out of the closet. Then she slipped through the snow to the garage, started the car and headed for Bumblebee Hill. Runnymede rested in darkness.

Cora never locked her door, so Celeste carefully

opened it and walked in. She couldn't decide which was ruder: waking Cora up or coming into her house uninvited. A daughter of departed Lillian Russell, Mabel Normand by name, let out a yowl. This played on Celeste's nerves. She jumped and banged into a chair. She couldn't see a thing.

"Who's that?" Julia called out.

"Celeste."

"Oh." Julia fell asleep in an instant.

Cora, hearing the noise and Celeste's voice, wrapped on her old robe, lit the gas lamp and carried it to the front room.

"Celeste?"

"Yes, it's me. Cora, I'm terribly sorry. Please forgive me for—"

"Is everything all right down at the house?"

"Yes, it's fine."

Cora placed the lamp on the table and noticed Celeste's worried face.

"Let me fix you some hot milk."

"No, no. Please, Cora, go back to sleep. I'm so ashamed that I came here and woke you like this."

Cora put her arm around Celeste's sabled shoulder. "Celeste, honey, don't trouble yourself over that. Many's the night I got up with the children. Let me start a fire."

"No, please. Go back to bed. Just let me sit here in your house." Her lower lip trembled.

Arm still around her shoulder, Cora got her on her feet. "Come on. You come on to bed with me. You look ready to drop."

"I couldn't possibly."

"You got a little case of nightsickness. Come on."

"Nightsickness?"

"Sure. Can't sleep. Dreams get you. Dragons growl under your bed."

"Something like that." Celeste obediently followed her upstairs.

"I get that, too. Had it terrible after Aimes died."

"What did you do?"

"Got up and worked and when I was too tired to work I laid in bed and tried to picture the sunrise."

Cora led Celeste into her small room. A bright quilt covered the bed. As she pulled down the covers, the full force of the fact that Celeste made love to women hit her. I'll chance it, she thought. Anyway, I love Celeste even if I don't feel that way about her. "You want a nightgown? Juts has an extra. I never sleep in them. Get tangled."

Sheepishly, Celeste declined. "I can't sleep in them, either."

Celeste threw her sable coat over the ladder-back chair and hurriedly stripped. It was so cold she wanted to get under the covers as fast as she could. Cora admired her beautiful body.

"I'll wake up tomorrow and laugh about being so silly."

"Getting scared's not silly. Sometimes it creeps up on you."

"Tonight mine galloped."

Cora laughed. "Isn't it funny how people are like snowflakes? No two alike and yet we are so common."

"Yes." Celeste kept her body still. She was afraid she'd touch Cora by accident and scare her.

"It occurred to me this evening that I'm forty-three. I'm not ancient but I'm not young. I'll never be young again." She fought back her anguish.

"Like everything else in the world. You don't know how good it is until it's gone."

"Do you worry about getting old?"

"Once in a blue moon. I'm thirty-seven. Hell, I'm thankful I got this far."

This made Celeste giggle. She inadvertently touched Cora's breast. "I'm sorry. I . . ."

"Lord, darling, you are wound up tighter than a drum. It's cold enough outside; don't freeze up on me. Come here." Cora pulled Celeste to her and hugged her. The divine Miss Chalfonte didn't know whether to shit, run or go blind.

"Celeste, relax. I'm not going to bite you. I'll hold you and you get to sleep."

Celeste rested her head underneath Cora's and let Cora smooth her hair. She could feel her heart pounding.

"Cora, are you afraid to die?"

This amused Cora no end. "The seasons pass. Why shouldn't I?"

Exhausted, Celeste fell asleep listening to the gentle rumble of laughter inside Cora. Cora kissed her like a sleeping child and dropped into a peaceful sleep as well.

May 22, 1980

Ev Most burst through the kitchen door, head still covered with little curls, only now they were white.

"Juts. Did you hear the news?"

"What?"

"Evel Knievel announced he's going to jump over Orrie's mouth."

"Ha!" Julia enjoyed that one.

"Got a plan yet?" Ev leaned over and whispered.

"Partly. We need to dope it out."

"You bet." Ev rubbed her hands together. "By the way, what is it all about?"

"Money. Money's green because Louise picks it before it gets ripe."

"Hell, Juts, that's no news. You just now getting mad about it?" Ev smirked.

"That's right, isn't it? I didn't tell you what Louise is up to on the phone. Well, the wires might be tapped. You never can tell about Louise, and if it ain't Louise it might be the FBI. They kept files on Nickel, you know."

Ev's mouth fell open. "What'd she do?"

"Pissed Nixon off, I guess. She sent for 'em. Saw them herself. 'Nicole Smith,' right on the page. Maybe Louise tied in with them to torment us."

"I doubt it. The FBI would never get a word in edgewise. Her and Orrie invented the original no-energy-loss system—their mouths."

"And she thinks her shit don't stink."

"Well . . . tell me. What's she up to?"

"Now wait a minute. Let me make sure Nickel's out there cutting the grass." Julia walked over to the back screen door. Her daughter was pushing away, whistling to beat the band. Juts lowered her voice. "Louise is sticking Nickel for sixty thousand dollars, so she thinks."

"What!"

"Sis is trying to sell Momma's farm for sixty thousand dollars. Now that's the God's honest truth."

"You can't mean it. Nickel knows the tenants moved out and she offered to buy Momma's place. You know Wheeze and I own it jointly. It ain't good enough for Louise to live in, but she won't sell her half out to my daughter. My daughter, the only damn one in the lot that made good."

"She'll sell it. Louise says one thing and does another."

"She says two things and does nothing, you mean."

"She'll come down."

"Greedyguts? If she was in the middle of a race track and someone dropped a dime, she'd hear it and pick it up. I think we got a real battle on our hands."

"You could be right. There's got to be some way to drum sense in her head. You got a price you think is fair?"

"I think between forty-five and fifty thousand is fair. The house leans a little. The barns lists like the Leaning Tower of Pisa. Land's good, though. And she can pay me my half month by month. No down payment on my half. If I was to die I'd will it to her anyway."

"Can't you will her your half now?"

"I thought of that, but what have I got to live on? That little rent each month put food on the table. My ironing business won't keep body and soul together. And I get tired standing on my feet those long hours."

"Aren't your new Adidas helping?"

"They're a darn sight better than those nurse's shoes,

but if I wear them out of the house Louise calls the fire department 'cause they're red."

"Gotta be something we can get on Louise Trumbull. Maybe we could get Ernst Cutworth to rezone her house."

"Huh?"

"All those Day-Glo Jesuses she has. We'll declare her house a plastics factory and a health hazard. Plastic causes cancer, you know."

This delighted Julia. "Think he'd do it?"

"If you squeeze his knee and a little higher up he would."

"Ev!"

"Heh, heh. Ernst's been sweet on you for many a year."

"Yeah, well, he can just eat Fannie Farmer. I wish Chessy was here. He'd reason with her."

"Chessy's been dead for nineteen years."

"I know, I know. He was my husband, wasn't he? I still wish he was here. He was the only one could calm her down or get an idea out of her head."

"Pearlie was next to no help." Ev sighed.

"She ran him like she tried to run everyone else. You couldn't find a nicer fella, but why he put up with Blowhard, I'll never know."

"Some folks like their life lived for them. Louise's specialty. Hey, maybe we could go to Father Scola. She listens to him."

"I'm not Catholic, remember? He'll side with her 'fore he sides with a Lutheran."

"Got a point there."

"Maybe I could bribe her."

"You could give her part of your share."

"Never. That farm's half mine. Giving her nothing. I was thinking more along the lines of my crystal candlesticks I inherited from Celeste. Louise slobbers for anything that belonged to a Chalfonte."

Ev opened the refrigerator door. "Eating some of your ice cream. Gonna stop me?"

"Ice cream? At this hour?"

"It's my stomach."

"I can see that."

Ev poured a ton of Hershey's chocolate over her ice cream.

"You know, I must be getting old, but things that used to rile me don't lift a feather now. I just want to be left in peace. As long as someone is nice to me I can be nice to them."

Julia eyed the gargantuan spoonful Ev had poised in front of her mouth. "Amen."

"Julia, I know that look. What are you thinking?"

"I swear that in the 1930s my sister gave herself up to the thrill of infidelity."

"No!" Ev's spoon stopped in midair, a lump of goo falling back into the bowl.

"I never said nothing because I couldn't prove it. But I could feel it."

"Who?" Ev relished this tidbit.

"Remember when she used to make buying trips to Philadelphia and New York for her job at the Bon-Ton?"

"You bet. How I envied her working for Bon-Ton. Then they found out old Shindel swindled the whole company. Dirt for days!"

"I swear to you, Ev, she had a fella in New York. She'd come back from those trips all moony and silent."

"Silent? Maybe she had typhoid." Ev now scraped the bowl with her spoon to get the last drops of chocolate.

"If we can just find some proof, we got her."

"Julia, I knew you'd find a way."

"You know what Momma used to say: 'If you can't find a way, make one.' I'll get my hands on love letters or something. Xerox 'em and threaten to go to the *Clarion* or *Trumpet* with the evidence."

"Julia, you're soft as a grape. They won't print love letters that are near fifty years old."

"They did for Eisenhower. And Louise thinks she's as important. We'll catch her on her high opinion of herself!"

"Hmm."

"Tomorrow at 8 A.M., when she's at mass, you go through her bedroom. Ransack it but put everything back when you're done."

"Why me? You do it. You two go in and out of each other's homes all the time."

"No, I don't want anyone to see me. She'll get suspicious."

"And she won't if the neighbors see me?"

"Put on a red wig. Everyone will think it's Orrie."

"I am not nearly as fat as Orrie. She's big as a house."

"I didn't mean that."

Ev wiggled in her chair. "Besides, what if she comes home early? Then I'm up Shit's Creek without a paddle."

"I'll sit by the phone booth two blocks away and ring you twice if she's coming."

"Julia, she'll see you. She's bound to know something is up."

"I'll disguise myself as old Patience Horney—you remember, Fatty Screwloose down by the railroad station?"

"Julia, Patience died in the twenties."

"I know, but Louise lives in the past. She'll drive by, see Patience and tell everyone she had a vision."

"I don't know." Ev's eyebrows squirmed as much as her body. "This is awful risky. I still think you should go in there and root around yourself."

"Ev, who fills her Valium prescription each month and gives it to you?"

"Now, Juts, you know I need that to calm my nerves. I'm a very high-strung woman."

"So why doesn't your doctor give 'em to you?"

"Well . . ."

" 'Cause you are an addictive personality—isn't that what he said? If it weren't Valium, it'd be dope."

"All right, Julia. I don't need you to tell me my own shortcomings, but I'm not an addictive personality. I like getting high, that's all."

"High? I never saw you when we were in our twenties without your hip flask stuck in your garter belt."

"So you manufactured the stuff. You should talk."

"Supply and demand. That don't mean I drank it. That was all so long ago. Who cares?"

"Those marijuana plants in your garden aren't so long ago."

"What have you been doing in my garden!"

"I got eyes, Julia Ellen."

"Nickel put them there for a joke."

"Once a bootlegger, always a bootlegger. You're gonna sell that stuff." Ev closed her hands as if in prayer.

"You keep this up and I'm gonna smash a caterpillar on your head."

Ev shrieked because she knew Julia was perfectly capable of it and would enjoy it in the bargain. Julia started for the door to go get one, just to hear Ev scream some more.

"Juts, no-o-o."

"Valium or breaking and entering. The choice is yours."

"All right. I'll do it." Ev acted as though resigned, but she couldn't wait for the next morning. Part of her friendship with Julia depended on being convinced for each caper. "Julia?"

"What?"

"Will you give me some of that marijuana?"

Julia put her hands on her hips and stared at her. Ev remained still. Juts started to laugh. "Yes."

Even as they spoke, Louise and Orrie, a few blocks away, were making plans of their own.

May 2, 1925

"Hi, Mom." Julia Ellen kissed Cora.

"How'd the day go?"

"Fine. During lunch break I ran into Yashew Gregorivitch—he works down in loading—and he told me a funny story."

"What?"

"Remember Ollie Buxton, who used to rent out a room in old Mrs. Gregorivitch's house?"

"I knew him by sight."

"Well, he skipped out on the rent some months ago and ran off to York. In the middle of last night the Voice of God tells him to go pay his back rent. He gets up out of bed and drives all the way down to Runnymede and bangs on Mrs. Gregorivitch's door. 'Wake up, wake up. God told me to pay the rent,' he yells. Old Mrs. Gregorivitch comes to the window, pokes her head out and says, 'Vell, he didn't tell me you vas coming.' Some punkins, huh?"

Cora shook her head. "I declare."

"I'm saving up all my earnings. I'm gonna buy us a radio."

"We don't need a radio. We got the piano."

"I can't play the piano."

"No, but your sister can."

"Mom, Wheezie comes by two or three times a week and she only plays on Sundays."

"Being married takes up a lot of time."

"She's been married three years. Don't you think she'd be used to it by now? Look at Fannie Jump and Fairy—they don't hang around their husbands much."

"They been married a lot longer than Louise."

"Uh-huh." Juts stared out the back door, gazing at the beautiful garden in the back of the mansion. Celeste, Ramelle and Spotts were playing croquet. The mallet was as big as Spotts. She squealed each time she hit the ball.

Julia worked at the Red Bird Silk Mill. She enjoyed all the ribbons, the colors, the dyes, the mixing with the other women. Efficient and good with people, she had been promoted to floor-walker. She trained new people as well as watched over the phases of ribbon production. She had even started reading business journals and newspapers. Ev Most worked in her department and they both had made many friends. Lunch hour with the girls was the best part of the day. On weekends the gang often ran around together.

Movies proved a favorite activity. She'd seen and memorized *The Sheik, The Prisoner of Zenda, Safety Last, The Perfect Flapper, The Big Parade*—in fact, Juts watched every movie that came to Runnymede. Ev grew wobbly thinking about Valentino, but Juts liked this new guy John Gilbert. Celeste had told her that along with real estate, Curtis had bought into a production company. Knowing of Julia's passion, he sent photos and posters to her. This made Juts the most popular person at the Red Bird mill.

Louise sniffed at Julia's "juvenile afflictions," she being a matron and a truly mature person. Louise had Victorian morality via Carlotta stamped permanently in her brain, although with coaxing she could be led to put it on the back burner. Juts, on the other hand, emerged a real flapper. The spirit of the twenties accorded perfectly with her own hell-raising bent. She kept Cora, Celeste and Ramelle in stitches. They never knew what would pop out of her mouth next or what she'd wear. One of her big trend-setting styles for the gang in Runnymede was to dress like "The Kid." In her bobbed hair she looked adorable in a big workman's cap and knickers. Girls in the high school strained to catch sight of her and would then copy her latest outfit. Louise prayed all the harder, seeking solace in the beyond. How Juts could be so favored shook her faith. Juts hadn't set foot in a church since her confirmation at Christ Lutheran. She had, however, set foot in every speakeasy within a twenty-mile radius of Runnymede. She won all the Charleston contests, too.

"Mom, who's pulling in the back driveway?"

"Hooch delivery."

"How come I've missed this?"

"He usually arrives earlier."

"Fannie Jump must be dropping over tonight."

"Celeste drinks very little. Fannie likes her stuff dropped off here. She thinks her husband don't know nothing that way."

A broad-shouldered, small-waisted man unloaded the truck, singing while he worked. His hair was blond and slicked back like a John Held, Jr., "sheik." As he turned and carried his burden to the back door, Julia Ellen beheld a beautiful square face and large luminous eyes. He tried to open the door but Juts stood there, immobile.

"Excuse me, miss."

She didn't move a muscle.

"Julia, move yourself," Cora called.

Startled, she looked at her mother. "Me?"

"No. Robert E. Lee. Move so the man can get through."

"I'm sorry." Juts took a few steps back and stared.

The handsome fellow heaved the huge carton on the counter. Then he had a long look at Julia. He didn't say anything, either. The two of them stared at each other like cats ready to pounce. Cora unloaded the booze. After a minute or two she fathomed the situation. A broad smile crossed her weathered face. "Chester Smith, this here's my youngest daughter, Julia Ellen."

"I'm pleased to meet you, miss."

"Likewise." Julia still stared.

"Julia, offer the man a cup of coffee."

"Mr. Smith, would you like a cup of coffee?"

"Yes, thank you."

Julia filled the coffeepot up, measured out the coffee, and forgot to turn the stove on. Cora turned it on while the two young people floundered for conversation.

"Do you take sugar?"

"Yes, thank you."

"Milk?"

"Yes, thank you."

"Cupcakes?"

"Yes, thank you."

Julia placed the items on the table.

"Thank you," Chester said one more time.

Julia sat across from him. More bulky silences followed. Cora whistled so she wouldn't laugh in their faces.

"Miss Hunsenmeir—" Chester gulped.

"Please call me Julia or Juts. All my girlfriends call me Juts."

"Juts?"

"Yes."

"Uh—is the coffee ready?"

"I'm sorry, Mr. Smith, I forgot."

"Call me Chessy. Call me anything," he blurted out.
Julia poured his coffee. He didn't drink it.

"Juts?"

"Yes?"

"Would you . . . pass me the sugar?"

She pushed it closer to him although it was easily
in reach.

"Juts?"

"Yes?"

"Would you like to ride with me while I finish my
rounds?"

"You bet!"

With that they both ran out and hopped into the
truck like two little kids. Cora felt a pang in her
chest of both delight and sadness. She knew she was
getting old.

Celeste, Ramelle and little Spotty piled in the back
door.

"Cora, did Juts just go off in the truck with our delivery boy?" Ramelle asked.

"Yes."

"What was that all about?" Celeste noticed the two
full and steaming cups of coffee.

Cora replied, "Love at first sight."

August 7, 1925

What a stinking-hot day. Even now, an hour before
sunset, the earth shimmered and the corn looked ready
to pop right on the stalk. Bumblebee Hill, being on
high ground, was a bit cooler, but not much. Today
was Chessy's twentieth birthday. Juts had promised him
a cake, so he drove his beloved Ford up to Cora's

house. Chessy and Juts spent as much time together as they could. He came from Hanover, where he worked as a butcher. His folks, being Dunkards, didn't know about his liquor deliveries, but they did know about Julia and they frowned on his keeping company with a worldly girl, as they called her. Chessy, not one to be held back by the refinements of religious prejudice, ignored Mom and Pop. As far as he was concerned, they lived in another century and he was a man of his time. To Juts' credit, she never acted any different with Chessy than she did with anyone else. Not for her the languid sighs of Louise when she was courting. She ran, jumped, danced and once even donned boxing gloves in a mock battle with Chessy. Louise deplored such behavior and remarked with pained dignity that Juts was no lady. Juts did everything but drive, and how she hounded Chessy to teach her! She even put on overalls and crawled under Bertha, his car, with him. Chessy and Juts were pals. This mystified Wheezie, who devoutly believed men and women were incapable of understanding one another. Sexual difference was part of God's plan and God's plan was dualistic: black and white, right and wrong, man and woman. It was very simple, too, which was why Louise embraced this revealed order with such fervor. She didn't understand Pearlie, nor did she try. Her energy ran in the direction of housebreaking him. Carlotta Van Dusen had darkly hinted during those days at Immaculata Academy that men were created in God's image but that Satan also was a man. Woman, the purifying force, must be ever vigilant lest her man enter down the paths of unrighteousness. Louise was vigilant. Pearlie worked so hard, the poor man barely had time to wipe his ass, much less be led into temptation. He dragged home from the factory only to find a mass of chores waiting for him. His reward for such labor was physical relations with Louise, carefully rationed. Pearlie, a quiet soul, accepted all this, for it relieved him of the responsibility of thinking ahead. Louise did that. This evening he sat on the porch railing, reveling in escape from duty. Louise played the piano, which was on the porch for the summer. She started off with a hymn, but Fannie Jump, tiddly, requested "I'm Just Wild About Harry," as that was the name of her latest conquest. Fairy fanned herself on the big swing at the other end of the porch. She and Fannie had ridden up with Ramelle, little Spotts and Celeste. The old Vassar gang had come to cherish these moments at Cora's place.

Ev Most helped Juts with the cake while Cora sat in her rocker and clapped in time to the music so Spotts would learn to dance. Celeste and Ramelle each held the child's hand and showed her the steps. Orrie Tadia, late as usual, plodded up the hill.

Cora saw her in the distance and exclaimed, "She got a red blouse, a green skirt and orange earrings. Lordie, that ain't no country girl—that's a miracle."

Celeste cracked, "No one will ever mistake Orrie for a TB victim."

"You are wicked," Fairy added, sorry she hadn't thought of it.

Chessy returned from admiring Celeste's latest Hispano-Suiza. "Miss Chalfonte, that's something."

"Why, thank you, Chessy. Juts tells me you love cars."

"Who doesn't?"

"Louise, don't answer that," Pearlie gibed his musical wife.

"Chessy—aw, Chessy!" Juts hollered from inside the house.

"What?"

"Close your eyes. Mom, make sure he closes his eyes."

"All right, Juts." Cora got up and put her hands over Chessy's eyes.

Julia walked out, carrying a large cake with twenty candles on it, lit.

"Ohhh," Spotts was thrilled.

"O.K., big guy, you can look," Juts told him.

Cora dropped her hands and Chessy's face shone when he saw his birthday cake. He couldn't think of anything to say.

"Cat got your tongue?" Juts said.

"Gee—it's beautiful. Thanks," he managed to stammer.

"Mom, this is getting heavy. Where should I set it down?"

"Here, put it on the top step. We don't need to be fancy." Cora helped her put the cake down.

"You have to make a wish and blow out the candles," Juts informed her friend.

"I wish—"

"Don't tell! It won't come true. You have to keep it a secret," she warned him.

Chessy's parents had never given him a birthday party. They had considered such things silly, mildly sinful, and it might spoil the boy's character. He didn't know about candles and wishes.

"Blow them out? Everybody stand back then." He waved them all aside, took a huge breath and blew them all out but one.

"Will take a year for your wish to come true," Cora said.

"I'll go get the plates." Ev hurried to the kitchen. From there she called out, "Juts, you don't have enough forks to go around."

"We'll eat with our fingers," Juts called back.

"I want a fork," Louise demanded.

"O.K., O.K.," Juts answered.

Fannie struggled to get the cap off her flask.

Chessy noticed her efforts. "Mrs. Creighton, don't bother with that."

"What? This is the elixir of the gods, young man."

"Huh?"

"Never mind."

"Save it." Chessy started down the steps. "I brought some stuff for the birthday party."

"You dear boy! Let me help you." Fannie was halfway to his car before he hit the last step. Together they carried back two gallons of good Canadian liquor.

Spotts had her hands on the cake. She couldn't resist. Her black curls shook with anticipation. As she bent over and put her head low, concentrating on the cake, she couldn't see anyone. She figured they couldn't see her.

"Spotts, what are you doing?"

Surprised, the child straightened up. "Nothing."

"Icing all over your fingers. Very incriminating." Celeste's eyebrow shot up.

Ev handed Chessy a knife. He cut the first piece and gave it to Spotts. As he cut the rest of the cake the people sang "Happy Birthday." Louise, at the piano, spiced the song with a few florid vocal additions.

The sun coasted toward the horizon. A deep golden light cast long shadows. Finishing her cake, Louise struck up "In the Good Old Summertime," everyone's favorite, especially on a day like this one. Then she remembered the "Charleston" and "Tea for Two." Pearlie perched on the banister. Celeste decided to sit there, too. Fannie, not to be outdone, sat by the piano. Since it was at the end of the porch, she could lean up against the post while sitting on the railing. She didn't trust herself without support. Ramelle sat next to the cake with Spotts in her lap. Cora rocked away, glad to be alive. She loved summer. Ev, Juts and Chessy horsed around in the front yard while Orrie sang along with Louise.

"Let's play catch," Juts challenged them.

"Too hot," Ev replied.

"Anyway, I ate too much cake." Chessy rubbed his stomach.

"Anyone want to play hide and go seek?" Julia addressed the porch folks. Their response ruled out that one.

"I know." Juts was full of beans today.

"Spare me." Ev sat down on the grass.

"Chessy, teach me to drive."

"Well . . ."

"Pulease, pretty please?" Julia punched his arm.

"Only if you do exactly as I say." Chessy wiped the sweat off his forehead.

"Julia listen to anyone? Ha!" Ev squinted.

"Ev!"

"Aw, Juts, I'm fooling."

"Come on, Chessy." Julia tugged at his undershirt. He had taken his shirt off in the heat.

"All right."

"I get to sit in the back seat." Ev raced for the car.

"Hey, everybody. Chessy's gonna teach me to drive," Juts announced.

"Remember, Julia Ellen, pedestrians come in two classes—the quick and the dead." Celeste was swinging her feet over the railing.

"With Juts at the wheel, they'll all be dead," Louise sang to the tune of "And the Band Played On."

"Mother, watch me."

"How can I help but watch you, unless you're driving to Baltimore?"

Julia was so excited she turned handsprings over to Chessy's Ford. Ev positioned herself in the back seat. Chessy cajoled Bertha into starting, put her in neutral and then pointed out the clutch, the gas pedal and the brake to Julia.

"I know all that," she gaily replied. Yes, driving a car. Independence, dash, speed. Julia saw herself heroically guiding an ambulance in World War I. She imagined flying down a country road scattering chickens or majestically rolling along Runnymede Square for all to see. First woman auto racer! She could just see it. Her picture in the paper. Goggles, scarf, grease, holding up a trophy bigger than herself. Transported by her ever-expanding sense of competence, she barely heard Chessy.

"Behind the wheel. I'll sit over here."

"Goody." Juts landed so hard in the seat the car rocked.

"Depress the clutch," Chessy said.

Julia pushed all the way down.

"Now put 'er in first."

"Up?"

"Right."

"Up and right?"

"No, honey, I meant yes."

"Oh."

"Julia, will you listen?" Ev realized she was a sitting duck.

"Now slowly let your foot off the clutch, slowly, and slowly give her a little gas with your right."

Bang! Juts clamped down the gas pedal and off they went.

"Take your foot off the gas." Chessy tried to remain calm.

Possessed, Julia heard no one. She forgot everything she'd ever learned, and terrified by the pace at which she was moving, she concentrated solely on steering.

"There she goes." Fannie slapped her thigh as the car roared in front of the house.

Julia headed around the house, with Chessy yelling, "Take your foot off the gas!" to no effect. She swerved to miss a hedge and pointed toward the garden. *Varoom!* she obliterated the squash. The red barn was her next target.

"I'm too young to die," Ev screamed, in genuine anguish.

Chessy, face ashen, gripped the right door. "Pick your right foot up. Turn left, Juts, for God's sake, turn left!"

She missed the barn by inches and tore back toward the front of the house. The gang on the porch heard the sound of doom approaching. Louise stuck to her spot, thinking the piano a good cover.

"Mother, she'll hit us," Louise yelled as the sound of the motor became louder.

"Just sit there and ignore your sister. You know she'll do anything for a laugh." Cora calmly rocked.

As the car leapt into view, Celeste jumped off the railing. "I don't think she's fooling. Every woman for herself."

Julia swung wide around the house and then turned toward it like a homing pigeon.

Celeste grabbed Ramelle and Spotts, who was applauding.

Pearlie gulped. "Hell's bells."

Fannie, seeing the car bearing down on her, crawled up the porch post like a monkey and grasped the roof, swinging her body over and up in a surprising display of agility.

"Brake, Julia, brake!" Chessy threw his hands over his head.

Her foot, leaden, never left the accelerator.

Ev pleaded, "Dear God, no. I'll stop smoking, I swear I will."

Julia's eyes engulfed her face. Smash! Chessy's dear Ford plowed into the corner of the porch and stopped. Fannie lost her hold as the post snapped, and hung by her fingernails over the edge of the roof. Louise, jarred, watched in disbelief as the piano rolled gracefully down the newly slanted porch to bump into Chessy's radiator.

"Save me!" Fannie bellowed, then lost her grip and plopped on the car's roof beneath her.

Chessy staggered from the car. Ev wiggled out of a window, chanting, "Thank you, dear God, thank you."

Julia remained at the wheel. Once stable on his feet, Chessy quickly opened her door. "Honey, honey, are you all right?"

Julia mutely nodded.

Fannie was assisted down from the Ford's roof by Celeste, who was laughing in spite of herself. Cora, once certain everyone was out of danger, sat on the bottom step of her injured porch and held her sides, she was laughing so hard.

Julia refused to get out of the car. This way they couldn't get a good look at her. Tears rolled down from her eyes.

Leaning over, Chessy put his hand on her shoulder. "Come on, honey."

She wouldn't budge. He lowered himself on his hunkers and gently encouraged her. "Come on, Julia, honey. Everyone is safe and sound."

"I busted your car—and on your birthday." Now she was truly sobbing.

Chessy looked at his prized possession and at a distraught Juts and sighed. He knew right then and there he loved Julia Ellen more than his car. "We can fix it together. You can help me."

"How can you let me touch it? How can you even speak to me?" Her chest heaved.

Chessy whispered, "Julia Ellen, it's just a piece of metal. We can fix it."

"Mom's porch." Julia gulped between sobs.

"We can fix that, too."

"You'll never want to see me again," a wounded Julia wailed.

"Yes I will."

"No you won't."

"Julia, I love you," Chessy whispered in her ear. "I want to see you forever."

"You do?" She stopped crying, shocked.

"I do." He spoke firmly.

"I do, too." Julia looked up at him, tear stains down her cheeks.

"Really?" No one had ever told Chester Smith he was loved.

"I think you are the best man that ever lived." Julia wobbled out of the car and hugged him.

Delighted, delirious, Chessy hugged her right back, while steam from his radiator spiraled skyward.

Louise, recovered from what she thought her close brush with death, entertained the assembled with a short prayer thanking the Lord for their collective deliverance. Observing Julia's cried-up face, she offered her sage advice: "Keep a stiff upper lip, Julia."

"If I want a stiff upper lip I'll grow a mustache," Julia flared.

Everyone knew Juts was fully herself again.

December 20, 1925

"Fairy's late again. Ever since our European tour this summer she's been irresponsible," Fannie Jump Creighton complained.

"Have you two made up since your falling out, truly made up?" Ramelle interrogated her.

"Yes, forgive and forget, but I tell you, Fairy was unreliable in France and she's unreliable here. Look at the time, How can we play bridge without her? Julia and Ev slave away at that damn silk mill. The whole world's going to hell."

"We can always play poker." Celeste shuffled the cards.

"You win too much." Fannie crossed her legs.

"I thought all Fairy did in Europe was look for a knight to go with her nightgown." Celeste's mouth twitched slightly.

"She struck out when I was with her."

"You, of course, hit many a home run," teased Celeste.

"In a manner of speaking." Fannie ran her hand over her hair, exuding superiority.

"I think she's taken a lover." Ramelle pitched that right by them.

"Don't be ridiculous. The woman's almost fifty."

"So are you and so am I, my dear," Celeste said.

"That's different." Fannie blinked.

"How so?" Celeste cut the cards on the table.

"We don't look fifty and we don't act fifty."

"Perhaps." Celeste dealt a hand for five-card stud.

"Celeste, let's give her another ten minutes. Besides, that gives me time to figure out how much I can afford to lose to you." Fannie checked her watch.

"Read anything interesting?" Celeste addressed Fannie.

"Certainly not."

"I just finished a book about the rigors of priesthood which strengthened in me my dedication not to become a priest." Celeste gathered up the cards.

"Father Chalfonte—ha, I can see it," Fannie remarked.

"What you should have seen was Celeste's face when Carlotta drove over to present it to her." Ramelle's light laughter brightened the room.

"No!"

"She came in here with the searching eye, as Cora

says. Most times we can fend off her advances, but every now and then she presents herself in the flesh." Celeste's lips drew together.

"What the hell did she want?"

"She said Christmas was upon us and she was redoubling her efforts for my soul. Then she distributed presents, including a gaudy rosary for Spotts, and left, miffed as usual."

"Darling, you aren't telling the whole story," Ramelle quietly prodded.

"Well?"

"Celeste, what did you do—revive the Knights Templar before her pontifical eyes?"

"All I said was that yes, I knew it was Christmas and that terrible pall of goodwill was again hanging over us. I also told her to spare me her limitless capacity for forgiveness and to beat it!"

"She never gives up." Fannie shook her head.

"What you all fail to realize is that if I were to convert, it would ruin my sister's spiritual equilibrium. She needs a sinner. As long as there is one soul to be brought into the fold she keeps going."

Someone knocked on the inside front door, then opened it and walked in.

"Fairy Thatcher, we've been waiting close to an hour for you," Fannie bitched.

"I'm sorry, really I am. Please excuse me."

"Let me take your coat." Ramelle helped her worm out of the heavy thing.

"Would you like a drink? Hungry?" Celeste offered.

"No." Fairy sat down at her accustomed place at the card table. She fidgeted.

"What's the matter with you? You aren't suffering from St. Vitus's dance, are you?" Fannie was irritated.

Hesitating, Fairy folded her hands. "I've got to tell you all something."

"Shoot." Fannie dealt a bridge hand with gusto.

Fairy looked at Fannie and stopped.

"Go ahead, Fairy. We'll listen," Ramelle encouraged her.

"I'm running away tonight."

Fannie froze in middeal. "What!"

"I said I'm running away tonight."

"Where?" Celeste wanted to head Fannie off before she exploded.

"Germany." Fairy held her head up.

"Germany! You're nuts. One month of bratwurst and you'll be back in Runnymede." Fannie was soundly irritated now, but she was also worried.

"Germany staggers under a Carthaginian peace, I should think that's the last place you'd want to go," Celeste said.

Suddenly animated, Fairy answered her, "No, that's exactly where I must go. The German workers will revolt. You'll see. It will be the beginning of world-wide revolution, just as Trotsky predicts."

"You can't be serious." Fannie's mouth fell open.

"I am serious. I've never been more serious in my life."

"Touring in Lenin? Fairy, you're a wealthy woman. Why in the world would German workers listen to you?" Celeste leaned forward.

"It's not me they'll listen to, but Marx. Anyway, I'll be working, not speaking. The Party needs workers."

"This is absurd!" Fannie erupted.

"You still haven't read Marx. If you'd only read him you might not think this is so absurd." Fairy stood up for herself.

"Well, I have read Marx," Celeste spoke. "He may have flowered but the frost got him. The information from Russia isn't all that reassuring."

"That's the whole point. Don't you see Russia is besieged? Alone. Ringed by hostile nations. Like France during the Revolution. Yes, exactly like France. But the trumpet is sounded. Germany will be next. Internationalism has begun." Fairy's eyes glittered with zeal.

"Oh, hell, the Church has been trying to unify the world since Jesus. What makes you think you can succeed where Rome failed?" Fannie surprised the others with her parallel. Fannie rarely gave the impression of thought.

"That's based on fantasy. Marx is based on fact."

"Perhaps, but people do cling to their rituals, no

matter how disproved." Ramelle wasn't trying to cross Fairy. She was merely involved in discussing the issue.

"Education will clear all that up," Fairy said hopefully.

"We are all living in the shadow of the guillotine. Education has yet to erase human capacity for brutality. Really, Fairy, do take a closer look at the French Revolution before you hop off to Germany," Celeste bent the corner of a card.

"I know what I must do." Fairy held firm.

"Are you sure you wouldn't like something to drink? Hot coffee, perhaps?" Ramelle invited her.

"Coffee, thank you."

Fairy leaned back in her chair, only to jerk forward again at Fannie's newest tack: "If Marx is for workers, what's in it for you? You're rich."

"I can't help that," but she did feel terribly guilty.

"How can you be rich and be a Marxist?" Fannie pressed.

"One doesn't need to be a memeber of the proletariat in order to crusade for the Revolution."

"If you're so keen on Revolution, why not start one here?" Celeste tested her.

"America's not ready. Germany is."

"I need a drink." Fannie lumbered to the cabinet and poured herself a stiff one. Fairy disturbed her. She offered to pour juice for the others, but they declined.

Fairy sipped at the coffee Ramelle brought her. "You can laugh at me if you want. I'm going and I'm going tonight. You American aristocrats can sit here and laugh. Go ahead."

"Aristocrat? Well, I like that." Celeste picked up a card. It was the four of hearts.

"You know perfectly well that you are of the Four Hundred," Fairy half accused, half stated.

"My family moved to Runnymede when the earth was cooling. Time does lend a name certain status." Celeste's voice rose.

"Status. You grew rich off the labor of others," Fairy warmed.

"Ha! The difference between a Chalfonte and anyone else is my family started stealing first."

"It isn't funny," Fairy grimly replied.

"For Christ's sake, you are holding me responsible for what my forebears did in the 1600s? That's hardly a way to attract converts. Smacks of Marxist Calvinism."

"Clever, ever clever." Fairy knew she could never outwit Celeste. "And what of the Indians and the coloreds? Their labor made you rich."

"I suppose we killed what Indians we could and gave the rest syphilis." Celeste, offended, retreated into sarcasm.

"That's rare, Celeste," Fannie approved.

"You haven't answered me." Fairy stubbornly returned to her accusations.

Baffled by Fairy's announcement, confused by her sudden thrusts, Celeste raised her voice, an uncommon event. "Goddammit, Fairy, I can't answer you. I read Marx, too. I know what you're after, but I didn't commit those acts. That I benefit from them is both my luck and my moral dilemma. Are you any different? Were your ancestors saints?"

"No. I'm sorry, Celste, I'm so nervous about leaving." Fairy drew a great breath. "But I am doing something. You should, too."

"I know I should do something!" Celeste was still angry. "Tilting at windmills is not to my taste."

"Ladies—" Ramelle didn't finish her sentence.

"You have a lover over there, don't you?" Fannie gloated. This was a reason she could understand.

"Fannie!"

"Don't Fannie me. We've known each other for nearly all our lives. You tell me the truth."

"Yes."

"I knew it!"

"I'd go anyway, Creighton."

"You would like hell."

Ramelle stepped in. "What's his name?"

"Gunther, Gunther Kreutzer. He works in Berlin."

"Is he Communist?" Celeste was curious, even though she knew the answer.

"Oh, yes. He's very important in the city. You can't believe how effective he is in the factories."

"Probably wants you for your money." Fannie hit a low blow.

"You should talk." Fairy quietly hit right back.

"I'm glad you've found someone you care about." Celeste knew Fairy meant what she said.

"Will you take me to Baltimore? If I get on the train here the entire town will know. I doubt Horace will chase after me. He hasn't noticed me in twenty years, but just in case, I want to throw him off the track."

"Yes, I'll take you," Celeste agreed.

"Will you come?" Fairy asked Fannie Jump.

Frowning, Fannie also agreed.

"My bags are inside the vestibule. Perhaps we ought to go now."

At the main railroad station the three childhood friends awaited the train. Fairy informed them she'd register on the ship under a false name. She'd obtained two sets of passports for this purpose. She had also packed all her jewels and withdrawn her money out of the bank, although the bulk of it was in her husband's name and couldn't be touched. She figured the jewels would keep her alive for a long time. She owned a great many handsome pieces. As the train pulled into view, each of the old combination of Hic, Haec and Hoc suddenly realized what a deep loss this would be.

"Write, wire if you need anything," Celeste urged her.

"I will. And I'll see you, Celeste. You return to Europe like a moth to a flame."

"Do you have Grace Pettibone's address in Paris?" Fannie mothered her.

"I've got everything."

Fannie's chin quivered, her eyes filled with tears. "I can't believe you're going. I can't."

Her eyes glazed with fought-back tears, Fairy hugged her long-time friend. "Come visit. Good-bye." She hugged Celeste. "Good-bye, dear, dear Celeste."

"Good-by, Fairy. Life won't be the same without you."

Fairy climbed the steps into the train. Fannie ran forward and gave her another hug. "God bless."

"God bless you, too." Fairy said. Somehow, "Marx be with you" wouldn't have sounded right.

"Good luck, Fairy," Celeste waved. "Give them hell!"

Fairy found her seat and waved from the window. All too soon the train was a tiny dot far down the track.

Riding home in the car, Fannie bawled like a baby.

"Pull yourself together. I'll start and you know I can't see if I cry."

"I can't help it. I can't believe she's doing this."

"I can."

"You can?"

"Yes, it makes a lot of sense if you think about it."

Fannie wailed. "I'm too upset to think."

"Here." Celeste handed her a handkerchief. "Fannie, we're all a cat's whisker from fifty. It's now or never."

Blowing her nose, Fannie mumbled, "Fifty is one thing. Besides, we've got another two years. But Germany . . . workers. Oh, I don't know, I just don't know."

"Life becomes more finite, the longer you live. Fairy can see her beginning and, now, her end."

"Don't get morbid on me, Chalfonte."

"I'm not getting morbid. But think about it. Most of our lives we drug ourselves with the delights of the future. Tomorrow. Remember what the White Queen said: 'The rule is, jam tomorrow and jam yesterday—but never jam today'?"

"I fail to see what jelly or jam has to do with Fairy hightailing it to Berlin. And who will be our fourth at cards, I ask you?" Fannie seized on this last sentence to blunt her sense of loss and the sense of what Celeste was saying.

"She's taking hold of herself. The Eternal Present. Few have the strength to live in it. Dear Fairy summoned all her courage. She is living now, right this minute, this second, this atom of breath!" Celeste squinted to get a better view of the dark road. "I'm proud of her. I hate to see her go, but I am proud of her."

Fannie quieted down and fell silent. She sniffled a few times and after a long pause of five minutes she said in her normal booming voice, "Well, yes. All right. I can understand a little." She lapsed into reflection once more, then snapped her head around to look at Celeste instead of staring out the windshield. "But with a man named Gunther? She could at least have chosen someone with a better name."

March 27, 1926

Juts and Chessy, with Ev Most and her date, Lionel Dumble, led the way while Louise and Pearlie followed with Orrie Tadia and her date, Noe Mojo. The two cars puttered along, a tiny caravan, heading for a glamorous speakeasy in York, Pennsylvania. Juts, Ev and Orrie had worked on Louise for days to get her to come. She had had a baby in January and named her Mary, of course. Since Mary's birth Louise hung a bit. Cora said that after birthing you do feel let down. Juts thought leaving her job bothered Louise. Wheezie had adored meeting people over the counter and exchanging gossip. She and Pearlie were worried, too, because her small salary had helped make ends meet. Now with another mouth to feed things were tight. Louise pounced on the idea that Pearlie should quit working at the factory and start his own business, house painting. He balked. No one could accuse Pearlie Trumbull of being a go-getter. Louise kept at him and he finally gave in. Better to risk the poorhouse than the wrath of Louise Hunsenmeir Trumbull. Shrewd in her own way, Louise contacted her old Immaculata pals who lived in the area. Rich girls marry rich boys and set up housekeeping in huge mansard caverns. Sure enough, many of them did need work done and were delighted to hire someone they could trust. Tonight the gang wanted to celebrate Pearlie's first finished job. Julia and Chessy had saved their pennies to give the couple a wonderful night on the town.

The club, Perroquet, was so jammed they drove around until finding a parking place two blocks away. Upon entering the club via the password, "Polly wanna cracker," the group was amazed. Men in tuxedos danced with glossy youth or with slightly older women acting like flappers. A black band on a raised dais tooted and thumped. Juts, a born dancer, thought it the best music she'd ever heard. Resplendent in a short silver-gray dress, a white orchid pinned on her left breast, Juts turned many a gentleman's head. It wasn't her clothes that did it, as she supposed, but rather her smile. She looked like a gal who had fun. She fit right in with the décor of this gorgeous club. No cheap joint, it boasted a centerpiece of carefully arranged flowers on each table, the colors offering a further accent to the club's décor. Orrie, overdressed, plopped at the table. Ev swam in deep purple, a flattering shade for her. The men, except for Noe Mojo, didn't own tuxedos but they dressed in their Sunday best and passed. Noe glittered like patent leather in his tuxedo. Being a Japanese American, he knew he must always be perfect because white people stare at you so. He was a man of culture and impeccable manners, and Orrie was nuts about him. In her young life no man had ever treated her with such respect. The crew could figure why Orrie gushed over Noe, but it was a little harder figuring it the other way around. Her open emotion, her unalloyed warmth, knocked him out.

"Wheezie, ain't it the bees' knees?" Orrie gawked.

"Snake's garters, all right." Ev giggled.

"What would you ladies like to drink?" Lionel inquired.

Julia quickly put in her order. "Old Fashioned."

"Me, too," Ev echoed.

"Lionel, I'd like a Pink Lady."

Louise stared silently at the flowers.

"Louise?" Lionel, a tall, willowy fellow, asked.

"Milk," Wheezie said in a soft voice.

"Milk?" Lionel was amazed.

"Are you tilted?" Juts fingered her orchid.

"Julia, you know I never reek of strong waters."

"Brother!" Ev slapped her thigh.

"Really, Evelyn, I don't expect you to understand."
Louise threw her head back.

Pearlie, wisely, kept his peace.

"Come on, Louise, this is a celebration," Chessy told
her.

"I told Pearlie when we got married, lips that touch
alcohol will never touch mine."

Orrie, wanting to kick up her heels, noted, "Well,
you order a drink and Pearlie can stay dry."

"I don't think drinking befits a Christian." Louise
would need a tent if she kept this up.

"Jesus drank hooch," Julia stated.

Louise, shocked, denied such blasphemy.

"Sure he did," Juts declared.

"That's impossible, Julia. Our good Lord never did
anything human."

"He drank wine, Louise. You ain't the only person
to ever read the Bible." Julia smacked the table.

The men were getting uneasy. They wanted to drink
and they wanted to enjoy themselves. If Louise was
going to pull her Saint Catherine number, the night
would be a bust.

"Jesus, son of God almighty, didn't guzzle no
wine." Angry, Louise lapsed into pre-Immaculata
grammar.

"What in goddamned hell do you think he drank
at the Last Supper? Coca-Cola?" Julia insisted.

"That's right, Wheezie." Orrie patted her hand.

Ev chimed in. "Yeah. 'Take, eat, this is my body.
Take, drink, this is my wine.'"

"Blood," Julia corrected her.

"Isn't that what I said?"

"Well . . ." Louise was dying to be convinced.

"Sweetheart, we wouldn't want you to cross yourself. Communion is wine. You can have a glass of wine," Pearlie soothed her.

"Well . . ."

Lionel, not a man to lose the moment, snapped his fingers and the waiter promptly arrived at the table. "We'd like two Old Fashioneds, one Pink Lady, one glass of chilled white wine—"

"Red," Louise interrupted him, then whispered to Orrie, "Blood's red."

"Pardon me; a chilled glass of red wine." Lionel knew the men's habits, so he continued: "Two Scotch on the rocks, one bourbon and one devil rum."

"Black and White or Green Stripe on that Scotch, sir?"

"Black and White." Lionel then checked with Chessy, who nodded.

As the waiter disappeared, Lionel informed them the stuff was cut only once here. Particularly fine brands weren't cut at all.

Pearlie asked Louise to dance. Juts sat with Chessy while the other couples danced, too. Chessy was cursed with two left feet. She knew that as soon as the first dance was over she could dance with the other fellows. Returning, Noe invited her to the floor and the two of them put on a show.

The drinks arrived and Chessy paid for them. Lionel protested, "Now, Chessy."

"You get the next round, bub. We can each take a turn except for Pearlie."

"You got to let me catch one fly," Pearlie said.

"Uh-uh." Chessy shook his blond head. "This is on us."

When the dancers returned, Chessy held up his glass. "To Pearlie and Louise's new business. May it thrive."

"Hear, hear." The others agreed and tossed their drinks down.

Louise gulped half her glass and smiled as it burned all the way to her stomach.

Julia hit the dance floor again, this time with Lionel. A dark man watched her with great interest.

Louise, wishing to become as close to Christ as possible in as short a time, ordered another red wine.

Glasses tinkled, firewater flowed, the night hopped with each hour. The dark man asked Julia to dance. He was an expert partner but there was something about him that she didn't like. After the dance she came back to the table.

"Another Old Fashioned? Did you order that for me, O Sheik?" Juts teased Chessy.

"I figured you'd need it, the way you're carrying on out there." Chessy smiled. He loved to watch Julia dance.

Noe and Orrie gracefully turned and twisted. The band got hotter and hotter. The dark man came back for Julia. She gave Chessy a frown but then got up to dance with him.

Ev gave Lionel, Chessy, Louise and Pearlie the entire plot of *Ben Hur* which the others hadn't seen. After Ev's lurid descriptions, none of them could wait. Louise wanted to know if they really showed Jesus on the screen. Ev confessed she couldn't remember. The naval battle and the chariot race obscured the finer points of religious sentiment for her. Julia was having trouble with that man on the floor and she started back for the table. As she neared it he grabbed her arm and held her. Chessy noticed this and called out, "Hey, leave her alone."

The man let go and advanced toward Chessy, who was seated. "You married or something?"

"No."

"Then mind your own business," the guy hissed.

"Just a minute, mister. She's my girl." Chessy was halfway to standing.

"Not anymore she ain't." The guy kicked the chair right out from under Chessy and he fell flat on his ass.

"Hey!" Julia slugged him.

In a flash the elegant clothes were forgotten and Perroquet had a brawl on its hands. Whether it was the moon, the booze or the hour, the place boomed like a match to gas.

"Yeck." Ev dove under the table. Orrie and Noe

found themselves stranded in the middle of the dance floor, among a sea of fists. Noe, a kendo enthusiast, grabbed the microphone stand and obliterated with great precision anyone who came in his path. Orrie dodged behind him. He'd swing and she'd duck. "You got 'im, honey."

Chessy and Lionel pounded away back to back. Louise was paralyzed on the spot. Ev tried to pull her under the table by the hem of her skirt but she couldn't move her. Julia, never one to duck out, boxed like a bantamweight. She caught one poor sucker right on a glass chin and he keeled over, cold. The dark fellow fought his way to her and grabbed her arm with every intention of hurting her or, worse, carting her out of there. A chair flew by Chessy and Lionel's heads. Julia, one arm pinned by the man's viselike grip, snatched the centerpiece and squashed it on his face. For a moment his grip loosened and she wriggled free. She bent over, stepped on his left foot while she grabbed his right leg, and in one swift motion pulled it as high as it would go and higher. His whole inseam ripped open. Enraged, he punched her on the chest. She wobbled back a step or two but kept her dukes up.

"Don't you dare hit my baby sister!" Louise shrieked. She picked up a broken chair leg and blasted it right over his head. He saw stars.

Julia grabbed Louise's hand. "Come on, Wheeze."

"Ev's under the table."

Without even looking, Julia and Louise reached under the table and yanked Ev out. The three bobbed and weaved for the door.

Noe, wielding his microphone stand, cleared a path over to Chessy and Lionel. Seeing him coming, Chessy yelled, "Mojo's a man on fire!"

Pearlie, besieged by two once impeccably dressed men, stopped to look and got pasted right on the eye. Noe wiped out all opposition in front of him and Orrie fed him constant information concerning his rear. She seemed glued to his back.

"Come on, fellas, let's get out of here," he ordered. They fell in behind him, Chessy and Lionel fighting a rear-guard action until all were safely out the door.

"Chessy!" Julia ran over.

"Am I glad to see you. I didn't know if you got out the door or not."

Louise growled, "I lost my shoes in that hellhole! Pearlie, you didn't see them, did you? Oh, Pearlie, what happened?"

"Two against one," he mumbled. His eye already was almost closed.

"Poor baby." Louise kissed him.

"Did you see Noe? Douglas Fairbanks couldn'ta done better." Orrie crowed.

Noe still had the microphone stand in his hand.

"I think we'd better get to the cars before the police get to us," Lionel wisely noted. He heard sirens way off.

They ran, limped, scurried for their cars and ducked in as the cops passed. Louise crouched by the side. She hadn't made it in the door. Once the paddy wagons whizzed on, the group howled like hyenas.

"Did ya see that guy I shoveled? Blood and snot all over his face." Pearlie slapped Chessy on the back.

"Ha! You shoulda seen Juts and me. We left that masher hearing birds." Louise beamed.

"Yeah, we knocked his dick up in his watch pocket," Julia roared.

"That's the God's honest truth. I saw them," Lionel concurred.

"Pick one up and knock one down," Julia bragged some more.

"Hell, I'm not traveling anywhere without you. You can protect me." Chessy put his arm around Julia's shoulders. Her dress looked like the guy in *Ben Hur* who didn't finish the chariot race, this was Ev's impression. In fact, they all had wrecked their clothes.

"I always say never throw the first punch. Throw the last." Louise studied her fingernails.

"We left many an aching breadbasket." Noe chuckled.

"This whole fight is your fault, Julia," Chessy said seriously.

"It was not! That creep wouldn't leave me alone."

"Chessy Smith, how dare you talk to her that way." Now Louise was mad.

"It's your fault because we aren't married," Chessy continued.

"Huh?"

"That's what the man said." Chessy smiled.

"He was three sheets to the wind." Julia shrugged.

"I don't want this to happen again. Do you, boys?" He looked to the other men, who all agreed it was a terrible event.

"Listen to them, will ya?" Julia marshaled her female support. "They only survived because Dempsey's got nothing on us."

"If you'd marry me this would never happen again." Chessy folded his arms.

"You're kidding," Julia said.

"In front of all our friends? I'm serious. Marry me. Besides, honey, with you around I'll never fear for my life."

The group stood, apprehensive, looking at Julia Ellen.

She paused, then slowly drawled, "O.K., Chessy Smith, but when you have a bad day, remember: you asked for it."

May 22, 1980

"Louise, I don't know if that's right." Orrie frowned. Near eighty, she still had fire-engine-red hair and she penciled in her eyebrows à la Marlene Dietrich. With Louise's blue hair and Orrie's red, they made quite a pair.

"Course it's right. Bible goes hard on these people."

"One thing I learned living here in Runnymede is don't take your trouble to outsiders," Orrie cautioned.

"This 'Save Our Children' bunch may be outsiders, but they can stir up a rumpus. Then I got Nickel and that high-and-mighty sister of mine where I want them."

"Didn't those fruit people merge with the Ku Klux Klan?"

"Not that I know of." Louise lowered her voice conspiratorially. "Unlessen they did it in secret."

"Maybe I got them confused with the Nazis."

"Orrie, they're in Germany. What do they have to do here?"

"No, there's an American Nazi Party." Orrie tried to sound like a librarian.

"That makes no sense. We got our own groups. Why imitate them? Besides, they lost the war. If you're going to imitate someone you ought to pick a winner." Louise rested on this political insight.

"Mark my words, Louise Hunsenmeir, you think twice about stirring up a hornet's nest."

"Fiddlesticks. I'll get Nickel all wired, then she'll come across with the money. And who else will sell to her after the news gets out about her being a pinko commie queer, I ask you? Worse, she's not a genuine queer. She likes men, too!"

"Runnymede's always had those kind of people and always will. Everyone knows anyway."

"Knowing and telling are two different things." Louise folded her arms.

"You sure you aren't mad about Nickel not putting you in her last book?" Orrie hit the nail on the head.

"I am not. I most certainly am not. Whatever gave you that idea? I'm relieved I'm not in that filth she writes. How could I hold my head up in this town? The very idea, the very idea, Orrie Tadia Mojo!"

"Thought you didn't read it."

Louise's eyes opened wide. "I didn't say I read it. I heard about it."

"Who told?"

"A reliable source."

"Louise?" Orrie's voice rose.

"None of your business. A girl has to have some secrets." Louise's little round rouge spots glowed even darker. Her Cadillac-red lipstick pulsated like neon.

"What about Julia's half of the money?" Orrie loved talking about money.

"I can't make Nickel pay her half if she don't insist—and doesn't that rub the wrong way! I guess it's just as well; money burns a hole in Juts' pocket."

"Life's short. Let her spend her dollars."

"Seventy-five isn't so short and she's been spending her dollars ever since she was tiny. Clothes. I never saw such a woman. Even now she goes out to Searstown and gets sundresses, then buys sandals to coordinate."

"My favorite is when she sent away for the mail-order tombstones."

"Ha! I'll never forget that."

"God, yes, she went on a frugality binge back in the fifties and ordered up those tombstones and got cement and a caster in the mail. I can still see that woman mixing those damn things up in her basement."

"Dumb Dora, she stirs them up on her cellar floor in a square like she's supposed to, but she didn't put wood underneath them. Two flat tombstones rock hard on her basement floor." Louise puffed up, recalling Julia's mistakes.

Orrie laughed so hard at the retelling, tears came to her made-up eyes.

"You know, she carved her and Chessy's name in them for spite! They're still down there, Orrie."

"No!"

"I swear it. Down there in her basement like giant cow patties." Louise whooped.

"Don't tell me." This was one of Orrie's favorite expressions.

"Know what she did when she heard Nickel was coming?"

"Bought Coca-Cola and made red-beet eggs?"

"She always does that. The best is she ran to every five and dime in town as well as the mall up near Hanover and bought every damn shade of nail polish on God's green earth. I mean it."

"She only has twenty nails. She got more than twenty colors?"

"Twenty! Her vanity looks like a Revlon counter. And at her age. Orrie, I tell you, she's got a screw loose."

"She's something else."

"She and Nickel do each other's fingers and toes. Get down on their hands and knees and put cotton balls between their toes so the nail polish won't smudge. This is the truth, I swear." Louise sparkled.

"Didn't that all start with Nickel and the women's libby movement?" Orrie wiped the corners of her eyes.

"I believe so. Nickel, on one of her annual visits, criticized her mother for wearing nail polish. She said it was pressive or something like that. Well! Julia Ellen twitched like a broody hen and told her in no uncertain terms that a political movement that worries about fingernails ain't worth two shits."

Orrie giggled. "Now they both wear polish all the time. Liberation! Such a pair."

"Two peas in a pod. Course, neither one will admit it, but you know what I always say: 'Like mother, like daughter.'"

Orrie discreetly failed to mention what had happened to both Louise's daughters.

"Know what else I think?" Louise was hitting her stride.

"What?"

"I don't think Nickel's a writer."

"What!"

"She don't wear turtlenecks. Every writer you see pictured in a magazine wears turtlenecks and smokes cigarettes at the typewriter. Nickel don't even smoke. Now what do you make of that?"

Orrie weighed that heavy evidence. "You've got a point there, Louise."

"I know I have—and more, she graduated from college an architect. You can't be an architect and a writer."

"But she can't get work."

"All that women's stuff. That and rattling her big mouth about lesbians."

"Didn't help, but you know this country's been having a tough time with new buildings."

"So?"

"No one's built a new house in Runnymede in near to ten years. The last business around here was that mall out Hanover way."

"Still keep up with business? I lost interest in house painting once Pearlie departed."

"I don't know. I read a magazine and it makes me feel close to Noe, dead though he is."

"Remember when you took up mah-jongg 'cause you thought he'd go for it?"

"That poor man. How he put up with me, I'll never know. I even get fed up with myself. Whatever was on the newsreels or magazines, I had to do it. My ceramic sugar bowls didn't turn out so bad."

"Funny how we get along better with our husbands once they're dead." Louise slipped.

Orrie, jolted, said, "You don't mean that."

"I do miss Pearlie—make no doubt about it—but I don't miss picking up after him and cooking his mother's favorite dishes."

"Pearlie was so neat."

"Neat! It took me a year to housebreak him, same as a dog."

"You were the stronger. With Noe, he was the strong one. When he died and I found out I couldn't balance a checkbook, I nearly followed him into the grave."

"Doing the business books kept me on my toes."

"And I thank you again for teaching me how to do those things." Orrie was grateful.

"Remember the time I taught Nickel how to make money? Juts and Chessy never did know how to manage money and I didn't want Nickel to grow up a numskull. Remember the lemonade stand? I told her she had to learn a trade."

"I can still see her, all of seven, down on the south side of the square with her little stand."

"Damn kid spiked the lemonade with a quart of gin." Louise laughed.

"I also remember when you got bit by the fried marble craze and made rosary beads. Nickel took them all and became the gangster of marbles round these parts. And all that time you thought she was getting religious."

"Humph."

"Why don't you wait before you seek out these anti-everything people?"

"No. I am driving up to York tomorrow. I think they got a chapter and I am telling them I'm being asked to sell my property to a commie, husband-stealing woman who's a homosexual." Louise accented the "mo."

"You're lucky Celeste Chalfonte ain't alive."

With that, the old cronies lapsed into gossip and behaved like two girls at a slumber party minus the slumber.

July 19, 1929

Eggs could fry on the sidewalk. Louise, determined to spite the weather, stood over her ironing board at one in the afternoon. Even the bugs had sense not to fly. If Louise missed her appointed rounds the world might tilt on its axis. Mary toddled about the house, creating havoc, and Maizie, not quite a year and a half, screeched in her playpen from prickly heat on her bottom. Early that morning Louise had faithfully done the books. It wasn't quite so hot then. Now, as she ironed, sweat rolled between her breasts, her hair stuck to the sides of her face, and the shirts, once pressed, immediately turned limp anyway. On a day like today she doubted that she loved her husband, her children, or anyone else, for that matter. Did other people feel this way or did the Evil One grab her by the ankle? Earth was hotter than hell, so maybe the devil was out and about. Such thoughts disturbed her. Marriage with Pearlie was uneventful. His only hobby was collecting figurines of naked ladies. Borrowing her red nail polish, he painted their nipples red. These eye-catching ladies filled the house. Even the art-nouveau standing ashtray did not escape Pearlie's skillful brush. Sometimes, when Louise would let him sleep with her, he asked her to rouge her nipples. She complied, sure this was her cross to bear. Louise was dying to know if other women's husbands behaved this way, but she could never bring herself to discuss the topic. Juts and Chessy were married just a little over two years. Chessy collected no figurines and as far as Louise could tell they did go to bed together, but how and when she didn't know. If only Julia Ellen would talk, but Juts was too busy cracking jokes and when Chessy was around the two of them fixed the car or built a new chicken coop. She couldn't imagine them making love. For that she conjured up steamy Nazimova and lamented Valentino. Also, they didn't have much money even with the hooch deliveries, so they lived up with Cora. She guessed privacy was dear. Once, when Julia was out delivering needle beer, Louise ransacked her dresser to find pots of rouge. She found just one little container on her dressertop. She even dared ask Julia if she wore rouge anywhere else and Julia said, "If I run out of lipstick I smear some on my lips with my little finger." Louise thought if Pearlie brought one more figurine into this apartment, she'd scream. Someone was piling flat tires on all the war monuments before patriotic holidays and this bothered Louise, too. She didn't know why.

"Mommy, I wanna play in the birdbath," Mary whined.

"No, it's full of bird droppings."

"I wanna."

"No. It'll cool off in time."

Mary wandered over to the playpen. Corralling her jealousy was beyond her tiny will power. On a day like today what little the child possessed vanished. Maizie was hitting new decibel levels for the human voice in her discomfort.

"Mommy, make Maizie shut up."

"She has a rash on her bottom."

"She can lay on her stomach."

"She's too little to understand. Leave her alone."

"I'll turn her over." Mary climbed over the playpen's sides and shoved Maizie on her stomach.

Maizie, small though she was, knew when her rights were violated. She socked Mary straight in the mouth.

Without a moment's hesitation, Mary took a round-house swing and flattened her baby sister up against the playpen.

"Girls!" Louise left her ironing and tried to separate them. It was no easy task because Maizie, screeching from more than prickly heat, wanted her revenge. Mary cried as much from her split lip as from fear of what Louise would do. In the struggle Maizie bit her mother's arm and drew blood. Now Louise had had it. She cracked Maizie one and belted Mary for good measure. They sat amid the baby rattles and wailed. Louise smelled smoke. The iron had burned through Pearlie's dress shirt. Running for the ironing board, she tripped over a cleverly placed toy and landed on her face. Frustrated beyond endurance, she turned on her side and kicked the goddamned ironing board over. The iron sizzled across the floor. Half hysterical, Louise stayed on the floor and sobbed. The children, viewing their mother's plight, quieted down. Then either out of fear that Louise was hurt or selfish pre-occupation with their own fate, Mary and Maizie continued their duet.

Cora sat on Celeste's beautiful back porch overlooking the formal garden while Fannie Jump, Ramelle and Celeste discussed Fairy Thatcher's latest letter. Spotty crawled under a black locust tree and read *Little Women*. She was a tall nine-year-old and every time Ramelle or Celeste looked at her they had to bite their tongues to keep from saying, *"Tempus fugit."*

"Fairy's nouveau poor. I have half a mind to sail over to Germany and set her straight." Fannie couldn't muster much conviction in the heat.

"She truly seems happy," Ramelle told her.

"Who can be happy living in a hovel in Berlin pawning your jewels? She's cracky." Fannie sucked the fresh mint leaf in her drink.

"One man's meat is another man's poison." Celeste rakishly opened another button on her blouse, revealing lovely sweating cleavage.

"I wish you wouldn't defend her. It makes me nervous."

"Fannie, it's not good to argue on a hot day," Cora suggested.

"I am not arguing. I am discussing Fairy Thatcher acting like a flaming asshole with some Kraut."

"She has the courage of her convictions. Don't belittle her." Ramelle gently corrected a wilting Fannie.

"I'm not belittling her. I'm worried. After all, Fairy and Celeste are my two best friends in the world." Fannie paused, then hoping not to offend present company, quickly added, "That doesn't mean you aren't dear to me, Ramelle; or you, Cora; but we all met in the crib. And I worry. Hell, she'll pawn her last bauble and wind up so poor she'll go to the zoo and pray the monkeys throw peanuts at her."

"What you don't have in your hand you can't hold." Cora wiped her forehead.

The sense of this expression escaped Fannie Jump, but she quieted for a minute.

"Right now Germany doesn't have much in her hand." Ramelle filled the conversation gap.

"What do you mean?" Fannie chewed another mint leaf.

"This winter when Celeste, Curtis and I took Spotty to Europe for the first time, we were all worried about Germany. Inflation is terrifying, the Reichstag hardly commands respect, groups of ruffians hide behind conflicting political ideologies."

Celeste added, "Even Curtis was appalled, and if any of us has a reason for vendetta it would be Curtis."

"Fairy's sitting on a powder keg," Fannie half growled.

"Yes, there she is. A little island of socialism in a sea of collapsing capitalism." Celeste undid yet another button.

"I still say she's happy, and if this heat doesn't subside we'll all be mad dogs." Ramelle fanned herself.

"Celeste, honey, why don't you put in a swimming pool? You know, like you see in the movie magazines?" Fannie changed the subject.

"Dearest, whenever it's a question of money being

spent, why are you always so eager to spend mine and save yours?"

"You know perfectly well Creighton keeps me on an allowance."

"It's hardly a pittance," Celeste sarcastically noted.

"Well, it's hardly enough for a swimming pool, either."

"Why don't you try saving it over a few months and cut down on trinkets for your handsome lads."

"Shut up, Celeste. That and gossip's all the fun I have in life. Anyway, you can do what you want with your money. It's your money."

"Yes, dear. That's one of the advantages of not getting married."

"Now you tell me." Fannie's good humor was somewhat restored. "Creighton's making money hand over fist on the market. I wonder what he's worth."

"You don't know?" Ramelle was surprised.

"Of course not. I get my allowance; the bills are paid out of his office. I don't know if we're worth a dime or millions."

"Do you have any money in land?" Celeste knew a great deal more about business than she let on. She had fought like hell to get her share of the Chalfonte money when her father died in 1897. Stirling, the oldest, wanted to manage Celeste's and Carlotta's shares. Stirling was no match for the two hounds of hell who descended upon him. Both sisters, however, agreed to keep a portion of their money in the business, and in fairness to Stirling, he guided the firm wisely.

"Our house."

"No, Fannie. I mean real estate. Acreage."

"I got my little piece on Bumblebee Hill. Land brings you close to the Lord." Cora smiled.

"I wouldn't know—on either count." Fannie frowned.

"Buy land, girl. If there's a war you can always fill in the potholes." Cora laughed.

"She's right," Celeste said.

"That's Creighton's worry, not mine."

"The stock market is a high-class form of gambling, sweetheart. It's great fun, but never gamble more than you can afford to lose. I play a bit, but most of my friends are in land and in the shoe business. Thank God for Yankees and the cold North. They need shoes."

"I'll think about it. Then what do I do? March in and demand to know where our money is?" Fannie swallowed a drink warmed long ago by the intense heat.

"Marriage is a partnership," Ramelle remarked.

"Ha!" Fannie disbelieved this heartily.

A squawk around the corner distracted them. Louise and her two recalcitrant offspring appeared next to the hydrangeas.

"Louise, honey." Cora got up to greet her.

"Sit down, Mother. It's too hot to move. You know the thermometer on your front porch reads ninety-eight degrees?" Louise informed them.

"Well, I'll be sure to stay off it." Cora chuckled as she opened the kitchen door to fix Louise and the children something to drink. "Any orders out there?"

"Let me help you." Ramelle joined her.

"Sit down, Louise, before you fall over." Celeste offered her a chair. Mary took Maizie out to Spotts. They liked being with a "big girl."

If Louise had had any intention of pouring out her heart to her mother, she rapidly forgot it. Sitting with Celeste and Fannie Jump inflamed her excitable social ambitions and by the time Ramelle and Cora came out with the drinks Louise was showing off her culture by saying, "You can't even walk in downtown Runnymede anymore for the filth. People walk their dogs on other people's property and in the park so the animal can illuminate."

"I'd like to see that." Fannie picked the new mint leaf out of her recharged drink.

October 29, 1929

Julia and Chessy sat on Cora's front porch. Both had been let off work early. People stopped each other in Runnymede Square to talk about the news on the radio. Aside from the disquieting reports from Wall Street, it was one of those days when the weather is fine but there's something in the air that makes people edgy. Julia didn't need any help. She was a day from her period. The bloat drove her bats.

Idabelle, wrapped in a shawl, one sock up and one sock down, rocked on her porch, fingering her accordion. The music drifted up to the top of the hill.

"Idabelle sure makes the sounds," Chessy said.

"If you can fold a road map you can play the accordion," Juts snapped.

They took off from there. No matter what Chessy said, Julia wised back. She had been spoiling for a fight. Now that she finally got one she felt hurt at Chessy's burst of temper, slight though it was, and ran upstairs to their bedroom, where she slammed the door and locked it for effect.

"Don't you dare come in here, Chessy Smith. Don't you dare."

He didn't answer. She threw herself on the bed and stared at the ceiling. I hate him, she thought. I never want to see him again. Who cares about Idabelle and her dumb accordion anyway? I don't. I never cared about Idabelle and her accordion. I don't hear him. Maybe he stalked off. Well, good then. I don't have to tell him to leave me alone. Men are such brutes. I bet he kicks down the door. I'll put the chair up behind it just for safety's sake.

She hopped out of bed and jammed the old ladder-back under the doorknob. Still no noise in the hall or on the stairway.

I hate him. I really and honestly hate him. He's as bad as Louise, only minus the catechism.

Five or ten minutes passed. Julia couldn't be certain of the time. Still no stirring outside her door.

He doesn't love me. He's not trying to get in. I could be dead in here. He doesn't care. Well, it's good I found out. Suppose I needed him. A friend in need is a friend indeed. I hate 'im.

A slight creak renewed her hope and apprehension. She jumped off the bed and got down on her hands and knees to see if she could see Chessy's feet. Nothing.

Musta been a floorboard aching. Change of weather always does that. He doesn't love me.

Another five minutes passed. Now Juts sat up on the bed and worried.

I wonder what he's doing out there, if he's out there. I don't hear a thing. Maybe he did himself in. Poor man. I didn't mean to be that harsh on him. I didn't hear a shot. Rat poison. That's it. He went out to the pump, filled a pitcher and took rat poison. They say that's an awful way to go. Do we have any rat poison? He coulda slit his wrists. All over the porch. Gruesome. Blood never washes out. Oh, God, Mother will walk up the hill and find him crumpled in his seat like red paper. Selfish. He didn't think of Mother or me finding him. Maybe he drove off and ran into a tree. Didn't hear the car start. I don't hear anything. It was rat poison. I know it. Even if we don't have any, maybe he walked down to Ida's and borrowed some. I'm not going to help him. I won't open this door to look. No, I won't.

In the midst of her grim reverie a shadow flitted under the door. Julia heard a rustle of paper. A white folded note slid halfway to the bed. She raced for it and read it on her hands and knees.

Chessy's expansive handwriting set down the following:

I know you mad at me.
Should I do
   1. Drop dead

2. Let you alone
3. Kiss and make up

Frantic, Julia searched the room for a pencil. She found a little piece of flat blue chalk Cora used for marking hemlines. She wrote on the back of the note:

You don't love me. I have my period, almost. I'm bloated and have a pimple on my face.

Your loving wife,
Julia Ellen

The shadow remained at the door. Julia dropped to her hands and knees again to push the note under. She stayed down there to look at Chessy's shoes. He got down on his hands and knees to pick up the note. He peered under the door and saw her squinting at him.

"I'm not talking to you, but you can read my note," Julia announced.

Chessy carefully unfolded the note to read out loud, which was the only way he could read. He put his nose under the door and tried to see Julia. There she was in the same position.

"Honey, I love you."

"No, you don't." Julia fought back tears. Louise might cry but I'll not stoop to that, she told herself proudly.

"I do." Chester was helpless before this challenge. All he could say was that he loved her.

"Do you?" Julia's voice rose slightly.

"You know I do," Chessy pleaded.

Julia, cagey, remained silent.

"I love you. I love you, I love you, I love you!"

"Say it again," Juts began to giggle.

"I love you."

The two of them burst out laughing, heads on the floor, asses in the air, the door between them. In the midst of all this Cora came upstairs.

"Do you do this often?"

"I . . ." Chessy stood up.

Julia was still giggling behind the door. Cora, ever one for fun, slowly lowered herself down and peeked under the door.

"I see you." Cora's voice sang out like in a children's game.

"Mother!" Now Julia really suffered a spasm.

Chessy tried to open the door but she still had it locked. "Honey, open the door."

"I can't. I'm laughing too hard."

Still down there, Cora chanted one of Julia's favorite childhood ditties:

"Life is a carnival,
     Believe it or not.
     Life is a carnival,
     Two bets a shot."

Julia joined her on "Two bets a shot." She clambered up and opened the door. Chessy gave her a big hug. Cora shook her head and laughed.

"Anybody home?" Louise called out even as she opened the front door, quickly followed by Pearlie and the two kids.

"We're upstairs playing hide and go seek," Cora called back.

"Yeah, Louise, you're it. Count to twenty and we'll all run and hide."

Mary and Maizie, thinking she meant it, squealed and tore off for the root cellar.

"Come down here. All hell is breaking loose," Louise ordered.

Still giggling, mother, daughter and son-in-law descended the sky-blue stairway.

"What are you talking about?" Cora asked Louise. "Hi, Pearlie. Come on. Let's go fix ourselves some coffee. Turning coolish now that the sun's down."

As they crowded into the kitchen, Louise continued, "The stock market crashed."

"We know." Airily Julia tossed off this calamity.

"Julia, you're such a child about these things. Our economic situation is garrulous."

"You mean 'perilous,' don't you?" Pearlie asked her respectfully.

Louise stated in her know-everything voice, "Yes. That's what I said."

"We still got Lindbergh. Can't be all that bad." Julia returned to her nonchalant manner.

"Really." Louise dismissed her and said to the rest of the adults, "I tell you the whole world is falling apart."

"It never was together," Cora answered her, hot pad in hand.

"Chicken one day, feathers the next." Chessy smiled.

"You two deserve each other," Louise pounced. Fortunately, Chessy was not a man to take offense at much. By this time he was accustomed to Louise.

"Reading the papers scares me."

Cora poured everyone coffee and turned her head to see two grandchildren emerge from the root cellar, bringing a can of spice cookies as a trophy. Cora looked Louise in the face and said in her rumbly voice, "If it's as bad as you say, you won't be able to afford a paper, so that'll rest your mind."

The others laughed.

"Mother." Louise pouted.

"You'll live through it," Cora told her with authority.

October 30, 1929

"Celeste, Celeste—wake up!"

Jolted from sleep, Celeste examined the clock on her nightstand: 2 A.M.

Ramelle, one eye open, the other shut, murmured, "What's the matter?"

"Celeste—wake up, goddammit!"

"That's Fannie. I'd better get the door." Celeste tossed on her robe and shouted, "Coming."

She opened the door to behold Fannie Jump Creighton, naked, her red fox coat wrapped around her shoulders and a glass of champagne held high in her right hand. Under her left arm was a large metal box. "Thank you, I believe I will." Fannie sailed into the house.

"Are you pixilated?"

"No, unfortunately."

"Then what in God's name are you doing here at two in the morning masquerading as Lady Godiva? Christ, it's chilly out there."

"Telling me." Fannie cautiously placed the metal box on Celeste's gorgeous hand-painted Chinese trunk, which she used as a coffee table.

"Would you like something else to wear or are you having one of your Nordic moments?"

"Bag it, Gladys." Fannie's square jaw clamped down.

"Is everything all right?" Ramelle called down the stairway.

"Yes, dear. Go back to sleep."

"Everything is most definitely not all right." Fannie gulped the last of her champagne with dash. She reached in her coat pocket and pulled out a note. "Read this. Creighton suffered a seizure of honor."

"He's leaving you everything and good-bye." Celeste's eyebrows drew together as she read. "How much is everything?"

"The house and a few hundred dollars."

"What?"

"Here, look for yourself. Along with the note came this key to unlock the box."

Celeste reviewed the contents of the strongbox. "Fannie, you're up Shit's Creek."

"Well put."

"Did you just find this?"

"Of course," Fannie affirmed. "You don't think I'd discover all this at eight-thirty and then decide to wake you up in the middle of the night."

"Another pretty thing?"

"Yes. He had lovely thighs."

"Maybe you could get a teaching post at Vassar: Seduction, Form I."

"Celeste, you are such a comfort to me in my moment of trial and tribulation."

Celeste patted her on the back. "That's what friends are for."

Fannie and Celeste were women who kept a tight rein on their emotions, particularly those associated with weakness. Losing face when the chips are down is the worst offense possible. Fannie knew she was broke, unskilled and confused. She also knew she would not compromise her honor. Money couldn't touch that. At this moment in her life she fully understood the importance of a code of behavior. Sometimes the form alone can save you until you can figure a way out.

"I think he ran off to manage a bawdyhouse," Fannie joked.

"That's really living on margin."

"I've considered my possibilities." Fannie spoke calmly. "I can sell the house, but who will buy it? I could always give it away and be thought a charitable old nut. You know, hand it over to some orphanage and live in the attic. Then they'd kill themselves trying to run that white elephant—homicide philanthropy."

"Saint Fannie. Yes, it has a ring to it."

"La Sermonetta needs a little competition. She's enjoyed the field to herself all these years." Fannie blithely let her fox coat fall open. She had nothing to hide from Celeste.

"You know I wasn't hard hit. Thank God. I won't let you starve."

"I know. Let's hope it doesn't come to that. I can't feature myself walking through life with my hand out."

"Perhaps we could find you a job in some office."

"I could always become an inventor. They can't be fired. Yes, I'll live off my patents. How about electric tomatoes, or better, an umbrella with a light bulb on the end so you can find your way home on dark and rainy nights."

Celeste laughed. "You could scandalize the horticultural world by growing roses thought to be homosexual. The notoriety might bring you funds."

"Roses have thorns."

"Fannie, we'll think of something." Celeste's voice was reassuring.

Leaning back, Fannie said in a whimsical voice, "I'm considering this a challenge. However, I'd rather this challenge had come when I was short of the half-century mark."

"Wasn't it you who said the twenty-five years between thirty and forty are the most interesting in life?"

"Ha! Now I'll have to prove myself wrong. Let's make it the twenty-five years between fifty and sixty."

"Hurrah for you."

"What surprises me is that Creighton left me a sou. I knew exactly where I was with him: he always let me down. Such a drastic change of behavior shocks my sense of order."

"Sneaking off in the night's a low thing to do."

"Celeste, you've solved my dilemma. He took one step forward and one step back. I needn't worry about him changing his ways."

"Virtue isn't habit-forming anyway."

"Did you hear about Hennings Gibson?"

"Yes. Can you imagine? Hanging himself on the huge Bon-Ton clock at quitting time!"

"I didn't see it, but I heard he dangled up there off the seventh story, eyes bulging like plums. He must have waited for the minute hand to go by his office window, tied the rope to it and then jumped out."

"The crash?"

"For him, yes," Fannie wryly noted.

"Hennings always tried to elevate himself."

"Celeste, you are wicked!"

"I fell in with the wrong crowd at a tender age."

"Did you think you'd live to see this? I never did!"

"There must be something we can do. Can you type?"

"No. About all I'm good for is talking and things modesty forbids I mention."

"Fannie?"

"No! I know what you're going to say."

"Now listen a minute. This paper here says you own that house free and clear."

"Fine. Now I need to pay the bills to live there."

"Why don't you convert the bottom into a high-class speakeasy? Your personality would make it succeed."

"You're not serious. At least you didn't suggest I open a home of ill repute."

"I mean it. People drive to York or Baltimore. A tasteful, lively place where conversation flows as readily as liquor would be a smash."

"I do know how to drink."

"And we both have the connections to fill the place up until word gets out."

"Spirits are a problem."

"Juts and Chessy sell goods."

"All they sell is needle beer and bathtub gin. Since the big operators took over, they can't get to the rum runners. I'd have to play ball with the juice barons."

"It could be worse."

"I'll reserve judgment on that. Do you think we could pull this off? What about Minta Mae Dexter? She's practically turned her Sisters of Gettysburg into a battalion for Carrie Nation. What a chance for her to get revenge on me and the Daughters of the Confederacy."

"More people want to drink than want to listen to Minta Mae."

"True."

"Besides, South and North Runnymede officials are never averse to contributions to their campaigns and other endorsements of their ambitions."

"Clever girl, our Celeste."

"I try to think of it as oil for the machinery of politics to run efficiently."

"Fairy'd lambast it as greed—the greed that fuels plutocracy hiding behind a democratic mask."

"Fairy isn't broke—yet. Morality is terribly comforting when food's on the table."

"I miss her."

"I do, too. And I'm afraid for her. Food won't be

on the table long." Celeste paused. "What do you think?"

"Well, why not? I'll try anything once." Fannie felt a sense of relief. "I can get used to living inside a question mark."

"That's what the twentieth century is all about." Celeste folded her hands.

"I don't know about that, but right now I wouldn't mind returning to the nineteenth. At least I was younger then."

Riding her train of thought, Celeste said, "That and the machine in the garden."

"What?"

"Think about it."

September 23, 1930

"Louise, Chessy's got a bug. Why don't you come with me while I make the rounds?" Julia asked.

"Deliver contraband? Certainly not."

"Come on, Wheezie, it's just a little gin and needle beer. I don't want to hit some of those dives alone."

"It's wrong."

"Please."

"Well . . ."

"I'll bring you some ribbon from the factory."

Louise softened. "I want you to understand that I'm only doing this to protect you. After all, I am your older sister."

"Thanks, Wheezie. You're a pal!"

As they walked toward the little black car, Julia headed for the driver's seat.

"I hope you don't think I'm accompanying you if you're driving."

"I can drive."

"Not with me in the car, you can't," Louise firmly told her.

Julia sighed. "O.K. You drive."

Louise sat behind the wheel, squirmed her fanny to get the proper seat and adjusted the rear-view mirror. On seeing herself, she exclaimed, "Julia, I can't go. I've got pin curls in my hair."

"We aren't going to the Waldorf. Nobody's gonna see you but a couple of boozehounds."

"You know I don't believe a woman should be seen in public unless her hair's in place, her shoes, bag and gloves match."

"You can't drive a car with gloves on."

"Oh, yes I can!"

"Louise, pulease!"

"All right, Julia Ellen, but don't ever say I didn't do anything for you."

The car puttered down the road, filled with Mason jars sporting pickle lables. For a special customer Julia strapped on her thighs two tins filled with uncut Scotch.

Fannie's house, dubbed Sans Souci, was thriving. At the end of a run Julia and Chessy would stop in for a short drink. Julia thought there'd be no getting Louise in there tonight. Strictly business.

Two hours later Louise stopped the car by a seedy crossroads. On one side was a gas station. The other corner carried a Baptist church. The third corner was the home of the Blue Moon Café. A blue neon crescent testified to this. The bar was painted flamingo pink, with dark-blue shutters and doors. On the last corner, under a shepherd's crook streetlight, numerous beat-up cars were parked or ditched.

"Last stop." Julia hurried out.

Louise waited in the car. Under the streetlight she noticed a white arm resting on a steering wheel. A puff of blue smoke curled from the window. She could make out, barely, a wide maroon tie with a silver moon on it. Lovers, she thought, indignant. How can people allow themselves to be seen in such surroundings? The shadowy form on the side of the car away from the light was leaning over talking to the driver.

Julia skipped out, glad the work was over. "There. That wasn't so bad, was it?"

"I still don't approve."

"I know. Thanks for coming along."

Louise rolled off the crossroads and pointed toward home. She asked Julia about the false license plates on the car.

"That's in case anyone gets nosy."

"Government agents?"

"Yeah, but hijackers are more trouble."

A few minutes down the road, Louise looked into the rear-view mirror. "I think that car is following us."

Julia twisted around to see it. "Well, step on it, and if they speed up, too, then we know we're tailed."

Louise fed the car a little gas. The other car, which was about half a football field's length away, picked up as well.

"Damn!" Juts cursed.

"We're being followed. Federal men. I'm giving myself up. I'm no bootlegger. You talked me into this, Julia."

"In for a penny, in for a pound."

This fired Louise. She tromped on the pedal. "Look neither to the left of you nor to the right."

"For Christ's sake. All they can see is the back of our heads."

"Yes, but if we gawk we'll look guilty."

"Speeding is worse. Besides, we are guilty."

Louise winced. The car was gaining.

"Damn thing must be souped up. Step on it!"

"Don't tell me how to drive. You're the one who tore out the front porch—remember?"

"This is not the time for that."

"Well, you watch your mouth."

"They're catching up! Faster!"

"It's floored."

"Shit."

"I wish you wouldn't be vulgar."

"Good God, Louise, this is no time to act like a lady."

"Carlotta Van Dusen always said—"

Julia interrupted her. "Up ahead, turn left."

"That's a dirt road." Louise was reluctant.

"I know where it goes," Julia commanded.

"How do you know that?" Even tearing down the road full blast, Louise couldn't imagine anyone knowing more than herself.

"Me and Chessy used to park there before we were married."

"Juts!" Scandal ran riot on Louise's face.

"Turn!"

Louise slowed the car, stuck out her left arm and hung a sharp left.

"You don't need to signal," Julia exploded.

"Shut up. I'm driving this car."

Potholes nearly rattled their teeth out of their arguing mouths. Stones flew up and scratched the paint job. Louise was screaming her pin-curled head off.

Julia outshouted her. "Now turn hard right!"

The damn car took that on two wheels.

"Now turn your lights out, Louise," Julia barked. "Not the motor, too. Oh, Christ."

"It's too late now. No use crying over spilled milk."

The pursuing car roared by. They could feel the wind rock their black car. The Feds or hijackers flew onto a little dock and off into the river. They never saw it coming. Louise and Juts could hear the men shout when airborne. The loud splash garbled the rest.

"We killed them. Oh, Hail Mary, full of grace."

"We'll be lucky if they are dead. Come on, we've got to get out of here." Julia kept a cool head.

"It's my Christian duty to save them."

"Your Christian duty might get you ten years or a fine."

"A fine?" This hit harder than the threat of jail.

"Yes. Now move it."

"It won't start." Louise's voice dropped to her shoes in despair.

Not wasting time to talk, Julia bolted out of the car.

"Don't leave me," Louise pleaded.

"Put 'er in neutral."

Julia pushed the front end with all her might and the car edged back onto the dirt road. She could hear the men bitching in the river. One was wiggling out the car window, no easy task since he had a belly on him. The other one was yelling, "Keep your weapon above water."

The fatter one spat back, "Weapon, hell—my head!"

Louise prayed, "Dear Lord, if you start this car I promise never to cheat on my income tax again." In case that wasn't good enough, she continued, oblivious to the fact that Julia, now behind her, was pushing like hell to get up speed: "Dear Heavenly Father, I know I am an unworthy soul. I am a sinful creature. If you start this car I promise to set one of my girls on the path to a religious life. A nun, Sister—"

"Pop 'er in second," Julia ordered.

Still in communication with higher powers, Louise decided to go whole hog. She called on Jesus and the Virgin Mary. She also rattled off a host of saints.

"Louise, if the Lord's as good as you say, he'll hear you if you pray silently. Now pay attention."

"What?"

"Pop the gear into second. When I yell 'Now.' "

"They're screaming out there like cats caught in the rain."

"Did you hear me?"

"Yes."

One of the men was swimming toward the dock. Another two minutes and he'd make it. He had his pistol over his head. Julia ran her legs off. The car jostled, but gathered steam.

"Now!"

Louise, all concentration, popped it into second gear and heard a sound more beautiful than the gurgle of her firstborn on the morning of her arrival. The motor started. Louise completely forgot Juts and started down the road.

Juts pumped after her. Her heels had broken off while she pushed the car, so she winced at every thud. "Wait up, goddammit. Wait up or I'll kick your ass into next week!"

A shot slugged a tree to Julia's right. That spurred Juts. She was drawing close to the car. Louise turned to see her and remembered her sister. She screeched to a halt. Julia leapt onto the running board and hooked her left arm on the window. "Step on it."

"Julia, get in this car. You'll catch your death of cold."

Another shot ripped off the outside mirror. Louise jammed the gas pedal. Julia hung on for dear life. Down the dirt road the old black car thundered. Louise slowed slightly, then hit the paved road and jetted left. Five miles later, she stopped and Julia got into the car.

"Are you all right?" Louise's face trembled.

"Yes. Listen, Wheezie, I think we'd better get off the road for a while. Go down by Bumba Duckworth's. We aren't far."

"Good idea."

Louise guided the car onto another winding dirt road. Then she doused the lights but let the motor purr. Julia quickly changed the license plates, then got back in the car and slumped on the seat.

"I thought you were leaving me there to get shot." Julia started laughing.

"Never. You're my little sister."

"Then how come you left your little sister down the road?"

"I slowed."

"Thank God for that." Julia unstrapped the Scotch from her thighs. They'd forgotten that delivery. She opened the cap and swallowed a mouthful. "I broke a world record tonight. Running with Scotch on the legs."

"Julia, you shouldn't drink in public."

Juts swallowed another mouthful in great relief, then readied to pitch the contents out the window. At this point she didn't give a damn about the customer.

Louise grabbed her arm. "You have a contract to honor."

Julia stared at her, unbelieving. Louise looked to the right, left and behind her. Then she took the Scotch from her sister's hand and treated herself to a much needed gulp.

"For medicinal purposes only."

"Yeah, that's what I always say," Julia quipped.

The two collapsed, laughing. Narrowly missing danger makes life all the sweeter. Their laughter was golden. A loud noise in front of the car cut short their hilarity. Louise's eyes outgrew her face.

"What's that?" Juts jumped next to her sister and held her. The two of them clung to each other like children. The noise came closer. A large something lurched in front of the car. If there's going to be a monster, better to have the car lights on than be devoured in the dark. Louise flicked the lights on.

"A cow!" Julia breathed.

"See—I told you it wasn't anything."

"You were too scared to talk!" Julia started laughing again.

The two sisters sat next to the cow pasture until sunup. They were full as ticks before finally getting home.

Bidding Louise good-bye, Julia slurred her words. "You know, Sis, I been thinking—we're like fried eggs in a pan, separate but together."

July 28, 1932

"I'm suffering the pangs of overrequited love," Fannie moaned.

"Who?" Celeste asked.

"Hans, the bouncer."

"He's rather handsome."

"Yes, for a man his age. He's forty, you know." Fannie waved as a familiar customer walked by.

"You're fifty-five."

"So what? I like my men median age twenty-five."

"That's silly."

Ignoring her, Fannie said, "After twenty-five, some of them grow up. If there's one thing I can't stand, it's a mature man. I might have to talk to him."

"You're impossible."

"No; I have nothing to say."

"Are you going to ditch him?"

"Not unless Douglas Fairbanks, Jr. comes along."

"What's wrong with Senior?"

"He's too old."

"Oh, yes, I forgot."

"I do like Hans."

"Fannie, I'm sure after exhausting all other alternatives you'll behave reasonably."

Sans Souci did a modest business during the week. Weekends were big. After paying staff, the cook and a small live band, Fannie kept her head above water. Gone were the days of careless money, but she had never been happier. The jewel-encrusted exterior of La Squandra sisters was not her style anyway. Fannie, at long last, was her own woman and she was in her glory.

She had kept most of her furniture but cleared out the ballroom, making it a real dance palace. Her house was one of those gargantuan extravagances with a balcony for an orchestra. Understanding the gentle arts needed for persuasion, she built a raised small stage in the ballroom for the band and used the balcony for very private couples. Sans Souci had the reputation of a place of taste, snappy conversation and good fun.

"I must say, Spotty is coming along nicely." Fannie switched ploys. "I can't believe she's twelve. She's as tall as I am. You and Ramelle did a good job with that child."

"Don't forget Curtis."

"Him, too. How's he doing?"

"Making money hand over fist. He says himself that it's insane. He's producing pictures full-time now. It might be a depression, but people are going to the movies."

"Escape."

"Perhaps."

"Where's Ramelle?"

"At the movies seeing Curtis's latest."

"I got a letter from Fairy today and she's pissed at you." Fannie nibbled a pretzel.

"Whatever for?" Celeste feigned ignorance.

"You know perfectly well what for."

"I got tired of her lectures, that's all."

"Um-hum."

"Is she really mad because I wrote her 'I don't do anything but I do it better than anyone else'?"

"Mad! Not only do you not show proper revolutionary spirit; she thinks you're hopeless."

"That's a good sign."

Fannie giggled. "She does drag on about majority rule."

"Dictatorship of the proletariat is not always majority rule."

"What's wrong with majority rule? If it's good enough for America, it's good enough for Germany."

"Majority rule presented us with prohibition," Celeste reminded her.

"That's just what I said. Everything's wrong with majority rule." Fannie ate another pretzel.

"Selfish. Give me one of those."

"Sorry." Fannie shoved the pretzel bowl toward Celeste. "Who do you think makes up the majority in America?"

"The dead. They outnumber the living in every nation." Celeste crunched a hard beer pretzel between her strong teeth.

"Ha! May I steal that? I must write it to Fairy."

"As far as I can tell, a great many of the dead cast their votes for Herbert Hoover."

Hans hurried out of Fannie's kitchen. "The cook heard over the radio that Hoover busted up the vets camped in the capital."

"The Bonus Expeditionary Force? The chaps who fought in the war?" Fannie wanted to get her facts straight.

"Poor bastards. All they wanted was advance payment on their bonus. Hell, it isn't due until 1945. They need to eat now." Hans was upset. He remembered the war all too well.

"How did Hoover break it up?" Celeste inquired.

"Got the army to do it," Hans answered.

"Fire on their comrades? I can't believe it!" Fannie marveled at the betrayal.

"Who would do such a thing?" Celeste demanded.

"Some creep named MacArthur."

Walking home, Celeste thought about those hungry men in Washington. I'm glad Spottiswood didn't live to see this, she said to herself. She still thought of her brother at least once a day. Time may heal the wound but it doesn't erase the memory. If love is strong, a friend may die but the living one still continues the relationship. Thinking about her brother slowed her gait. She studied the Confederate memorial on the south side of Runnymede Square. Three soldiers fought in the thick of battle. One slumped toward the ground, his hand over a wound in his side. The other Confederate hooked his left arm under him, holding his gun in his right hand. The third man stood upright and kept firing. As those things went, it was a fairly dynamic statue. While Celeste looked up she suddenly realized that the generation that had bled at Manassas, Gettysburg and Vicksburg was passing from the face of the earth.

May 23, 1980

At seven in the morning, Julia Ellen and Ev dabbed each other's faces and squealed like kids at the circus. They had to be careful not to make too much noise because Nickel was sound asleep. Ev, appropriately padded, considered which inflammatory garments to put on.

"How about this gypsy blouse with bear-claw beads?"

"That's an Orrie Tadia outfit if ever I saw one. Here, try this gathered skirt with a big cinch belt."

"The skirt's dark purple, the blouse is red."

"You'll look more like Orrie than Orrie."

"Thanks a lot. All I need is for this pillow over

my behind to slip out while I'm walking up Louise's front drive."

"We can always start a rumor that Orrie had a miscarriage on the path, just like Pope Joan."

"Gimme a hand here with this wig, will ya?"

Juts fiddled with the neon-red wig. Of late Orrie had taken to wearing a modified pageboy with long pointed ends. When putting on her white gloves and party manners, she fell back on her old standby, a French twist. "Maybe we ought to put this up."

"No. Orrie reserves that for special occasions. Remember after she first married Noe, she wore her hair like a geisha and stuck chopsticks in it?"

"I figured an eye operation would follow."

"Julia!"

Juts laughed at her own joke while combing Ev's wig. "That Noe was a good guy. You know, Orrie ain't so bad, neither. She gets all influenced by Louise the Big Cheese. Away from the saint and she's O.K."

"Yeah, I like Orrie fine. Funny how you miss people who are dead. I was thinking about Chessy and Noe and Pearlie. We had a gang." Ev started singing "Ain't We Got Fun."

"I miss Mom and Celeste. But you expect older people to die. I never expected any of us to die. God, Ev, now we're older people. Think of it. I'm seventy-five. I bet I ain't got but ten years left."

"I try not to think about it. You'd better be damned sure these last ten years are going to be worth something," Ev said with conviction.

"Right. I am listening to nobody or nothing. Who's gonna arrest a little old lady? I am doing whatever I please."

"You said it, Juts. We earned it!"

"Quit shaking your head. I got a rat's nest here to smooth out. You know, Ev, you're the only one of us with a husband left alive."

"That's a matter of opinion."

"Ha!"

"I still get the urge, but Lionel lays on his back like a beached whale."

"I still wonder how Pearlie and my sister produced two children."

"Me, too. I can't feature Louise randy."

The two of them exploded with laughter, then "Shh"ed each other for fear of waking Nickel.

"Time for you to get in your duds, Julia."

By the time Juts adorned herself, she looked like Raggedy Ann gone wild. The fright wig added the crowning touch.

"A paint store hit by lightning." Ev admired the handiwork.

Julia never minded acting the fool. She figured it was one thing if you did it yourself, quite another if someone did it for you. If anyone stopped and asked her why she was dressed like Patience Horney, she was prepared to tell them she was a refugee from permanent press. That sounded loony enough to satisfy anyone and set them on their way. Patience had often said things that sounded off the wall until you started thinking about them. In the old days everyone called Patience a nut. She'd heard it so many times she'd sit at the railroad station and chatter like a parrot: "Nature provides the nuts. You gotta crack 'em yourself." Julia imagined she was going to enjoy playing old dead Patience for an hour.

"Hey, remember when Patience had her twins?" Juts practiced walking with the sashay step she recalled the old lady doing.

"What a scene. She named those poor things Dyslexia and Effluvia because she thought that sounded classy. I think Lexi never did forgive her."

"Funny, though. Here Lexi and Fluvi grew up with a nut, Fatty Screwloose. They turn out just fine and look what happened to Mary and Maizie."

"Mary's end was no fault of her own. Maizie— well, that's a different story." Ev shook her red head, which made her sad expression somewhat comical.

"I still say that two years in the convent gave her a touch of the melancholy."

"We'll never know, Julia, we'll just never know."

"You're right. Who wants to think about that anyway? Are you ready?"

"Ready as I'll ever be." Ev took a deep breath.

"Ten, nine, eight, seven, six, five, four, three, two, one—blast off!" Julia raced for the door, followed by Ev.

Sneaking through the back yards and alleyways, they made it to the phone booth in five minutes. At few dogs complicated their speedy progress, but once they smelled it was Juts and Ev, the beasts let them go on their way. Julia plopped down on a creosoted telephone pole laid by the telephone booth next to the road. Ev hurried to get to Louise's, no small task in gold lamé high-heel sandals. Another three minutes and she sank her heels into the frontyard grass. They had about forty-five minutes to pull off the job. Louise dragged her carcass to mass every morning at seven-thirty, sure as the sunrise. Today was confession day, so she'd be a little longer.

Julia danced around the phone booth. She'd read about method acting, so she tried to get into Patience's character. Then she sank on the log again and watched a few heaps roll by. No one took much notice. In fact, Dillard Flexnor absent-mindedly waved. This blocked Julia's bowels. She resolved to give a command performance.

> "I sat next to the duchess at tea.
> It was just as I feared it would be.
> Her rumblings abdominal
> were simply phenomenal
> And everyone thought it was me!"

She sang this as loud as she dared. Not a car passed by. Too early, she thought. It's just as well. I don't want to jeopardize Ev. You'd think someone would notice. Juts sang to herself on the log and clicked her fingers.

Meanwhile Ev Most was in danger of decapitation from low-hanging rosary beads. The hallway into the bedroom glowed with an illuminated picture of *The Last Supper*. When guests came, Louise always turned the picture on. The wine in the cups sparkled. Juts would usually whisper into anyone's ear that it wasn't the Romans that killed Jesus, but Near Eastern cooking. This never failed to get a rise out of Patty Piety. Everywhere the eye could rest some religious object hung. Her entire house was decorated in Catholic rococo. The only relief was a wobbly-headed statue of a Philadelphia Eagles football player. Everyone in Runnymede rooted for the Washington Redskins, so naturally Louise rooted for the Eagles.

Fortunately, Ev had been in the house many times. Otherwise her mission would have been slowed by the dazzle of Day-Glo Jesuses, sacred heart Marys, Saint Christopher carrying his load, and countless rugged crosses. Knowing Louise as they did, both Julia and Ev figured her love letters from this long-ago affair would be in her bureau drawers. They were certain she'd be mushy enough to tie them with ribbon. Ev raced through each bureau drawer and found nothing but twenty pots of red rouge, each a slightly different shade. Ev assumed Orrie, overrun by her beauty potions, had dumped some of her rouge supply on Louise. The bureau yielded nothing.

Ev teetered over to the closet. How Orrie walked in these things with her bulk began to amaze Ev. Until now she had never realized what a triumph over gravity Orrie Tadia truly was. Louise's closet looked exactly like Julia Ellen's: neat. All the dresses were hung according to both season and style plus color. The shoes were on a rack and even the sweaters and shawls were arranged. Cora taught those girls proper, Ev thought. Nothing in the closet. Even Louise's sewing basket was neat. No folded letters, no hidden codes. Orrie was about to give up. The bed; mustn't forget the bed. She pulled off the covers. Nothing. She rooted under and in the pillowcases. Nothing. She looked under it. Nothing. She slid her arm in under the mattress as far as it would go. She felt something. Didn't feel like letters. Straining, she got her index and middle finger on it. She pulled it out. Felt like a magazine. She stared at the cover in disbelief. Ev had in her hands a piece of genuine pornography. Fired up, she reached in again and swept the whole bed in an arc. She unearthed two more. She crawled to the other side of the bed and repeated the motion. More. A gold mine!

Bored, Julia Ellen had drifted off into that zone where children go in similar circumstances. She hummed and looked out over the road. She sang limericks to herself. Her favorite was:

> "Nymphomaniacal Jill
> Used a dynamite stick for a thrill
> They found her vagina
> in North Carolina
> And bits of her tits in Brazil."

It wasn't until she hummed "tits" that she noticed Louise's rear license plate down the road. Her sister had slipped past her. Frantic, she rummaged in her pockets for a dime. Found it.

The agreed-upon signal was two rings on the telephone. Ev would clear out on hearing this. Julia, nervous, dialed the number. It rang once. On the second ring, Ev picked it up.

"Hello."

"Asshole! What are you doing answering the phone?"

"Oh, I forgot."

"Louise slipped by me. Hurry and get out of there."

"Julia, you were supposed to watch."

"I did, but you know Louise. She's shrewd. Hurry."

Ev gathered up the evidence. As she was flying out the back door, her pillow shook loose. She ran with it half hanging down her legs. Under the bushes in Louise's yard, it fell out. Ev was so scared she left it and ran through four back yards. Then she stopped to yank the damn sandals off and ran the rest of the way to Julia's.

Julia trotted home, too.

"Did you find them?" Julia asked before she closed the door behind her.

"No."

"Piss."

"I got something better." Ev cradled the precious cargo.

"What?"

"Look at this." Ev handed one over.

Not accustomed to viewing such literature, Julia blankly turned the pages. She finally made the connection. "What in God's name?"

Nickel called out from her room. "Mom, are you O.K.?"

Julia cupped her hand to her mouth and put the magazine behind her back. "Yes. You go back to sleep."

"Some apples!" Ev smiled, appreciative of her own talents.

"Ev, you oughta get a medal for this. Do they give Oscars for discovering dirty books?"

"No."

Julia held one out at arm's length and slowly turned the pages. Ev covered her eyes but peeped through her fingers. The photos were shameless. After a minute or two of horror, they dropped their poses and sat next to one another discussing the contents of this incriminating evidence.

"My sister, who when she scratches her head has to be careful not to cut her fingers on the thorns! Now I got her dead to shit!"

"I never in a million years woulda thought Louise would go for this stuff. Can you believe it?"

"I can believe anything. Ha! Once news of this gets out, even the flies won't hang around her."

"If she gives up on twisting Nickel you won't tell."

Julia paused for a moment. "No, I won't tell, but what a test of my will power!"

Nickel, awakened before her usual time by the hysteria in the kitchen, shuffled into the bathroom. She saw Julia and Ev in those ridiculous costumes. "Huh?"

"Take your shower."

"What are you two doing?"

Juts and Ev leaned over the magazines, but a few corners showed.

"None of your business. Go take your shower. This is big-lady stuff," Juts ordered.

Half asleep, Nickel shook her black hair and closed the bathroom door behind her. As soon as the sounds of teeth being brushed reached the kitchen, the magazines were carefully studied again.

"Look at this." Ev pointed to an interesting endeavor.

"People must be made out of rubber to do that."

"Are you going to call Louise up?"

"No. Hey, look at this one."

"Do you suppose Louise tried any of this stuff?"

Julia yanked her fright wig off her head. It was getting warm. "Who's she gonna try it with?"

"Let's see—who's living and single?"

"Single. You're sure giving her credit." Juts smirked.

Initially shocked, Ev composed herself. "I guess after seeing this stuff I can believe anything."

"I still say she had an affair before the war."

"Which war? We've had so many." Ev sighed.

"Two."

"Who cares? What you've got on her now is hotter."

"It's just that I can't stand the thought of Louise raising some hell. I mighta missed out on something."

"You never cheated on Chessy?"

The very thought so surprised Julia that she blinked and stopped. "No, why would I do a thing like that?"

"Plenty do," Ev tossed off airily.

"Ev."

"Mind your business."

"Ev."

"Never, never, never."

"Ev."

"No."

"Evelyn Most, don't lie to me. You know you are a rotten liar."

"I did no such thing as you are suggesting."

"Ev."

"Once."

"I knew it!" Julia clapped her hands.

"Oh, shut up."

"Who?"

"You don't know him. He's from Baltimore."

"Tell me everything. Every syllable."

"I most certainly will not."

"Will you at least tell me if it was fun?"

"It was fun until it got serious. It's hard to keep these things"—Ev thought for a minute—"unserious."

"Hmm. Did you tell Lionel?"

"Of course not. How dumb do you take me for?"

"I never did anything." Juts pouted. "Now it's too late."

"Nickel's making up for you." Ev laughed.

"She slowed down once she hit thirty," Julia solemnly assured her bedecked friend.

"You ought to get her to talk."

"She's worse than you. I can't get nothing out of that kid. She was always like that, from little on up. She makes her mind up about something and watch out. She never gives up and she don't talk."

Ev sighed. "What a pity. We could do with some fresh gossip as opposed to this printed stuff."

Julia flipped through another trophy. "It might be printed, but it's better than nothing."

"Well, what are you going to do now, Juts?"

"Get out of this paraphernalia. It's turning hot."

"No, I mean what are you going to do about these magazines?"

"Nothing."

"Nothing?"

"She'll find them missing. You know Louise will come around with the searching eye or send Orrie out poking."

"This is gonna be rich." Ev rubbed her hands together.

Julia sat back and folded her arms across her chest. "We can sit and wait."

"The mountain comes to Mohammed."

"Christ Jesus, Ev, don't you go getting religious on me."

February 2, 1937

Fannie paced in the railroad waiting room. Celeste's train was late. As usual after Christmas, Celeste had sailed for Europe. This time she hadn't gone for fun and frolic. She had traveled to find Fairy. Neither Fannie nor Celeste had heard from Fairy for a good four months. Busy as she might be, their old crony always managed at least one letter a month. Celeste sent weekly telegrams to Fannie: "TRAIL COLD"; "SLIGHT SCENT"; "GARBAGE"; and "COMING HOME FEB. 2. 4:02 P.M." Fannie couldn't figure out the garbage message, but she'd get all the details from Celeste.

When they first became seriously worried they wired the consulate, only to receive evasive replies. Curtis contacted his business associates in Berlin. They advised him to let well enough alone. In desperation Celeste went to Washington to speak with Spottiswood's old commanding officer, now a general. After noting the Chalfonte family resemblance, he told her Germany was tightly sewed up by the National Socialists. Given Fairy's politics, the general bluntly said, Fairy would either be deported or be dead. Shaken, Celeste came home. Fannie paled upon hearing this hypothesis. She was burning to go to Germany with Celeste, but Celeste forbade her to accompany her. Besides not having the money, a weak excuse because Celeste would have given it to her, Celeste figured one of them in danger was enough.

The bitter cold intruded into the waiting room. The wooden benches offered little comfort. Fannie felt a rushing in her head. She feared she'd start screaming or weeping uncontrollably. The tension, not knowing, the feeling of helplessness, were worse than a verdict of death. Sam Renshaw, the ticket salesman, and

Patience Horney at various times tried to divert her attention. A few other Runnymede people chatted. It was all Fannie could do to keep a civil tongue in her head.

A blue flash on the tracks alerted Fannie to the arrival of the train. She charged out on the platform and shivered. It took the train another five minutes to pull into the station. Fannie thought those were the longest five minutes of her life. A few cars away, the erect, familiar figure of Celeste stepped down.

"Celeste, oh, Celeste. I'm so glad to see you." Fannie hugged her with all her might.

"I never thought I'd see anyone again." Celeste buried her head in Fannie's neck.

"Darlin', let me get you out of this cold. Come on." Fannie picked up one of her bags and shepherded her into the station. She knew she'd never be able to drive until she found out what was what. "Did you find Fairy?"

"Not a trace." A tear rolled down Celeste's cheek.

Fannie was shocked. In all the years of their friendship, over a half a century, she'd never seen Celeste cry. "Darlin', sweetheart, honey. Let me get you something."

Celeste's strong hand grabbed her forearm. "No, please. I'll be fine."

"My God, what happened?"

"Wherever I went, people who I *knew* knew Fairy and Gunther pretended they'd never heard of them. Communist headquarters were long gone."

"What about our people?"

"The embassy? All they're good for is licking asses."

"Oh, God." Fannie's lower lip trembled.

"You can't imagine what Germany is like, Fannie. You simply can't imagine. Electing Hitler was like prescribing suicide as a cure for the common cold."

"What do you mean?"

"I mean the streets are clean, the highways are marvelous, but the people are catatonic, in a trance. It's unnerving."

"Is there widespread violence?"

"No. The bratwurst tastes delicious. The women are

beautiful—I do so love German women. Everything is orderly. No violence. But something worse lurks under the surface. Whatever that something is, it got Fairy."

"Don't say that, Celeste, please don't." Fannie covered her eyes with her hand.

"I don't know what to say. I don't know what to do."

"Do you think she's dead?" Tears streamed down Fannie's square jaw.

"I don't know. I even bribed people, Fannie. About all I could get is that one night neighbors heard the police trucks outside. I went so far as to go to the government and demand information."

"What happened?"

"The official was smooth, courteous and opaque."

"We should never have let her go," Fannie accused herself.

"No. She was right to go. If she is dead, she died for something she believed in. That's more dignity than most of us manage when the book is closed."

"I can't bear to think about it." Fannie cried as silently as she could.

"I'm afraid Fairy Thatcher has disappeared from the face of the earth," Celeste said.

Sam Renshaw and Patience came over and tried to help the two old friends. Upon hearing of Fairy's disappearance, they, too, grew silent.

"Is Cora at my house?"

"She's been working away. She's so excited you came home before March," Fannie told her.

"Take me home. I want to see Cora. She's the one person in the world who can make me feel as though I won't fall through the other side of the mirror."

Cora, seeing the car drive up, burst through the door into the bitter weather, her apron strings blowing in the wind. Celeste catapulted into her arms, sobbing. Fannie followed behind, tears almost turning to ice on her face. Once inside, Cora got what she could of the story between sobs. She cried, too, quietly. The three women rocked and hugged each other.

"I understand the politics of this. I do." Celeste

wiped her eyes. "But beyond that it doesn't make sense. Fairy was so kind, so gay. Who could harm her? Why?"

"There's gotta be a reason." Fannie attempted to calm herself and be logical.

"Life's much older than reason." Cora held their hands. "Most of what people do to themselves or to one another's got precious little to do with reason."

April 20, 1937

Maizie and Mary, after a serious uprising, fell asleep at last. Louise padded into the small bedroom, only to find Pearlie rummaging in her bureau drawers for rouge. That could mean only one thing. Like many a Catholic woman before her, Louise worried about sex. All the "no"s before marriage were supposed to dissolve into a happy "yes." Louise never reached the stage of the happy "yes." She wondered if Pearlie would love her without such activity. Secretly, she believed that was all any man wanted from a woman. The rouge confirmed this secret in her mind. If Pearlie loved her, truly loved her, why would he need to improve on her body? She sat down on the bed, exhausted from the pitched effort with the kids.

"Do you know what Maizie asked me today?"

"No." Pearlie searched for the right color.

"She asked me if I loved Mary more than her. I said I loved them both the same. And she says, 'Well, I don't want to be even with Mary, so you can love me a little less.'"

"Those two." Pearlie held a pink rouge pot in one hand and a deep red in the other. He studied them carefully.

"Orrie and Noe are driving down to the Blue Ridge this weekend." Louise figured if she talked long enough he'd get tired. Sometimes he even closed his eyes in midsentence and dozed off. "I asked Ramelle if raising children gets easier as they get older. Spotty's seventeen now, so she's been through nine and eleven."

"Doesn't seem like the girls should be that old. They grow so fast." Pearlie picked the dark red.

"Ramelle says it doesn't get easier; it just gets different. Isn't Spotty beautiful? She's begging her father to put her in the movies."

"She's a looker."

"He doesn't want to do it. Not a healthy life. After all, look at Fatty Arbuckle and the dope. Did you know that Mabel Normand, one of my youthful favorites, is on dope?"

"No, Louise. I can't say as I knew that."

"Wait until I tell you about Garbo."

"She on dope, too?"

"No, but——"

"Louise, I'm not interested in Garbo. I'm more interested in you." He handed her the rouge pot.

"I'm tired."

"Come on, honey. It's been nearly two weeks."

"That reminds me. Mary has that sweater I bought her close to two weeks ago and it's already got a hole in the elbow. She wants a new one. Absolutely not. I told her: Use it up. Wear it out. Make it do or do without."

He sighed. This was going to be a long siege. Pearlie didn't know why this wasn't as much fun for Louise as it was for him. Since he'd never been good with words, this was one of the only ways he had for conveying affection. That his imagination was somewhat limited in physical areas was not entirely his fault.

"Oh, I almost forgot to tell you. Julia and Chessy are putting down planks on Momma's dirt floor, you know, there in the pantry. Won't that be nice? Now that the weather's good, Chessy's going up on the roof with some new shingles. Guess Juts will crawl right up there with him. That girl don't know her place."

"It's kinda nice that they do everything together."

"He even does the laundry with her. I don't think it's proper. Men do men's things and women do women's. Who's to say what will happen to the world if they get mixed up? I mean, how will people tell who is who?"

"Juts and Chessy don't have much trouble telling who is who." Pearlie put his hand on Louise's shoulder, hoping.

She pretended not to notice. "I say it's not right. All this modern business. And they don't go to church, which is a terrible sin. The Lord won't smile upon a marriage like that."

"Lord seems to smile a lot in their direction."

"That's on the surface. Underneath I bet they're miserable." Louise rolled "miserable" around in her mouth.

"They're happy and so's your mother. Can't you take anything for what it is? You're fishing in muddy waters."

"Is that so? Married all these years and that's what you really think of me."

Pearlie had lost his chance. A fight would keep her busy for days.

"Well, I'm just glad I found out, Pearlie Trumbull." She hadn't given him time to reply.

"I didn't mean that."

"Yes you did. You don't really love me."

"All these years together and I don't love you?" He was frustrated.

"See, you don't care. You don't remember exactly how many years."

"We got married after the war."

"See, see, you're all alike. Men think only of one thing."

"Huh?" Pearlie's mind was not running in the same direction as Louise's at that moment. "What's 'one thing'?"

"You know what." She nudged the rouge pot on the bedspread.

"Louise, that's natural. That's being married."

"Ha! You don't have to be married to do that. Look at Ramelle and Curtis or Ramelle and Celeste. Such degradation."

Pearlie was not a man of highly developed prejudice. It made little difference to him if Ramelle was married to Curtis or if she made love with Celeste. Ramelle lived her life, he was trying to live his. "Not five minutes ago you said nice things about Ramelle Bowman."

"She's a nice woman, a very beautiful woman."

"Then why call her degraded?" He stumbled over "degraded."

"She violates the Lord's law. You can be nice and violate God all the same." Louise was in her element now. "Look at Jews. Asa Bleichroder is a good man, but he belongs to those people who killed our dear Lord, and if he doesn't accept Jesus he'll go to hell all the same."

"I don't believe that. Good is good. What church they go to makes no difference."

"Asa don't go to church. He goes to a temple and wears a skullcap."

"So you wear a hat when you go to church."

"That's different. I'm a woman."

"Louise, you aren't making sense." Pearlie, after many years, was finally getting agitated.

"Sense! What did I marry—a heathen? It's all there in the Bible, if you'd take the trouble to read it."

"The Bible tells you to wear a hat? Shit."

"Pearlie! I'm going to talk to Father Dan about you."

"Don't bother."

"You are in need of remedial Christianity."

"No, I'm in need of my wife."

"See, men only want one thing." There's satisfaction in having your bad thoughts confirmed. It proves you're right.

"I'm sick of all this back-pedaling. I'm your husband. I don't need no lectures on God. I met men from all over in the service. Christians and Jews and even people from countries where they got different religions than that. And they all die the same, Louise."

"Yes, but some go to heaven and some go to hell."

"You can just go to hell." He stalked out of the room, taking his hurt with him as well as his exasperated virility.

"Where are you going?" Louise ran after him.

"For some fresh air. It's stale in here."

"You come back here, Paul Trumbull. You come right back in here."

He paid no attention. He slammed the door of the old paint truck with "Trumbull" painted on the side in rainbow colors. As he started out the driveway, Louise, in a fury, threw the rouge pot at the truck, where it splattered on the door.

By eleven that night, some three hours later, Pearlie still hadn't returned. Louise swallowed her pride and called Julia. Cora answered the phone.

"Mom, what are you doing up so late?"

Cora laughed. "What are you doing calling so late?"

"I want to talk to Juts."

"Your mother's not good enough?"

"No, but I remembered something I want to talk to Julia about before she goes to work tomorrow."

"All right, honey, but you come up here and see this beautiful floor they laid down for me."

"I will."

Cora called out for Julia, who slowly came down the stairs.

"Julia?"

"Yeah, Wheezie, what's up?"

"Pearlie left me."

"What?" Juts rubbed her eyes. Cora stood by her and Julia shrugged her shoulders. Cora sat down and waited it out. She knew her daughters.

"He drove off in a huff."

"He'll be back with the morning milk."

"I don't know. He was violent."

"Pearlie?" Julia could scarcely believe that.

"Yes, he said unkind things to me."

"I'm sure you said unkind things right back."

"This is no time to be smart, Julia Ellen. I need sympathy, not smartness."

"What can I do about it?"

"Lend me Chessy."

"What?" Julia put her index finger to her temple and made a circle, indicating she thought her sister was nuts. This opinion was not new to Cora, who'd heard it many times from an irate Julia. She put her hand over her mouth and hid her smile.

"Lend me Chessy."

"What the hell for, Louise?"

"He can go find Pearlie."

"Pearlie will slink home. Wait."

"I'm worried. Suppose he gets hurt."

"The man's thirty-seven years old. He can take care of himself."

"Now there you're wrong. He can't take care of himself. You know as well as I do men can't do anything for themselves. First their mothers take care of them and then their wives. Pearlie can't even make change."

"He's not helpless."

"Yes he is, oh, yes he is. I'm married to him—I ought to know."

Julia knew that underneath all this arguing, Louise was shaken. "Chessy's in bed. Let me go ask him. Here, talk to Mother some more." She handed the phone to her mother and vaulted the steps two at a time. A few minutes later she came down and took the phone from Cora.

"He says he'll go look for him but you shouldn't worry, Pearlie probably tied one on."

"Damn Roosevelt for repealing prohibition."

"Hell, Louise, that makes no difference."

"You tell Chessy to bring Pearlie home. You hear?"

"Yes. Don't worry." Julia hung up.

"I can't recall those two ever having a good fight."

"Me neither, Mom. I don't think Louise ever let him get a word in edgewise."

"Well . . ." Cora didn't like to side in these feuds unless it was necessary.

"Louise never learned that it's not just what you say, it's how you say it."

Chessy drove down to Sans Souci. Fannie told him that Pearlie had wandered in and drunk a bucketful. She had been amazed to see him; Pearlie never lingered in public places. Chessy thanked her and decided to go up and down all the town blocks on both the south and north sides. Pearlie was nowhere in sight. Then Chessy, a logical man, figured he'd sweep the back roads in wider and wider circles. If he didn't find Pearlie by Hanover on the north or Westminster on the south, then he'd worry.

About ten minutes up on the north ridge near Rife Munitions, he saw Pearlie's truck parked in front of Green's dairy. Old man Green thought a giant cow on his front lawn would amply advertise his product. There was Pearlie, drunk as a skunk, painting the cow's udder bright red. Chessy coasted over quietly, turned his motor off and got out.

"Chessy!"

"Shhh."

"Whatcha doing?"

"Looking for you, bub."

"Heh, heh." Pearlie giggled.

"Louise 'bout had a fit and fell in it."

"Heh, heh." Pearlie liked that news.

"Come on, fella. You'd better pack up or Green will tan your hide."

"Wait a minute. One last touch on this tit here."

"O.K."

"Pretty, ain't it?"

Chessy decided to humor him. "Gorgeous."

"Louise don't appreciate me. She don't like my painting."

"Let's talk about this at home."

"No. I'm not going back there."

"Well, let's get out of here."

"Wanna go up at the top of the ridge? We can see all of Runnymede from up there." Pearlie left his can of paint and his brush and lurched over to the truck.

Chessy gathered up Pearlie's materials and put them in the back of the truck. It occurred to him that he couldn't let Pearlie drive in his condition. If they left the truck here, Green would know for sure who'd decorated his giant prize cow. Better to have the old man mad than Pearlie dead. He drove the truck up the road a few yards and parked it saefly under a big chestnut. Pearlie wobbled and watched. Then Chessy helped him into the front seat of his Dodge.

"Pearlie, if you gotta puke, tell me. I don't want you smelling up my car."

"Yeah, yeah." Pearlie rested his head back on the seat.

"Here's the ridge. Can you get out?"

"Yeah, yeah," Pearlie mumbled.

"Let's sit over here."

"I ain't never going back to Louise."

"Everyone fights now and then."

"You and Julia fight?"

"You shoulda seen the one we had a time ago. She locked herself in the bedroom. Had to write her notes and slip them under the door."

"That right?"

"Sure."

"You two get on, though."

"Juts is my best pal," Chessy said, but caught himself before he started bragging on his Julia Ellen. That would make Pearlie feel worse.

"Louise ain't no pal. She says all a man's interested in is one thing." Pearlie slurred his words a bit.

"The way some men act, you can't blame a woman for thinking that."

"What's that one thing again?" Pearlie, dimmed by juice, forgot.

"Bed."

"Oh." He wrinkled his nose. "Louise thinks all I wanna do is screw?" Pearlie's voice rose in a question.

"Do you?"

"Wanna screw?"

"Yeah." Chessy tossed pebbles over the ridge.

"Sure. She's my wife."

"There's a lot more to marriage than that."

"What? Paying bills and working your ass off. Then I come home and listen to the girls scream and holler. And Louise trying to turn them into nuns."

"Don't you and Louise go to the movies or anything?"

"We don't do nothing without the children and we don't have much time. Well, I don't have much time."

"You married Louise. She comes first. Children come second. Seems like people forget that."

"That's easy for you to say. You don't have any."

"We will."

"Good luck." Pearlie was feeling bad.

"Buck up, Pearl. Try talking to Louise. Maybe she feels you're taking her for granted."

"What about taking me for granted? I got feelings, too!"

"Then show them."

"Huh?"

"You aren't made of wood."

"Gets confusing."

"Being a man?"

"Shit, yes. If I show my feelings I'm a sissy. If I don't I'm a brute. If I tell my wife what to do, I'm ugly. If I don't, I'm henpecked. What the hell."

"Do what you want. Who cares what anybody else thinks? It's your life."

"My life." Pearlie considered this.

"No one's gonna live it for you but you."

"Ain't that selfish?"

"No. If you aren't happy, how can you make Louise happy? Or Mary and Maizie? Unhappiness rubs off like coal dust."

"Chessy, do you think Ramelle is demen—I can't remember that word. Do you think Ramelle is bad?"

"No. Why'd you think of that?"

"'Cause Louise brought it up in the spat."

"I admire her and Celeste. They go about their business and trouble no one. Them and Fannie's happy people, I think. Cora, too. Except for that news about Fairy Thatcher."

"Ain't that something?"

"No nothing. No clue."

"Funny her running off like that, wasn't it?"

"I don't think she ran off. I think she ran to something. Maybe you ought to think about what you really want, Pearlie."

"You happy?"

"Yes. I got no complaints, although I could stand more money. Being a carpenter don't bring in the dough."

"Hmm."

"Hey, let's walk a little. I'm getting stiff out here in this dampness."

"O.K." Pearlie stood up. He wasn't so looped anymore.

"Looks like lights up at the factory there over the hill. Can you see it?"

"Yeah. Let's go see."

A ten-minute walk brought them outside Rife Munitions. The guard was asleep. Chessy and Pearlie snuck in and peered through the tall factory windows. Inside stood Julius Caesar Rife and his younger brother, Napoleon Bonaparte Rife.

Their grandfather, Cassius, had been heavy-handed. Brutus, their father, had been only slightly more subtle. But in Julius and his brother Napoleon, the breed reached perfection. Julius, in particular, cemented ties with other industrialists, most particularly the rubber industry and Detroit. In the late 1920s they tried to run trolleys out of Runnymede and put in a bus line. The town resisted. Buses took you to the town line and stopped. There the trolley picked up. People learned you can give ground but not give way. The murder of Brutus stiffened the community. They weren't as afraid of the Rifes anymore. And the Rifes had amassed such an enormous fortune from World War I they didn't need to be crass.

"It's the middle of the night and they're working," Pearlie whispered.

"What's over there, Pearl? You were in the war."

"Looks like some kind of antiaircraft gun."

"Why work at night?"

"Guess there's a market. Always a war in some corner of the globe or other."

"I don't know. Something doesn't sit right."

"Hmm." Pearlie scanned the interior. Some things he could identify, others he couldn't.

"They must be working round the clock up here."

"Has to be pretty recent or we'da heard about it."

"I wonder." Chessy paused. "Come on, let's scram. I can't feature explaining you went on a drunk to the guard if he wakes up."

Pearlie smiled and followed Chessy as they tiptoed past the snoring man.

Walking back to the car, Chessy said, "I don't like it."

"I dunno." Pearlie shrugged. "Let me off at Green's, will ya?"

"I'm supposed to deliver you to Louise."

"I'll deliver myself. I'm O.K. now, really. I want to paint the cow."

"You did that."

"You know, I want to fix it up. Old man Green'll have a heart attack if he sees what I done."

Pearlie was still there when Celeste breezed by on her sunrise ride. He had got inspired and put a coat of fresh paint on the cow, spots and all. Old man Green woke up with the roosters and was delighted to find Pearlie hard at work. Surprised but delighted. Celeste trotted up about an hour later, discovering Pearlie fast asleep. She woke him, put him in the saddle, although he protested, climbed up after him and rode him back to Louise. Pearlie fell asleep on the horse.

May 2, 1937

Celeste and Ramelle walked arm in arm through their formal garden. Dennis, as usual, had things blooming, pruned, arranged.

"Do you know what day this is?" Celeste asked.

"The day before we send Spotty off to California for this damned movie business."

"Heartless."

"It's not our anniversary. That's months away, and it's not your birthday—that's not until the end of November."

"Thirty-two years ago on this very day I met you for the first time." Celeste smiled.

"At Roosevelt's party in Washington, yes."

"No, we met in New York City. Remember I told you I'd swim in the Plaza fountain for you?"

"Celeste, I'm sure it was Washington and you made some aside about Washington throwing a dollar across the Potomac."

"A dollar went a lot farther in those days. I recall the sentence but I'm certain we met in New York."

"It doesn't matter. We stayed mad for each other." Ramelle squeezed Celeste's arm.

"How about just mad?"

"Now who's heartless?"

"Darling, do you think of me as old?"

"You? Impossible."

"I'll be sixty this year."

"Celeste, you don't look a second over forty-five."

"Flattery will get you everywhere." Celeste plucked a colorful flower and presented it to Ramelle. She didn't look older than forty-five, but in her mind she felt the full sixty years of her life on earth. Not that she felt old, but the years weed out camouflages of character, leaving a truer self.

"What about me? Do I look old to you?" Ramelle questioned her. "I'm fifty-three in case you forgot."

"Time cannot pass through the door. When I look at you, it's as it was all those years ago. Your voice still runs up and down my spine, a delicious sensation."

"Now who flatters?"

"Nonetheless, it's true." Celeste patted Ramelle's arm.

"What I do remember is being overwhelmed. I never met anyone like you in my life. It also took me quite a while to realize your desires were not entirely intellectual."

"I was perfectly honest in my approach."

"Yes, but mothers fail to teach daughters of such approaches."

"Mothers make countless mistakes." Celeste sighed in mock sadness.

"The first time I visited here I nearly suffocated from your elegance."

Celeste's eyebrow shot upward, her telltale sign of a cognizance deeper than her words. "I doubt civilization has known elegance since the outbreak of the industrial revolution."

"And it was just such statements as that that used to freeze me. I thought I was so dumb and you were so smart."

"And you've changed your mind?" Celeste's lips twitched.

"Yes. I think you are still quite smart but so am I."

This reply pleased Celeste enormously.

"And something else, Miss Chalfonte. Inanimate objects can exert an influence just as people can. Your house was overwhelming. Now I'm accustomed to it, of course."

"Darling, it's your house, too," Celeste said.

"Not really. You were clear-cut when I met you and so was the house. I haven't minded that, actually."

"What I remember most is wondering how long it would be before you allowed me, both of us, actually, nocturnal rhapsodies."

"Tart." Ramelle laughed.

"You took your time. Sigourny Romaine wrote her first novel in the time you took. I found it an interminable semicolon." Celeste breathed in. "And Grace Pettibone finished her first series of paintings which resemble the bottom of Lake Erie."

"Oh, Celeste, you haven't changed in all these years." Ramelle sighed.

"You wouldn't want me if I had."

"Dearest, I love you now and forever, but you can get arch."

"Arch?" She pondered this. "I suppose you're right. However, let's not get off the track. We were talking about how long you wavered."

"You were talking about my tardiness; I wasn't. I had a great deal to think about before flinging myself in your arms. Of course, your beauty speeded up the process."

"Speed? Gradually, as in 'Gradually the ice age ended,' you came to your senses!"

"Ha! Let's just say you offered me a new deal long before FDR."

"Damn jockeying between corporate power and demagoguery." Her black eyes darted about the garden. "I suppose it must have seemed as though I was offering you original sin."

"Original sin was original so many years ago I think we can drop the adjective." Ramelle laughed. "See, you have rubbed off on me. But I often wonder have I rubbed off on you? You are complete. You've always been complete. I wasn't, you know. I was young and unformed."

"I was young, too, and you, sweetheart, were beautifully formed. Still are."

"Masher."

"Forgive me my lurid energies. I keep forgetting women aren't to have them."

"Yes, well, you cured me of that, too. But I was behind you. Somewhere along the line you grew to be independent, self-sufficient, a bit cocky."

"Ramelle, my father and mother didn't believe in anything but independence. They fought a war over it. As for being self-sufficient, my God, I was given everything in this world: wealth, education, travel. I would have had to be utterly incompetent not to be somewhat interesting."

"My family wasn't exactly heading for debtors' prison. I've tried to pinpoint it over these many years. Why you went your own way and why it took me so long to find mine. I think underneath it I didn't really want the responsibility for my life. Can you understand that?"

"No."

"No matter; I do. I never have thanked you for helping me grow up. Thank you, dearest." Ramelle kissed Celeste's smooth cheek.

"You did rub off on me. I show it less."

"How?"

"You softened me. I was raised with the expression: 'There are a thousand reasons for failure but not one excuse.' All Chalfontes are raised on that. If someone failed I was contemptuous. I learned, through you, that success isn't external. There is an inner life, a life deeper than intellect. Finding that chord might mean failing in the outer world. I can't say I still don't value success . . . but I am listening to a cosmic heartbeat. I owe that to you and, yes, to Cora."

"Do you know when I first moved here to make my life with you I was terribly jealous of Cora? When I think of it now I could die."

"Dear Cora." Celeste's voice lowered. "If I could choose a sister I would choose Cora. Our tragedy was to be born at opposite ends of the social spectrum. This is the only way we can be part of one another's lives short of revolution."

"Strange. Life."

"Strange, unjust, cruel, beautiful, inspiring, exciting —all at the same time." Celeste laughed.

"Too bad they don't teach complexity in school. It's right or wrong, black or white, good or bad. I can recall only a few occasions where something was that clear. Brutus Rife was one. You know, dear, I always suspected you killed him."

Celeste continued walking, not breaking her pace. "What a silly idea."

"Oh, Celeste, you are filled with secrets. I never shall know them. That's one, but in my heart I know you killed him."

"All these years with a murderer?" The light mocking tone crept into her voice.

"Liberator."

"Ramelle, I'm not Robin Hood. And I'll never answer such a bizarre question."

"You do have secrets."

"Everyone does."

"Tell me one."

"If I tell you, then it will no longer be mine."

"After thirty-two years you can divulge one. You've

had so long to collect them. One secret can't bankrupt you."

"All right. Whenever I begin reading a book I must read as many pages as my years in one sitting. As my years have advanced, you can imagine this becomes more and more difficult. There!"

"That's wonderful!"

"Your turn."

"Celeste, I have no secrets from you," Ramelle kidded her.

"Fair's fair."

"I add up numbers all the time. I don't know why. For instance, the street number of this house is 34. That adds up to 7, a respectable number if ever there was one. But I tell you I hate the number 5. If your house number had been 14 I might never have consented to live with you."

"I rather like that one. Do you have any more?"

"Of course, but I'm not telling." Ramelle skipped along, dragging Celeste with her.

"You know, it took you an extraordinarily long time to go to bed with me."

"Celeste."

"Yes, it did. As I recall, I said something to you paraphrasing Jefferson about the pursuit of happiness. For some reason that did the trick."

"You can't pursue happiness. It isn't a grouse."

"You didn't say that."

"I said yes, that's what I said. I think what touched me most was when you wrote me, 'Let's push each other along the road to eternity.' "

"Did I write that?"

"In 1905."

"We're a great deal closer to eternity now." Celeste shaded her eyes and looked up at the sun. "Darling, memory is a form of prophecy."

"What's that supposed to mean?"

"Since we met thirty-two years ago today, we ought to celebrate."

"What did you have in mind?" Ramelle knew anyway.

"Let's take a bottle of champagne, some strawberry shortcake and go to bed."

"If you wanted to go to bed with me all this time, why didn't you come right out with it?" Ramelle put her hands on her hips.

"This way is ever so much more fun."

August 29, 1938

"Julia, did you hear the news?" Louise caught her as she walked through Runnymede Square on her way home from work.

"What news?"

"Minta Mae Dexter's husband died."

"He was pushing eighty, wasn't he?"

"Yes." Louise took a breath, eager to tell of her social graces. "I conversed with Minta as she came into the Bon-Ton today. She always comes by my department, you know. So I said, 'You're lucky your husband is dead. At least you know where he is.' I thought that would cheer her."

"Did it?"

"It seemed to. Elmo Dexter was a notorious run-around, don't you know. He might of crossed over the far side of eighty, but he visited the bawdyhouses sure as clockwork."

"Louise, how do you know about bawdyhouses?"

"I am a woman of the world." Louise tilted her nose in the air.

"How far out into the world did you get?" Julia sneered just slightly.

"Don't be vulgar, Julia."

"You been waiting here on the square for me?"

"Yes. I thought you might want to catch the latest."

"Fred Astaire and Ginger Rogers—is the movie here yet? I love white-telephone movies!"

"No, the latest gossip."

"Oh." Juts stopped to press her nose against a store window. "Say, Wheezie, those are dandy shoes."

"You spend too much money on clothes."

"I do not. I make most of what I wear. Anyway, it's none of your goddamned business what I spend my money on."

"I'm your older sister. I feel somewhat responsible for you."

"Huh?" Julia wasn't sure her ears were working.

"Obviously, Chessy is not prepared to handle finance or make his way in the world. I feel it is my duty to help you with these matters."

"What? Are you around the bend or something?"

"Don't insult me when I'm trying to help."

"When help ain't asked for it ain't help."

"Julia, don't be proud. You and Chessy live up there with Mother and the house doesn't even have indoor plumbing. Only last year you put down a new floor in the pantry, shingles on the roof and changed over Mother's wood-burning stove in the kitchen. I don't call that living. You might as well be camping out."

"You were raised in that house. Now it's not good enough for you?"

"One is to move up in life, not stay the same."

"Piss on your teeth."

"You have no ambition. This is America. What's wrong with you?"

"Nothing's wrong with me. Rockefeller can live his life and I'll live mine."

"Don't be a child, Julia. I've learned a lot with our painting business. Now that the girls are old enough to take care of themselves I have my job back at the Bon-Ton, but I can still do the books. This way I can send them to Immaculata Academy, where they develop useful contacts and learn social graces."

"They'll learn to pray at an ice-water tea. Some social graces." Julia never could endure Louise's snob moments.

"You're jealous because Celeste sent me and not you."

"Up your ass."

"I wish you'd restrain yourself."

"Look, Louise, me and Chessy get by. We go out with the gang, we laugh, we're happy. I don't need a lot."

"Better to have it and not need it than need it and not have it."

"Keep it up and I'll tear your thumbs off." Julia scowled.

"You're thirty-three years old. Do you want to pump water for a bath in a wooden tub when you're fifty?"

"I might not live that long. And if I'm pumping water it'll be good exercise."

Louise took another tack. "Mary's playing Delirious on the piano now. You know, the composer."

"Rooty-toot-toot."

"The religious life doesn't interest Mary but I think Maizie will hear the call." Louise puffed up.

"Sister Maizie. Ah, it has a ring to it."

"Infidel."

"Asswipe. For all you know, the priest could pee in the holy water. You'd still put it on your forehead and drop to your knees."

"Julia!"

"Shit, Louise, what do you expect? You insult me and Chessy. Tell me to my face I'm dumb about money and gonna wind up in the poorhouse. I live my life, you live yours."

"What would you have me do—say you're dumb about money behind your back?"

"You do that, too."

"I do not. I most certainly do not."

"Come on, you sling mud at me every time you see Orrie."

"Did Orrie tell you that?"

"I'm not revealing my sources."

"Big mouth!"

"See!"

"Wait until I get my hands on her."

"Noe will flatten you out, girl."

"Now take Noe Mojo, for example. He's smart. He's a good businessman. He runs that meat warehouse, as well as his small restaurant right next to Fannie's. The two of them worked it out, you know. This way Fannie's patrons go to the next house for good food and come back in the club when they're done. That Noe is a smart man. He and Orrie are going to Japan this September for a solid month. That's what planning ahead can do for you."

"I don't want a solid month in Japan. I'm happy on the front porch listening to the crickets."

"Now you sound like Mother."

"I'm my mother's daughter."

"I didn't say that. You're discontented, Louise. As far back as I can remember you've always been discontented. You want to be high and mighty and rub shoulders at the Ritz. I don't care about that."

"You should."

"I don't want to be better than anybody else. I just want to be myself; that's plenty good enough."

"I can see you're recalcified. There's no talking to you."

"What's recalcified? I like to know my insults."

"It means you're stubborn, won't listen to reason."

"Is that so?"

"That's so." Louise pressed her lips together. "And furthermore, Bon-Ton is sending me to New York City on a buying trip. You can sit here and listen to the crickets. I'm going to Fifth Avenue."

"You know what you are, Louise?"

"Successful."

"No. You're a worm's turd."

Walking home, Julia fumed over Louise's lecture. She didn't give a damn about status or money, but she was tiring of an outdoor toilet and pumping water in all weather. Climbing up Bumblebee Hill, an idea hit her. Chessy, Noe and Lionel had bought a game called Monopoly. Last weekend the whole gang played it. Julia loved games of any sort. If two blackbirds were sitting on a telephone wire, Julia naturally had to bet on which bird would fly away first. Monopoly was a matter of skill as well as luck, an irresistible combination to Juts. As soon as she was inside the house, she ran to the telephone and called up Celeste Chalfonte.

"Hello."

"Celeste, hello. It's Juts."

"Do you want your mother?"

"No, I want you."

"How flattering."

"Celeste, have you played Monopoly?"

"Spotty gave it a whirl before she left."

"Do you like it?"

"It's not as much fun as poker."

"Suppose you played it with real money?"

"Julia, what a splendid idea."

"I propose that you host a Monopoly party this Saturday afternoon. All comers must bring cash."

"Let's see. Fannie will come, even though she can't really afford it. She'd never miss a chance like that. Ramelle will go along with it. Who else?"

"Ruby, Rose and Rachel Rife." Julia's voice was firm.

"They're three years older than God."

"Celeste, they can't be much over sixty-five."

"I'm not having a Rife in my house socially. No."

"They share a brain between them. Think of all that loot."

"Clever, these Hunsenmeirs."

"They'll be so overjoyed at the invitation they'll play. Money means nothing to them anyway."

"Let me think about it. I'll call you back."

Twenty minutes later, after checking with Fannie Jump and Ramelle, Celeste called Julia back.

"Julia, Celeste again."

"How about it?" Julia's palm itched.

"Yes."

"I have another proposition for you."

"What?"

"You advance me the cash. If I lose I work it off, no matter how long it takes. I'll work it off every weekend. If I win I give you back your investment and I keep the rest."

"Julia Ellen, what are you up to?"

"I'm not telling."

Celeste paused a moment. "I'm game."

By Saturday afternoon Runnymede buzzed with the news. Celeste set up the board in her formal garden under a tent. Noe, who had a passion for Monopoly, catered the affair. Fannie Jump supplied oceans of booze, hoping to lull her opponents into mistakes. Orrie and Noe, Ev and Lionel, Chessy, Cora and Fannie's bouncer boyfriend, Hans, were on hand before the game even started. La Squandra sisters arrived, separately, each in a different-colored Rolls-Royce. Ruby's rubies glowed on her wrinkled breasts like pigeon blood. The acid green of Rose's emeralds could burn out your eyes. Rachel's pearls were big as pears. They pulsated. It had taken them sixty-some years to get invited to Celeste Chalfonte's, but they'd finally made it. The curious began to wander into the garden, until it resembled center court at Wimbledon.

Julia picked the little pewter iron for her mark. Celeste grabbed the high hat, Ramelle the Scotty dog and the rest disappeared in a minute. Fannie bitched because she wanted the high hat. They rolled the dice to get their order. Julia was fourth. She knew with this many players the property would go fast.

The kitty money was fronted by each player, as well as the standard amount to start. This way every player put up the same amount. The first go-round of the board, Celeste got Pennsylvania Avenue. Julia winced. She wanted those greens if she could get them. Fannie landed on the Reading Railroad and bought it up in a twinkle. Juts knew if Fannie got her hands on the railroads or bargained for them, she'd be hard to dislodge. Ruby bought Oriental Avenue, no threat. Rose snatched the Electric Company. Rachel landed on Community Chest and received ten dollars for winning second prize in a beauty contest. Rachel thought this was better than buying property. Ramelle grabbed Indiana Avenue. This worried Julia. By luck, Julia landed on Park Place. She shelled out the money for it while the others watched with a wary eye.

Fannie motioned for Hans to pass out the booze.

Julia wisely stuck to Coca-Cola. The second round saw more properties get scattered. Fannie, however, secured the B & O Railroad. Fannie was already dangerous this early in the game. La Squandras spent themselves on Baltic and Mediterranean avenues. Rachel refused to buy any property. "My late lamented brother, Brutus, always said put your money in stocks." Her pearls heaved up and down with her breathing.

Celeste plucked Illinois Avenue. Ramelle got Pacific and Fannie quickly disposed of North Carolina. Julia managed to scrape up Tennessee before landing in jail on a Chance card. She hated those damn Chance cards. On these beginning runs around the board, with so many players, a missed turn could spell disaster later. Noe was sweating as he watched the board. No sooner did Julia free herself from jail, not an easy procedure, than she landed on the goddamned Chance square again. This is it, she thought. I'll be working for Celeste Chalfonte for the rest of my life. She turned over the orange card while the players and crowd stopped murmuring.

" 'Advance Token to Board Walk!' Look, that's what the card says."

Julia raced to Boardwalk and purchased the dark-blue card. Now she would figure out her resources and begin putting houses on her property. But she didn't want to leave herself short. She had to pay rent every time she landed on someone else's property, although she was the first on the board to have a hegemony on lots. But Fannie garnered the Short Line Railroad in addition to her scattered property holdings. Fannie was getting extremely dangerous. Julia put up one house each. The trouble with Park Place and Boardwalk is that they are the most expensive places on the board but people don't land on them that frequently. Once they do, for those not in sound financial condition it can mean bankruptcy.

Rachel, keeping her departed brother's counsel, was out on her ass by the fifth pass at the board. She unwisely lent her two sisters money and they refused to pay it back when she needed it. With Rachel out of the game, Ruby and Rose's collective IQ resembled a good golf score. They'd hang on for another half hour or so, but they couldn't possibly keep up with Fannie, Ramelle, Celeste and Julia.

Louise, horrified at the gossip about her sister's gambling with the elite of the town, snuck around the back of Celeste's property, only to discover a crowd. She also discovered Pearlie, content amid the rubbernecks. She edged up, hoping to be overlooked, which was not likely since she was dressed to stop traffic. *Gold Diggers* movies had gone to Louise's head. Her outfits were either out of date or outrageous. Louise never could find the middle road.

"Louise, hi!" Ev Most ran over and pulled her into the throng.

Julia glanced up, said hello, then got back to her concentration. Ruby was on the verge and she held the Pennsylvania Railroad. Julia didn't want Fannie to make a deal with her, but Fannie was slippery. She got the railroad.

Rose divested herself of the utilities. Celeste bargained for them. Celeste, shrewd and clever in games, was building up middle-income properties. She was one lot away from controlling the red block and she finagled the light blues out of the defeated Rifes. Ramelle, never very competitive, knew she'd go down in less than an hour. Before her last gasp she'd have to buy out her debts by giving away her properties. She had Pacific, a green, and Julia wanted to get that lot away from her before Fannie took it in trade. If Fannie controlled the greens, the yellows and even piddling Baltic and Mediterranean, with those railroad lines, she could choke Julia out. The battle now raged in earnest.

Each pass on the board, each tripping on a Chance card or a yellow Community Chest card, brought forth oohs and aahs from the crowd. Fannie landed in jail. That gave Julia a chance to deal a little with Ramelle. Ramelle gave her Pacific. Fannie nearly blew a fuse.

Another hour of play found the three remaining women deadlocked. Celeste's luck landed her on Boardwalk and Julia had a hotel on it. That was a technical knockout. Celeste could hang on for another half hour, but she would never regain her former strength. Now it was Fannie versus Julia.

Back and forth and back and forth the two fought. Those railroads did considerable damage to Julia. There was one on every side of the board. After a while it adds up. Neither Fannie nor Julia would trade properties they held to give the other an edge. Fannie collected two reds from Celeste, on her way out. However, Julia hustled for the remaining one. This split the block. But Fannie put hotels on the light blues and the yellows. The greens were split. Julia held the dark blues and the utilities. She put houses on the orange block and she had collected in payment of debts States Avenue, Virginia Avenue and St. Charles Place.

Six o'clock and the two grimly battered one another. The crowd stayed with them. Fannie forgot to drink. Celeste gulped two glasses of champagne to soothe her loss. She was terrifically tense, because if Julia lost, Celeste would lose twice. Ramelle, also, was glued to the board.

Chessy got so nervous he took a walk around Runnymede Square, accompanied by Pearlie, trying to calm him. Noe repeatedly wiped his brow with his immaculate white handkerchief.

Fannie Jump landed twice in a row on Park Place. Turning the corner from her last shock, she ran into St. Charles Place with four houses on it. That severely rocked her. The end was in sight. By seven-thirty, Julia Ellen had cleaned everyone out.

Fannie, a good sport, shook Julia's hand. Celeste almost fainted from relief. La Squandras wandered around making polite conversation, oblivious to the bundle they had dropped and ignorant of what that meant to everyone.

Noe sprinted to Runnymede Square, where Chessy and Pearlie were pacing. "Chessy, Chessy, she did it! She did it!"

"No." Chessy went white.

"Yes!" Noe slapped him on the back.

"I can't believe it." Chessy tore back to the garden, closely pursued by a jubilant Noe and Pearlie.

"I won!" Julia jumped into his arms.

Louise, stunned, collected herself and stood in line to congratulate her sister. The garden was bedlam. An impromptu party hit high gear. People were wild now that the tension was over.

"Congratulations, Julia." Louise shook her hand.

"Here's the indoor plumbing and a first-class bathroom and shower." Julia held the money out for her sister to look at.

"How nice." Louise was both glad and pained.

"Louise." Julia smirked.

"What?"

"There's more than one way to skin a cat."

September 1, 1939

For Spottiswood Chalfonte Bowman things came too easily, and that's a curse in itself. Her first film drew attention to her beauty; her acting suffered by comparison, but no one was comparing. In time she'd learn her trade. Curtis was pleased for her, though he would have been far happier if she'd chosen to become a doctor. Ramelle took it all in stride and hoped Spotty would keep a good head on her shoulders. Celeste fumed about how embarrassing it was to have an actor in the family. After all, in Restoration times such women sold oranges to the audience before graduating to the stage and dukes' bedrooms. She omitted how many times she'd chased after such sullied violets in her youth. Ramelle suspected Celeste's explosions on this fallen profession were an elaborate feint to get everyone's mind off Europe.

Louise joined in exploding. She screeched because Mary, not yet fourteen, fluttered around Extra Billy Bitters. He was eighteen years old. Since Billy's birth had not been planned—four brothers and two sisters had preceded him—his name became Extra Billy. Violent, handsome, mildly stupid, he struck fear in the hearts of mothers all over Runnymede. Sober virtues rarely attract protected young ladies. Mary was lost to the nunnery; Louise felt it in her bones. Maizie, however, progressed as planned. Obedient, quiet and passive, Maizie showed great potential for an inspirational order. Even as Louise moaned over Mary, she carefully put down the groundwork to get Maizie, in good time, into a rich girls' convent as opposed to an ordinary one. If you're going to serve Christ, better to serve him with people of quality than with poor girls in simple habits. But Louise, too, sensed a sinister twist in the air.

On this Friday, all their fears focused, for the German army attacked Poland.

Cora crouched over a bowl peeling potatoes. Celeste and Ramelle ought to be back in half an hour. They were out riding. Celeste was breaking in a beautiful spirited gray mare, since her old bay had been put out to pasture. Louise burst through the door. She'd just gotten off work.

"Mother, Germany invaded Poland."

"Shut the screen door, honey, you'll let the flies in."

"Aren't you upset?"

"Yes—but it doesn't matter if the rock hits the jug or the jug hits the rock: the jug still gets it."

"What's that supposed to mean?"

"Means Germany lost the last war and Germany will lose this war. God help all the innocents that are bound to die."

"We could be some of them. They got airplanes, you know. It isn't like the last war."

"Louise, don't worry about it right this minute. The Atlantic Ocean is wide."

Julia yelled before she opened the door, "Mom, war. Gonna be another war." She slammed the door behind her. "Hi, Louise."

"Louise told me."

"You think we can stay out of it?" Julia asked her sister.

"I don't know. Not for long."

"I hope Chessy doesn't get called up."

"He's too old," Louise comforted her.

"He's thirty-four." Juts' brow furrowed.

"They only take them that old if we're really in dutch," Louise said.

"I hope so, Momma, what do you think?" Julia absent-mindedly picked up a potato and started peeling it.

"I don't know what to think. I don't understand why people can't leave one another alone and live in peace."

"Me, too." Julia peeled a bit more vigorously.

"Me, too." Louise sat down. "Did you see Spotty on the cover of *Screen Gems* magazine?"

"I can hear Celeste now." Cora laughed. "She'll say there's nothing more vulgar than publicity."

"Nothing like starting at the top. Spotty's got everything: beauty, money, movies."

Cora sighed. "Louise, don't count any woman lucky until her life is lived."

"Are you sure Chessy's too old?" Julia tapped Louise's forearm.

"Yes. The problem is not him getting called up but him enlisting."

"What!" Julia went white.

"If he goes down to enlist, the army might take him. He's big and strong. Anyway, if it's Ted Baeckle doing the signing up, he'll take Chessy."

"No." Julia bit her lip.

"Honey, don't get riled up. The U.S. ain't in this shooting match yet." Cora's voice was soft.

"Mother, Chessy will go down and sign up. You know how men are."

"I think Pearlie will pass. He's forty and the last war cured him of curiosity." Louise spoke with half-hearted conviction.

"Who knows? Once one man signs up they all do. Then we never see them again." Julia cut into the potato.

"Will you two stop." Cora reprimanded them.

"Would you go if women could fight?" Julia leaned over and peered into Louise's light-gray eyes.

"No. Men make the wars, let men fight them."

"I never thought of that." Julia flopped back.

"If you want to kill people, go to Chicago," Cora wryly noted.

"It's not the same." Louise decided to pitch in on the potato peeling, too.

"Oh, no?" Cora's voice rose upward.

"I'd go," Julia announced. "If America's in danger I'll fight. If they come here I'll really fight."

"Of course, if they come here everyone will fight," Louise affirmed.

Cora filled a large pot with water and threw the potatoes in it.

"Mother, when I came by from work the town was so quiet you could hear a pin drop," Julia informed her.

"Everyone's worried. I never saw it like this," Louise added.

"You all don't remember, but when Wilson declared war last time it was testy."

"I remember running through Celeste's front door. I thought that was exciting." Juts rested her chin in her hand.

"Well, us old fogies didn't think it was so exciting."

"Mom, aren't we about the age you were then?" Louise asked.

"Yes."

"History repeats itself," Julia brooded.

"I've got an idea." Louise brightened.

"You gonna call Hitler?" Julia played with the edge of the table.

"Listen. Let's you and me go down to Ted Baeckle and tell him to ignore Chessy if he comes in. I mean, if we get into this war. Let's do it now, then you won't worry."

"Louise, I can't talk to him. I'll die of embarrassment. And if Chessy found out there'd be hell to pay."

"What have we got to lose?"

"Face." Julia shifted in her chair.

"If face is all you're worried about, go," Cora urged her. "Ted Baeckle's got a closed mouth."

"Come on, Juts. You'll feel the better for it."

"You'll really do it?"

"Yes," Louise answered.

True to her word, Louise spoke to Ted. She didn't plead or bargain or harangue. She said that Chessy, should we go to war, would probably try to enlist. Would Ted please pass on him as long as other men filled the ranks? If our country was invaded or if a manpower shortage should hit, then he could take Chessy. Sitting amid the army recruitment posters, already outdated, Baeckle was a kindly fellow. Given Chessy's age and the fact that he was married, he didn't anticipate trouble. If the U.S. ran up against it, well, that was another matter. He bade the women good evening and told them not to worry.

"Thanks, Louise. You're a pal." Julia impulsively kissed her sister as they walked back to Celeste's.

"Sure." Louise inhaled deeply. "You know, I make two trips a year to New York. Gives me a lot to think about."

"Yeah." Julia didn't get the connection.

"I come back knowing I'm not as perfect as I'd like to be. I spend so much time worrying about little things. Every now and then I see that and I . . ." Her voice faded. Either she had lost her train of thought or she couldn't bring herself to say it.

"Half the time I can't see the nose on my face." Julia, puzzled, sought to ease the strain on Louise.

"Julia, I don't show it, but I do love you," Louise blurted out.

"I love you, too." Juts put her arm around Louise's waist and continued walking.

May 23, 1980

The lavender afterglow of sunset shimmered on the horizon. Juts, in high spirits, rolled a joint. She wanted to smoke it before sitting out on the front porch, as she did every evening in good weather. Front porches vibrated with gossip and Julia didn't want to miss a thing. Nickel leaned against the screen door, laughing as her mother licked the paper.

"What are you laughing at?"

"You."

"What's so funny about me?" Juts lit up and took a grateful drag.

"You're the most alive person I know."

"If I wasn't the flies would be here." Her wrinkles folded in deep laugh lines around her eyes.

"Don't you know that people are supposed to get conservative and unadventuresome when they get older?" Nickel tormented her.

"You're most conservative after a full meal. Here, want a puff?"

"No, thanks."

"What's wrong with you? You don't drink, smoke or smoke-smoke. Come on, girl, climb down off Mount Rushmore and have a little toke."

To please her animated mother, Nickel inhaled.

"There, now you're a little more human." Julia reached for the weed.

"Since when does humanness connect to vice?"

"Vice? I knew you shoulda never gone to college. This is relaxation, accent on the lax." Julia was in an extraordinarily good mood. "You don't relax near enough, you hear me? I swear, girl, you pushed in your cradle. Come on, life's short."

"Sex is my only vice and I don't have much time for that. I'm bisexual in name only. I'm too busy to practice what I preach," Nickel mused.

Julia's ears perked up on the word "sex." "You can tell your old mother all about it."

"What's to tell?"

"Who, what, when, where and how. Ain't that the newspaper way?"

"Why, Mother, I thought you didn't care for this tacky stuff." Nickel enjoyed teasing her.

"I didn't. Not until that orange juice lady went berserk. I figured anything that's got that many people screaming and hollering about it must be good." Julia held a mouthful of smoke after that.

"Just be glad America won the Revolutionary War."

"What's that got to do with it?"

"If we lost, Anita'd be singing 'God Save the Queen.'" Nickel took the marijuana out of her mother's hand and breathed in another load of cheer.

"Ha! I love it! Hell, what's wrong with people? You live your life and I live mine. If everybody felt that way, there'd be no more wars."

"Inclined to agree." Nickel let smoke out. She wasn't as practiced at this as her mother.

"I'm still your mother and I'm still right." Juts slapped her thigh.

"You're right that I need to relax more."

"Sometimes you remind me of Celeste Chalfonte with an engine on your back."

"Huh?"

"You don't show emotion, like her. You're smart, I gotta give you that, kid. You're smart. Celeste, oh, my, she was witty. Once you rest you're pretty sharp yourself. Wish you coulda met her."

"Fanny Jump Creighton told me that once, that I reminded her a bit of Celeste. Funny. I figured I was like you and Dad."

"You get your brains from me." Julia patted herself on the back and both women burst out laughing.

Nickel looked out the screen door. "Mother, there's a large, colorful object approaching."

Julia craned her neck. "Christ, it's Orrie. I'll never get rid of the smell before she gets here."

Turning up the sidewalk to the old house, Orrie was a kaleidoscope. She wore a kelly-green polyester pantsuit. Her fingernails were painted mocha frost. A breath away from eighty years old, she piled her scarlet hair on top of her head like lasagna. Around this brilliant mop she tied a sheer yellow scarf. Large dangling earrings threatened to pull off her lobes and an enormous necklace hung around her neck. It was made from fried marbles. No doubt a gift from Louise back in the 1950s, when the marble craze hit her. She sang "You Must Have Been a Beautiful Baby" to herself. Her kelly-green espadrilles climbed the front porch steps. Rather than knock on the door she let out a "Yoo-hoo."

Julia sprang to the front door. "Why, Orrie Tadia Mojo, what a pleasant surprise. Let's just sit out on the front porch, as there's a foul odor in the living room."

"A foul odor?" Orrie wrinkled her nose.

"Yes. Half the people wouldn't have indigestion if they wouldn't be ashamed to fart." Juts steered her out on the porch, secure in the knowledge that such an explanation would both offend and satisfy Orrie.

Nickel put her hand over her mouth and coughed.

"Miss Orrie, can I interest you in something to eat or drink?" Nickel politely asked her.

"Why, thank you, no."

"Mother, how about you?"

"I'll pass. You come on out here and sit with us."

Orrie settled herself in the white wicker rocker while Juts and Nickel plopped on the big porch swing.

"Orrie, you're dressed up fit to kill."

"Thank you, Julia. It's all the latest thing. I wash it and hang it up and it's ready to put right back on."

"They must have killed six Du Ponts to make that suit," Nickel admired.

"Have you done any redecorating now that you have Nickel here to help you?" Orrie was fishing to get in the house.

"Hell, no."

"Mom figures the 1940s will come back in style, so she's leaving everything as it is," Nickel explained.

"If it don't come back in style, then I can charge admission as a museum," Juts cracked.

"Julia, you're a card." Orrie genuinely liked Julia. However, she was Louise's bosom buddy and had to walk the line. Louise was always jealous of Julia.

"Nickel's planning to move back here. Did you know that, Orrie?" Julia asked slyly.

"I heard something to that effect. Be good to have you back, Nickel."

"Thank you."

Orrie paused, not knowing how to bring up the subject, so she stalled a bit. "You planning on opening up a business?"

"I'd like to reconstruct a lot of old homes around here and then sell them or fix them up for the owners. There are great buildings in this area. If people don't have money, maybe we could barter, you know?" Nickel was enthusiastic. Having made up her mind to return to her roots, she couldn't wait to do it.

Orrie's eyes opened underneath all the eye shadow. "I think that's wonderful. I wish Noe were here. He'd help. Noe loved this early-American architecture."

"He was a good guy." Julia pushed the swing with her bare foot.

"Yes. They don't make men like that anymore." Orrie sighed.

"How's that?" Juts knew Orrie had come with the searching eye, but she'd dangle her as long as she could.

"Gentle men." Orrie loved talking about large categories. "You look on TV today. It's all pop, snap, crunch. Men wear three-piece suits and carry guns. Or they wear T-shirts and carry guns. Violence. Being a man means assuming responsibility. I think men today don't know that." Her ample bosom heaved.

"Don't you think being a woman means assuming responsibility?" Nickel asked her.

"Yes, of course." Orrie paused, then spoke again, like a motor ready to roar. "What I mean is, when I was young people knew one another. Understand? If a fella tried to act like King Kong, everybody laughed. You were supposed to be part of the group. You took care of your own." Orrie's thoughts were garbled but her message was clear.

"Now people don't even know who their own is and if they do know they don't care," Julia said in agreement.

"Just writing my whole generation off, are you?" Nickel's black eyes danced.

"I didn't say that. I said I'm sick of men acting like boys. A real man is quiet, responsible and gentle." Orrie spoke this with great conviction.

"You're right, Orrie. My Chessy, God rest his soul, was a gentle man. I could have done without him dying in 1968."

"No wonder you bounce around, Nickel. If I was a young girl I wouldn't look at these flaming assholes." Orrie had put her foot in her mouth.

Nickel knew her well enough not to be offended. She also knew that the older you get, the less you expect to be understood. "Now, Orrie, I don't think all men in their thirties are such duds. I know some pretty decent guys."

"Seeing is believing." Orrie folded her hands.

"Guess I'll have to import some men so you two don't keep on assailing my generation," Nickel kidded them.

"You know any Japanese men?" Orrie's face brightened.

"I know a few fellows from New York City. I know a lot of Chinese people from San Francisco. Remember when I went out there on that job?" Nickel turned to her mother.

"I love Japanese men. You bring me one." Orrie giggled.

"Isn't the sky beautiful?" Julia pointed to the deepening purple in the west.

"Say, did you talk to Louise today?" Orrie asked.

"Not so far. I was out most of today." Julia rocked some more. It was difficult to contain her urge to jump up and down.

"Louise thinks someone broke into her house." Orrie's eyebrows, thin painted lines, knitted together.

"You don't say." Julia could have shown a little more concern.

"Did they take anything?" Nickel, who knew nothing, was worried.

"Not that I know of." Orrie hedged. She knew something was missing, but Louise certainly didn't spill the beans to Orrie. That would be like putting an ad in the *Runnymede Trumpet*.

"Makes no sense that someone would break in and not steal anything." Julia played Sherlock Holmes. "She's got some nice pieces of jewelry, my sister does."

"How's she know someone broke in?" Nickel asked.

"Uh—she found a pillow under her bushes in the back yard."

"Someone could of left it there from playing Santa Claus." Julia was most helpful.

"I hadn't thought of that." Orrie stopped.

"In May?" Nickel glanced at her mother. She felt Juts was up to something.

"Practice makes perfect," Julia shot back, unruffled.

"Well, Julia, I should be getting back to Knuckles. Time to feed him." Knuckles was Orrie's beautiful Akita dog, a sort of Japanese German shepherd.

"You keep me posted, Orrie. I'll call Louise right now to console her," Julia said.

"It was good to see you, Mrs. Mojo." Nickel put her hand under Orrie's elbow and helped her down the porch steps.

Orrie drove immediately over to Louise's.

"Well?" Louise stood quite still.

"Nothing."

"Did you look around the house?"

"Juts said there was a bad smell. I couldn't get in," Orrie reported.

"That sister of mine is behind this, I know it."

"Exactly what did she take?" Orrie couldn't figure out why Louise was so worked up if nothing was missing.

"Papers."

"Insurance, stuff like that?"

"Well . . ." Louise hedged. "Not exactly."

"Julia said she was going to call. Did she?"

"Yes. I hung up the phone as you came through the door. She was all concern, my baby sister."

"What are you going to do?" Orrie wondered.

"I'll have to see her myself or sneak through the house when she's not there. Let me think about it. Damn!" Louise then said rapidly to herself five "Hail Marys" to atone for swearing. Why trouble the priest at confession with such a little thing? He has enough on his mind.

October 17, 1939

Each year the volunteer firemen of South and North Runnymede threw a Harvest Moon Ball to celebrate themselves and to raise money. Both Chessy and Pearlie were volunteers for South Runnymede since they lived on the Maryland side. North Runny firemen were full of themselves because with the help of Julius and Napoleon Rife they had recently bought a fire truck with a seventy-five-foot ladder. Of course, the only thing in Runnymede that was seventy-five feet tall was the water tower. Odd years the ball went to the North; even, the South. Both sides helped decorate. No matter what the theme, the fire hall wound up choking in crepe paper, Indian corn and pumpkins. This year proved no exception.

Maizie primped for hours, stealing some of her older sister's nail polish. When Louise saw those painted nails the fur flew. Mary, a quiet girl, fussed for two solid hours over one curl on her forehead. She normally wore football socks, which were the rage for teen-age girls. For this special occasion she forswore her socks and squeezed her feet into pumps dyed to match her little gloves and dress. Extra Billy had told her he'd come to the ball, pay his dollar at the door and seek her out for a dance. Extra Billy thrilled her. He did not thrill Louise. However, because this was a public to-do, she didn't fear for her precious Mary.

Since Fannie Jump's Sans Souci remained so popular, Fannie showed up at events like the Harvest Moon Ball. Before going into business she had ignored such things, not because she disapproved but because the aristocracy didn't attend, although they donated money. She found she enjoyed mixing with people from different backgrounds. Now sixty-two, she was more alive and adventuresome than in her youth. She and Hans shared a table with Julia, Chessy, Louise and Pearlie. Mary, looking very grown up, danced with her father and made faces. Maizie cut in constantly to torment her. Pearlie, the center of all this attention, presented a dashing figure in his fireman's uniform. Cora sipped some cold October beer while waving at everyone.

"You know that Carlotta died this morning?" Fannie told the group.

Louise, fond of her teacher, choked back a tear and said she'd heard.

"The best part is what Celeste said." Fannie enjoyed retelling Celeste's ripostes as much as hearing them for the first time. "She said, 'Maybe now she'll be happy. Carlotta always thought she was too good for this earth.' "

"Celeste was always heartless to her sainted sister," Louise replied.

"Now, now, Louise, she's being proper and not appearing in public. Don't be too hard on her. Those two never got along."

"Carlotta's the only person I know who'll feel guilty about resting in peace," Julia quipped, then she nudged Chessy. "Do you remember your lines?"

"I think so." Chessy, in charge of entertainment, feared he'd forget his part in the little skit they were doing.

"War memorial's full of used tires again." Fannie giggled.

"I wonder who's doing that," Louise asked. "Always happens before a big holiday or something patriotic."

"Rubber lasts longer than flowers and the tires are round as a wreath," Juts joked.

"Julia, memorials are serious business," Louise admonished. Pearlie tugged her to get her to the dance floor.

"Here comes Mary's boyfriend," Maizie sang in the taunting manner of a child.

"Don't be silly." Mary turned up her nose.

"The Gas Alley gang? I hope not. Those dumb

bastards get sozzled straining Sterno through a cloth," Hans informed them.

Ev and Lionel, Orrie and Noe were at the adjoining table because the gang couldn't get a big enough table for all of them. Ev cupped her hand to her mouth. "Juts, some crowd, huh?"

"Yes, this is the best Harvest Moon ever, and wait until you see the entertainment. Chessy wrote a skit, you know—with help from Pearlie because the Yankee fellow got sick and none of the North boys would fill in."

"Cora, did you ever see such a crowd? No one will be awake tomorrow before noon." Fannie clinked glasses.

"Half of Runnymede is asleep by eleven. The rest never close their eyes." Cora kidded her since Fannie fell in the latter category.

Orrie bustled over to whisper in Juts' ear. "See Beulah Renshaw over there? She doesn't know old Ben's cheating on her with that Sweigart girl."

Julia quickly whispered right back: "Of course he's sleeping with Sweigart. Beulah didn't marry a pansy."

Extra Billy, already slightly looped, strode toward Mary, who valiantly pretended not to care.

"Hi, Mary."

"Oh, hello, Extra Billy. I didn't see you in this mob."

"Wanna dance?"

"Sure." Mary flew off her chair with amazing speed.

Louise, on the dance floor, saw her daughter with Extra. "Pearlie, I want you to get her away from him."

"Louise, leave her alone."

"That boy is no damn good."

"He's wild. At that age. He was sure good at stuffing potatoes up the exhaust pipes of Rife's buses." Pearlie spun his wife around.

"Be that as it may, you tell her after this dance, no more. You're her father."

"All right. All right. Let's finish the dance."

Back at the table Ev, Lionel, Noe and Orrie quickly shoved both tables together even though they weren't supposed to and chattered like blue jays.

"Lordie, over there's Patience's girl Dyslexia. I never will forget the time she blew her nose in church through her veil! Even stopped the preacher." Orrie roared at her own story.

"That's as bad as the time one of the Gas Alley boys put on the church tablet—yes, right out there in front of the Lutheran Church—'Jesus Saves. Moses Invests.' " Ev wrinkled her nose.

"Hi there, Bumba." Fannie waved to Bumba Duckworth. "Nice guy, but what an Old Glory."

"What?" Julia asked her, leaning over to hear her in all the noise.

"He's an Old Glory—so ugly you have to throw a flag over his head to fuck him," Fannie boomed.

Minta Mae Dexter passed by just as Fannie uttered that rude word. She stopped, for effect, stared, but before she could play the Puritan, Fannie quipped, "Why, Minta Mae, where's your flag? Don't tell me the Sisters of Gettysburg are falling down on the job!"

Furious, Minta stalked off.

The entire table exploded. Louise, on the dance floor, scowled. She hated missing anything, especially if it would offend her.

Extra Billy dipped Mary. Maizie wriggled in her chair. Poised on the line between childhood and adolescence, she acted a baby one minute and grown up the next. The music ended. Bill kept Mary on the floor waiting for the next song. Louise chewed on Pearlie's ear the whole way back to the table. He seated his wife, then reluctantly walked out onto the dance floor.

"Honey, may I have this dance?"

"Oh, Daddy, no. Bill asked me first."

Stymied, Pearlie thought for a minute. "Save the next one for your old man. O.K.?"

Louise was twitching. Pearlie walked back to the table and told her to behave herself. He had the next dance.

Extra Billy liked Mary as much as he was capable of liking anybody. His boisterousness and innocent brutality arose from a combination of stupidity and the fact that he never, not once, stopped to think what it felt like to be in the other guy's shoes. Mary, to him, was high-class stuff. Gas Alley was as low as you could go in Runnymede. After the dance he properly escorted Mary back to the table. She introduced him to the throng. Then he rejoined his increasingly drunk companions. He threw down two quick belts to make up for lost time. After a fifteen-minute wait he again approached Mary. She desperately wanted to dance with him, but Louise sniffed at him and in so many words told him to get lost.

"Louise, let her dance," Juts recommended.

"I don't need your advice on raising my children. You don't even have children." Louise, angry anyway, took it out on Juts.

"Have it your way, sister." Julia decided to ignore her.

Extra Billy, now truly bombed, delighted his seedy companions by drinking a neat shot of whiskey, then putting a match to his tongue, breathing out the fire and quickly dousing it with a beer chaser. His dragon act received loud applause.

A drum roll alerted the audience that entertainment followed. North Runnymede's fire chief announced the sequence of events in a droning voice. The first act on the bill was a talent show, the talent provided generosity of the wives. Eva Skolowski warbled a hot version of "Anything Goes." Another wife danced on roller skates, to muted appreciation. Chessy and Pearlie sweated it out backstage. Their act was a satire on both fire departments, with different fellows playing the bigwigs. No one would get riled, as it was all in good fun. The little raised stage rumbled under the onslaught of Tessie Trenton's roller skates. Once she finally speeded into stage left, there was a moment's hesitation. A moment too long in this instance.

"Hey, I gotta talent." Extra clambered up on the platform. Blotto though he was, he stood up tall. Mary's eyes widened. Louise utilized this golden opportunity to embarrass her daughter by telling her what a drunken sot Bill Bitters was. Fannie, Juts and the rest of the group watched with their mouths open.

"What's going on out there, Pearlie?" Chessy adjusted his fake mustache.

"Extra Billy Bitters is on the goddamned stage."

"I didn't know he was in the talent show."

"He ain't," Pearlie told him.

"Yeah?" Chessy pulled back the curtain to see for himself. "Where's the chief? He's master of ceremonies."

The chief at that moment was ardently telling the roller skater that she had a great future ahead of her. After all, Ginger Rogers had appeared in a movie on roller skates. This compliment was interrupted by one of the North boys, giving him the bad news. The chief pulled down the bottom of his coat, puffed out his chest and started out on the stage.

"Chessy?"

"What?"

"I forgot my line." Pearlie looked stricken.

"Fire."

"Fire . . . fire . . . fire," Pearlie repeated to himself.

Extra Billy fended off the chief with one long arm. He was young, tall and strong. Chief Ackerman, replacing aged Lawrence Villcher, was short, middle-aged and of average strength.

"Watch this!" Bill yelled. He threw down a shot of whiskey, struck a safety match on his shoe, hopping on one foot to keep Ackerman at bay, then lit his tongue. Out poured a stream of fire. The crowd gasped. Extra Billy was just tall enough on the raised stage to be near the crepe paper. That quick the damn stuff caught fire.

"Fire," Pearlie repeated.

"There really is a fire." Chessy ran out on stage. Pearlie was one step behind. The pudgy-faced chief bellowed, "Fire! Women and children out first!"

Chessy knocked out a staggering Bill with one well-placed blow, threw him over his shoulder and ran backstage with him, tossing him out in the alley for safety. Pearlie made use of his line: "Fire."

All that thickly hung crepe paper blazed up by the rafters. The firemen kept their heads and the folks were herded out in an orderly fashion. That took a good seven or eight minutes. Chief Ackerman revved up the new fire truck with its seventy-five-foot ladder.

The truck was so damn long that he jackknifed it backing it around the corner so he could get close to the fire hydrant. Chessy, now outside with his wife and the rest of the family, appreciated the problem.

"Pearlie, grab Doughtery. He's got the keys."

Pearlie found their man. They raced for Chessy's car and tore down to the South Runnymede fire station. The small old engine coughed, then popped out of the station, Chessy at the wheel. They reached the North Runnyede firehouse in time to save half the roof. As the South boys collected their equipment, Chessy, in his fire helmet, clapped a sorrowing Chief Ackerman on the back. "Aside from that, Mrs. Lincoln, it's a great show."

Once all was said and done, Extra Billy had to help rebuild the roof during his free time. He didn't have a minute to sneak around and see Mary; the firemen worked his tail off. Louise breathed a sigh of relief. She figured that put an end to it.

March 1, 1940

Celeste, wisely deciding not to go to Europe, had stayed in Runnymede for the winter. Wrapped in a fabulous quilted silk maroon jacket with matching pants, she could have walked out of one of her brother's movies. Fannie Jump harumphed in her seat and picked up the deck of cards.

"Gin?" Fannie asked.

"You already reek of strong water," Celeste advised her.

"There are more old drunks than old doctors. I mean gin, as in cards."

"Sure. Before we get going, do you want any refreshment?" Celeste inquired.

"Cora, I could do with a tasty cup of tea," Fannie called to Cora, who happened by the room.

"You bet." Cora headed for the kitchen.

"Miss Europe this season?"

"Yes and no." Celeste kept a sharp eye on Fannie's dealing. Fannie dealt like a pro, off the bottom of the deck as fast as from the top. You had to watch her every minute.

"Nothing's happened since Poland. Maybe they'll all forget it and go home."

"No one's left their home but the Germans," Celeste replied.

"England and France declared war." Fannie sang "Rule Britannia, Britannia rule the waves."

"Will Britannia waive the rules?"

"What?" Fannie broke her dealer's concentration.

"Forget it. Dear, I wish you wouldn't wear pink. It makes you look like a sausage."

There was some truth to Celeste's criticism. Fannie peered down over her bulging chest. "Maybe I could wear black and yellow and look like a bumblebee."

Cora reappeared, carrying a tray full of tea, cakes and little sandwiches. She would arrange them once the game got hot. "Here, ladies."

"Thank you." Celeste smiled. She adored conspiracy.

"Yes, thanks loads, Cora." Fannie shoveled a tasty little cake into her mouth. "Maybe the Germans won't go home. The Nazis are powerful."

"Power is not a permanent substitute for skill." Celeste's nostrils flared.

"Guess poor Fairy had neither." Fannie studied her hand.

"I wonder if we'll ever know. Not a day goes by that I don't think of her at least once, or my brother, Spotts. If you truly love someone they're always with you."

"I think of Fairy, too. However, I never think of Creighton." Fannie sipped some tea. "I hope there isn't a war. All that destruction and death so someone can sing a new national anthem."

"Mary Baker Eddy was responsible for more deaths than the Kaiser." A sly smile played on Celeste's face.

Fannie threw down a discard. "If they do get into a war they're nuts, all of them."

"Perhaps logic has gone the way of oil lamps, so few people seem to be using it these days."

Fannie concentrated. "Hmm?"

"What I'm saying is don't count on individuals or nations behaving reasonably. Given the horror of the last war, people will have to outdo themselves in this one, once it gets started. This will then be portrayed to us as progress." Celeste's cool voice echoed.

"Well, I hope we stay out of it." Fannie eyed Celeste's discard.

Cora arranged the sandwiches and quietly told them, "It's the fools who defeat you, not the clever ones."

"Afraid you're right." Fannie poured herself more tea from the large silver pot on the tray.

A descendant of Madame de Récamier padded into the room, a cloud of blue-gray fur. Cora scratched her ears.

"Did you know cats used to rule the earth until they taught people to do it for them?" Celeste smiled.

"Say, why didn't you go to the Daughters of Confederacy benefit last night?" Fannie drew a card from the pile.

"My eyes need a rest from the glare of sequins."

"You should've seen the crowd, Celeste—husbands, sons, us. The Sisters of Gettysburg will have to top this one."

"It must have looked like a convention of your exlovers." Celeste laughed.

"Don't be a twit," Fannie remarked.

"Is that the present tense of twat?"

"You are wicked, as Fairy used to say." Fannie loved Celeste when she was in this mood.

"Really? I've always thought of myself as boldly nonchalant." Celeste paused, then smiled triumphantly. "Gin."

"You shit." Fannie got up to fix herself a drink. "Cora fell sound asleep on the sofa."

"All that wrangling with Louise over Mary and Extra Billy Bitters exhausted her." Celeste gazed at Cora. Now how would she win?

Fannie returned to the card table, glass brimming with spirits. "You know, of course, that Diddy Van

Dusen is taking over Immaculata Academy since her mother's death?"

"As to children, Carlotta had a single unsavory specimen. I hope never to see or hear from Diddy Van Dusen again."

"Don't be too hard on her, Celeste. She's still recuperating from her childhood." Fannie eagerly grabbed her cards as Celeste dealt a new hand.

"At thirty-seven?"

Fannie arranged her cards according to suit and number. This could take her a few minutes. "Louise must be on one rampage about this Extra Billy business. Listerine ought to get him to do a magazine advertisement in front of North Runnymede firehouse."

"That's good, Fannie. Why don't you send it in to the *Trumpet* or the *Clarion* under a false name?"

"Yeah." Fannie's eyes gleamed with devilment. "Sending Mary to the academy hasn't affected the child much, although Maizie is trying to be Mother Cabrini."

"If Louise would shut up, Mary'd forget about that barbarian in time. This way it's a point of honor to stand up to Wheezie."

"Someone ought to warn Mary that before you meet the handsome prince you kiss a lot of toads." Fannie cast off a two of hearts.

"You ought to know."

"Damn you, Celeste."

"Now that Carlotta's dead and gone, we can look forward to Louise glowing periodically with a pentecostal flame." Celeste's elegant voice skipped over the words, making them crisp and perhaps funnier than the content.

"If only you'd sent Louise to Fox Run School for Young Ladies. The woman hungers for conventionality. At least then she'd be crackers about horses instead of Jesus."

"Mea culpa." Celeste struck her breast. "I say, Fannie, that was a shifty discard." Without her code, Celeste struggled. Fannie could win as easily as she could now.

"It's my hand, Chalfonte. I can do as I please. God,

that Bill Bitters is about as attractive as a steaming goat pellet."

"True enough. But you and I weren't daughters raised by domineering mothers. I'm afraid Mary will take the path of least resistance for her rebellion." Celeste sighed.

"What's that?"

"Her body. Whenever a young thing wants to be free minus serious thought, she gets pregnant and then gets married. *Voilá.*"

"You aren't going out, are you?" Fannie clutched for a moment.

"*Voilá* is not gin." Celeste shifted in her seat. "Pour me a cup of tea, will you, dearest?"

"Ramelle due back on time?"

"End of March. I hear Spotty's face is on the cover of all those dreadful movie magazines."

"Yes."

"Gin!" Fannie smashed her cards down.

"Piss." Celeste junked her cards on the middle of the wood-inlaid table.

"My deal." Fannie scooped them up, delighted. She didn't often win with Celeste. She knew Celeste must be cheating, but her system had never dawned on Fannie. Mrs. Creighton wasn't that subtle, so she couldn't begin to imagine it.

"Grace sent me Sigourny Romaine's latest book, *Arise Artemis.* Did she send you one?" Fannie gleefully asked Celeste. This subject never failed to rile the great beauty. It had burned her at Vassar and it burned her to this day.

"She did, of course. Imagine Sigourny wallowing in the tea leaves of literary triumph? The toast of Paris. Ugh. She's illiterate in two languages, ours and theirs."

"Tsk, tsk." Fannie shook her head.

"The absolute worst line in the book was 'Her wings beat against my breast like an avenging angel.' Romantic tripe." Celeste slammed a card on the table.

In a voice ringing with girlish innocence, Fannie asked, "Didn't Grace beat against your breast at Vassar with the wings of an avenging angel?"

"Fannie, that is beneath you." Celeste's voice hit her toes.

"No, dear, you were beneath her, or was it the other way around?"

"I was very young."

"You weren't so very young when you had a wild fling with Clare in that very same Paris." Fannie bore in.

"A mere babe; I was just out of college. You sucked miles of cock on that European tour, as I recall."

Fannie's mouth flew open. "Hic!" She castigated her by their childhood name. "You are too beautiful for words but not for arguments."

"Even the gods are fools in love."

"The test of a love affair is what the participants say afterwards." Fannie grumbled, picking up a card from the deck.

"I've had many affairs. I felt it was my duty to my biographers." Celeste snatched Fannie's discard.

"Ha! I knew you kept a pot on the stove in France." Fannie rejoiced at this evidence of frailty on Celeste's part.

"I'm too old to care now. It's true. Ramelle's love for Curtis shook me initially. I believed it was right for her and it didn't hurt me, but I needed to know I was beautiful to someone."

"Ramelle worships you, then, now and forever." Fannie sipped her drink.

"Good taste, Ramelle." Celeste's lips curved upward. "But we'd been together years at that time. I needed a new jolt. I found one. It was all airy, light and sunny."

"No regrets?" Fannie questioned.

"No regrets," Celeste confirmed. "And you?"

"None whatsoever. I wish I could come back a baby and start all over again."

"If reincarnation is true you will."

"Do you believe that?"

"No, but I don't disbelieve it, either. I'd like to come back as a rhinoceros. They have such thick skins."

"Grace never would go to bed with you once she met Sigourny, would she?"

"No, the fool." Celeste studied her hand and then sweetly called out, "Gin."

"Damn it to hell."

Shuffling the cards, Celeste looked at Fannie. "When it comes to sex, women don't have the sense God gave a goose."

"We make out all right."

"We are the exceptions that prove the rule." Celeste dealt another hand.

"Well, I never was one of those creatures who thought the road to higher truth lay through my vagina," Fannie Jump drawled.

"Hear, hear."

"Do you know what has always irritated me most about Sigourny?"

"What?" Celeste asked.

"She's always crowing about being a self-made woman."

"It's big of her to take the blame. Sigourny Romaine is an aesthetic prophylactic."

Fannie picked up her glass and toasted Celeste. "Here's to people like us."

"I was thinking of throwing a party to defend Western values." Celeste introduced this new topic to lull Fannie.

"How's that?"

"Gin!" Celeste trounced her.

"Bad luck! I'll get you next time." Fannie's voice rose and woke Cora, who heard the phrase "Bad luck."

A touch groggy, Cora told them, "Good luck and bad luck are like your right and left hand. You gotta use them both."

Celeste, sparkling from her small victory, grinned. "Cora, you are outrageously sane."

September 11, 1940

Cora rocked on her front porch, shucking fat white ears of corn. Julia trudged up the hill, a bit late from work.

"Hi, honey."

"Hi, Mom." Juts collapsed in the old wicker chair next to the rocker.

"Look at this corn. Juicy." Cora blinked as a well-fed corn spider jumped out at her from all the silk.

"Ha!" Julia picked up an ear, twisting the tassel off.

"Got hungry for chicken corn soup. How about you?"

"Want me to go get some eggs and parsley?"

"Rest. You look tired."

"It was one of those days. A dye lot fouled up. How'd you like a few tons of splotched orange ribbon?"

"Never know when you can use it." Cora smiled.

"Louise's such a priss. Boy, did they have a row last night."

"I heard."

"Extra Billy hit Pearlie so hard they had to peel him off the wall," Julia said.

"Terrible. They're not going to stop that girl, so they might as well let her be." Cora rocked.

"Lie down with dogs, get up with fleas." Juts borrowed the paring knife from her mother.

"That may be so, Julia, but Mary's set on him."

"Since they're carrying on over in Europe, maybe we'll get into it and that's one way to be rid of Extra Billy."

"Don't say such a thing. There's good in everybody." Small frown lines dotted her forehead.

"Oh, Mother," Julia said in a resigned voice. What Cora believed she believed totally. "This ugly duckling will stay an ugly duckling. I'm with Louise. Bill Bitters is no damn good."

"If you'd keep your nose to the grindstone you wouldn't have time to stick it in your sister's business." Cora watched a hen and her biddies scurry past the porch. They looked like puffs of dandelions with legs.

"I miss Idabelle's music, don't you?"

"She was a sweet soul. But we all got to go sometime." Cora stood up and shook out her apron.

"Saw Orrie Tadia Mojo today. She wore high waters."

"What?" Cora asked.

"Pants too short for her legs." Julia's eyes betrayed her solemn face.

"Hand me those ears, will you?"

Julia gave her mother the corn. Cora disappeared inside and came out again in five minutes.

"Gee, that was quick."

"Had it all laid out. Just needed the corn. Here, honey, I brought you some lemonade."

"Thanks." Julia reached up for the tall glass. "Now that Louise is having all this trouble with Mary she'll lean on Maizie full force. She'll get that girl in a nunnery yet."

"If Maizie goes it's her own doing."

"It's hard to go against your mother." Julia sighed.

"Why, Julia Ellen Hunsenmeir, I never though I'd hear you say that!" Cora rocked vigorously.

"Now that Louise can't get into the Daughters of the American Revolution she'll go whole hog on the Catholic Daughters of America." Julia had ignored her mother's comment, preferring to imagine herself the perfect daughter.

"Poor Louise." Cora squinted up at the sun, putting her hand over her eyes. "All that work tracing our family."

"Only to find out we're leftover Hessians!" Juts let out a war whoop.

"It is kind of funny." Cora rubbed her elbow. "I feel like I been out in the rain and rusted."

"Got aches and pains?" Julia teased her.

"You just wait. You'll remember your old momma

when you're old." Cora reached over and touched Julia's arm.

"A light heart lives long. You'll live forever." Julia held her mother's hand.

"Wouldn't that be grand?" Cora noticed the old round wooden tub exploding with black-eyed Susans. She could enjoy such sights into eternity. "I tell you, I'm ready to go when the time comes. Hate to leave the sun and the flowers and you, but a new crop will come up after me."

"Mother, don't talk like that."

"Honey, everyone's got to face their own death sometime. Better to be prepared in your soul than go out uneasy."

"I'm not prepared for your leaving or for mine. We ought to make it to one hundred, at least." Julia spoke just a little too loud. Maybe to scare off Death in case he was hanging around.

"Listen to your old mother. Prepare your soul. If you're at peace with yourself the world is so beautiful. Now ain't that odd? If you're ready to go, to give it all up, why, everything is . . . sunshine." Cora's arms curved outward in an expansive gesture.

"It would be easier to go if I left something behind. I've got no children." Julia's voice quieted down.

"You're young yet," Cora reassured her.

"Momma, I'll be thirty-six next March."

"There's time."

"I went to the doctor today after work. About having babies." Julia fiddled with her hem. "He said there was nothing wrong with me. I can have babies."

"I know that."

"But that means there's something wrong with Chessy."

Cora held her peace.

"It does. After all this time, we'd have a baby," Julia continued.

"Send him off to the doc," Cora advised.

"I'm afraid to ask him."

"Lordie, he's your husband. If you can't talk to your husband, what's the use in being married?"

"He'll go. I can talk to him. I'm afraid to find out and I'm afraid not to." Julia bit her lower lip.

"You talk to Chessy. He's no lace-panty job. He'll do the right thing."

"You're right."

"Suppose it comes out true? Suppose he can't have children?" Cora thought she'd test the water.

"There's nothing I can do about it. Can't blame the thermometer for the temperature," Julia replied.

"The world's full of children that need somebody to love and care for them."

"Adopt?" Julia was surprised.

"Why not? It ain't birthing that makes a mother. It's the raising up of the child," Cora firmly told her.

"What about Chessy? I thought men had to have their own. I don't think they're like women. I mean, women love children. Men have to have it be their own."

"Fiddlesticks. Do you think for one minute Chester Smith is that selfish?"

"No."

"Where do you get such ideas?"

"Louise told me that. After all, she is a mother."

"And so's our house cat. All these years I raised you and you're worried about a thing like that? People aren't like grapes, girl, you don't weigh them in a bunch. You got to take every person one by one. You talk to Chessy and get this thing ironed out."

"O.K. But if it is him, I'm not walking down to Runnymede Square and taking the first baby I see," Julia said defiantly.

"I hope not."

"I'll know when it's right."

"Like anything else. You get a feeling." Cora rose from her chair and placed both hands on the small of her back. "Think I'll go check the soup."

"O.K."

Before she opened the screen door Cora asked, "Where is Chessy anyway?"

"I stopped by the store and he said he'd be home in twenty minutes, but you know Chessy. If he says he'll be home in twenty minutes it covers anything from twenty minutes to ten days."

December 7, 1941

Louise, frazzled with wedding preparations, finally collapsed in her pew next to Pearlie. Julia, Chessy and Cora sat immediately behind them. Although Mary wouldn't be sixteen until January, things had progressed to such a state that Louise had no choice but to let the girl get married; otherwise the progression would protrude and all could see. This fall from grace on Mary's part strengthened Louise's resolve to never, ever, let Maizie get out of hand. During the simple but lovely ceremony, Louise, still furious, forgot decorum and whispered in her husband's ear, "She won't amount to a hill of beans and he won't amount to a pint of piss." Pearlie squeezed her hand since he couldn't very well put it over her mouth.

As the bride and groom descended the church steps, everyone waited with handfuls of confetti and rice.

Louise grumbled to Julia. "Why do people throw rice anyway? It's a waste of food."

"Supposed to mean fertility." Julia readied a load.

"Looks like maggots." Louise dropped her handful on the ground. She felt that she was the something old, the something borrowed and the something blue for this wedding. As to what was new, she couldn't think of anything.

It wasn't until Mary and Extra Billy safely drove off in an old Plymouth trailing tin cans that the wedding party learned of the something new. The Japanese had bombed Pearl Harbor. Father Dan had heard it just before he went out to perform the ceremony. He thought it best to keep the terrible news to himself until after the newlyweds departed.

Extra Billy heard the news as he turned on his

car radio. The next morning at 8 A.M. he stood in line to enlist as a marine. Chessy Smith and even Pearlie went down to the recruiter. Pearlie wanted to reenlist in the navy and Chessy said he'd go wherever they needed him. Ted Baeckle, remembering his distant talk with Julia, informed both men they were a bit too old. Instead he suggested that Chessy head up the Civil Air Patrol with Pearlie. He reassured them if enough younger men did not enlist he'd take them.

When Louise learned of Pearlie's action she threw a giant hissy fit and pulled all her drapes off the windows and the telephone out of the wall. It was bad enough Mary leaving for that lout; now her own husband wanted to desert her.

March 27, 1944

"Mother, this is a disgrace!" Louise whipped through Celeste's back door, nearly taking it off the hinges.

"What?" Cora was covered in flour.

"Rillma Ryan is pregnant!"

"Oh, hell. I ain't got the strength to be bothered with that."

"I do. What about our family name?"

"You think you scrubbed it clean by marrying Mary off in the nick of time?"

That stung. "That union is sanctified in the eyes of the Lord God almighty."

"You sure set store by a bunch of words."

"Mother, it's unnatural that a daughter should have to instruct her mother in morality."

"Yes. Why don't you shut your trap and rest your mind?"

"Aren't you going to do anything?" Louise was bug-eyed.

"When Rillma came here from Charlottesville she properly visited us and we properly found her a job and a nice place to live. She comes by about once a week and what she does is her own business." Cora slammed the dough on the table.

"She's your niece. You're responsible." Louise clung to her outrage.

"I haven't seen Hannah in years. My mother remarried when I was out on my own. Hannah's fifteen years younger than me. Momma settled in Charlottesville, raised Hannah, and died. Hannah got married, raised Rillma, and now Rillma's fixing to raise another."

"It's a disgrace."

"Having a child is no disgrace. It's natural." Cora belted the dough.

"Out of wedlock it's a disgrace. Common as dirt."

"Just because you're born average don't mean you got to be common." The large woman shot her daughter a wicked glance.

"For all you know, the father could be black as spades."

Cora quietly replied, "Don't matter if a cat is black or white as long as it catches mice."

Julia opened the door, came in and shook the mud off her boots. Before she could sweep it up, Louise hit her with the bombshell.

"Rillma's pregnant."

"Good for her." Juts sought out the broom.

"You're as bad as Mother."

"I'm my mother's daughter." Julia carefully swept the clods into a dustpan. "Happy birthday. I brought you a present."

"How can you even think of celebrating at a time like this?" Louise wailed.

"There's a war on, sister. Women are bursting like seed pods. So what else is new?"

"Ugh." Louise rammed her butt into a kitchen chair and folded her arms across her chest.

"Ran into Orrie Tadia today. She retold me the story for the three thousandth time about how she whapped the Fed over the head with her umbrella when he came to take Noe away."

"I hate violence." Louise put her hand over her heart.

"If they carted Chessy away because his relations are German I'd punch their lights out, too."

"We're all mongrels." Louise tossed her head.

"I thought you were tracing us back to Count von Hunsenmeir who fought with Charlemagne." Cora whacked the dough again before pulling it into little muffin-shaped globs.

"Which reminds me." Louise tapped her finger on the table like a schoolteacher. "The father of this bastard is that Frenchman, Bullette."

"Handsome fellow." Cora nodded.

"Yeah, well, the handsome fellow is on his way back to France now that it looks like the Allies will win the war," Louise sneered.

"Come on, Louise. He did good work raising money for the underground." Julia untied her boots.

"How do you know? Maybe he pocketed the whole shebang and ran to Canada."

"Live and learn." Juts shrugged. She wasn't going to play If with Louise.

"Thought you didn't know who the father was?" Cora asked her.

"Yes, I know. I also heard that Julia and Chessy are thinking of taking the baby," Louise steamed.

"Maybe." Julia tried to sound noncommittal.

"I don't want no damn French brat in this family." Louise tapped the table again, an irritating gesture.

"What's it to you?" Julia flared.

"Those people gave up their country without a fight. They lack moral fiber. We don't need one." Louise sniffed.

"Louise, the baby's not even on earth yet and you blame it for the fall of France?" Juts put her hand to her forehead in disbelief.

"They eat snails." Louise trotted out this evidence of depravity.

"So?" Julia eyed her mother, who was opening and closing kitchen cupboards more briskly than usual. That meant the old lady was getting mad.

"I still say no one of French blood should be in our family. They welcomed Hitler with open arms. If he came here I'd fight until my last breath." Louise pounded the table like a melodramatic orator.

"If he came to America you'd welcome him with open arms. Hitler is Catholic." Julia told the honest truth.

Louise screeched, "Liar, liar, your pants are on fire!"

Cora banged the cupboard door shut and yelled, something she rarely did. "Just a goddamned minute, both of you! I have had enough. If one suffers, all suffer. That poor Rillma's young and scared. Put yourself in her shoes. She been turned every way but loose. She can't keep the baby. She knows that. Now what good do we do this world if the baby gets put in a home because it was born without papers, I ask you, Louise?"

Louise, terrified at her mother's display of temper, moved her mouth but not a word came out.

Cora continued. "I don't care if Adolf Hitler is the father of this little one, or Bullette the Frenchman. A child gets born, needs love and care, and grows up as best it can. If Julia wants this baby then she'll have it. Do you hear me, Louise Hunsenmeir!"

"Yes, Mother." Louise cowered.

Cora turned toward Juts. "You are doing the right thing, Julia, but you and Louise wrangle. It takes two. If you two are going to pull each other's hair out, do it outta my sight. You understand your old momma?"

"Yes, Mother."

Celeste, aroused by the uproar, had tiptoed to the kitchen door and opened it a crack. Cora, still riled, yelled, "All right, Celeste, get your sweet ass in here."

Celeste jumped through the door as if she'd been shot. "I couldn't help but hear the family hour."

"Looks like Julia here will take Rillma's baby when it's born in November. Now you know, so that puts an end to it." Cora marched over to see how her rolls were rising.

"Julia, I think that's splendid." Celeste beamed. "Perhaps there is such a thing as the milk of human kindness after all."

"She's so full of it she moos." Louise smarted.

Julia zoomed right for her. "Louise."

"I take it back. I take it back."

Knowing Louise, Celeste thought she'd needle her since she had been so busy tormenting Juts. "Louise, dear, I forgot to tell you—the paper says there's to be no Easter this year."

"What?" Louise stammered.

"They found the body." Celeste smiled.

Cora, Julia and Celeste howled. Louise sent aloft a fervent prayer for their salvation. The sisters stayed for supper. Louise attempted to make up for her churlish behavior by being overly polite. At the table she sweetly said, "Please pass the chicken bosoms."

November 27, 1944

Celeste skipped across the cold earth to Fannie's Sans Souci. She'd be sixty-seven tomorrow. Rillma expected her baby tonight or tomorrow. Celeste found herself strangely excited about the baby. She hoped it would come forth tomorrow. She was tired of sharing her birthday with William Blake and Friedrich Engels. Celebrating earthly renewal with a new person might be fun. Her tall, erect figure darted among the last leaves of autumn. Last night had inflamed her imagination. She might be getting up there, but she and Ramelle could still roar like tigers. She imagined herself a rampaging tart on the plains of pleasure and laughed at herself.

Fannie didn't open up for business until six in the evening. They would have plenty of time to chatter.

"Celeste, happy day before your birthday." Fannie checked out her cash register and rang up a few items.

Celeste stopped dramatically, put her gloved hand on Fannie's forearm and whispered, "Listen. They're playing our song."

"You!" Fannie led her to the upstairs, where she lived. "Did you hear?"

"What?"

"Minta Mae Dexter died last night in the Capitol Theater."

"Alas, poor Minta Mae perished amid the juju bees." Celeste appeared forlorn.

"She was a bother, but I'll miss hating her. Wonder who will take over the Sisters of Gettysburg?"

"The ghost of Lincoln, just to haunt you."

"Celeste, you look twenty-five today."

"Love keeps me young." She removed her soft gloves.

"Me, too, but I tell you, Celeste, this business of watching our old cronies and enemies push up daisies is tiresome."

"Reincarnation. They'll all be back," Celeste lightly informed her.

"Well, at least you aren't going to give me a lecture about God," Fannie mumbled.

"God is someone who comes after menopause."

"And you, of course, haven't endured the swan song of the ovary." Fannie's eyes gleamed with merriment.

"Why tell you?"

"Doesn't seem to have slowed down your appetite for Ramelle." Fannie admired her friend's continuing lust.

"To few much is given and much expected," she cryptically replied.

"Shall we toast today?" Fannie broke out a bottle of champagne, Celeste's favorite year.

"Irresistible." Celeste collected the glasses while Fannie popped open the bottle. "I guess you heard that Louise is turning Maizie into a holy virtuoso."

"Maizie can't make up her mind whether to be a nun or Dale Evans."

Celeste held her glass high and touched the rim of Fannie's sparkling glass. "Prosit."

"Prosit." Fannie relished the first sip. "Nice to know Latin is good for something."

"Rillma's baby is due today or tomorrow."

"I'll root for tomorrow." Fannie smiled. "Rillma still pining over that French jerk?"

"So I gather." Celeste savored the champagne. "Anyone who ever died of love deserved it."

"Heartless."

"You'll never guess what arrived in the post today."

"Fresh fruit from Curtis?"

"Fannie, how mundane. No. Never mind, I'll tell you. Another book by Sigourny Romaine."

"My God, she's inexhaustible."

"Quite."

"What's this one about?"

"Inner motivation. She set it during 1870, hoping to slide by whatever censors are left in Paris."

"Inner motivation? Might that be a laxative?" Fannie poured more champagne.

"Oh, what can we expect of a pretty girl who married herself out of a small town in Minnesota?"

"You mean Grace Pettibone?" Fannie looked slightly perplexed.

"After all these decades, what else can you call it but a marriage?"

Fannie reflected. "Yes, I suppose. God knows you all did better than I did on longevity and love."

"Mixed marriages never work, dear. That was your first mistake."

"Celeste, you should have been the writer."

"I have nothing to say." She appeared surprised.

"Nonsense. You've such an original mind."

"Ah, if I could find a solar verb, yes, then I would write." Celeste gave herself up to the soft sofa.

"More?" Fannie held the bottle.

"A tad. Thank you. Back to this Sigourny business. Life shrouds its mainspring. Can art, if truth is the goal, be any different?"

"No, but I'm not the reader you are." Fannie felt warm inside. She didn't know if it was a conversation with her dearest friend or the champagne or both.

"Whatever the art form, a self-conscious culture is inauthentic. I'm convinced of that."

"I tell you you ought to write."

"Flattery will get you everywhere."

"Yes, I know. It already has." Fannie nodded. A lovely sapphire ring graced her left hand. It was about all she had left from her jewelry. Having hocked everything to get Sans Souci off the ground, she found, once it made money, she no longer had any interest in jewelry.

"Devil." Celeste enjoyed another sip of liquid.

"Speak of the devil, did you hear about Juts and Napoleon Rife?"

"No."

"He's been going around giving pep talks. Invited by other factory owners, you know? He showed up down at the mill, Red Bird mill."

"We own it, Fannie. The new manager apparently does not yet know our policy concerning the Rifes."

"I forgot. Isn't that funny?" Fannie stared out the window for a moment, shocked at her blanks when it came to other people's sources of income.

"Well, what happened?"

"Pole gives a little wartime hoohaw. Then he starts bitching about the workers up at the munitions and how they misunderstand him, blah, blah, blah."

"At least Julius is intelligent." Celeste ran her finger around the rim of her glass.

"Juts tires of all this bull and yells out, 'Now you know how Marie Antoinette felt.' "

"No!"

"I swear. Ev Most told me when I ran into her on the square."

"Julia Ellen never was one to back down." Celeste recalled the little girl who used to do her homework in the kitchen. "We grow old so fast. I can see her at seven as clearly as I can see that ring on your finger."

"Where does it all go?" Fannie wondered.

"When we were young, society was as frozen as the hierarchy of playing cards. But now the slow striptease of history has left us bare. I wonder how it will be for young people maturing after this war?"

"I suppose they'll back into the future instead of walking into it," Fannie quipped.

"Maybe that's how we all did it."

"My life didn't turn out as I expected, but then if everything ran according to plan think how bored we'd be."

Celeste paused a moment, then said, "You know, I've been thinking a lot about the Amish lately."

"Whatever for? Chessy comes from Dunkards."

"I remember that. I'm beginning to believe that of all of us, the Amish are the wisest. The rest of us listen to the radio, drive automobiles, plug in vacuum cleaners, etc., ad nauseam. Not our Amish brethren. We rush for anything mechanical. They refused all that. They insist upon living their lives, defining their lives, by their standards. We find ourselves tangled in a mass of electrical wire, of telephone lines. We've concentrated on the means to life and forgotten about life itself. This grotesque war convinces me of that more than ever. The Amish are the only intelligent people in America."

Fannie reflected on this. "Maybe. But all these conveniences make life easier."

"Do they? Do they really, Fannie? You finish your wash in half the time and then propel yourself madly into another chore. What's gained? What's happened to the graceful, majestic rhythms of nature? Everyone is listening to Edgar Bergen and Charlie McCarthy. Something's terribly wrong."

"Celeste, you've never done the wash in your life!" Fannie laughed at her.

"I'm observant. North Runnymede looks like an electrical rash with all that inexpressibly vulgar neon. I hardly consider that progress. My doing or not doing an endless succession of petticoats doesn't weaken my observations."

"Well, I'm not giving up radio to make you happy."

"All right, Fannie Jump Creighton, all right. But mark my words, we took the wrong turn at the crossroads of intelligence. This way madness lies."

"You still haven't forgiven Queen Elizabeth for ending the Tudor line." Fannie winked at her.

The two talked, argued and laughed for another hour or two. Celeste walked back home, invigorated by batting ideas about with Fannie and by the crisp, biting weather. She sailed through the front door and told Ramelle she was taking a short ride. She always rode in the morning, but she felt so much surging energy she had to burn some off. Ariel held still while she saddled up and trotted out in the twilight.

Celeste loved the hills around Runnymede. Riding cleared her mind, gave her new ideas, quickened her pulse. She thought about the war. Perhaps this war by the magnitude of its brutality will rip away the last pretense of civilization. If we see ourselves for what we are, perhaps then we can begin to improve ourselves. Humanism does not consist of cultivating illusions. She smiled at that thought, sorry she couldn't thrash it out with Fairy Thatcher.

As the light faded, the chill deepened. The low line of hedges just off the road leading back to her house challenged her. Celeste adored jumping. Anything requiring skill and daring tempted her. She might be sixty-seven tomorrow, but in her mind she would rise to physical challenge as though she were thirty-four. Ariel, a good mount, sensed her mood and pricked up his ears. Celeste and Ariel took the first row of hedges like champions. The light was tricky. As they soared over the second row Celeste knew she had misjudged. As she fell she seemed to float for an eternity. She knew midair that she would never get up from this fall. She saw Spottiswood, accompanied by a figure of unearthly light. She cried out at the sight of her brother. Celeste regretted she would never be able to tell Ramelle what she had seen in that last millennial second. She was not afraid.

The incredible shock of Celeste's death was relieved only by Celeste's sense of humor. Anticipating her end, although she figured she'd be good until a hundred, she clearly specified in her will that her estate be left to Ramelle Bowman on the condition that Ramelle erect a tombstone with this epitaph: "Now I'll Really Raise Hell." Celeste's light heart would reach beyond the grave for whoever stopped to read that inscription.

Cora was half mad with grief and contained herself only for Ramelle's sake. No one had ever conceived of Celeste Chalfonte's dying. She seemed indestructible, eternal. After the funeral, as the closest friends comforted Ramelle at home, Cora told Fannie, to cheer her, of Celeste's system for cheating at cards. The next day Fannie Jump Creighton put a deck of cards amid all the flowers on Celeste's grave.

November 28, 1944

At 3:45 A.M. Rillma Ryan delivered a healthy but small girl. She named her Nicole but didn't bother with a last name since she wasn't going to keep the baby anyway.

Julia Ellen and Chessy raced to the hospital in the early morning as soon as they heard the news. They were numb from Celeste's accident, but their drawn faces brightened when they first saw their new roommate.

Rillma had to stay in the hospital a few days, but Juts and Chessy arranged to pick her up on her release day, take the baby and drive Rillma to the train station. She had no desire to stay in Runnymede.

But Rillma snuck out of the hospital in the middle of the night, taking Nicole with her. No one had a clue to her whereabouts or why she did such a thing. Julia, already battered from Celeste's passing, sank with this news. She had loved that baby at first sight. She couldn't believe she would lose the child. Chessy strained not to cry, but both of them walked around for days, tearing uncontrollably.

In the midst of all this sadness and uncertainty Louise Hunsenmeir Trumbull came through with flying colors. Julia's misery touched her to the bottom of her heart. Louise determined to track down Nicole No Last Name.

January 8, 1945

Louise searched high and low for Rillma's baby. Grateful for anything that would take their mind off their deep loss, Ramelle and Fannie Jump Creighton pitched in. Juts had contracted pneumonia and was slowly recovering. Since religion loomed so large in Louise's mind, she did know Rillma was a Catholic. Because the girl was young and in a sorry situation, Louise figured sooner or later she'd tell a priest or dump the kid in a Catholic orphanage. With Ramelle's connections and Fannie and Louise's hard work, they kept tabs on orphanages in Maryland, Pennsylvania, New York and Virginia. Now, in winter, Rillma couldn't get much farther than that. Besides, she was broke. Sure enough, Nicole turned up in a Catholic orphanage in Pittsburgh. The sister in charge informed Louise, over the phone, that the baby weighed the same as when it was brought in, around five pounds. It was her expert medical opinion that the child wouldn't live another three days. When Louise asked her what was wrong with the infant, the nun replied that nothing was really wrong except that the place was jammed. Many infants won't drink their bottles unless held. There were too many children for that. All the sisters could do was prop the bottle next to the baby and hope the little one would suck.

Louise told Ramelle and Fannie Jump. They strongly advised her not to tell Julia, who was depressed enough. When Chessy came by after work for the daily report, he was informed.

"The baby's not dying," Chessy declared.

"Why not?" Louise slumped into a chair. She didn't know what to do next.

"Because I'm going to fetch her."

"Chessy, we can't get her out without the mother," Louise said.

"Juts can be the mother."

"Chester, you can't take Julia on a trip like that in this foul weather. She'll have a relapse," Ramelle cautioned him.

"Besides, it makes no sense for Julia to be the mother if she's your wife," Fannie boomed. "Why would you dump your own child at an orphanage at the other end of Pennsylvania?"

"Then one of you come with me," Chessy demanded.

"I'll go." Ramelle started rooting around the house for gas rationing coupons, money and other necessaries.

"Ramelle, you're sixty years old. Not that you look it, dear," Fannie forthrightly noted. "Someone's got to spring this kid who is still in breeding range." Fannie lit up a cigarette.

All eyes turned on Louise, who, though forty-three, could pass for her late thirties. She pretended not to notice, then squirmed in her seat.

"I know what you're thinking." Louise's lower lip protruded.

"Louise . . ." Fannie's voice hit her shoes.

"Yes, really, Louise," Ramelle chimed in.

"And ruin my reputation as a Christian woman? How could I face my children?" Louise stammered.

"Who cares who you fuck in Pittsburgh?" Fannie exhaled.

Louise, shocked, stuttered. Chessy was too worried to laugh.

"What about cooking Pearlie's supper tonight?"

"Louise, he's a big boy. One night he can fix his own supper." Fannie laid that escape to waste.

"What about Maizie? Think how this will affect her impressionable mind."

"Maizie's in the convent. What she doesn't know won't hurt her." Fannie shot down another feeble excuse.

"Louise, you simply must do this for your sister's sake and for the sake of that tiny baby—and for

Celeste's sake. She so looked forward to this little girl."
Ramelle rested her hand on Louise's shoulder. Louise
remembered that gesture from the day when she had
played the piano by ear in this very living room.
There was no way out.

"I'll have to go home and change my clothes. These
are so chintzy."

"The baby can't see your clothes. Come on, Louise,
let's go." Chessy put his strong hand under her arm.

"Wait five minutes, Chessy." Ramelle motioned for
Fannie to get up and follow her. "We'll pack food
for you."

"I'm not hungry. All I want is that baby." Chessy
was nearly desperate. "I don't care about food."

"I do!" Louise was pulling on her boots. "Anyway,
we need milk and a baby bottle for the baby. If she's
that far gone we're going to have to feed her every
three hours."

"It's a twelve-hour ride and the snow might slow
us even more." Chessy frowned.

"Then we'll do our best, but we've got to keep that
kid fed around the clock." Louise finished with her
boots.

Fannie and Ramelle loaded them up with blankets,
thermos mugs of hot coffee and plenty of milk as well
as sandwiches. Fannie wanted to go along to help
with the driving, but Louise feared three people might
look suspicious.

Chessy and Louise took turns driving. The snow ham-
pered them slightly but they made it to the orphanage
by morning. A wrought-iron gate with a curved "St.
Rose of Lima" inscribed on the top greeted them.

Whoever Louise had spoken to on the phone wasn't
kidding. The place was wall-to-wall babies. A small
Italian nun showed them Nicole. Chessy recognized
the girl immediately.

Louise gave a command performance. She cried, she
lied, she appeared contrite. Here she had carried on
with her sister's husband. Oh, deed most foul. But her
Catholic conscience had overcome her carnal nature.
She'd come to claim her baby and raise it in her own

home, bringing it up a good Catholic, of course. To give weight to her oath, Louise produced a rosary and laid it in the scrawny baby's hands. Chessy kept his eyes downcast. The nun couldn't hide her judgment upon Louise, fallen woman. This demonstration of motherly love may have convinced her to release the child to Louise and Chessy, or perhaps it was that one less mouth to feed would lighten her load. Once she felt secure that Louise and Chessy had sufficiently humbled themselves, she had each of them sign Nicole's release papers.

The two of them were so excited they nearly ran out of the orphanage. Louise wrapped Nicole in the baby blanket Ramelle had given her and stuck the baby under her coat. Once inside the car and a block away from Saint Rose of Lima, Chessy and Louise flushed with victory. Chessy was so thrilled he kissed Louise on the cheek, he kissed the baby, he kissed Louise again and then he started to cry.

"Chessy, now watch the road. Here, maybe I ought to drive." Louise couldn't feature them in a snowbank.

He sniffled. "No, no, I'm O.K. I'm so happy. I—"

"We got a lot of work to do before you celebrate, buster. This little thing looks like something the cat drug in. God knows if she'll live or not." Louise cuddled her docile bundle.

"She'll live!"

An hour out of Pittsburgh, a snowstorm brewed. Dark swirling clouds whipped the battered car. They plugged on.

"Chessy, we've got to heat up some milk for her. Maybe we can stop at the next gas station."

"If I see one through this pea soup."

They drove on a little farther. Louise called out, "Red Horse gas station up on the right."

"O.K."

Chessy pulled next to the gas pump and waited for the man to come out. When he did, Chessy ordered gas and asked if they could use a hot plate if the attendant had one.

"Sure. Got one right over by the cash register. Come on in." He led the way, a squat man in a thick plaid jacket covered with grease.

Louise poured out some of the milk Fannie and Ramelle had packed and heated it in a saucepan Ramelle had also included.

"Looks like you got a little soldier there." The fellow smiled.

"Yes, she's been through her own war." Louise rocked her.

The greasy man hovered over the tiny bundle like a protective angel. When the feeding was finished and they started to leave, he fished a rabbit's foot out of his pocket. "Here, ma'am. Bring her luck."

"Thank you." Louise felt the tiny rabbit claws in her hand and gently placed the foot in her pocket.

All across half of Pennsylvania and half of Maryland Louise and Chessy pulled in to feed the baby. Old people, young people, white people, black people, poor people, rich people—wherever they asked for a warm corner, a burner on a stove, they got it. People were glad to help. Nicole owed her life to people she would never see, never even know.

Exhausted, Louise pulled into Ramelle's driveway, with Chessy holding the baby. Everyone had agreed that the child and Juts should stay at Ramelle's until both recovered. Julia should have remained up on Bumblebee Hill, but nothing could have kept her there. With all of them at the big house, people could take turns feeding Nicole around the clock. It was almost midnight when they opened the back door and stumbled in. They'd been twelve hours going and sixteen hours coming back. The entire crew—Julia Ellen, Cora, Ramelle, Pearlie, Fannie, Ev and Lionel, Orrie and Noe—awaited them in the front room. The relief on their safe arrival quickly changed into wild curiosity over the baby. Chessy walked the length of the living room and placed Nicole in Juts' arms.

"Honey, here's our baby." He stood there and started bawling in front of everyone.

Julia couldn't see, either, for the tears. Everyone cried, even Lionel and Noe.

Cora joked. "To look at all this weeping in here you'd think we had another funeral on our hands." She glowed every time she peeked at the baby, in Spotty's first baby blanket.

Of course, each individual wanted to feed her right then and there. They would have stuffed her until she burst. Much buzzing occurred over schedules and sleeping places and diet. The only one who didn't talk was Julia. She was so enchanted by the little dark head, the huge black eyes, that she forgot to join in. Chessy was glued to her side. He forgot how worn out he was.

"Juts, what are you going to name her?" Orrie asked.

"Nicole's a nice name and she is French—half anyway," Julia replied.

"She has to have a second name." Fannie was fluttering over the whole crowd.

"Her middle name is Louise," Chessy stated.

Louise was stunned. She started to bawl all over again. Julia reached out and held her hand. "Thanks, Sis, I can't say anything but thanks."

Louise sniffed and huffed and blew into her hanky. Pearlie patted her on the back and gave her his wide white handkerchief since she had used hers up. "I was glad to do it." She collected herself. "Juts, you wouldn't have believed that nun's face!" Then she got up and rummaged around in her coat pocket.

"What are you doing?" Pearlie wondered.

"Here, I almost forgot this. This is the baby's first present." She handed the worn rabbit's foot to Julia.

Sometime in May, 1945

At the beginning of the assault on Okinawa, some three hundred and fifty miles south of Japan, nothing happened. It looked like a piece of cake. Ushijima, the Japanese officer in charge of Okinawa, wisely reinforced the southern sector of the island, where natural terrain aided defense. In time the Americans learned their piece of cake was bitter indeed. They fought yard by yard in this hellhole. Overhead, Kamikaze pilots splattered into the earth, glad to die for the Emperor and delighted to take U.S. soldiers and sailors with them. Extra Billy Bitters, Sixth Marine Division, found himself overwhelmed with heat, flies and the stench on Sugar Loaf Hill. Extra Billy and his buddy, Corporal David Levy of Burlington, Vermont, were too far forward, cut off from their unit. A wicked burst of machine gun fire hurried them into a small entrenchment, not more than a glorified foxhole really. They landed on two very dead Japanese.

"Oh, Christ," Bill exclaimed as he felt a dead man's ribs crack under his weight.

"The worms crawl in, the worms crawl out, and we'll play pinochle on your snout." David curled up his nose. The stench was unbearable and the maggots didn't confine themselves to rotting flesh.

"Let's see where those bastards are." Bill put his helmet on the tip of his rifle and slowly edged it over the side of the hole. An instant blast of fire left him with an air-conditioned bonnet. "Shit."

"Looks like there's nothing we can do except wait until the guys catch up with us," David sighed.

"If they catch up with us."

"Extra Billy, have you no faith in the United States Marine Corps?" David lit a cigarette. Let the Japs shoot up the smoke.

"I got a lotta faith in the U.S. Marines. I also got a lot of faith in those Nips up there."

"Funny those guys don't surrender. There's no way off this piece of real estate." David studied his blue cigarette smoke.

"From what everybody says, the sons-of-a-bitches don't believe in surrender. They die and go directly to the Imperial Digs," Bill snorted.

"Funny." David took a deep drag.

"What?"

"That human beings can be so different from one another. Doesn't make sense."

"Fuck, I can't stand this smell. Think we can push these carcasses over the side? Be kinda protection." Bill grimaced.

"Yeah, if they don't fall apart." David peered underneath him at the disgusting sight.

"How long do you think they've been dead?"

"Not more than two days. In this climate it doesn't take long, you know?" David crouched low and slid his arm under one soldier's waist. "Crawl around here and get this guy's shoes."

Billy obeyed. "Goddamned bastards have such little feet. You can't strip them for nothing useful."

They edged the body over the rim. Maggots rained on them.

"One more. Hold it in, Billy Boy, don't puke. This hole is in bad enough shape."

"I can't look at the guy's face. The rest I can take, but not the face."

"Know what you mean." David tried to pull his shirt over his nose.

With a struggle they pushed the second hunk of rancid meat up and over. The men slightly above them blasted into the decaying hulks. Flesh splattered like rotted persimmons. David and Billy crouched in the hole, their hands holding tight onto their helmets.

"Welcome to the South Pacific," David joked.

"Land of hula girls and eternal sunshine," Billy chimed in. He liked David. They'd already been through a hell of a lot and David was a man who'd lay his ass on the line for you. At first Extra Billy shunned him because he was Jewish. Once he got used to it he had a hard time remembering why he had shunned David in the first place. Runnyede had a few Jews. They were industrious, clean and marvelously good-humored. For some reason Bill had got the message early in life that Jews were different, different meaning bad, and stay away. All that seemed so far away and so stupid now.

"You looking at Mary again?" David asked.

Without realizing it, Bill had pulled Mary's picture out of his pocket and was staring at it. "Huh?"

"Hey, Romeo, don't show your wife these sights."

"Yeah, yeah." Bill thrust the photo back in his pocket.

"I forget what women look like." David put his hands behind his head and looked up at the sky.

"I don't forget what they feel like." Bill laughed.

"I hear the Russian women are fighting same as the men. And Poles and people like that have whole units made up of women. Nazis won't fight 'em," David told him.

"Why the hell not?"

"They're more ferocious than we are. No shit."

"I can tell you my mother-in-law ought to be in one of those units. Sweet Jesus on water skis, that woman can bitch. Put a gun in her hand and she'd clear out a battalion."

"Please Louise, huh?"

"Yeah. Nothing I do satisfies the old biddy."

"Don't take it to heart. Most mothers aren't overfond of losing their daughters. If I saw you coming down the aisle I'd run put my girl on a train for San Francisco."

Bill growled, "You really know how to hurt a guy."

"Thanks, Bill. I didn't think you cared." David pushed Bill's thigh with his boot.

"I guess I was kind of a bastard when I got married. Still wet behind the ears. I was so dumb I thought every wall was a door."

"Whatta ya mean, 'was'?" David laughed. "You're the meanest son-of-a-bitch I ever met. A real meshuga."

"What's that?"

"Meshugana. Crazy, man, you are crazy. You've been busted down to a buck private twice in one year. Slug one more sergeant and you'll be out on your ass."

"Yeah, well, this ain't exactly the Chalfonte mansion. I could do with an eviction notice."

"No way, buddy. I'm here to watch over you. You

get a piece of shit like that on your record and you'll leave World War II to join the ranks of the unemployed," David advised him.

"I'm not so sure I'm ever going home again." Extra Billy was forgetting to be flippant.

"Everybody has ups and downs. This happens to be very down—we fell off the continental shelf and are approaching the lowest point on earth." David fished around in his pocket for something.

"Whatcha looking for?"

"Candy bar," David told him.

"Iron guts. How can you eat with our protective wall up there?" Bill jerked his head upward.

"Couple of dead Japs aren't going to get me off my he-man diet."

"Levy, you're something, you know that?" Bill rooted around in his back pocket and fished out a very melted chocolate bar. "If you can eat this I swear I'll take you to Fannie Jump Creighton's Sans Souci and buy you the best meal in the entire state of Maryland." Bill handed him the mess.

"You're on!" David unwrapped it and licked the paper.

Three hours later David and Extra Billy were still cramped in their sloppy hole. Lieutenant Kaneko, not half a football field away from the two stranded Americans, was having his own problems. He'd lost over a third of his men in two days. A cultured, handsome young man, Kaneko knew not one of them would ever see his homeland again. He had married just before the war started, a brilliant match socially. He imagined what it would be like if he could live to 1960. Kaneko was an expert horseman. He dreamed of himself taking jumps in full-dress uniform. He dreamed of his wife, her skin the color of fresh wheat. He dreamed of children he would never father. He would die here on Okinawa. He believed in a greater Japan. It was worth dying for. Still humans dream of life. He had written a long letter to his wife. He prayed that the American who found his body would have the decency to deliver the letter. He wondered about the two men pinned below him. Every now and then he could hear rippling laughter fly out of the foxhole. Incredible men, he thought. He had been trained to think that Americans were monsters. The weeks of fighting had led him to believe they were men much like himself. They had different ways, perhaps they weren't as cultivated, as educated, but they were worth respect. They fought like demons for men who had no emperor, no hall of heroes. That he could not understand. Why did they fight? From what he could gather, the average GI had as much political dedication as would fit in a thimble. It didn't slow them down in the field. Lieutenant Kaneko regretted he would never visit America.

Private Suga wanted to send another round into the bodies of their comrades. Kaneko stopped him. "Save your ammunition for the living."

Lieutenant Kaneko didn't like killing. He wondered if anybody did, truly. Even the Yanks.

Night crept around Extra Billy and David. In the twilight you could see, but not for long.

"Shit. Looks like we are spending the night here," Bill exclaimed.

"We still got daylight in us. It could be worse." David tried to make himself more comfortable.

"You know what really burns my ass, Levy?"

"What?"

"Man, I hate being called a Yank. I'm from the South. I hate that so bad I want to drop leaflets on every Jap on every island in the South Pacific."

They took turns watching and sleeping. Deep in the night David was on watch. He thought he heard a slither. He softly shook Extra Billy awake.

"They're coming."

Bill woke, wild amounts of adrenaline pumping into his bloodstream. David pointed to the direction from which he heard the sound. Either it was men or it was the largest snake on earth. "What do you think?" Bill asked.

"I say let's stay here in the hole and let them come over the side. We can kill them. If we crawl out of here they'll blast us from the machine gun nest. At least this way we've got a fighting chance."

"Roger." Bill checked his rifle and pulled off the bayonet in case he couldn't maneuver the rifle in such close quarters.

The slither drew closer. Bill went wet with fear. Oceans of sweat rolled from his armpits. David held his mouth tight. If he'd opened it his teeth would have chattered. Waiting seemed worse than combat. Closer and closer the sound came The next instant three Japs flung themselves over the side. Bill ripped one with his bayonet. The other two were at David. Levy fired and took half of one guy's face off, but not before the other Jap plunged a knife deep into his left armpit. Bill shoved his bayonet in the guy's back. Not content with that, he stabbed him six or seven more times. He also stabbed the other two Japanese to make certain they were irretrievably dead. He then rested David against the side of the foxhole. He could barely see in the dark.

"Tell me how you feel," Bill said in a trembling voice.

"Can't tell if they punctured my lung or not. Losing a lot of blood, Billy."

"O.K., I'll tie a tourniquet and take it off every twenty minutes. We'll pull through. Don't worry, David. Don't worry." Bill hastily ripped up his shirt and applied pressure under the arm and slightly over the shoulder. The wound was in a devilish place. He slowed the bleeding slightly but not enough. They both knew it.

"Extra, search those guys and see if they got anything good on them before you throw them out of our apartment." David wanted to take some of Bill's attention away from himself.

Bill started ransacking the Japs' pockets. "Hey, here's a little picture of a Tokyo honey." He handed the picture back to David.

"You dumb bastard, how can you tell in the dark?"

"I can just feel it."

"Shit, man. If a dog shook its ass right you'd fuck it."

"Only live once, David."

"Yeah, I know."

Bill could have bit off his tongue. He saved the Japs' shirts and a few trinkets before heaving the bodies over the side, creating a larger wall.

"Hey, Bill?"

"What?"

"Don't let the maggots get in my wound. Watch me, will ya, Billy?" David's voice shook slightly.

"Sure, buddy. I'm head of maggot patrol."

They stayed quiet for a time. At last dawn suffused the hills with a light-gray presence. Bill could see David's wound much better now. If a medic didn't show up soon, David wasn't going to make it.

"Ever read about the battle of Bull Run?" David asked.

"You mean Manassas?"

"I mean Bull Run, you rebel son-of-a-bitch. We won the goddamned war, so we get to name the battles."

"Ha! We just let you win because we knew you damn Yankees would be lonesome without us. Only Southerners know how to give a good party."

"You got a point there." David smiled. "Well, it seems there was a fellow from North Carolina. Was July, that battle, and hot. Hot like here. This guy took a wound in his head and a fly laid eggs in it. Happened to lots of guys. But in the head. The docs couldn't get them out. The maggots ate his brain out for five days before the poor bastard died. They should have killed him. They shouldn't let people suffer like that." David was covered in sweat.

"You're right. You're right."

"Billy, don't let the maggots get in my wound. Please, Billy."

"Don't worry, buddy. Don't worry." Bill shoved one of the corpses with the barrel of his gun. It drew fire from Kaneko's men. "Christ, don't those guys ever sleep?"

Another hour passed. The sun was making itself felt. From the rear Bill heard sounds. "Hey, David, David, I think some of our guys are coming up."

"Great. Great."

"You'll be fine." Bill rocked him. He'd been holding him in his arms all night.

"Ah, Extra Billy Bitters. I should live so long. I'm gonna die, I can feel it. I was scared before. Maybe I still am, but I'm getting used to the idea."

"Hey, man, don't talk like that."

"Bill, I'm nobody's fool." David blinked.

"Those dumb bastards behind us sound like they are coming into Runnymede Square. They're gonna get the shit knocked out of them if they don't pipe down."

"Fire off a round or two. Maybe that'll warn them," David told him.

"Yeah." Bill cracked off a few volleys in the air.

"They're hollering and running this way. Christ, they musta just got off the boat." David tried not to touch his wound.

Immediately a barrage from the Japanese halted all sounds of merriment. Now the next wave of guys were pinned down and crawling forward.

"Think they know the Jap position?" David asked.

"No. Another hundred yards before they can see much."

"When they get in range, you run back to them," David told him.

"No, you put that in the shit can, boy. I ain't leaving you."

Cleverly David reassured him: "No, go back for a medic."

"No."

"Come on, Bill. I got to have a medic."

"I ain't leaving."

"Extra fifteen minutes might be too late."

Bill knew this was true. God, he felt awful.

"Bill, you gotta."

"O.K."

As the Americans drew closer they waited.

Still not close enough. When I can hear clear I'll know I can make a run for it, Bill said to himself. He couldn't look over the foxhole or he'd have a bullet in the back of his brain.

"Soon," David gasped. He knew, medic or no medic, he wasn't going to see the United States again. He resolved to die like a man, but he had to get Bill out of there first.

"Another five minutes." Bill patted him. He was desperate to get help to David.

"Now, Bill." David gripped his hand.

"Yeah, O.K." Bill paused and then said in a sheepish voice, "David, can I kiss you?"

"Shit, you mean I been spending all this time with a cocksucker?" David whispered. "Yeah, you can kiss me, but you can't kiss and tell."

Bill leaned over and kissed him on the forehead and then quickly, fearfully, on the lips. "See you in a few minutes with a medic."

"Move out, buddy."

Bill shot out of that hole like a bat out of hell. Since the Japanese were waiting for the next wave of Americans, he got a few seconds on them. A burst of machine gun fire took a hunk out of his side but he still tore up the sod. With his back turned, he couldn't see David crawl over the side and lob a grenade at the nest. He had no hope of tossing it near them, but he gave it a heave hoping to attract the marines' attention in case Bill didn't reach them. No reason why more good men should die here, he thought.

Bill made it to the advancing line, screaming, "Medic! Medic!"

"You hit?" A lieutenant snarled and then saw the blood all over Bill's side.

"I don't know. I don't care. I need a medic for my friend."

The looey pointed to the rear. He saw the grenade explode and the Jap machine gun spit. He now knew where the enemy was positioned.

Frantic, Extra Billy located a medic. He had to wait until the line advanced before the medical officer could go forward into the foxhole. The minutes taunted Bill. Every one dropped into his brain like acid. The medics calmed him as best they could. He tried to start running back to the foxhole, but a quick tackle by one man put a stop to that. This unit had a bazooka. As soon as they were in range they brought it up and loaded. The first shot went wide of the mark. The second one was a bull's-eye. Lieutenant Kaneko exploded in three parts.

By the time they reached the foxhole, Bill saw what David had done. He knelt over David's body and noticed that the skin was blown away from his skull, revealing a creamy translucence that glowed with ebbing life like a candle. Extra Billy Bitters bent over his friend and sobbed like a wounded animal. It took four men to get him to give up David Levy's body.

When the blowhard boy that left Runnymede returned, he returned not the best of men but, a man nonetheless. After the war Bill found he no longer enjoyed hunting, formerly a favorite pastime. He couldn't bring himself to kill animals. Their dark eyes reminded him of David Levy.

April 30, 1947

News from Germany filtered back to the United States in fits and starts. The Allies bickered like thieves. From the rubble that was Berlin reports sometimes turned up, missing persons were sometimes found or at least their destinies revealed. Fairy Thatcher was such a missing person. Both the *Clarion* and the *Trumpet* ran a report of Fairy, judiciously omitting some of the more gruesome details.

As Celeste had suspected, Fairy and Gunther were hauled off to a concentration camp, the bulk of whose prisoners were there for political reasons. As conditions worsened, so did the lot of these unfortunate people, who soon had their ranks swelled with human beings whose only fault was having been born Jewish. Gunther died early. Perhaps his heart was already broken by the futile squabbling in the Communist camp or by the Stalin-Hitler pact. Fairy clung on in this strange land, with foreign words on her lips. She worked at every loathsome task assigned her. Her unflagging endurance and sad, silly sense of humor endeared her to all the other inmates. When an escape was planned, the old lady was invited to make a run for it with the others. She declined this honor and opportunity. Instead Fairy Thatcher took it upon herself to create an unholy racket while the others fled. Because even the guards respected her, she was hopeful it would be a few hours before they discovered her instant insanity act had been a decoy.

Discover they did. Fairy was paraded before the entire camp, assembled for the purpose of her execution. The commandant of the camp detested this labor. At the time he did not know more grisly work was in store for him. The war was young. Fairy's hands were bound behind her back. The commandant thought her public execution would crush the spirit of the other inmates. She refused a blindfold. As the rifles were raised to greet her, Fairy let out a yell. If she had ever once imagined this scene in her entire life, she might have pictured herself at her final moment heroically shouting, *"Viva la Revolución."* But the cry that sprang from her was unrehearsed, a surprise even to her. Before they mutilated her body with bullets, Fairy Thatcher blasted in a voice that reverberated against backbones, "America! Amer—"

When the camp was liberated at last, the few survivors from those early years recalled the dainty American woman. She seemed the least likely candidate to inspire admiration and a toughening of the soul. Perhaps that is why these wretched Germans, flayed at the hands of their own people, remembered her.

Courage comes from many different people and in many different situations. For most of her life Fairy was a disconnected, searching person. She found something she believed in, and right or wrong, the cause gave her dignity. And her Southern upbringing made her understand honor. Fairy Thatcher died with honor.

Fannie Jump, the last of the three, felt an anguish that froze her lungs when she read the report of Fairy's death. She upbraided herself for the times she had bullied Fairy. She cursed her dismissing of Fairy's politics, no matter how foreign they seemed to her. She staggered under the blows of these last three years. She had lost Celeste, dear Celeste, who could walk into a room and command it with one sweeping gaze; Celeste who held the long view, who spoke of centuries, not years. And Fairy. What terrible loneliness to lose the people you love most in this world! What a ruthless curse to outlive one's friends! Fannie wanted to die, to join them if there was a life hereafter or perhaps to return, reincarnated, as she and Celeste used to laughingly suggest. But to remove herself from life, no matter how painful, was not the course of honor.

Fannie could not belittle Fairy's magnificence or Celeste's joy for life by taking her own. Did not people live through the Middle Ages, diseased, enslaved and ignorant? They suffered but they lived. They bequeathed something to succeeding generations. At seventy years of age, Fannie began to understand the compact between the living and the dead. It was her duty to live. No matter how shattered her heart, no matter how besmirched the world, no matter how inhuman the lessons of World War II, Fannie must live. As long as she could draw breath she must. Fannie knew this burgeoning faith was not intellectual. No complex ideology fortified her. When worlds collapse, the flourishes of the mind evaporate. What's left is the raw meat of one's own flesh. Fannie decided to live what was left of her life to the fullest, to do what good she could for her neighbor. She would honor her friends by her actions. Life is the principle of the universe.

All through Runnymede, both South and North, good people faced the heavy emptiness of the postwar world. Some filled themselves with music. Others with booze. Some hid from the future but many, as most people everywhere, cautiously walked forward to meet it. And in this strangest of times these people spawned a generation that would rock America to its very foundations. As they rode their red tricycles and collected baseball cards, they looked the way children always do. But these children had Hiroshima for a birthmark and Auschwitz for a christening gift. Fannie was not alone, but she would have to wait for the toddlers to catch up to her.

May 24, 1980

Juts whizzed around the house singing "I'm Looking Over a Four-Leaf Clover." She laid her trap with care. Since Orrie had nosed by yesterday, Julia knew Louise would come by today. It wasn't enough to sit and talk to her. Juts wanted to put some skin on the baloney. Last night she had told Louise that she and Nickel were riding up to the big potter's barn in Hanover. Said she'd be gone most of the afternoon. Louise would come snooping for sure.

"Is your ass in gear?" she called out to Nickel.

"Yes."

As they got in the car, Julia gave Nickel strict instructions in her conspiratorial voice. "You drive me by my sister's and Orrie Tadia's. Then swing around the back way and let me off."

"What for? I thought we were going to Hanover."

"You're going to Hanover. I got plans." Juts struck a Douglas MacArthur pose. All she needed was the pipe.

"Like hell I will. Mother, you've been sneaking around like the cat that ate the canary. What's up?"

"None of your business."

"In that case, we'll sit here in the car, because I'm not starting it." Nickel folded her arms over her chest.

"I'm your old mother and I'm gonna be your old

mother right up to the end. You start this car or I'll give you such a smack!"

"Nope."

Julia punched her in the arm. Nickel pinched her mother right back.

"Ouch!" Juts spat.

"I'm my mother's daughter. You tell me or you'll never see your false teeth again as long as you live."

"Some daughter you are. You are disgusting mean." Julia feigned upset. She was beginning to enjoy this tussle. Nickel gave as good as she got.

"You can always trade me in on a new model. I hear Korean orphans are big these days."

"So that's the thanks I get." Julia's eyes narrowed. "You're gonna miss me when I'm gone."

"Are you going to spill the beans or do we sit here in this tin can and roast?"

"All right, smartass. I got the goods on my sister. If you do as you're told I can get the price of the farm down, so help me."

"Mom what'd you get?"

"I'm not telling. You'll put it in a book."

"You can tell me."

"Not until I force Louise into an agreement."

"Mother, I swear. Scout's honor. I won't put this in a book."

"You got bounced out of Girl Scouts, remember?"

"I won't tell." Nickel crossed her heart.

"Loose lips sink ships," Julia warned. She took a deep breath, lowered her voice even more and said very fast, "Found pornography under Wheezie's mattress."

If Nickel hadn't been sitting in the car she would've fallen on the ground. *"No!"*

"Yes. That's the God's honest truth."

"Ol' Louise climbed down off the cross, did she?"

"Slithered." Juts licked her lips.

"O.K. Mom. You're on." Nickel started the car.

Driving past Louise's and then Orrie's, they attempted to appear casual. As soon as they passed Orrie's royal-blue door, Nickel cornered and sped to the rear road behind the house.

"Good luck, Mom."

"Come back around four." Juts waved good-bye to her. She raced for her back door, grabbed the pornography, which she had carefully hidden in the freezer compartment of the refrigerator, and then stuffed herself in her clothes closet. She fully intended to jump out at an unsuspecting Louise. She didn't have to wait long.

Louise walked into Julia's house bold as brass. Since she was her sister and everyone was accustomed to her trailing in and out, she didn't worry about neighbors. The neighbors were used to the two of them anyway, after all these years. Louise checked the kitchen. She didn't expect to find the magazines in the kitchen, but she felt it was her responsibility to be thorough about this. Those damn rags had to be in this house somewhere. TV shows sometimes had murderers put clues in obvious places because people overlook the obvious. She flipped through all the magazines in the living room. The bedroom was the place. After all, that's where she had hidden them. Still as a mouse, Julia heard the *clop-clop* of Louise's wedgies come down the hall. She heard a groan as Louise got down on her hands and knees to look under the bed. A sweeping of the hands could be heard as her sister checked beneath the mattress. Bureau drawers were pulled open and closed. A low mumble, "Shit," wafted under the closet door. The wedgies approached the closet. The door opened.

"Boo."

"Aaaah!" Louise screamed at the top of her lungs and staggered back. She considered a heart attack, then clearly saw her sister. She'd live to thrash her.

"Looking for something?" Julia held out the magazines.

Louise lunged for them and Julia took off down the hallway. "You can't catch me. You can't catch me."

"I'll pull out every hair of your head, so help me, God!" Louise tore after her.

Julia, four years younger and faster, kept ahead of

Louise, flashing the magazines before her eyes. "Now you see it. Now you don't."

"When I get ahold of you you're going to look like the tail end of bad luck," Louise screeched, her face like rumpled paper.

"Tail. That's what these magazines are all about." Juts danced an irritating two steps ahead of panting Louise.

"The stork didn't bring you. It was a vulture."

"Yeah, a horny toad brought you."

"Gimme that! Gimme that!" The veins in Louise's neck stood out like purple earthworms.

"You're a dried booger," Julia sang out, in that lilt children use when tormenting a foe.

"Oh, the pain." Louise clutched her heart.

"It's easier to bear pain than the itch," Juts brayed.

"This is killing me." Louise lurched dangerously forward, stopping her fall by grabbing onto a kitchen chair.

"Only the good die young. You'll live forever."

"I'm going first, Julia. This is it." Louise's knees hit the floor. She didn't move.

"All right, Louise."

She still didn't move. Julia's face got reddish.

"Louise!"

Nothing.

Now Julia was scared. She tiptoed over to Louise. Not a twitch. Bending down on her hands and knees, she put her head on her sister's heart.

Whap. Yank. That fast Louise liberated a huge chunk of Julia's hair. "Fool around with me, will you?"

"Owww." Tears filled Julia's eyes.

Louise latched onto the magazines. Julia wouldn't release them. Back and forth they seesawed on the floor. First one would dominate, pulling her sister off the floor, and then the other would brace her foot against the table and pull the other up in the air.

"Gimme that!" Louise grunted.

"Never!"

"First Amendment says I can have those magazines." Louise strained.

"First Amendment says I can read 'em." Juts gave her a wicked jerk, but Louise didn't lose her grip.

"Does not."

"Does too."

"Does not!" Louise bellowed. "Private property."

"Yeah, well, the church says you gotta give me these." Julia was switching gears.

"You're full of shit." Louise could barely get the words out, she was pulling so hard.

"Gotta share, remember? It's Christian. That's what you said when you took my hair ribbon, you son-of-a-bitch." Julia gritted her teeth.

"I never took your hair ribbon."

"You lie, Louise." Julia jerked again.

"I can't remember that far back." The exertion made Louise sweat. "After all, that was 1909."

"I thought you didn't remember!" Julia crowed, and summoned all her might for another pull. Louise let go and Julia Ellen skidded across the room. Now it was Louise's turn to laugh. Juts started to laugh, too. Louise got up and was surprised to find all her parts got up with her. She walked stiffly over to Julia and offered her a hand up. Julia quickly put the magazines behind her back.

"Quit hanging over me, blowfly," Juts snarled.

"Come on, I'll help you up."

"I don't trust you. Go over to the fridge. Then I'll get up." Louise obeyed and Julia scrambled to her feet. The women glared at one another. "Now, sister mine, let's sit down and discuss the sensitive nature of these magazines." Julia's eyes jumped in her head.

"Give me those magazines."

"Not so fast." Julia kept them in her lap so Louise couldn't grab them and run out.

"Julia!"

"Quit bellyaching. I'll give you these magazines if . . ."

"If what?"

"If you sell the farm to Nickel for forty thousand dollars."

"Chiseler!" Louise pouted.

"Pornographer!"

"I am not. I don't know how those magazines got under my bed." Louise wiped her brow.

"The good fairy brought them." Juts snickered.

"The good fairy lives with you."

"How would you like to eat a bug," Julia threatened.

"She is." Louise glowered. "Nickel is the black sheep of the family."

"Yes, but she has golden hooves." Julia smiled.

This caught Louise, who expected a vehement denial. "Well . . ."

"You know, Louise, for someone who hates sex you're making an awfully good job of it." Julia tantalizingly waved one of the magazines in the air, opened to the shocking centerfold.

"I'm not fit to drive a hen from the door." Louise faked a swoon.

"Recovering from your recent bout with good health?" Julia tormented.

That quick, Louise snapped back, "Don't rub it in, Julia. What's the harm in a few magazines at my age?"

"What's the harm in Nickel's love life at her age?"

"You know perfectly well."

"Better than a shotgun wedding, to my way of thinking."

"There you go throwing Mary in my face again. Why the Japanese ever let Bill Bitters get away is beyond me." She sighed like a furnace. "There's no justice in this world."

"So bring the price down to forty thousand dollars. When you sign the papers you get the magazines back."

"Julia!"

"Not before."

Glumly Louise shifted her weight in her seat.

"Louise." Julia dragged her name out as long as it would last.

"I'm thinking."

"I never know what you're thinking—probably because you don't know yourself."

"Oh, shut up."

Julia congratulated herself. "This is my high-water mark."

"Yeah, you left a ring around the toilet."

Juts rolled up a magazine and leaned across the table to knock her. Louise ducked and stuck out her tongue.

"Don't make me laugh, Louise. I'm supposed to be mad at you."

"We're what Nickel would call loony tunes."

"What's her other one?" Julia concentrated for a moment. "Ozone cookies, that's it. We're ozone cookies."

Louise sighed, then bargained again. "What about forty-five thousand?"

"Louise!" Julia went to smack her once more.

"Give me one day to think it over," Louise requested.

"All right. One day."

February 14, 1950

Juts smashed her face against the reality of raising children. Nicole did not turn out to be Shirley Temple, as Julia had ardently hoped. No wonder Louise used to look like death eating a cracker on bad days. One child was driving Julia to distraction. God knows how Louise managed with two. Now that they were full grown, Louise still endured their problems. Mary squatted out on the north side of town in a shack, which was a polite term for it. Extra Billy farmed weeds and neurosis. The man couldn't adjust. His oldest boy, OdeRuss, worked alongside his father. David, born in 1946, started doing chores, too. Maizie did not exactly set the world on fire, but she did put a match to one wing of the Holy Humilities of Mary. They eighty-sixed her. Since that outburst Maizie had languished back home with Mother. She read Roy Rogers and Dale Evans comic books. She also colored all their coloring books with her Big Chief crayons. Maizie was just shy of twenty-two.

In the midst of all this, Nicole—Nickel to everyone —was relatively O.K. She would turn six in November. Unbeknownst to Julia, the qualities that most infuriated her in Nickel were the qualities the child picked up from her. Like Julia, Nickel proved herself independent, flippant and bursting with entirely too much energy.

This morning, with an ice storm raging, Nickel had barreled outside and crammed snow into every available orifice. In the summers she'd pop tar bubbles. In the spring, mud adorned every inch of skin. In the fall she'd already begun playing football, tearing her clothing and other kids' hair. Aside from tremendous energy, Nickel displayed an early intelligence that baffled Julia. At three years of age she had sat in the middle of the living room and read the newspaper to Cora, Chessy and Juts. Julia Ellen rushed her to the doctor, since children weren't supposed to read until first grade. Old Doc Gibbons told her to leave the kid alone.

At breakfast today Nickel had rattled on about whatever danced into her small head. She wanted to know if butterflies could wear earrings. Julia didn't feel like listening to this. She told the child to shut up. So Nickel sat there and talked to her Rice Krispies.

Julia schemed. If she took her downtown and walked her all around, she could exhaust her. Then, a few moments of peace and quiet. By early afternoon the storm passed, but Bumblebee Hill and all Runnymede was coated with icing. Juts bundled up herself and the child and then waxed the sled runners and zoomed down the hill. At the bottom they left their sled on the other side of a big snowbank and started into Runnymede Square.

"Mother?"

"What?"

"What was Aunt Wheezie talking about last night?"

"Herself, as usual." Julia slipped along.

"She said something about God." Nickel persisted.

"She said God couldn't be everywhere so he invented mothers." Julia said to herself: Unfortunately he also invented children.

"I didn't know you were invented. I thought you were born."

"How do you know I wasn't hatched out of a giant egg?" Julia teased her.

"Because you don't have feathers."

The logic of this struck Julia. The two clung to the iron railing in front of Christ Lutheran Church on the corner before Runnymede Square. A few paces in front of them, a well-dressed woman struggled also. Her high-heeled shoes barely dented the ice. Her feet were covered in light-gray plastic boots but the heel of one shoe pierced through. Wind slashed them all in the face. Julia was determined to walk through the Bon-Ton and to buy a hot fudge sundae. Once Nickel arrived, she had stopped working. Staying inside the house drove her bonkers. She figured Nickel would start first grade this fall and she'd go back to work. She liked working.

"Mother, that lady dropped her panties."

"What?" Juts, engrossed in her thoughts, had missed the spectacle in front of her.

The woman's elastic broke and her underpants bombed down around her ankles. On this treacherous ice she was like a hobbled horse. First she'd shake one foot and crash into the fence. She couldn't lift either boot out of her undergarment. Naturally, she wasn't going to bend over and release it. She had to pretend the underpants clutching at her ankles were not hers but rather a pair lost by some other woman.

"Lady!" Nickel called out.

"Shut your trap."

"But, Mother, she dropped her pants."

Julia squeezed her little arm. "Quiet. You'll embarrass her."

"What's embarrass?"

As Julia strained to answer that one, the woman succeeded in freeing one foot, at the cost of ripping half the pants. The other heel seemed nailed to the white thing.

"Uh—embarrass is when you wish you were some-body else."

"I don't ever want to be anybody else." Nickel's dark eyebrows knitted together.

"If your pants drop right off in Runnymede Square you'll wish to high heaven you weren't you."

"Everyone's got to wear drawers."

"Can't you leave well enough alone? I told you what embarrass is. Now hush."

Up ahead, the mortified woman stepped on the of-fending undie with her free left foot and liberated it, only to have it now stick against the left foot. She cursed a blue streak. Julia laughed. It was rude but she couldn't help it. After a mammoth tussle, the woman cleared herself of the leechlike obstacle and started to run away. The ice made escape impossible. She fell flat on her face. Nickel was distressed by the spectacle and worried that the woman forgot her pants, because Julia had taught her not to throw anything out. Even old clothes could be made into rags. Thinking she was being helpful, the child skated up to the pants and picked them up.

"Nickel, *no!*"

Ignoring her mother, Nickel hurried to catch up to the woman, now crawling on all fours to get away.

"Nickel, you come back here."

"Lady! Lady, you forgot your drawers."

The woman glanced back, a look of horor on her face as she observed Nickel heading toward her waving the damned pants like a flag. She rolled like a polar bear, trying to get her feet under her.

"Nickel, drop those dirty drawers right this minute!" Julia tried to catch up with the child, but she, too, skidded, and landed on her behind. When she at-tempted to rise she landed right back down again. The ice bruised her bottom. She decided to crawl along.

As Nickel came closer to the woman, she saw her efforts were not appreciated. The enraged woman waved her away.

"They're not mine."

"How could someone else's underpants fall from under your coat?" The child was puzzled.

"They're not mine." The woman crawled faster.

Juts gained on Nickel, who was about six feet from the sliding creature. "Nicole Louise, come back here."

"Mother, she says these are someone else's pants."

"Get back here!" Julia yowled.

Nickel threw the pants, which landed right on the woman's face, and raced back to her mother, on all fours, who raised up on one arm and cuffed her with the other.

"Ow!"

"You listen to me."

"I was. You said, 'Waste not, want not.' "

"Don't get smart with me, young lady. I told you to drop those filthy pants and you didn't."

The woman managed to crawl around the corner, leaving what was left of the panties trampled in the snow and ice.

"Mother."

"You listen to me, hear?" Julia demanded. "Or I'm gonna open up your Oreo cookies and spit in the middle of every one."

May 30, 1952

Ever since Celeste's death Cora had religiously checked in on Ramelle every day. The three months she visited California each year, Cora kept the house. Fannie dropped by frequently also. Today blistered. Once Cora finished her chores she joined Ramelle on the back veranda overlooking the beautiful formal garden.

"Before I take this load off my feet, would you like a lemonade?"

Ramelle glanced up from her book. She was sixty-eight. Her hair was totally gray and laugh lines creased her lovely face. Her eyes had lost none of their unusual luster. "Cora, let's sit back here where no one can see us and drink a beer. God, it's hot."

Cora fetched the cold drinks, put the tray on the wicker table between them and sat down, wiping her forehead with a lovely hanky Nickel had valiantly tried to embroider.

"What a riot of color," Ramelle said, noticing it.

"Nickel."

"She's indefatigable."

"I don't know about that, but you sure can't wear her out." Cora grinned. "What are you reading there?"

"A Midsummer Night's Dream. It was one of Celeste's favorites."

"That's the only thing I regret about my life. I never did learn to read." Cora tucked her hanky between her breasts.

"If only I could be as calm as you."

"You don't look as though you're breaking out in hives."

"No, but I wander between the past, present and future. I ought to stick more to the present."

Cora really didn't understand this. "How's Spotty doing?"

"Fine. She's sensationally bored with Hollywood. My granddaughter is six years old. I never once thought I'd be a grandmother."

"Little Hallie is six? Time flies. Nickel is near to eight and near to driving Julia around the bend."

"They're a great deal alike." Ramelle closed her book.

"Six of one, half dozen of the other. Nickel is as bullheaded as her mother and every bit as ready to get into trouble. If mother and daughter aren't scratching each other like cats, you can bet they're ganging up on someone else." Cora shook her head.

"How about Fannie Jump and the Gas Alley affair?"

Cora sat up. "She's got the tiger by the tail. Writing up an article for the *Trumpet* and the *Clarion* about how those alleys are unsanitary and how conditions got to be improved."

"The fact that the Rifes own every building on both Gas Alley and Frog Alley makes this a heavyweight bout." Ramelle squinted into the sun.

"She's grand. Seventy-five years old and raising hell

with what she has. Ever since she got word of Fairy, she's taken on the whole world. Any little thing that Fannie thinks ought to be corrected gets corrected. I tell you I wouldn't tangle with her." Cora approved of Fannie's actions.

"She goes about despotically improving our lot. If only Celeste were here to see it."

"Maybe she is. Who knows what happens when you cross over the river?" Cora mopped her brow again.

"I'd like to think so. She's in my mind every day, every hour. Achilles absent is Achilles still." Ramelle remembered Cora didn't know who Achilles was. "I mean, even dead, Celeste fills the rooms."

"Speak of the sun and you see its rays."

"Yes, exactly." Ramelle sipped some beer.

"She inspired me to pick my tombstone out."

"Oh, Cora!" Ramelle was shocked.

"My tombstone is going to say: 'Born: Yes. Died: Yes.' "

"When Fannie dies we'll have to inscribe the stone: 'At last she sleeps alone!' " Ramelle said.

Cora playfully smacked Ramelle's arm. "Aren't you awful!"

"You know what Celeste used to say: 'Angels can fly because they take themselves lightly.' "

Cora's eyes glistened. "I know when one falls out, one steps in, but Lordy, there will never be another like her."

Ramelle grasped her hand. "She loved you, too. Very, very much."

Cora dabbed her eyes with her handkerchief. "Love keeps on growing. I don't know about all them miracles in the Bible, about Lazarus and such, but in this life I've seen plenty of miracles, yes I have."

"Me, too." Ramelle swallowed hard.

Cora changed the subject so the two of them wouldn't have to sit there and bawl. "As I came on down here today the war memorials were full of old tires."

"I wonder who is doing that? This has been going on since right after the Great War."

"Every holiday plus a few wild-card times in between."

"It must be a soldier who resents the statues or the army or what?"

"Damned if I know." Cora laughed. "I wish they'd catch him. Curiosity is hard to bear over all these years."

"Cora, speaking of curiosity, I've always felt in my heart that Celeste killed Brutus. Does that surprise you?" Ramelle threw out that grenade.

Cora hesitated, drew a long breath. "No. I figured it, too. I always kept it to myself."

"Yes." Ramelle cupped her chin in her hand. "Murder is supposed to be wrong, but you know, I respected her for killing him. I'm afraid I'm a little too impatient to wait for heaven to judge. How do I know the heavenly judges aren't also susceptible to gold? I prefer justice right here on earth."

"Well, I don't know. Can't say as I miss Brutus, though."

"The absurdities of this world threaten to engulf me on some days." Ramelle's mouth pinched together.

"Mother Nature didn't want everything to be perfect. Even the sun has spots," Cora reassured her.

Ramelle paused, digested Cora's wisdom and ventured forth on another long-hidden topic. "Could you talk to Aimes?"

"Most times."

"You know I love Curtis. He is a compassionate, gentle, humorous man. To be loved by two Chalfontes really was and remains quite an honor. With Celeste I could say anything. She knew what I was saying and what I wasn't saying. But with Curtis . . . sometimes he doesn't know what I'm talking about."

"None of 'em do. You have to take them as they are."

"Hmm."

"Look who's whipping around the hydrangeas," Cora called out.

"Hello, Louise," Ramelle greeted her.

"Mother, drinking beer in public!" Louise hissed.

"Oh, hell, Wheezie, leave your old mother alone."

"Would you care for one?" Ramelle asked her.

Seeing that Ramelle was drinking, too, changed Louise's mind. "Well, all right."

"Sit down, Ramelle." Cora put her hand on Ramelle's arm. "Louise, go right on in the kitchen and fetch one. Neither one of us is moving our bones."

Louise reappeared and wiggled herself into a chair.

"Well?" Cora knew Louise was fuming about something. She might as well let the shoe drop.

"Well, what?"

Ramelle opened her book again, pretending to read.

"Louise, your bowels are blocked about something."

"Mother, must you be so vulgar?" Louise patted her lips dry after a sip of beer. "I'm simply nonplused over Julia's performance in the Capitol Theater today."

"Juts performing? You know she can't sing," Cora reminded her daughter.

"No, Mother. We went to see *An American in Paris*. Everything comes so late here. It was in Baltimore ages ago. I couldn't wait. Well, the movie was wonderful."

"Really? Perhaps I'll go down and see it myself." Ramelle thought out loud.

"Don't go with Juts. She loved it so much she wants to go again."

"Now what in God's name is wrong with that?" Cora asked.

"Nothing, except that after the movie Harvey Spence played the movie music over his loudspeaker in the theater. Trying out a new technique, he says. Just wait." Louise held up her hand for silence. "Julia hears the music and asks Noe Mojo to dance. Orrie was along, too, and Ev and Lionel. Everyone. Noe thinks this is funny, so he dances with her. Then they split up and tap other people on the shoulder. Before you know it, everyone was dancing in the aisles. I was so embarrassed I could have nearly died," Louise huffed.

"That's marvelous!" Ramelle exclaimed.

"It's not so marvelous if you get stuck dancing with

Yashew Gregorivitch. He's so dumb he'd steal a bag of dirty laundry. Besides, he stinks like rubber tires. Ugh!"

Ramelle blinked; the thought passed.

"Louise, you take all this too serious. You know Juts is full of the devil," Cora admonished her.

"If Yashew wasn't bad enough, first I had to dance with Diana Williamson." Louise's eyelashes fluttered.

"What's wrong with that? Diana Williamson is ravishing and, my dear, she's half your age." Ramelle smiled.

"She's a girl. I don't want to dance with girls." Louise was adamant.

"Really? I used to do it all the time."

"I don't think it's so funny. Julia got all the good partners. I got all the flotsam. Besides, it's hard dancing in these high heels. I know she did that just to spite me because she knew full well I had blisters." Louise gulped a cool drink.

"High heels were invented by a woman who had once been kissed on the forehead." Ramelle snapped her book shut and glanced wickedly at Cora.

September 20, 1955

"Open sesame." Nickel fluttered her fingers like a magician. A towel wrapped around her head gave the effect of a turban. David, Extra Billy's boy, studied her with his mouth hanging open.

"Open sesame," Nickel repeated in a louder voice.

Juts came to the back door to call them in for early supper. "What are you doing?"

"Nothing," Nickel answered. She turned her back and faced the barn door once more. "Open sesame."

"Are you having fits?" Julia put her hand on her hip.

"No."

"Auntie Juts, she's opening the barn door by magic. Just like in the books."

"That towel on her head is overheating her brain."

"Mother, you're disturbing my magic powers."

"I'll disturb more than that if you don't get in here and eat your supper. And give me my towel back."

Reluctantly, Nickel plodded toward the house. "She interrupted. I bet if Mom hadn't called us in, that barn door would have swung wide open."

"You really think so?" David's voice rose.

"Sure, I can do anything."

Once they were inside the house, Juts put the milk on the table.

Extra Billy and his older son, OdeRuss, were working down at Fannie's fixing the shutters. Billy took odd jobs. He was too abrasive to hold down a position at any of the Rife factories. Extra Billy got fired as easily as other people got colds. These days he picked up whatever work he could. Fannie employed him as often as she was able. She and Extra Billy shared a hatred for the Rifes in general and Napoleon Rife in general. Napoleon commanded workers while Julius took care of all national and international deals. Pole brought in outsiders, threw up shanties and tied the poor bastards into the company for life. To spite the south side of town he focused all his "improvements" on the Pennsylvania side. Fannie put on her war paint and daily wrote scathing columns for both the *Clarion* and the *Trumpet*. Sans Souci had been running large ads in both papers since the great crash of '29, so they gladly printed her columns. Of course, Napoleon put pressure on them, but the editors were flinty men themselves and stoutly defended freedom of the press. Fannie knew that though she could never run the Rifes out of town, at least she could try to clean up their slums. It was part of Napoleon's cunning to bring in disadvantaged groups who were unaccustomed to fighting for their rights, as Fannie advocated. He underpaid them as well. When Fannie discovered she couldn't rouse the workers, she turned to the remaining aristocrats and harped on their sense of noblesse oblige. Demands were being made about improving living conditions and Pole was fit to be tied.

The kitchen poured out smells of corn on the cob, mashed potatoes and chicken.

"Nickel, you haven't touched your mashed potatoes," Julia said in her mother voice.

Smash. Nickel slapped her hand right into the goo. Potatoes oozed between her fingers. David froze.

"You little shit." Juts collared her. "Now clean up this mess and do all the dishes before you go outside."

"All right, all right." Nickel agreed since Julia dangled her in the air.

"Damn you, showoff. David wasn't impressed." Julia glowered at David. "Were you?"

"No, Auntie Juts."

She cleared the table and did the dishes under the watchful eye of Juts. David sat at the table and did sums.

"I'm done."

"Not so fast, young lady. I want to inspect these dishes." Juts carefully searched each one for a speck. "Not bad. Go on—get out of here."

The two children raced for the door.

"Mother, we're going down to help Uncle Billy."

"All right."

As they skipped along the dirt road, Julia had to laugh.

David held Nickel's hand while they skipped. He was a solemn-faced little boy without much initiative, but he was as loyal as a dog. OdeRuss was four years older, so he wasn't very close to his brother. Nickel was his pal.

When Extra Billy and Mary would drop by Bumblebee Hill, Billy would teach Nickel judo and how to shoot a gun. Then he'd pit the kids against one another to see if they could think on their feet. It embarrassed him that Nickel had more grit than either of his ɔys, but the boys weren't cowards. He could at least ɔe proud of that.

"Nickel?"

"Yeah?"

"Did you ever look under Blanche Bozana's desk?"

"No, she sits in the back of the room."

"You should look. She sticks all her boogers under her desk. Honest injun. Looks like a picture of the moon."

"Yuck." Nickel held her nose.

"Blanche is a real cootie."

"Yeah."

"A real boom-boom face." David enjoyed this.

"Yeah." Nickel put her hand above her eyes and observed Extra Billy and two large men gesticulating on Fannie's lawn. Napoleon Rife stood off to the side with a superior air. "David, look at that guy."

"Where?"

"Down there with your father. The bald one. He is the biggest thing I've seen that doesn't run on wheels."

David squinted. "Hey, let's get down there. Daddy looks mad."

They drew close enough to hear Billy snarl at the giant. "Man, you tear my ass with boredom."

The goon, hired by Napoleon to take care of the difficult types, socked Bill square in the middle. Napoleon had obviously decided to now intimidate anyone who helped Fannie Jump Creighton. Bill rolled over and felt a kick from the second goon. OdeRuss, barely fourteen, jumped the smaller man on the back.

David rushed in without a thought for himself and how small he was. He bit the huge man on the leg. The goon kicked him clear across Fannie's yard.

"You can't hurt my friend." Nickel went right for the monster, but Napoleon grabbed her by the shoulder with a viselike grip. "Julia Hunsenmeir's bastard brat, I see."

"Batshit," Nickel screamed. It was the worst thing she could think of. She squirmed but Pole held her tight.

David was crying over near Fannie's front door.

Extra Billy, smaller but quicker, remembered his marine training. The big man lunged for him and he threw him on the ground. As the heifer raised himself slowly, Bill kicked his teeth in. The smaller man still struggled with OdeRuss on his back. He moved for Bill but too slowly.

"Beat 'em, Uncle Billy. Beat 'em," Nickel shouted.

"Shut up, kid. I hear tell your father was a nigger." Napoleon smiled a slimy smile. He was a low-rent type who enjoyed calling Jews "kikes," Italians "Wops," along with the usual garden variety round of other racial slurs.

"Yeah. I'd rather be all nigger than part stupid like you." Nickel twisted and kicked him square in the balls. Pole bent over double and she crashed both fists on the back of his neck as Billy had taught her. She was too small to put him out of commission. Pole, enraged, dashed his fist into her face and broke her nose. Blood poured over her orange-striped T-shirt. Tears welled up in her eyes. Nickel was smart enough to know she couldn't take him, but she wasn't going to leave the fight. She picked up a rock out of the street and sliced it over his left eye. He bellowed like a bull.

Billy was holding his own with the big man, but every time that giant connected Bill thought his guts would fly out of his mouth.

Fannie, hearing the rumpus, burst through her front door and fired a volley in the air. This put an end to it.

"Napoleon Rife, get the hell off my lawn or I'll make Swiss cheese out of you."

The gunfire scared the combatants. Bill ran over and checked David. Pole called his men and sullenly left, holding his left eye. "Goddamned blueblood. I'll stop her one way or the other."

"Davy, you O.K.?" Nickel knelt down, oblivious to the blood gushing from her nose.

David smiled. His front teeth were forever gone.

Fannie leaned her rifle against the front door. "Come on, Bill, get in here. I'll take care of this. OdeRuss, how are you?"

"I'm O.K. He knocked the wind out of me."

"Good work, son." Bill clapped him on the back. Then he took a good look at Nickel. "Jesus H. Christ on a raft, girl."

Fannie patched them up and called Julia.

"Julia, you'd better come down here and tend to Nickel. I think her nose is broken."

"Is that damn kid scrapping again? Fannie, she has to fight her own battles and pay the penalty. She can just walk home by herself."

"Just a minute, Julia. This time she tangled with Napoleon Rife."

"What?"

"You heard me."

"God in heaven, Fannie. I'll be right down."

October 31, 1955

All the kids were Halloweening. Mary stayed at home in the small rickety wooden house on the north side of the line. Bill hurried to finish up another piece of work, since Mary had been feeling poorly. She complained of pains deep down in her chest. The doctor prescribed medicine which made her drowsy. He hoped she'd be asleep but he was afraid children might play pranks on this night.

As he drove home he noticed a glow in the direction of his house. Then he heard the fire engine roaring behind him. A cold sweat bathed his thighs. He let the engine pass, then followed it. He arrived in time to see what was left of his house. Mary had burned to death in her sleep.

A routine inquiry was held. Bill knew Napoleon was behind it, although three witnesses proved he was in York at the time. The two goons never showed their faces in Runnymede again.

Julius Rife was livid. He sent his brother away to

Europe until things cooled down. He cleverly tried to repair what fences he could, such as encouraging his middle management men to frequent Sans Souci with their wives. Fannie wouldn't let a Rife pass through the door, but she couldn't stop people whose only sin was working for him.

Bill and his sons were stranded. Fannie took them in. She couldn't heal their sorrow, but she cared for their bodies.

Louise was hysterical. The doctors had to sedate her. Cora, Julia, Ramelle, Orrie, Ev and Maizie took turns sitting with her around the clock. They feared she'd take her own life. Chessy, Noe and Lionel watched over Pearlie as best they could. He was gruff about it, but during the day he'd find himself on the ladder, painting away, and he'd suddenly burst into sobs.

Bill Bitters vowed he'd kill Napoleon in good time, in good time.

April 12, 1956

"Come on, wake up." Cora gently rocked Nickel awake.

"Hmm."

"Come on. You said you wanted to see the sunrise with me."

"O.K." The child crawled out of bed, put on her clothes, brushed her teeth and bounded downstairs.

"Shh. Mom and Dad are still asleep." Cora put her finger to her lips.

"Sorry."

"Here, carry the blankets. I'll carry our breakfast."

"Where are we going?"

"To the top of the hill behind the house. Best view of the sunrise for miles." Cora trotted lightly toward the back door.

Birds called to one another as the two figures climbed the little hill. A silver band appeared in the east. Creatures could be heard running and a lone owl swooped overhead, gliding toward rest.

"Here. Now ain't this something?"

"Yeah, Gran. You know all the best places."

"See you put on red and yellow. You know what that means?"

"What?" Nickel's eyes gleamed with anticipation. She loved Cora, who was full of stories and fun.

"Red and yellow, catch a fellow."

Nickel looked down at her jacket and pants, half expecting forty boys to suddenly appear on the hill.

"Did you ever have a fellow?"

"I was married once. That's how I got your mother and Louise. He ran off and I then had a fellow named Aimes Rankin."

"Was he nice?" Nickel asked.

"He was a good man. Why, he was like a blade of grass busting up through the sidewalk. Special." Cora emphasized "special."

"Like Daddy?"

Cora stopped for a moment, then slowly replied, "In a way. Chessy is a fine man, too."

"Gran, how old are you?"

"I'll be seventy-three in the fall. I like to look ahead." Cora laughed.

"That's a lot, huh?"

"Yes, but Fannie Jump is ahead of me by six years. She was born in 1877 and I was born in 1883."

"I was born in 1944."

"I know. Years are your wealth, darlin'. I'm a rich woman." Cora reached in the basket for rolls and butter. "Here."

"Thanks. Gran, I try to think ahead, too. I am thinking about going to college when I'm grown up."

"That's wonderful. Put your money in your head. No one can ever take it from you then."

"That's what Mom says, too." Nickel gobbled a roll.

"That's my daughter."

"Me and Mom fight a lot." Nickel paused. "We're

bullheaded. That's what Daddy says. I never fight with Daddy."

"She's a good mother. You listen to her."

Nickel's mouth twitched at the corner. "Yes, m'am. When she's right I'll listen."

"See, there you go again."

"Not me, Gran." Nickel hung her head and giggled.

"You'll go far, child. I can see that. If you put that bullheadedness in the right direction, nothing will stop you."

"I am going to go far. Just watch." Nickel's eyes blazed.

"I hope I'm here to see it, sweetheart."

"Gran, you'll live forever."

"Wouldn't mind that a bit. I sure hate to think of missing anything." Cora popped a roll in her mouth and put jam on another one.

Nickel peered intently at Cora. "Why did Aunt Mary have to die?"

"Only the good Lord knows that."

"How can he be good if he lets Aunt Mary die and Napoleon Rife live?"

"He knows things we don't, I guess."

"I don't believe that."

"What?" Cora held Nickel's hand for a minute.

"I don't believe in God."

"Child, don't say such things."

"You never see him. You can talk to him but he doesn't talk back and he lets Aunt Mary burn to a crisp and me get a bloody nose. There's no God."

"Nickel, someday you'll be in big trouble and then you'll discover the Lord or whatever is up there."

"I hope I live to see it." She mocked her grandmother.

"Here, smartypants, have a little peach."

"Aunt Louise goes to church every day now, you know?"

"Yes, I do know that. She was always inclined that way. Gives her comfort."

"Yeah, I don't mind if it gives her comfort, but she tries to drag me along with her."

"I can tell you she didn't appreciate you putting a goldfish in the holy-water font."

"Fish need baptism, too."

"You're a bag of beans, kid." Cora opened a thermos of hot tea. "Try to remember that Aunt Louise lost one of her daughters. That's a terrible thing, outliving your children. Parents expect their own to put them in the ground."

Nickel grew quiet. "I don't want to outlive Mom and Dad."

"You must, honey. That's life. You go on."

"Gran?"

"What?"

"You don't go to church."

"This here's my church." Cora pointed to the land. "You can't buy a sunrise. It's a gift."

"Yeah." Nickel, too, had caught her grandmother's deep love of nature.

"What'd you and David do yesterday?"

"We sat by the side of the road and counted Pontiacs."

"I declare."

"I won," Nickel proudly bragged.

"You watch over David. He's missing a few lights."

"You mean he's dumb?"

"No, I wouldn't say that. The boy's a little slow and now with his Momma gone he's sorrowful. You help him out."

"Yes, m'am." Nickel agreed. "Davy's good in a fight, though."

Cora swallowed some hot tea. "That hits the spot. Celeste Chalfonte used to get the best tea."

"I wish I could have met Celeste. Everyone talks about her."

"You got her birthday, you know."

"I know. What was she like?"

"First, she took your breath away when you looked at her. Celeste and Ramelle were the two most beautiful women I ever laid eyes on."

"Tell me more about Celeste," Nickel pressed.

"She was witty, powerful smart, and she was strong. Yes, that woman was strong. When something had to be done in bad times, Celeste was the one to carry the load. And her eyebrow used to go up like the curtain at the Capitol Theater." Cora tried to make her eyebrow shoot up.

"I hope I grow up to be like Celeste."

"I do, too, but people are like snowflakes. No two alike. You be you. That would please Celeste and that would please me."

Nickel got up to look for the sun. "Not here yet."

"When the good Lord made time, he made plenty of it. The sun hasn't failed yet. Hold your horses." Cora poured herself more tea.

"Did Aunt Wheezie give you some fried marbles?"

"Um-hum. She made me a bracelet. Very pretty."

"Don't you think Aunt Wheezie and Mom are different? They don't seem like sisters to me."

"Those two are like two kids on a seesaw. They bicker and carry on. One keeps the other up in the air, but I tell you, if either one ever jumped off the seesaw the other would crash to the ground. People show love in their own ways."

"Oh." Nickel didn't quite understand.

"And as for you. You go as far as you can in this life, but don't you forget where you came from. You hear your old granny?"

"I hear you." Nickel leapt back on the blanket.

"We're all dumb beasts on Noah's ark," Cora mumbled to herself.

"Getting rosy."

"Won't be long now."

Nickel was silent for a long time. When she spoke, it was with great concentration. "Where do people go when they die? Where is Aunt Mary now?"

"I don't know. You only die once and I ain't accomplished that as yet."

"Don't ever die, Gran." Nickel was intense.

"When the trumpet sounds I got to go. You, too."

"No, Gran, don't leave me. Promise you won't leave me." Nickel hugged her.

Cora wrapped her strong arms around the wiry child. "I won't leave you—not if you keep me in your heart. You see, then I will live as long as you live."

"I will. Forever and always."

"There it is!" Cora clapped her hands.

"Ohh." Nickel stared, transfixed by the blood-red arch that had just peeped over the horizon.

"Hello, sun. It's me again," Cora called out, waving.

December 24, 1958

For weeks Ramelle lay in the hospital, dying of lung cancer. She wanted to get it over with. A spike through her lungs pinned her to the bed. Fierce pain would not let her go. She lay there, observing fluttering nurses tiptoe around her. She saw the faces of Juts, Louise, Fannie and Spotty every day, but she could barely speak. Sometimes she thought she saw Curtis, too, but then she remembered he had died four months before of a heart attack. He seemed so real. She saw Nickel, child eyes enormous with fear and wonder at death. The light from those faces, were they friendly beacons to the beyond?

Today the pain intensified. A beating overhead startled her. The glistening wings of a giant bird undulated. A silver eagle's talon smashed through the ceiling and reached for her.

Ramelle raised her hand to welcome the intruder. The monster ripped into her, then vanished. The spike through her lungs was gone. Perhaps he had seized the pain, she thought.

The room became hazy. Ramelle began to float. She saw herself young, golden hair crowning her head, as she wore it in 1907. Surrounded by beautiful hills, six soft breasts of earth, she climbed the seventh hill. Each hill was smothered in a solid color of tulips. One hill ran red, another yellow, yet another purple. The tulips were singing. Their transparent veins surged rhythmically with opalescent blood.

Her hill, the seventh, dazzled her clear eyes by having all the colors mixed together. What secrets they sang to her, a universal throbbing. Spring breezes filled her and made her feel light. As she drew near the crest of the hill, a cascade of butterflies released their tiny feet from the tulips and swirled around her head. The music pulsated louder, fanned by the butterfly wings.

Ramelle was panting from her climb.

"Ramelle! Beautiful, beautiful friend," a voice called to her.

On top of the hill, arms outstretched, black hair lustrous, stood Celeste. All the energy of the world danced in her smile.

Ramelle's rib cage shattered. Her joy was so great that her heart exploded out of her body. She dashed for Celeste's embrace. Smooth arms encircled her waist and she buried her face in Celeste's elegant neck.

"Darling, oh, darling, I love you for eternity," Ramelle sobbed.

"We have eternity," Celeste whispered in a voice deep as Jupiter, and kissed her amid the tulips and butterflies.

November 24, 1961

"Where is she? Do you see her yet?" Julia wiggled in her seat, a blanket wrapped around her legs.

"No, honey, I don't see anything yet." Chessy put his arm around Julia. After all these years she was still the most beautiful woman in the world as far as he was concerned.

"Well, I wish she'd hurry up. This darn half-time band is giving me a headache," Louise bitched.

The Runnymede Grays swooped and spun in the middle of the football field. Each year at homecoming, the South Runnymede High Grays played the North Runnymede High Blues. In Nickel's senior year she enjoyed the honor of being voted homecoming queen by her classmates. Both Juts and Louise were as puffed up as if they were the queen themselves. Louise saw fit to tell everyone around her, and everyone knew everyone anyway, "That's my niece, Nicole Louise Smith. She's homecoming queen, you know."

This would be followed by a firm statement from Julia: "Well, I'm her mother."

"But I traveled all the way to Pittsburgh to get that poor dear out of Saint Rose of Lima's orphanage."

"I raised her," Julia hotly butted in.

Chessy and Pearlie attempted to concentrate on the band competition before them. The women were always uncontrollable anyway.

Down on the field behind the goal posts, obscured by the Blue band forming up, Nickel and her attendants fussed. She was to sit on the back of a convertible, arms full of long-stemmed roses, and wave a gloved hand. She felt like a flaming asshole, but you couldn't very well be prom queen in combat boots. The attendants were to follow in another convertible. A squabble ensued and the girls all demanded to ride together. Nickel's reason to the head of the cheerleaders, Sylvia Yelton, in charge of this extravaganza, was that if she had to sling her tits in the cold, she wanted her friends around her for warmth. Miss Yelton, not the slightest bit of a prude, thought this so funny she gave Nickel her own way. The two runners-up, Elaine Spaulding and Sydney Rachel Goldstein, arranged their flowing skirts on the back seat. The student body was holding its breath. Something had to happen with those three girls in the same car.

Elaine Spaulding puffed a forbidden cigarette. "When we drive by I want to announce to our parents and friends that I've been offered the lead in a movie."

Sydney, plumping up her teased hair, said, "What?"

The Pubic Hair That Wouldn't Die," Elaine cracked.

"Do you eat with that mouth?" Nickel punched Elaine.

"Don't get her started, Nickel. You know violence

goes to her head." Sydney tried to maintain a minimum of dignity. She stayed cool because she knew exactly what they were going to do to make this homecoming unforgettable.

"Is your mother up in the stands?" Elaine asked.

"Mother, Aunt Wheezie, Dad, Uncle Pearlie, and I think Orrie's up there with Noe and Ev and Lionel are squashed in there someplace. The only one who couldn't make it was Cora. She and Fannie say they're getting too old for crowds."

"Fannie Jump Creighton is two years older than God," Sydney said.

"Yaweh, Sydney—you're Jewish," Spaulding provoked her.

"Wasp," Sydney rasped. "Elaine, do you know what minks hope to buy?"

"What?"

"A floor-length Wasp." Sydney smiled.

"I told you that joke yesterday." Nickel stuck a finger in the rat's nest Sydney Rachel had built up for herself.

"My hair! Watch it, Smith." She rearranged each strand lovingly.

"Why don't the Blues blow it out of their ass? I'm sick of sitting here in the cold." Nickel shivered.

Miss Yelton walked by the car. "All right, girls. We're ready to roll. Now I know you've planned something. It's all over the school. I'm driving this car. You do anything while I'm behind the wheel and so help me, you won't graduate."

"Yes, Miss Yelton." Three sweet voices chimed in unison.

"Better watch it when you turn the ignition key. You know what happened to Napoleon Rife last week." Sydney said.

"Why? Is someone planning to blow me to kingdom come?" Sylvia switched on the motor.

"Hey, where's David?" Elaine remembered. "He's supposed to come out of the locker room to wish you well." She laid heavy on the "well."

Miss Yelton felt a slight heart palpitation. What in God's name were these three rascals going to do?

"Maybe the team is still winning one for the Gipper back there." Sydney suppressed a sneeze.

"David's doing pretty good for a halfback. We can always give him all back." Elaine tossed that one off.

"Boo." Nickel held her nose. "Did you ever think about leaving home?"

"No, I always thought I could provoke my parents to leave."

Sydney grew deadly. "All right, you all. Here we go. Smile."

Sylvia Yelton coaxed the chrome hog out from behind the goal post. First they drove by the North Runnymede side of the stands. Polite cheers. As soon as they hit their home side, wild cheers, confetti, pandemonium ensued.

"There, there, that's my Nickel!" Julia stood up.

"My niece! My niece!" Louise tried to outshout her.

"There's Debby Brown of the Thin Thighs. Over there with Arnold Reisman. I'm going to cut up a biology frog and put it in her purse," Elaine hissed.

"Arnie's worth that much trouble, huh?" Nickel called out to her between grand and gracious waves, evening gloves up to her boobies.

"She's on my reserve shit list," Sydney growled.

"Why? What'd she do to you?" Elaine asked.

"Clipped my term paper and put her name on it. Yesterday, I swear."

"Minus two points for Debby Thin Thighs." Elaine started to wave, then remembered that was Nickel's prerogative.

As they pulled behind the far goal post, Miss Yelton breathed a sigh of relief. Nothing had happened. A puzzled silence filled the stands. A lot of kids thought the three must have chickened out. Julia and Louise basked in their competitive glory.

David Bitters loped out with the rest of the Grays. He came close to the car and handed something to Nickel. This was not lost on Miss Yelton, but she figured her job was done. She prudently disappeared.

As soon as she was out of hearing range, Sydney grabbed Nickel's hand. "Let me see." A Volkswagen key twirled from Nickel's forefinger.

"Hey, you remember Georgette DePalmo with the spray-starch hairdo?" Nickel innocently inquired.

"Lasagna legs?" Elaine asked.

"She died last night from scalp infection," Nickel continued.

Georgette, however, was alive and well in the stands, although you had to sit three rows behind her before you could see the game.

"What are they doing out there?" Sydney, less easily distracted, peered out from under the scoreboard.

"Still a tie. But the third quarter should be almost over. Ready?" Elaine put on her glasses to read the scoreboard at the far end of the field since they couldn't see the one they were under.

"Ready!"

Three young ladies whipped behind the locker room where the football players parked their cars and crammed themselves into David's Volkswagen. Dresses slammed in the door. Ruffles of white, blue and peach stuck out.

"O.K. Know your part?" Sydney quizzed them.

"Yeah. I get to sit in the back and blow a trumpet." Elaine fished for the trumpet David had stuck there.

"Here we go." Sydney's heart was beating a mile a minute.

"You guys, we're gonna get a week's suspension for this." Nickel inhaled.

"It'll be worth it," Sydney said.

The little bug grumbled and sputtered. Sydney drove out from behind the goal post. Right in the middle of a pass play by the Blues, Goldstein hit the accelerator. Out onto the field of play roared the three homecoming honeys. The North Runnymede receiver could not believe his eyes. The football slowly arching toward him, a perfect spiral, bonked the poor guy right on the head. The fans were screaming on both sides of the field. South Runnys knew, at last, their queen and her court had not let them down. Coach Maltby lost his scrotum. The North Runny coach, Maxie Sasadu, lost his self-control.

Nickel bolted out of the tin can, scooped up the still live football and dashed back into the car. This time half of her dress hung out the door. Sydney gunned the motor while Elaine blew her trumpet out the window. "Charge!"

The girls ran straight down the middle of the field, under the goal post, and scored a touchdown. The scoreboard registered the feat. Now Maxie Sasadu was collaring Maltby.

The kids kept going. They knew not to stick around at the scene of their crime.

"She's adopted. She's no blood relation. She's not really my niece. Never saw her before in my life," Louise ranted.

"Shut up, Louise," Julia admonished her.

"I told you never to adopt that kid. French blood. Does it every time."

"Shut up, Louise."

"Wild. Those foreigners are wild. Passed down in the bloodstream."

"Louise!" Julia yanked her down on the bleacher. "Calm yourself."

The two sisters rattled and haggled the whole way home. Louise had recently purchased a wall-to-wall carpet, of which she was inordinately proud. As the adults walked into the living room, Louise was still hitting her one note.

"Julia, we are disgraced."

"Maizie runs all around town in a cowboy outfit. Leave Nickel alone."

"Alone! Why, they could have killed somebody."

"Sydney Goldstein is a good driver."

"That's what comes of hanging around Jews. I bet that little smarty planned the whole thing."

"The only difference between us and Jews," Juts informed her sister, "is they have more arms on their candlesticks."

"Did you know about this?"

"No."

"It's bad enough she's a bastard. Then you influence her. She's as bad as you were when you were young."

"You, of course, were a saint."

"You said it, I didn't." Louise hopped up and down.

"Louise, put some coffee up." Pearlie tried to distract her.

"No."

"Well, you come into the kitchen with me and help me do it." He winked to Chessy.

"Men are so helpless." Louise put her hands on her hips, but she did go into the kitchen.

A loud "Julia" ricocheted into the kitchen. Chessy possessed good lungs.

Louise raced back in the living room to find her sister adjusting her skirt. Julia latched onto Chessy's wrist and pulled him to his feet. She made haste for the door.

"What's that puddle on my wall-to-wall carpet?" Louise blasted.

"Piss on your rug." Julia zoomed out the door.

August 15, 1962

Roses climbed over the trellises. A warm sun moved westward. Cora pulled up her rocker on the porch and surveyed the world from Bumblebee Hill. She placed a bowl in her lap and began shelling peas. Her old gray tabby snoozed in the shade on the porch.

In a week Nickel would be off to college. Cora was thrilled. Here she couldn't even read and her grand-daughter was going to become an architect. Celeste had left a provision in her will for the Nickel she never saw. If the child could get accepted at Vassar, all expenses would be paid. Nickel's grades were fine. She got in and Vassar made arrangements with Yale so she could take architecture courses over there. Such mutual arrangements between women's and men's colleges were rare, but they were being done.

Cora rocked and threw the pea pods into a wicker basket. Once Nickel learned her trade she could fix up the old house. Cora imagined improvements, additions. Houses are almost as much fun to raise as children.

The black-eyed Susans in the old tub wavered gently in the breeze. The valley below sparkled in the sunlight. She was an old woman. On a day like today Cora could forget the mirror. She felt seventeen again. Summer rejuvenated her. Seeing the fruits of the earth restored her faith in her labor and her neighbor's labor. Hearing the animals and birds deepened her faith in the Good Lord on High, as she called That Person to herself. Life was magic.

A blue jay swooped low and yakked about the sleeping cat, then just as quickly spun off. Cora shook her head and grabbed another handful of peas. A dark shudder made her drop the peas into the bowl. Another stab made her gasp. She put her hand on her heart, for that's where the pain lay. Cora knew she was too old to withstand the attack. At last, her time had come. She rose as if to greet this powerful visitor, but sank back, heavy. The bowl of peas clattered on the worn porch. The cat, startled, stretched herself and then rubbed against Cora's leg. The gasping woman reached down to stroke the fur and she heard a rewarding purr. Slowly she lifted her right hand as if to touch the sun one last time, and she murmured, "Thank you, God, for all of it."

A few weeks after Cora's death, Julia asked Chessy if he would mind moving down into town. She used as an excuse the fact that Bumblebee Hill was steep and she was no spring chicken. Such memories flooded each room. Juts felt surrounded by bruised shadows. She couldn't get used to going into a room and not finding her mother there. With Nickel off at college, the emptiness was even more profound. Chessy agreed. Louise and Julia, who now jointly owned the house, rented it out.

Louise helped Julia pack and move. As the two sisters walked away from Bumblebee Hill, Julia fought back the sobs.

"Louise, now we're really alone."

"We got each other." Louise slid her arm around Julia's waist and quietly walked her sister to the car.

May 25, 1980

Orrie Tadia flamed in. Ev Most was hot on her heels. Word was out that today was D-day; hit the beaches for Louise or else. Orrie didn't know what the "or else" meant, but she sure didn't want to miss out on the fun. Juts and Nickel prepared for their arrival. Sometime between noon and sundown, Louise would straggle in with the house papers.

"Big day," Ev said, smiling. The secret knowledge tasted delicious on her tongue.

Orrie, bedecked in pedal pushers, a peasant blouse and mountains of jewelry, made small talk. "Nickel, exactly how old are you now?"

"Thirty-five, but I'm big for my age."

Juts buzzed around her two guests, seeing to their physical comforts.

"Julia, sit down. You're busy as cat hair," Ev commanded.

"Just a minute. We need potato chips." She zipped into the kitchen and came back with three different kinds of potato chips. "Here, feed your face."

"Say, wasn't it around this time in '75 that Maizie had her accident?" Orrie wondered.

"Yes, I believe so," Julia answered her.

"No one knows if it was an accident or not." Ev had put her foot in her mouth. She and Julia discussed it in hushed tones between themselves, but not in front of Orrie.

"That sure was weird, her calling up Aunt Louise and singing 'Happy Trails to You' before pulling the trigger." Nickel added fuel to the fire.

"Maizie never was playing with a full deck." Julia decided to steer this conversation away from such subject matter. "The doctor believes she thought it was a cap gun. Poor thing."

"Poor thing," Orrie agreed, satisfied with her having dug information out of both Julia and Ev.

"This town has everything in it." Nickel crossed her legs.

"Ain't that the truth." Orrie's smile was like a crack in old plaster.

"How's the car doing?" Ev inquired of Julia. Any chance to brag on her new car made Juts happy.

"Runs like a top. I'm so glad Nickel bought it for me. That other heap was a pip. Every time I took it in for repairs it was Ali Baba and the Forty Thieves."

The buzzing voices obscured Louise's footsteps. The door opened and she stepped in. "What's this? A convention?" She wore battle uniform for the occasion, all her Catholic Daughters of America medals pinned to her dress.

"Louise, your left tit is going to fall off from pinning all that metal on it." Julia pulled a chair over for Louise to sit in while she sputtered. "Now, Wheezie, don't get testy. It was a fair fight."

"Fair!" Louise snorted. "Well, I suppose this is the right thing to do." She plucked the papers from her purse. "So many people that we know are dead and gone. It's time for a new generation to take over."

Julia handed her sister a pen.

"I got one. Thank you." Louise found a ballpoint in her purse.

"If you don't mind, I'd like to use my Mont Blanc pen. It's lucky," Nickel stated.

"Suit yourself." Louise folded her hands in her lap. As Nickel went back to the bedroom to get her pen, Louise said, "I wonder who she is, really."

Julia knew this line of thinking by heart. Nickel was one of us but she wasn't one of us. There were times when she thought she'd strangle her sister over that. Today she was in too high a mood to let Wheezie catch her. "Maybe she's Jack Benny. After all, we've never seen them together."

"Here." Nickel reappeared and handed the pen to Louise.

Louise was in no hurry to sign the papers granting the house to Nickel. The young woman had her checkbook in her hand.

"I got aches and pains today," Louise grumbled, hoping to slow the proceedings.

"Getting old is hell," Orrie sympathized.

"Fannie Jump Creighton lived to be one hundred years old before she finally died in her sleep in 1977. She used every minute of life. Think I'll see if I can't beat her record," Julia sang out.

"Go to it, Mom." Nickel laughed. "Being old has its drawbacks, but being my age isn't without problems."

"Like what?" Ev leaned back, waiting.

"Well, a friend of mine got so carried away with the birth movement she made a stew out of her placenta." Nickel's voice was lowered confidentially.

Orrie Tadia decided she'd have to pay more attention to Nickel if she was good at collecting such dirt.

Grandly and with much ceremony, Louise raised herself and paraded to the kitchen. There she sat down and put the papers in front of her. The others nearly got stuck in the door running for the kitchen.

"Nickel," Louise intoned, "I hope you make good. You've done pretty good so far."

"I'm trying to roll Auntie Mame and Mao into one." Nickel smiled broadly.

"One for the money, two for the show, three to get ready, and four to go." Juts handed Nickel's lucky pen to her poised sister.

The pen scratched loudly on the paper. Louise handed the pen to Nickel. Nickel signed. Then she pulled out her checkbook and wrote out twenty thousand dollars to Louise Hunsenmeir Trumbull.

Observing the sum, Julia cracked, "Isn't education a wonderful thing? If you couldn't sign your name you'd have to pay cash."

"Done." Nickel handed the check to Louise.

"I have my half. You can work out your mother's half with her."

"Congratulations." Juts shook her daughter's hand. The other women shook her hand also and then decided to kiss her on the cheek as they always did.

"Julia Ellen." Louise stayed in the chair at the kitchen table.

"Oh, yes." Julia opened the freezer and took out a plain brown wrapper.

Louise snatched it from her hands. "Thank you."

Orrie was dying to know what was in that packet.

"Celebration!" Julia opened a bottle of champagne she had bought to surprise her daughter.

As they lapped up the stuff, Julia bet Orrie and Ev one hundred dollars they couldn't staple two potato chips together. Louise, in a rare moment of self-revelation, whispered to Nickel amid all the uproar and cracking of chips, "I don't know what gets into me. I do love you. Sometimes I can't see the forest for the trees."

"I know, Aunt Wheezie, I know."

September 21, 1980

"You are going up there?" Julia squinted and peered at the barn roof.

"Needs fixing. Anyway, the weather vane is crooked." Nickel pulled thread off her denim cutoffs.

"You be careful, hear?"

"Mother." Nickel climbed up the ladder and worked her way along the spine of the roof to the weather vane. "How's Aunt Louise today?" She grunted as she tried to bend the vane back into shape.

"That piano fart had the nerve to tell me my glasses make me look like a dried apple trying to be a teenager."

"God, Mother, how you talk!" Nickel wiped the sweat off her forehead. The sun was blazing.

"Piano fart really gets to you?"

"Yes!"

Julia yelled up, "Just imagine how enormous a piano fart would be."

"Then why not call her an elephant fart?" Nickel called down.

"You don't see elephants. You see pianos all the time."

A car scratched up the hill. Louise tumbled out. Each day she found herself at Bumblebee Hill, curious as to the work Nickel was doing.

"Don't you fall," Louise called before she was even out of the car.

"There she goes again. Telling everyone how to live their life." Juts groaned, but she was glad to see her sister.

"Nickel, you're doing that wrong." Louise stood next to Julia and shaded her eyes.

"Aunt Wheeze, I'm up on the goddamned roof. Not you."

"All right, all right. I'm just trying to help."

"Yeah, well, thinking is so difficult, the majority prefer to judge instead." Nickel grunted again as she gave the weather vane a twist.

"Piddle." Louise scuffed her foot in the grass. "You're tetched to be up there in this hot sun."

Julia elbowed her sister. "One out of four persons in this country is mentally unbalanced. Think of your three closest friends."

"You, Orrie and Ev," Louise said without hesitation.

"If they seem O.K., then you're the one." Julia cackled.

Watching Nickel work, Julia said, "You know, Louise, I didn't do a half-bad job with that girl."

"Depends on the day," Louise hedged.

"For that matter, Momma did O.K., too."

"Our poor dear mother was a saint." Louise looked pious.

"Louise, you say that about everyone once they're dead."

"Don't get an attitude, Julia. It's too nice a day."

Overhead, the sun beat down on Nickel's uncovered head. The sounds of the two bickering sisters floated up to her, a well-trained duet. "You know, you two are a pair, a real pair."

"Are you making fun of me?" Louise shaded her eyes again.

"No, just stating a fact."

"You'll miss us when we're gone," Juts shouted up at her.

"Yes, I will. No argument." Nickel waved in agreement.

This reply pleased the two groundlings considerably. As they stood there bickering but glowing and the sun poured into Nickel's body, she felt an incredible euphoria. She felt lifted, inspired. She suddenly trusted the future. She had always trusted herself, but now she trusted the future. Hearing the comments, catcalls and laughter from the ground, she knew in her heart she could trust the future because those two women had given it to her. She opened her arms wide like a bird and gathered the sunlight.

"Don't fall up there!" Juts yelled.

Crying with happiness, Nickel replied, "Everything is possible. Pass the word."

ABOUT RITA MAE BROWN

She was born in Hanover, Pennsylvania just a few miles north of the Mason-Dixon line—to her eternal regret. Being orphaned was bad enough, but being a Yankee orphan was really too much. Happily, her luck changed! She was adopted and eventually the family moved to Florida where she was raised, in her own words, "in a blazing pink house on the wrong side of the railway tracks."

Though she grew up with little money, Ms. Brown managed to attend the University of Florida, but lost her scholarship and was subsequently expelled for participating in civil rights activities. She ended up at New York University where she earned a degree in Classics and English, and then a doctorate in political science from the Institute for Policy Studies in Washington, D.C.

According to Ms. Brown, she seriously became a full-time writer after meeting at a party Alexis Smith who "convinced me to get out of the fog of political rhetoric and propelled me toward my typewriter."

The first result was *Rubyfruit Jungle* (dedicated to Miss Smith). "I took it to publishers and I took it to agents and got every door slammed right in my face," she comments. It was finally published by a small feminist press and ultimately purchased by Bantam Books for a mass market paperback edition which has already sold over 350,000 copies.

When she isn't writing, Ms. Brown is touring the country speaking to women about success. "There's nothing wrong with it. It's a forbidden topic; people will talk about sex before they'll talk about success or money," she states, adding, "I'm not so sure that having a dishwasher is so bad."

Rita Mae Brown has published two books of poetry, a book of feminist essays and five novels, the most recent of which is *Sudden Death*, published in hardcover, and *Southern Discomfort* in paperback, both by Bantam Books.

Ms. Brown is currently retracing Stonewall Jackson's steps during The War Between the States in preparation for her next novel.

When recently asked if success had changed her, Ms. Brown answered; "It's hard to be one of the jet set when you don't fly."

THE LATEST BOOKS
IN THE BANTAM
BESTSELLING TRADITION